Anne Goring was born i[n] ... until she married. She tr[avelled ...] to Singapore where they lived for six years before returning to the UK to live in South Devon. Her three previous West Country sagas, also available from Headline, are A TURNING SHADOW, A SONG ONCE HEARD and RETURN TO MOONDANCE.

Also by Anne Goring

A Turning Shadow
A Song Once Heard
Return to Moondance

The Mulberry Field

Anne Goring

HEADLINE

Copyright © 1998 Anne Goring

The right of Anne Goring to be identified as the Author of
the Work has been asserted by her in accordance with
the Copyright, Designs and Patents Act 1988.

First published in 1998
by HEADLINE BOOK PUBLISHING

First published in paperback in 1998
by HEADLINE BOOK PUBLISHING

10 9 8 7 6 5 4 3 2

All rights reserved. No part of this publication may be reproduced,
stored in a retrieval system, or transmitted, in any form or by any
means without the prior written permission of the publisher, nor be
otherwise circulated in any form of binding or cover other than that
in which it is published and without a similar condition being
imposed on the subsequent purchaser.

All characters in this publication are fictitious and any resemblance
to real persons, living or dead, is purely coincidental.

ISBN 0 7472 5181 9

Typeset by Avon Dataset Ltd, Bidford-on-Avon, Warks

Printed and bound in Great Britain by
Clays Ltd, St Ives plc

HEADLINE BOOK PUBLISHING
A division of Hodder Headline PLC
338 Euston Road
London NW1 3BH

For Dot, Heather and all the Thursday Scribblers.
And in loving memory of Irene Northan.

Prologue 1752

The room was cold. No more than a handful of smoky coals glimmered in the grate and the one narrow window admitted only mean slivers of March sunlight. The harsh white walls and the few pieces of utilitarian furniture set stiffly in place did nothing to create an illusion of warmth. Or welcome. For not even a flower or an ornament or a curtain softened the austerity of the room. As though, the visitor thought, any such frivolous, cheerful object would have been an affront to the purpose and responsibility of the woman seated opposite her, on the other side of the plain deal table.

The visitor shivered within the folds of her brown cloak. As she had hastened through the maze of narrow streets after the chairmen had set her down she had regretted the burdening weight of the cloak, of necessity the heaviest, the most concealing that she owned. Gusts of wind had caught the deep brim of her bonnet and threatened to tear away the swathes of veiling that she had carefully arranged to hide her face from curious eyes. She had railed at being forced to stop and waste precious minutes repinning and readjusting the wretched veiling. Had cursed the flapping, hampering cloak. But now, in this cold room, under the unblinking scrutiny of the woman opposite, she was grateful both for the warmth of her clothes and the anonymity the heavy veil bestowed.

'To what do I owe the pleasure of this call, Mrs . . . Smith?'

The visitor caught the infinitesimal pause. For a moment she wavered, feeling guilt must be stamped like a brand across her forehead. But guilt quickly gave way to anger. She had not taken the chance to come here, risking so much, to be intimidated by a person of inferior standing, and a sour, ill-dressed old maid at that.

'I make this errand on behalf of a friend.' She ignored the disbelief in the other woman's eyes. Let the old crone think what she would. 'It concerns one of your charges, Angeli— Emily Wroe.' Almost, almost a slip. She saw that the stumble was noted. *Merde!* She must be calm. Put away anger and fear and urgency. They were useless emotions that would tangle her thoughts. She took a deep breath. Said, more slowly, 'The girl is an orphan, I am informed, who was left as a baby in the care of your establishment, Miss Edgar. Some ten or eleven years since.'

Ten years, two months, to the day. A dark January morning with a bitter, killing wind from the east. The land iron hard, streams and rivers locked with ice. Small birds had died where they slept, claws frozen to black twigs. And something within her own heart had frozen and died in those hours, never to be revived.

'My friend's many charitable acts have always been performed quietly and anonymously, as the Bible exhorts us all to do, which is why she charged me with this duty.' The well-rehearsed lies slid easily from her tongue. 'Many persons over the years have benefited from her kindness. As did the infant Emily – left so sadly without a relative to care for her. She was found a place in this orphanage together with a generous sum of money for her keep.'

'We allow no favouritism here. All charitable donations are put to the general good.'

'That is only to be expected,' she agreed meekly.

But she had hoped, so hoped, it might make some difference when she had learned – far too late – where

Uncle Pierre had placed the baby. Not with a kindly family as he had promised. But in a home for foundlings.

'So what is your business here?' Miss Edgar's fingers rapped an impatient tattoo on the table. 'You will understand that your unexpected visit has diverted me from pressing duties elsewhere . . .'

'Of course. I will be as brief as maybe.' She was careful to keep her tone level and polite though she seethed inside. Such insolence! And there was nothing she could do about it. Nothing. She must bear it if she was to accomplish what she had set out to do. 'I am charged to enquire the child's state of health and her general progress.'

'Her health is robust.' A pause, then with a baring of long, yellow teeth in a smile that held both slyness and malevolence, 'Wroe is fortunate in that she enjoys rude good health, which is an advantage that we may present to a prospective employer when the time comes. As to the rest, we at the Lady Eleanor Home for Foundlings and Orphans never cease from rigorously instilling in our girls the principles of industry, obedience and modesty laid down by our charitable founder two hundred years since, though often, as in Wroe's case, the material we work on is, shall we say, not of the best quality.'

'In what way? What do you mean by that?' The questions were too sharp, too imperious. With an effort she softened her tone. 'My friend will demand from me the fullest possible account of the girl's character. I would be obliged for your co-operation.'

'Then you may inform her that though Wroe has in the past displayed a regrettable tendency towards idleness and mischief, she has recently begun to display a more sober and willing attitude. She is not clever, beyond a certain coarse cunning which doubtless derives from her parentage – which if my memory serves me right was said to be of low rustic stock – but if she continues to be diligent we may make something of her yet.'

Low rustic stock! *Mon Dieu*, may the old bitch's tongue rot in her head! But that was the tale the servant had been paid to carry here. She had done her duty well... No sense in rising to this old maid's bait. Discretion. Discretion. That must be her watchword...

'And what will that "something" be?'

'Girls leaving Lady Eleanor's are much in demand among discriminating employers in Bristol and my recommendation, as overseer, carries considerable weight with the charity's Board of Trustees whose responsibility it is to place the girls in suitable employment. A select few, whose behaviour and industry merit it, receive the accolade of an apprenticeship to a suitable trade, such as stay-making or dressmaking or millinery. Most of the others are found places as kitchen or laundry maids in respectable households where they may advance themselves in the due course of time to the ranks of upper servants.'

'And those who do not conform to your high standards?'

'A strong, healthy twelve- or thirteen-year-old may be usefully employed in work which requires brawn rather than brain.'

'Such as?'

An indifferent shrug of the bony shoulders. 'There are many hostelries in the town where she may be employed about the sculleries or stables. Or there is the brickyard...'

'My friend would certainly prefer the child be found a place in a gentler environment than a brickyard.' This time she made no attempt to disguise the sharpness of her tone and she let her gloved fingers move deliberately over the reticule that lay in her lap. 'Indeed, I am instructed to satisfy myself that when the time comes, she will be found employment of as superior nature as is possible in the circumstances. It is on receipt of this assurance – and only then – that I am to present you with a further donation. A very *generous* donation,' she added softly, alert for any change of expression on the other woman's face, and recognising, thankfully, a flicker of greed in the pale eyes. 'My friend is a thorough person and has made extensive enquiries among the better sorts of dressmaker as to their terms. This has enabled her to make ample provision for Emily Wroe's indentures with a further sum to be used by the Board of Trustees as is thought appropriate.'

'You ask me to favour one girl over another?' Miss Edgar pursed her lips. Yet her tone was less aggressive than it had been and her gaze was drawn and held by the small doeskin bag the visitor drew from her reticule and placed on the table between them.

'My friend would wish you to seek out a high-class establishment where the apprentices are well-fed and well-treated, not a back-street establishment where the girls might be overworked with little care for their health.' A careless movement of her hand caused the coins within the purse to chink softly together. 'All it needs is your word, Miss Edgar. Your promise to do your very best for Emily Wroe and find her a good place where she will be comfortable and happy... However, let me make it clear that I do understand your dilemma and I shall quite understand if your principles will not allow you to take advantage of my friend's more-than-generous offer. But please do think carefully before you refuse. I am sure that an experienced person such as yourself, whose word is so much trusted and relied on, could manage the whole business discreetly, with no untoward reflection on yourself or this charitable foundation.'

Kid-gloved fingers nudged the purse encouragingly towards the centre of the table. Lace-mittened fingers moved involuntarily an inch or two towards it. Stopped.

'Your friend desires complete anonymity?' Miss Edgar dragged her gaze reluctantly from the purse. Her narrowed eyes were wary and calculating.

'Have I not made that plain? All I require is your hand to a receipt for the monies. Thereafter, I would expect you to honour your word, once I have it, in regard to the apprenticeship.'

'And if I did accede to this . . . this request, would you give me your assurance that there will be no further interference? No more untoward visits?'

'Of course.' A pause. Then, lightly: 'Indeed, if you felt it politic to keep the matter entirely in your own hands, without recourse to a higher authority, then I believe that would be perfectly acceptable to my friend. After all, you have the responsibility for the day-to-day running of this establishment. There must be occasions when you have unexpected expenses. How tedious it must be to have to go cap in hand to the Board of Trustees for every penny. It seems to me that a few pounds kept discreetly in reserve – to be used as you think fit for the benefit of all who reside under this roof – might not come amiss.'

That was as near as she dare go to hinting that she was offering nothing more nor less than a bribe. For the rest she could only trust that the money – carefully hoarded year after year – would persuade this old maggot into favouring the child.

And was it really enough? She breathed a silent prayer that it was. It had been a hard struggle to fill that purse, though lately with the connivance of her friendly dressmaker to whom she had recommended many of her friends and which had resulted in a generous commission, it had grown satisfactorily weighty. Her husband did not see the need for his wife to have any dealings with money. Even the little ready cash he allowed her each month must be meticulously accounted for, though she had grown wise to ways in which she might scrimp a penny here, a sixpence there. Was she not, he reasoned, generously provided for by him in every way? Food, clothes, servants – she wanted for nothing. So long, that is, as he approved of it.

She had learned in the early months of her marriage that it was best to conform to his wishes, his taste, his opinions. To do other was to invoke the weight of his rage. His was a volatile temperament. A sunny, charming mood could change with alarming speed should he be crossed or thwarted and such punishments that he devised for her were rarely direct and always subtly unkind. Not necessarily to her, but to those whose helplessness undermined her own strength and will: his young children, and the servants. The only way to protect them was to be all that he required in a wife. She must look up to him with admiration, obey him, submit meekly to his demands by night, be an ornament to his household and an example to his children by day.

She did her best. More than her best. What other choice had she? In the eyes of the world she appeared the most fortunate of women, cosseted as she seemed. But sometimes she would wake in the night with tears on her face, aroused from a dream in which her lost child called piteously from the black shadows of a ravine and she was powerless to go to her, for Uncle Pierre stood before her, a great looming shadow, his words implacable: 'You will do as you are bid. I will not have this disgrace upon the family name. You will wipe everything that has happened from your memory. We have a new life, in a new country. The past must be forgotten. I have made arrangements for you . . .' Then her husband's heavy hands would fall upon her shoulders and in the dream she would feel herself dragged away, the child's cries growing fainter, more desolate . . .

She would wake then. And in those stark waking moments she would know herself to be in little better case than a prisoner condemned to a house of correction, for all that her cell was hung with velvet and satin.

'If you would give me a moment to consider...'

Miss Edgar stood up abruptly and paced to the hearth and back, her heels ringing harshly on the floorboards. She maintained an attitude of deep thought, head bent, hands clasped earnestly at her waist, as though in private prayer. But the visitor was not taken in by these manifestations of a conscience wrestling with itself. She had seen the near-imperceptible quirk of the thin lips, the gloating smile hastily suppressed.

It was done. She had achieved what she had set out to do.

She was suddenly bone weary, as though all the nervous energy that had sustained her so far had drained suddenly away. She was scarcely able to murmur an acknowledgement as the other woman confirmed her desire to be of assistance in this delicate matter and swiftly removed the purse before seating herself to scribble the receipt and push it across the table top.

The visitor took it.

She knew she must go now. She had carved out this brief time of freedom, luck on her side for once. It was providence that had brought the family briefly to Bristol, providence that had kept her husband engaged upon important business affairs for the day. She could not press luck too far. Yet pushing the receipt into her reticule, her fingers encountered the second package.

Should she? Could she bear it?

As if from a distance she heard her voice, surprisingly cool and clear.

'Is it possible that I might meet the girl?'

She wished the words unsaid almost as she spoke them. She knew at once that she should rise to her feet, explain that she had changed her mind and leave. Walk briskly away from this room, this building, these memories...

But her voice was clogged in her throat, her body too heavy to move from the chair. And in the long slow minutes between the maid being summoned and shuffling off in search of Emily Wroe, her mind slipped back, back...

She saw herself a wilful child again, rebelling against the need to be meek and quiet and not cause offence to their Catholic neighbours, even those who seemed kindly and tolerant. The whispered tales of purges and slaughterings of Huguenot communities by wild mobs seemed too remote from the ordered life she knew in the quiet Languedoc market town to be believable. Were not Papa and Uncle Pierre, his elder brother, respected for the employment they gave to so many people in their mill? Were not Maman and Aunt Jeanne admired for the kindness and generosity they showed to anyone in the district who was ill or in trouble? If the grown-ups wished to worry their heads about such things, let them. She would not! At six years old it was far more important to evade old Marie in order to spend an afternoon paddling in the stream where she was forbidden to go alone.

Then she was ten years old, railing against the annoyance of being the youngest, least considered in the family, and planning devious schemes to get her own back on her brothers when they ignored her or teased her. Another swift flick through the coloured pictures in her head and she was fourteen and gripped with the passion and pain of love.

Even here in this cold, austere room and after all these years, the long fingers, encased in the fine grey doeskin of her gloves, curled against her palms as though in a rictus of remembered grief.

How had she been such a fool as to believe him? Why had she not been obedient like her friends, who would not have dreamed of being other than dutifully virgin until their parents had arranged marriage into a suitable family?

Why had she allowed herself to fall under the spell of someone who represented everything her respectable parents deplored and feared? That he was Catholic was bad enough, but he was also wild and arrogant. Worse, he was from degenerate stock. His father, the Comte, like his father before him, lived a life of reckless spendthrift debauchery while the elegant château in which he and his dissolute friends gambled and drank and entertained whores, rotted and crumbled about their ears.

But she had not wanted to know or see any of that. She saw only his bold, handsome eyes, the broad-shouldered grace of his body, was bemused by his easy promises, by the excitement of intrigue and by the wanton responses of her own nature. Nothing else mattered all that languorous, wild-flower-scented spring except their secret, passionate meetings. Louis adored her. He told her so a thousand times. And, of course, he would protect her and her family against the new outbreak of hatred that was once more abroad. His family had influence. He swore that he would never allow anyone or anything to harm her . . .

Hah! Had she not been so gauche and trusting, so dazzled by his ardour, she would have looked deeper, seen that it was all a game to him. He had whiled away a few dull country weeks teasing and seducing a pretty, silly country girl. Yet, at the time, it had not seemed like that at all . . .

But overnight he was gone, borne off by his father to the headier delights of Paris society.

Louis. She had no recourse but to believe that he had used her, deceived her, abandoned her. And, as though the stern God who ruled their Calvinist household had waited this moment to deliver punishment for her sin, his departure was the signal for her small, comfortable world to dissolve to unimaginable chaos.

In that chaos, the women – Maman, Aunt Jeanne,

herself – fled to the coast under Uncle Pierre's protection, travelling by night, hiding by day. They had crammed into the filthy hold of a fishing boat, praying for Papa and her two brothers, who had stayed behind to salvage what other valuables they could from the house, to join them quickly. But the hours had dragged on with no sign of them, until the hatch opened to admit a chink of grey dawn light and the whispered message that it was no use to wait any longer. Word had come that Papa and his two sons had been taken by the dragoons.

They were scarcely out of La Rochelle before the wind turned contrary, the herald of the storms that drove them far to the west. It was three weeks before they made landfall on the south coast of Cornwall. They were rowed ashore with their pitiful bundles of belongings and stranded in a deserted cove like so much flotsam left by the tide. She remembered how she had looked at the other three as they stood in the yellow rays of the lowering sun and had scarcely been able to smother the hysterical laughter that rose in her throat. Were these two unkempt women – their hair wild, clothes salt-stained and stinking from the bilgewater that had constantly slopped about them – really her once plump and immaculately dressed maman and Aunt Jeanne? Was that gaunt, bowed, dishevelled figure really proud Uncle Pierre or some scarecrow who had taken his name?

The urge to laugh died as quickly as it had arisen as the others dropped to their knees. She followed suit. Uncle Pierre offered up a prayer of thanksgiving for their survival. Then, in a long and impassioned appeal, begged that those dear ones they had been forced to leave behind in France might soon be spared to join them and that the Lord would bring down retribution on their enemies.

But her own prayers, most fervently offered, had gone unanswered. Before the hurried departure from home she had begun to suspect her condition. During the voyage the nausea and vomiting that had overtaken her had been little worse than that which had laid her mother low. But it was not *mal de mer* that ailed her. She knew for certain now that she was with child. Louis's child.

She gathered up her bundle and trailed slowly after the others over the coarse yellow sand. However eager the others were to make their way, the road ahead was for her to be a stony one indeed.

That night they were sheltered by a kindly farmer. Within a week they had taken lodgings in Plymouth. Maman hoped wistfully that they might settle there to await news from France. The rush of events and the privations of the journey had left her ill and bewildered. She needed time to rest and recover, and for a while it seemed that Uncle Pierre was agreeable to her pleadings. It was a bustling town and had the advantage of an established community of Huguenot settlers. He immediately began enquiries among the congregation of the How Street chapel as to where he might profitably set to work the family money with which he had been entrusted.

These hopeful plans changed with dreadful suddenness.

The interview when she had blurted out her news was written indelibly on her mind: her mother's sobs, Aunt Jeanne's hysterical screeches, Uncle Pierre's wrath. Then she was locked in her room and not allowed out of it until the day they left for the secluded house Uncle Pierre had found for them where, he had decided, she would be incarcerated until the child was born. If they were careful, he reasoned, nobody need ever know of this disgrace. The tale he would put about to the few acquaintances they had made was that both his niece and sister-in-law were suffering from a weakness of the lungs brought on by the privations they had recently suffered. To prevent the condition becoming morbid, the physician had advised complete rest away from the noise and miasmas of the town. By the spring, he reasoned, and with the child disposed of, she would be fit to present to decent society once more when, in the absence of her father, he would endeavour to find her a suitable husband.

But winter must be got through first.

A winter in which Maman became genuinely ill. The final blow – the news that her husband, refusing to renounce his faith, had been hanged on some trumped-up charge of plotting treason, and her sons dispatched to the galleys – was too much for her mind. She grew vague and fanciful, her appetite shrivelled. She moved about the gloomy house like a wraith, sighing and smiling by turns, scarcely noticing where she was. There was no comfort to be got from Aunt Jeanne, who grew more sour by the day, or Uncle Pierre, or the discreet widow woman they employed as a servant.

A winter in which a child was born as snowstorms whirled down from the moorland heights. And in the days before the snow cleared and the child could be removed to a wet nurse the widow woman knew of, as had been planned, she must feed the baby herself, nurse it, allow herself the indulgence of such overwhelming love for this scrap of new life that when the snow shrivelled away in the bitter wind and the roads were passable for the widow woman to travel, she thought herself like to die from the pain of separation . . .

'Ma'am?'

She started. As though still locked in the past she saw Louis's eyes staring into hers. Eyes she would never forget. Irises of such a deep velvet brown that could darken with passion and desire to the intensity of jet. They still haunted her dreams. Eyes that had drawn her into sin. Yet, in sinning, there had been such lightness, such joy, that it had felt perfectly natural, perfectly right. A world apart from the rough unpleasant act that went with a wedding band and respectability. His eyes in a young girl's face.

She took a grip on the chaos of her thoughts. Slowly, the cold bare room, the serving maid standing attendant at the door, the slight figure of the girl bobbing a curtsey before her came properly into focus.

Louis's eyes, yes. And more. She recognised the clear-cut, sensual curve of the upper lip, the fine-drawn line of the nose. She herself had surely bequeathed the round chin with its hint of wilfulness, the square, stubborn set of the shoulders under the grey serge of the ugly dress. And, with a tremor of pain, she saw the glint of silver-gilt hair exactly the colour as her own drawn back under the starched cap.

Yet she also recognised – and it was no less painful – that there was something in this child that was very different to either herself or Louis. There was no easy, laughing, carelessness here. She was too watchful, too wary. A wariness forged in a harsher environment than either Louis or herself had known as children. It veiled whatever strength and fierceness of spirit lay within, much as the dark veils now masked her own features. There was a gravity about Emily Wroe that gave her a maturity beyond her years.

She reached out and took the child's hands in hers. She could not stop herself. Such red, rough little hands, still damp from whatever task she had been called from, a half-healed scab on the thumb. She had an aching to smooth and warm them, to draw the girl into her arms and hold her tight. Remove the shrouding veiling and reveal her own features. Instead, remembering that other matter, she stood up abruptly, still holding Emily's hand.

'Come to the window,' she said. 'The light is poor here.'

Once away from the desk she fumbled in her reticule for the second package, concealing it in the palm of her hand. When they halted by the window, she kept her back to the room, shielding Emily from Miss Edgar's gaze.

'Now, tell me of your day, how your time is occupied,'

she said clearly, then mouthing in a faint whisper, 'I am a friend. Take this. Keep it secret,' before adding again loudly, 'Speak up! I wish to know everything that you do. Begin at the beginning. At what time do you rise?'

The girl began haltingly, her fine brows drawn into a frown as she felt the package squeezed into her palm.

'Please, ma'am, we are woken at six o'clock in summer and seven in winter.'

'And then?'

'Then we have duties before prayers and breakfast.' She spoke in a flat little voice, carefully weighing each word. 'Turn and turn about we help with the babies and little ones, or go to the kitchen or laundry. When breakfast is cleared we get on with what we have been set to do for the day... cleaning or washing and ironing.'

'And what of schoolwork?'

'We have an hour set aside before supper to learn the scriptures and help the little ones with their letters and numbers.' For an instant it seemed the brown eyes darkened with some secret pleasing thought, though her voice was still expressionless as she said, 'After supper there is the sewing and mending to be done.'

'At which Wroe is particularly inept,' Miss Edgar interrupted, thrusting back her chair and rising to her feet. 'As she is at most of the tasks she is set. Her nature inclining her, as it does, to a regrettable lack of application.' Her skirts swished irritably as she crossed the room to take a grip on Emily's shoulder. 'I fear I must curtail this interview, Mrs Smith,' she went on coldly. 'I can no longer defer the pressing duties which require my immediate attention. I believe that the object of your visit has been achieved in that you have been able to observe Wroe as healthy and well cared for.'

The visitor stood silent for a moment, before she slowly inclined her head by way of acknowledgement.

'Then I will bid you good day, Mrs Smith.'

The woman did not answer, though a sound – a sigh, a faint choked sob, hard tell which – escaped her. The child heard. Miss Edgar, calling to the servant to show the visitor out, did not.

The girl bobbed a curtsey. Unguarded curiosity sparked briefly in the depths of her brown eyes before she hastily lowered her long gold-tipped lashes. Her fingers curled against the skirt of her dress, concealing the packet.

The visitor, her back ramrod stiff, followed the old servant out of the room. She did not glance backwards. She walked briskly down the short passage to the front door. Only when she was once again out in the narrow street did she allow her shoulders to sag and her steps to falter. And as the blustery wind caught at her cloak and veils, it seemed to the maid closing the heavy door behind her that she was bowled away and out of sight with no more resistance than a shrivelled, dead leaf left over from winter.

'What was it? What did she give you?' Miss Edgar shook Emily Wroe so violently that her head snapped painfully back and forth on her thin neck.

'Nothing, miss . . . Please, miss . . .'

'Do not lie to me! Open your hand!' She prised back the small, work-scoured fingers that clutched desperately at the packet. 'Do not think, miss, you can have secrets from me . . . There. I have it. Now off about your work. And if I find the scullery floor is not to my liking when I inspect it, you shall forfeit your dinner while you scrub it again. Do you hear?'

She gritted her teeth against the urge to box the girl's ears. She did not wish to waste time on Wroe when she longed to be alone to gloat over this unexpected piece of good fortune. But Wroe need not think she had escaped lightly. Later she would order her to be locked in the coal cellar for a few hours. No – better – overnight. That would teach her to tell lies, the insolent hussy. Though she doubted even this punishment would reduce Wroe to satisfactory screams and tears as it did the others. There was something deeply stubborn and infuriating about Wroe. Even the way she walked away now was an irritation – that steady, unhurried stride where another child would have scurried, the tilt of the head that spoke dumb defiance instead of remorse . . .

The door closed. Evelyn Edgar banished thoughts of Wroe and allowed herself a satisfied smile. A good morning. Yes, indeed. That stupid woman with her cock-and-bull tale – and a foreigner, to boot. Her speech, though swift and fluent, had a different intonation to that of an honest Englishwoman. Transparent as glass. Come to ingratiate herself in the hopes that her by-blow would be treated better than the rest. As though the bastards of the rich should take precedence over bastards of the poor. Faugh! She despised the lot of them if the truth were told. Still, with this nice little sum to add to her nest egg, it would not be long before she could kick the dust of this wretched place from her heels and take comfortable retirement in a little cottage near the Avon.

Now, what had the foolish woman tried to sneak to Wroe? . . . She broke the seal on the packet and two gold coins fell out. Better and better. Evelyn Edgar smiled as she slipped them into her pocket, her smile deepening at the comfortable clinking sound they made as they nestled with their fellows. She peered at the square of folded paper which had wrapped them. Such minute writing, and crossed at that. Her eyes, troublesome of late, were not up to the deciphering of it, even if she had wished to do so. Which, she swiftly decided, she did not. It was of no account to her. Her only interest was in the money and the urgent need to remove it to the compartment under a loose floorboard in her bedchamber where it would be safe.

So, pausing only to toss the still folded letter onto the smouldering coals, she hastened about her urgent and exciting errand.

The serving maid, busying herself in brushing up the dust that had blown in when the front door had been opened, watched Miss Edgar hurry away in the direction of her private quarters. Then moving more swiftly than she allowed herself under the overseer's eye, she slipped back into the room.

Martha Monday had lived in the home all her life. First as a foundling, named for the day she was discovered wrapped in sacks on the doorstep; then as a servant when a previous overseer, aware of the willing heart in the misshapen, hunched body, had decided not to send her out into an uncaring world where her looks would be likely to call down ridicule. Her whole life had been bound up in this building and the orphan children it sheltered. Little that went on under this roof escaped her, for she made it her business to observe and listen. Not out of idle curiosity, but out of interest in the little ones, such as she had once been.

She knew as well as anyone that charity could have a cold, hard face and she tried her best to bring what she could of softness and warmth to the children of Lady Eleanor's, even if it was only with a smile and a friendly word, though often she could help in more practical ways. She was always first to offer to sit all night with a sick child. She concocted soothing salves to spread on chilblains and bruises or the weals raised by Miss Edgar's busy cane, and many clumsy-fingered girls had reason to bless her for whisking away the darning they had been set and returning it fit to pass Miss Edgar's inspection. Emily Wroe among them, for Martha had a particular fondness and sympathy for those whom Miss Edgar disliked and who suffered most severely from the overseer's sour temper.

She had had her eye to the keyhole and her ears sharp for the muffled conversation during the interview with the visitor, and had scuttled back from seeing her out to listen and watch by the door again, determined to learn what she could and, if it were possible, to turn that knowledge to Emily Wroe's advantage.

She went directly to the fireplace, snatched up the paper from the coals and pinched out the flames that had taken hold. As she did so, something slipped out from a fold of the paper, clattering to the hearth.

Her first triumphant thought was that Miss Edgar had missed a gold coin. In a wave of disappointment, she saw it was only a small brass key. Oh, and she'd so much hoped there'd be something better to pass onto the poor little moppet. Sadly, she turned the key in her calloused palm, then looked again at the charred letter. Not much left of it, but perhaps there was enough of the writing to tell about the key. She wasn't scholar enough to make anything of it herself. 'Twas as much as she could do to draw the letters of her own name. Emily was sharp as sharp, though. She'd be able to read it. Such a little key. It was no bigger than the one which Miss Edgar used to open the box where the tea was kept, or the one on her nightstand where she put the locket with her mother's picture at night. Excitement fluttered in Martha's chest. Perhaps it was a jewel box the key opened, full of precious things . . . treasures intended for Emily so's she'd be rich when she growed up – and the paper would tell where it was hid and who her real ma was . . . Oh, this was better than a few gold coins.

With shaking fingers she put the key into her apron pocket and refolded the charred scrap of paper. Then she went in search of Emily Wroe.

Chapter One

When my reluctant feet carried me over the doorstep of the Thorn Tree on that raw January evening in 1754, I was perfectly convinced that I had died and been conveyed to Hades.

I stumbled after old Martin, the orphanage watchman, who had been instructed to fetch me to the inn, into murky light scarcely brighter than the inky rural blackness outside. The yellow glimmers from the candles set along the walls in holders mounded with ancient tallow made little impression on the thick fog of tobacco smoke which assailed my eyes and nose along with the ripe stink of dirty clothes, unwashed bodies and sour ale. And the noise! Such a bedlam of screeches, drunken guffaws, the crash of pewter pots on tables, a bawdy song yelled out by a shrill female voice . . . I wanted to turn and run, but Martin grabbed my arm and tugged me through the press of bodies, his own cries of, 'Make way, blast'ee,' adding to the din.

How could I not have been appalled and terrified? For all that I had longed to leave the orphanage – that place where chill silence dominated, and fear and repression ruled – it was not to this. I had never been able to please Miss Edgar in any way, however I tried, but I had clung to the hope that when the time came her conscience might prick her into finding me a decent place. Even Martha Monday had encouraged me to believe so, having imparted to me the secret knowledge that the overseer had taken money on my account. But I saw that Miss Edgar had meant to torment me to the last and she had sent me here as a final, dreadful punishment. She knew that as I possessed nothing in the world save the clothes I stood up in, together with the three new pennies, the spare petticoat and stockings, the night shift and comb that each girl leaving Lady Eleanor's was entitled to, I was in no position to do anything but accept my lot.

In that moment I hated her with an intensity I had always tried to keep under control. It fired my blood as fiercely as the heat that met me when Martin hauled me into the kitchen and looked about for the person to whom I was to be delivered. This was the hellish heart of the inn, a place where a huge fire in a vast stone hearth spewed leaping shadows into the beams overhead and dark figures rushed to and fro in a demented fashion with steaming bowls and pans and heaped up platters of food. I half expected to see the devil himself complete with horns and toasting fork waiting to thrust me into the flames.

But it was not the devil who was peering into a cauldron suspended over the fire, but an enormously fat woman, who turned to scowl malevolently at us through clouds of steam.

'That'll be her,' said Martin, with satisfaction. 'That'll be the cook, Mrs Hill, as I've to speak to.'

It took all the power of my will not to cling to Martin and beg him to take me away. But as I watched the fat cook waddling towards us I held instead to the hatred I had of Miss Edgar. I would not submit to despair! In a strange, instinctive way I had always known that to cower and weep before someone whose pleasure lay in cruelty and repression was to make her the victor. Miss Edgar had consigned me to this place of noise and dirt and confusion, and though she could not see me now, I still could not bear to think that Martin would take back any word that would cause her to gloat over my predicament.

I would not give in.

There had been times, locked in the lightless cellar with unseen creatures scuttering and rustling among the coals, when I had nearly succumbed and pleaded for release. But there had always been something – someone – to hearten me in my isolation. To give me the strength to endure. Martha Monday usually managed to find an excuse to pass the door and whisper a few comforting words. Another girl had once slipped into my hand a daisy she had picked on the Sunday walk to church. It was sadly wilted when I was let out, but the memory of its white petals and yellow heart, the cool, sweet feel of it, had bolstered my flagging courage. Sometimes I told myself stories, or repeated the verses we learned from the Bible, or remembered a comical dog I had seen chasing its tail in the churchyard and imagined it was my dog and we went on long walks together and lived in a splendid house.

I needed something like that to cling to now. Something to give me strength and fire my courage . . .

'This her then?' The cook's massive shape blotted out my view of the forbidding kitchen, though she herself was no pleasanter a sight. Her sacking apron was stiff with the congealed traces of many meals and her grey hair hung down in rat-tails from under a grubby cap She brushed a trickle of sweat from her red face with the back of a meaty red hand, scooped up several of these rat-tails and twisted them back under her cap, before she thrust her head forward to inspect me. 'Namby-pamby little thing, en't she? Not a patch on poor wronged Polly I was obliged to put off this very week. Weepin' fit to break your heart, she was. And this puny article is all that I gets in 'er place, is it?'

'Her's stronger than her looks,' Martin said defensively. 'And her's used to hard work. All Lady Eleanor's girls are . . .'

'Lady Eleanor's girls,' the cook mimicked in a high, scornful voice. 'We all knows whose idea it was to bring in one o' they. Mistress Nose-in-the-Air!' She hawked and spat onto the greasy flags. 'Bringing her high-flown ideas along with her fancy clothes and pernickety manners. Pity Master Harry ever clapped eyes on her, I say. 'Twas all nice and comfortable here afore she got her claws into him. Men!' Her scowl deepened so alarmingly that Martin took a step backwards. 'Once what lies in their breeches calls the tune their brains gets addled . . . Well, give 'im a month or two and p'raps the novelty of having his bed warmed reg'lar will have wore off. Mistress'll have to learn her place then and all will be as 'twas afore they wed, wi'out her plaguing us and interfering . . . Now you,' to me, 'into the scullery and set about those dirty dishes!' She jerked her head to a door in the far corner of the kitchen. 'I en't got time to waste gossiping. And you,' to Martin, 'out of my kitchen! I'm not in the mood to be generous, so you needn't think you'll be refreshin' yourself with victuals afore you leaves.'

Martin was already edging away, looking as though escape from this dragon was more on his mind than a free supper.

'I'll bid you good night, ma'am,' he said, but she had already turned her back on us and was waddling away.

'I'll be off then, maid,' he muttered to me.

'Good night, Martin.' From somewhere my voice came out clear and strong. I had something to cling to after all. Mrs Hill had unwittingly given it to me: the information that the Thorn Tree had a new mistress who was demanding change. There was hope – there had to be – in that. 'And, Martin, would you give a special message to Miss Edgar for me?'

His eyes swivelled nervously to the door. ''Tis no use asking favours. You're put here and here you must stay.'

I laughed. It did not sound in the least false.

'I don't need to ask a favour. I just want you to say to Miss Edgar how very pleased I am to have been found such an . . . an *interesting* place. I shall be very content and comfortable here . . . Now, be sure to tell her that, won't you?'

He nodded uncertainly.

I felt in my pocket and drew out one of my precious pennies.

'Promise me, Martin,' I said firmly, pressing the penny into his palm.

He looked down at it in surprise.

Then, brusquely, he thrust the coin back at me. 'I thank 'ee kindly, maid, but I don't need your penny to remember to speak as you tells me. You has need of it more'n me, I reckon.'

He cast a last apprehensive look at the cook, bestowed a kindlier – perhaps a shamefaced – one on me, and was gone.

So I had my little victory, hollow though it was.

For once I had crept with my small bundle of belongings into the dank, fetid scullery and seen the squalid mess that awaited me, I wished with all my heart that I had weakened and begged Martin to take me back.

'Wake up! Rouse yourself, you lazy bitch!' Pain shot through my shoulder as a hand gripped my arm and yanked me upright. ''Twill be the worse for all of us if Cook comes down and finds the fire en't ready nor the water fetched.'

I ground my knuckles into my eyes, blinked, tried to remember how long I had been locked in the cellar . . .

Memory returned with a frightening rush. This was not the cellar at the orphanage but the room at the Thorn Tree where I had collapsed to the straw-filled pallet so short a time ago and had sunk instantly to oblivion. I had but the blurriest recollection of being shown to this cubbyhole off the kitchen where I was to sleep. Now I remembered this girl. She had been laughing – no, there'd been two of them jeering and scoffing – as I removed my clothes in the modest way I'd been taught, struggled into my nightgown and, despite my exhaustion, carefully folded my day clothes and laid them square and neat on the rough shelf above my straw pallet.

'Proper fancy, en't she?'

'Too grand for us.'

'P'raps her thinks the bugs'll be too respectful to find their way under that nice clean night shift.'

'But her'll be sadly mistook. An' I daresay the ones Polly left behind'll be glad of a drink o' new blood.'

Their shrieks of laughter had chased me into the swift dark embrace of sleep. Now, as my arm was loosed and my tormenter turned away, I saw in the flickering light of the tallow dip that I had not slept here alone.

There were two other pallets besides mine, the three of them taking up nearly all the floor space. The only other furnishing was the rough shelving running the length of each wall and the chamber-pot in the corner behind the door.

'Where is the washstand?' I ventured timidly after a moment, thinking – hoping – that there might be some private corner set aside where I could spend a few moments collecting my wits while swilling my face to banish the muzzy effects of too little sleep.

'Washstand, is it? Well, 'er highness upstairs do have such a thing.' The bigger of the two girls turned a surly face towards me. 'You may stick your 'ead under the pump when you fetch the water, if you've a mind to it.'

The other girl stopped yawning and peered at me from under draggles of unkempt hair. 'Finicky ways won't find you no favour 'ere,' she said in a more kindly tone. 'Don't forget too much washin' is weakenin' in cold weather an' it'll set Cook in a temper if 'er finds you've took an ague on account of deliberately layin' yourself open to such.'

I looked from one to the other of them as they stretched and scratched and did up the strings and hooks of the grimy clothes they had slept in. The animal smell of them hung sourly in the atmosphere yet they seemed entirely uncaring of their noisome, grubby state. I wondered with a shudder how soon I should become like them.

At Lady Eleanor's the virtue esteemed above all others was that of cleanliness and we slaved from morn to night in its cause, for apart from Martha Monday and Cook there was no other indoor servant kept. No speck of dust was ever allowed to rest for long. Floors must be scrubbed daily, walls scoured, furniture moved to ensure that no spider's web lurked unseen. Bed linen and body linen were rigorously and regularly laundered, the mattresses on our beds turned and aired every day, the pewter plates we ate from and the utensils used in the preparation of our food washed, sanded and polished after each meal. For fleas or lice Miss Edgar had no mercy. Any such creature having the temerity to enter the orphanage was hunted down and eliminated instantly, and from infancy we were compelled to strip and wash ourselves from head to toe twice in the week and examine our clothes to ensure that we were not harbouring anything untoward. In summer it was a pleasure to be fresh and clean. In winter when we had to break the ice on the washbasin and submit our shrinking flesh to the rigours of cold water and the harsh soap we made from grease and ashes, it was a considerable penance. But to disobey was to court punishment so we had no choice but to steel ourselves and to become hardy in the worship of the gods of cleanliness and order.

I could not easily dismiss the habits ingrained into me.

Though the other two did no more than push their tangled hair under their caps by way of making themselves neat, and did not give a backward glance at the state in which they had left their beds, I felt compelled to dress as carefully as I could before I straightened the two ragged blankets that had been my covering and followed the other two into the kitchen.

The girls were named Amy and Cass, both older than me by several years. They were quick to advise me of their superiority.

'Bear in mind that we'm above 'ee,' said Amy, setting the tallow dip on the big table that stood in the centre of the kitchen and proceeding to light others from it. 'You'm only a scullion and me an' Cass is kitchen maids. So if we tell 'ee what to do, you does it without argufying, d'you hear? First off, get that fire going and stir the gruel afore 'ee goes to fetch the water.'

There was a good supply of small faggots kept near the hearth. I found a few red embers under the heaped ashes and with the aid of the bellows soon got the fire to a good blaze. The cauldron of oatmeal and water, which had hung all night over the embers, was now reduced to a smooth cream. I gave it an appreciative stir with the wooden spoon, realising suddenly that I was famished. I had not been offered supper last night and even if I had been, I think I should have refused, for the revolting and smelly mess I had had to tackle in the scullery had turned my stomach. My spirits sank at the prospect of having to face the scullery again. And not only today but for the weeks and months ahead.

'Don't think you gets your breakfast yet,' Cass warned me. She was the kindlier-mannered of the two. Amy was pretty in a hard, sharp-featured way, but Cass had a round face and limpid blue eyes which seemed altogether pleasanter to me. 'None of us eats until the men comes in and Mrs Hill is 'ere – an' 'er don't come down until me and Amy's set the kitchen to rights. An' you'd best hurry about fetchin' in the water. If the kettle's not boiling for the toast-and-water she reckons sets 'er up for the day, her'll take the broom to your backside.'

If I had not felt so unhappy and confused I daresay in the next few minutes I should have fallen prey to the giggles, for I could imagine our old cook at the orphanage would have swooned right away at the paltry efforts of the pair of them.

Amy pushed a clutter of pans to one end of the table, then wiped a rag in a languid fashion across the cleared space before carelessly throwing down spoons, knives and bowls together with a brace of fat loaves and a crock of butter she fetched from the pantry. Cass meanwhile took a few swipes of the broom across the floor and briefly opened the back door to whisk her meagre catch over the step. She shut the door hastily against the cold and shuffled back to the fire. Here she drew two stools to the hearth beside a wooden rocking chair that I presumed was Cook's own and presently both girls settled themselves before the blaze.

Was that it? Could they not see the curtains of smoke-grimed cobwebs dangling from every beam? Or the gruesome state of the flagstones? Or those mouldering remnants lying under the table? Evidently not. Nor, apparently, did they have any intention of putting themselves out further. They both drew their skirts back over their knees to make the most of the heat and settled to gossiping.

I had already made acquaintance with the pump in the yard. Last evening I had been obliged to make several journeys there to refill the cistern kept by the scullery sink. I had done no more than scuttle there and back as quick as I could, for Mrs Hill had bellowed at me that I should not be allowed to bed until every dish was washed and dried. This was a daunting enough task in itself, but what gave me greater horror than the tottering mounds of plates and bowls and cooking pots, was the surroundings in which I was expected to perform this miracle. Every level surface was clotted with greasy filth and I could feel the slippery pull of spilled detritus under the soles of my shoes as I stepped across to the slime-encrusted wooden sink.

I could not even find a place to leave my cloak and bundle where they would not get soiled. I settled in the end for leaving the door to the yard open a crack and suspending cloak and bundle from the top of it, and though in consequence an icy draught streamed in, I was able to bear that better than the closed-up stench of the scullery.

Gingerly I had searched among the clutter for something to aid me in my task but could find nothing but a ragged bunch of twigs. There was not even a washball of ferns, nor a handful of bran to help clean off the grease, leave alone the luxury of fine sand or good whitening. I had already been told I was forbidden to interfere with the activities in the kitchen by begging for hot water. 'There's no call to be particler,' Mrs Hill had bellowed. 'Our customers en't proud. They'm more concerned wi' their victuals than what they eats off.'

It made a deal of extra work to empty the sink so often (I did not even bother to ask where the slops should be discarded, but threw them willy-nilly over the grass that fringed the cobbled yard outside) and refill it with clean water. For some reason it had seemed important that I did make this one small stand, though a futile one it appeared this morning when I went into the scullery for the buckets, and my nose and eyes informed me that my efforts had made very little difference. The plates and bowls might now be ranged in some sort of order in the racks on the walls where I had set them last night, but the scullery itself was as filthy as ever and I could hardly think where I should begin – and with what means – to make it any better.

I hefted up the wooden buckets and opened the door to the yard, misery and self-pity hanging like a solid weight on my shoulders. But I got no further than the step, stopped dead in my tracks by the sight that met my bemused eyes.

Last night the yard had been very dark, the trace of light from the scullery door being the only illumination by which I could find my way to the pump. I had expected nothing different this morning, for it was not yet dawn.

I could not have believed such an alteration.

Some time during the night there had been a light fall of snow, though the sky was now clear and cloudless. The snow, the frosty glitter of stars and a near-full moon had transformed the yard, the huddle of outbuildings surrounding it and the leafless branches of the trees rising above the roofs. It was magical. Silver on black. A landscape glossed with pure cold light, mysterious and beautiful.

Perhaps it was that very unexpectedness that seemed to bestow the atmosphere with the quality that struck deep into my heart – a sign of such significance that I instinctively knew that I must hold to this moment and imprint it on my memory. I stood there, transfixed, slowly becoming aware of the depth and silence of the countryside beyond the inn, something I had never experienced before.

From the drying yard behind the orphanage we saw nothing but the backs of other houses. Our short walk to church on Sunday was through narrow old streets with few gardens to break the monotony of stone and brick. We knew of the importance of Bristol as a sea port, we knew of its rich merchant venturers, and of the fashionable people who came to be cured by the waters of Clifton Hotwells. It was in the households of these people we might be lucky to find employment, or an apprenticeship in some trade which relied upon the patronage of such gentry. But our lives being so greatly circumscribed, I had never clapped eyes on the river or glimpsed the splendour of the great cleft of the Avon Gorge until yesterday when I left Lady Eleanor's for good. Even then, Martin had hustled me on when I might have dawdled to soak up all these unfamiliar, exhilarating sights, for it was a long walk. Indeed, by the time we were well out on the country road it was already dusk and my feet were so sore and my nervousness about my destination grown so intense that I was scarcely aware of the scenery.

Now, standing at the scullery door and a mere step away from the squalor that reigned within, I was transported to a landscape of dreamlike purity. And I seemed to feel the living presence of the land – the deep secret earth, the trees and plants in the fastness of their winter sleep, all the wild creatures that the land nourished – pressing close about the walls of the inn.

I felt very small and vulnerable. In this silver-washed darkness I was alone, caught and held by something beyond my understanding. Yet I did not feel afraid. Rather, I felt the strangest elation, as though I was on the verge of some important discovery. I found myself looking up at the moon as though I half-expected a message to come whispering down through the icy air . . .

All was silent

And water must be fetched or I should fall foul of Cook's temper.

The spell shattered. The icy air nipped peevishly at my face and fingers. I had been caught up in a fantasy that was both foolish and harmful, for I should surely catch my death if I dawdled here much longer. Shivering, I slipped and slithered my way across to the pump, the icy moonlight seeming not so much beautiful now as hard and unfriendly.

I cranked fiercely at the handle. It was a larger, heavier pump than the one in the orphanage yard and it took a moment before the water began to flow. It was in those seconds before the water gushed out that the thought came out of nowhere.

That deep under the yard – which I did not doubt to be any more savoury than the rest of the inn – was a spring that ran fresh and crystal sweet, no matter what desecration lay above. And close on the heels of that thought came another: that this source of water was like hope in the human heart, always there, always reachable. And as water sustained the body, so hope sustained the mind and spirit. That was something I needed to remember.

I filled the second bucket more slowly. It was pure imagination to believe this was a message borne of the magical moonlight, yet it comforted me to accept it. And I knew that from wherever the message did come, it was a true one. If I gave way entirely to despondency and gloom I was lost. I was very young, I was strong and I must cling tenaciously to the anticipation of better things to come . . .

A noise. The crunch of a shoe on the snow. I jerked my head round to the direction of the sound. There was someone – a shrouded figure – watching me from the inky moonshadow at the angle of the outbuildings.

Now I did feel fear. Was it an intruder intent on villainy? Or someone who would sneak to Cook that I was dawdling? I snatched up the buckets and made for the scullery door.

Speed was my undoing. My feet slipped from under me and down I went, landing flat on my back and banging my head on the ground. I lay there winded and dazed, feeling the spilled water seeping into my skirt and stockings, and momentarily unable to do anything about it.

'Are you hurt? Here, let me help you up.' A woman's voice, calm and unflustered. An arm about my shoulders, as I sat up too quickly and the moonlit yard spun dizzily about me. 'You went down with a thump enough to break bones. Are you able to stand? There . . . lean on me and I will help you inside.'

'The buckets,' I said weakly. 'I must refill them . . .'

'That can wait,' the woman said in a tone that brooked no argument. 'It is more important to see what damage you have done to yourself.'

I was glad to do as I was bid. My head was throbbing so badly that my chief concern was to get back to the kitchen and sit down before I swooned right away from the pain of it. I just hoped Cook was not yet down and I should be given a moment or two to recover my wits.

We shuffled into the scullery and then through the linking door to the kitchen. As we did so a missile came hurtling at us, missing me by a whisker, and Cook's voice bellowed, 'What's 'ee been up to? Where's the water, you misbegotten, idle young toad? . . . Oh . . .' Her voice died away to a stunned silence. Then, 'Oh, Mrs Yelland, ma'am, I didn't see 'ee.'

'Evidently not, Mrs Hill,' the woman said drily.

Mrs Yelland! My throbbing head could scarcely grapple with the information that my rescuer was the woman who employed me, the new mistress of the Thorn Tree.

'Perhaps, Amy,' she went on, nudging the missile with her foot, 'you could bring yourself to leave the comfort of the hearth in order to replace this piece of wood on the log pile. Then retrieve the buckets and fetch in the water.'

The icy sarcasm of her tone caused all three of them to rise as one from where they had been sitting so cosily ensconced by the fire. Amy, head down, scuttled across to retrieve the missile. Cass grasped the broom and took a deep, sudden interest in sweeping up the ash from the hearth. Mrs Hill bent intently over the porridge pot, as though her life depended on inspecting its contents.

I saw them all through a grey, sickly veil as Mrs Yelland half dragged me across the kitchen and pushed me down into the rocking chair that Mrs Hill had vacated. It was a few moments before my head stopped spinning enough for me to take a proper look at my rescuer.

She was a small, plump, straight-backed woman of perhaps a little over thirty. She had thrown back the hood of her dark cloak to reveal a crisp linen cap set on glossy brown hair. A pair of sharp green eyes regarded me with concern.

'You are very pale. Are you still in pain?'

'Just where I banged my head, ma'am. It's easing, now.' I gingerly touched the back of my head and managed a shaky laugh. 'I've a lump as big as an egg.'

'Let me see. Indeed you have. And you are soaked to the skin.' To my astonishment she went on her knees on the flagstones, unbuckled my shoes and placed them on the hearthstone, then peeled down my stockings. She wrung out the worst of the wet and hung them over one of the trivets above the fire where they proceeded to steam gently. 'Do you have spare clothes?'

'A petticoat and stockings, ma'am,' I said, astounded that she did not seem to think it beneath her dignity to attend me like this.

'Fetch them,' she said sharply to Cass.

By the time Cass returned I was feeling recovered enough to unfasten my damp petticoat, slip it off, retie the clean one round my waist and pull on the dry stockings.

But Mrs Yelland was still not satisfied. She made me sit down again.

'You will feel more comfortable now, but you must stay by the fire until that damp patch on your dress dries and you are feeling stronger.' She brushed vigorously at the crumbs and ashes that now decorated her own skirts from kneeling on the floor. 'I will not have it on my conscience that you took sick on your first day here. Do you understand, Mrs Hill? The child – Emily Wroe, is it not? – has had a nasty shock. See that she rests here until you have all breakfasted.' She frowned at me. 'I think she would benefit from a little more flesh on her bones, so you must ensure that she eats well. Cass, you may then fetch her upstairs to see me before she begins her day's work.' A pause, then, with a caustic glance around the kitchen: 'I see, Mrs Hill, you have not yet had time to put in hand the improvements I wished made in here.'

'Oh, 'twill all be done soon, Mrs Yelland, ma'am.' Mrs Hill's fawning smile was no more pleasant than her scowl, for it revealed four yellow fangs in her otherwise toothless mouth. ''Tis just that with losing Polly so sudden and now 'aving to train up a new girl . . .'

'Polly was a harlot and a thief. She brought trouble on herself. If she had spent her time about her proper duties instead of obliging customers on her back in the hay loft or skulking in corners intent on picking pockets, then I would not have had reason to dismiss her. I repeat what I told you yesterday. I will not tolerate dishonesty and whorish behaviour.' She looked hard at Cass and Amy as she spoke. Cass's round face turned pink. Amy seemed in a mind to stare back brazenly but quickly lowered her eyes under that piercing green gaze. 'Do you understand?' They shuffled their feet and muttered that they did. 'Good. And as to instructing Emily, Mrs Hill, I believe you will find that she is already well trained in the duties of a scullery maid. Or so I am reliably informed. I shall make my own assessment of her worth in due course, but in the meantime I should be obliged if you would employ less rigorous methods of encouragement than throwing objects at her. She has already received one blow to the head this morning. Another might have addled her wits completely.'

I fully expected to be cuffed from Cook's chair when Mrs Yelland had departed, saying coldly as she went out that she hoped to see a considerable improvement in the state of the kitchen when she should see it again. But as Mrs Yelland closed the inner door behind her Mrs Hill was distracted by the men shuffling in by the back door for breakfast. She immediately sat herself at the table and settled for throwing me a poisonous scowl before launching into a highly coloured version of what had happened. Amy's glare was no less fearsome as she ladled porridge from the pot over the fire and carried the brimming bowls back to the table.

''Ten't my business to be waitin' on 'ee,' she snarled in passing. 'You can go 'ungry for all I care. Sittin' there like a fine lady. 'Ten't right, while those 'ee should be serving has to do the work.'

But Cass, kindlier – or maybe because her fear of the mistress overrode her fear of Cook – brought me a tankard of small ale and a bowl and spoon when she fetched bread to toast at the fire.

'Help yourself to gruel,' she whispered. 'Much as 'ee likes. Now watch what I does, for making Cook's toast water is rightly your job and you must do it tomorrow.'

The porridge was superior to any I had ever tasted, bearing no comparison to the watery stuff doled out at the orphanage. I ate slowly, relishing every mouthful while I watched Cass break up the toast into a jug, tip boiling water from the black kettle onto it, then cover the jug with a scrap of muslin.

''Tis to be left standing on the marble slab in the pantry until 'tis properly cold. It don't take long this weather. Then 'ee strains it through this muslin into a mug and takes it to Cook. Her says 'tis healthful for the bellyache she's a martyr to.'

'Is it the bellyache that makes her so cross?' I ventured.

'Her's not such a bad ole stick, as a rule,' Cass said comfortably. 'An' her's a grand cook, as you'll find out. I never ate so good in my life till I come here. 'Tis just that her's had her own way for all the many years her's been here. Makes all this talk of change proper upsetting for her.'

She went off bearing her jug and I refilled my bowl from the porridge pot, still bemused by the concern that Mrs Yelland had shown to me. Though I seemed to be the only one to have an appreciative thought towards her. The mood at the table where two elderly men had seated themselves either side of Mrs Hill was very different. Mr Yelland's marriage was evidently an aggravation to them all.

'Poor Master Harry,' sighed the man addressed as Enoch, spitting out mouthfuls of breadcrumbs as he spoke. 'Kept hisself out of women's hands all these years and now to fall prey to such a managing wench.'

'Aye, and her's already seen one husband off,' said Albert, a small bony man with a sharp-featured face. 'I hear tell the stepson wanted shut of her after his pa died, her was such a nuisance. I favour he's well pleased someone else has the handling of her now.'

Cook gave a disparaging snort. 'A pity Master Harry ever went to her poor husband's funeral and fell into her clutches.'

'He was bound to go, I suppose, bein' kin.'

'No more'n a distant cousin to him as died,' she said. 'And them living so far off, there was no obligation.' She hesitated, then leaning forward, lowered her voice to a penetrating whisper. 'Seems to me as though someone meant for him to be there. As though he'd been *called*. Think on it! Think of the way he was took so sudden with a fancy for her. Why, he come back from that funeral a changed man.'

'How changed?' said Enoch, bushy grey eyebrows drawn to a frown.

'Different. As if . . . as if his thoughts was all mazed and he couldn't put his mind to aught.'

'Mazed, that's it 'zackly!' Albert thumped his tankard down on the table, his long nose quivering with excitement. 'Be damned if you en't put your finger on it, Mrs

Hill. Said to you, Enoch, didn't I? Master's proper tetchy, I says. Forgettin' things hisself and making out it's our fault. And him usually so easy-tempered.'

'You says a lot o'things, Albert Huggins,' said Enoch. ''Alf of 'em doesn't make sense.' He sucked his teeth reflectively. 'Still, this time, I has to admit you might be right.'

Mrs Hill pursed her lips. 'Whatever happened to poor Harry her's at back of it, I wager. There's something about her that en't quite Christian to my mind.' She nodded portentously. 'Something that en't rightly... *natural*...'

A log fell suddenly to the hearth. Ash and smoke gusted over me in a fine grey cloud. Amy and Cass both jumped, squeaking like frightened mice. Even the men looked momentarily disconcerted, as though the sound had added emphasis to Mrs Hill's pronouncement.

I picked up the poker and pushed the log back into the blaze. I told myself stoutly that I would not believe their superstitious gossip. They were unpleasant people who were out to blacken the new mistress's name because they were afraid of the changes she was set on. From what little I had seen of the Thorn Tree, I could see nothing but advantage in a few alterations.

For all that, I was glad when one voice spoke up in Mrs Yelland's defence, for uneasy thoughts, once they were implanted, bred others. I could not help but remember how her dark-cloaked figure had merged with the moon-shadow and how she had scared me, standing there when I thought I was alone...

'Speak as you find, I say,' said the voice defiantly. 'Mrs Yelland's spoken kindly to me and given me one of Master's old shirts. I'll not think evil of her.'

I had almost overlooked the red-headed boy at the far end of the table. He had been silent and devout in his attention to his breakfast, though where he put the weight of porridge and bread I could not tell, for he was thin as a wire, with long bony wrists protruding from the sleeves of his ragged jacket. I remembered now that I had glimpsed him last evening staggering out of the kitchen with a loaded tray looking as if his lean shanks might buckle under the weight of it.

'No one asked 'ee, Luke Gilpin,' said Enoch, fetching him a buffet across his ears. 'Sup your ale and less of your lip.'

''Tis the truth,' the boy persisted.

'And what does 'ee know, eh?'

'When my ma was living, she taught me to speak the truth and fear nobody. So I'll not hush up about saying my piece if it's right and proper.'

'Pity her didn't learn 'ee not to interrupt your elder and betters, you young bugger,' Enoch growled, bunching his fists for another blow.

But the boy was too quick. He slid like quicksilver from his chair and dodged out of range, grabbing a last slice of bread as he went.

'Can't stay dawdling here,' he called, grinning. 'I've logs to take up to Master's parlour before I tends the pigs. If I meet Mistress, I'll give her your regards, shall I, Enoch? Perhaps then she won't be so inclined to bewitch you into a bluebottle or a dung beetle for speaking ill of her, for I daresay if she is what you say she is, she knows all that goes on down here... You'd best think on that, hadn't you, before you start gossiping about Mrs Yelland again?'

He was out of the kitchen, laughing, before Enoch could summon breath for a few choice oaths, while Mrs Hill shook her head and muttered darkly about young imps who were too cocky for their own good.

But Luke Gilpin's little outburst had altered the atmosphere. I for one was pleased. His plain speaking had brought a breath of common sense that stirred the company, perhaps a little guiltily, into movement.

There was a shuffling and coughing and scraping of

chairs. The men departed, Amy snuffed out the now redundant candles. And I looked at the wintry light filtering through the grimy little windows and envied not a little the cheerful cheekiness of the red-headed boy.

The Thorn Tree was old. A building that had the feel of something ancient that had sprouted out of the earth in a haphazard fashion. As a tree year by year puts out new twigs and branches, so the inn seemed to have added bits to itself – some half-timbered, some brick or stone – to no discernible pattern. The result was a jumble of interlinking rooms and passages, with steps and staircases in unexpected places. I would in time come to know every inch of the inn and appreciate its idiosyncratic architecture, but that first morning as Cass led me up to the Yellands' parlour I was more oppressed by the deep gloom cast by the low ceilings and inadequate windows than curious about its dilapidated charm. Where a glimmer of light did filter through the dirty panes it revealed only peeling plaster, crumbling wainscoting and rough, uneven floorboards, and even on the upper floor there was no escape from the clinging aroma of stale tobacco smoke and ale lees with an underlying rankness of grime and neglect.

So my first sight of the Yellands' parlour came as a surprise. I realised then that I should have listened more attentively to what Cass had been telling me on the way up; that though Mrs Yelland had been here barely a month she had spent most of that time arranging her immediate surroundings to her own satisfaction.

'Had me and Amy up here two whole days, a-scrubbing and a-scouring,' she grumbled. 'And howsoever we laboured, nothin' was right for her. Got into a proper temper when Amy missed but a speck of dust in a corner where nobody'd ever notice. Packed us off back to the kitchen, saying we was more trouble than help and she'd sooner do it herself and know it was done proper.' Cass's round face was crestfallen. 'I had hopes as the missus' might have need of a housemaid, and I should be asked, for I've been here longest and I've been used to tidying round for Master Harry when he's had need of it an' *he's* never complained. But *her's* a different article altogether. Me and Amy don't suit her ideas, that's for sure.'

Having witnessed a sample of Cass and Amy's working methods, I was less than surprised at this, though I managed a sympathetic murmur before she went on, 'Poor Master Harry, 'tis he I feels most sorry for. Missus had most of the furniture that had been his pa's – and his pa's before that – put out in the yard to make way for what her brung from Devon. All her let him keep was his armchair and the big bed – for 'tis a grand affair, all carved wi' strange beasts. Not that her give tuppence for the bed curtains. Tore 'em down and fired 'em in the field at the back along with master's old hoss-hair mattress. Now the pair of 'em lies snug as fleas on a dog's tail on *two* fat feather mattresses, one atop t'other, *and* her's makin' new hangings though there was naught wrong with the old beyond a bit of moth . . . Now, can 'ee manage the door latch? Knock afore 'ee opens the door, though, and wait to hear her bid us enter, or we'll catch the sharp edge of her tongue.'

We were carrying a laden tray each and I nearly dropped mine in astonishment as I stepped across the threshold. It was in that moment, as I stared about in wonderment, that I began truly to understand that the new mistress of the Thorn Tree was a force to be reckoned with. Whatever the state of the room previously – and I had little doubt it had been as frowsty as the rest of the place – there was no question that this was now a handsome and elegant parlour.

It was a long room with a window at one narrow end and a closed door, which presumably led to the bedchamber, at the other. The window itself took up almost the width of the end wall, its tiny panes of uneven greenish glass spilling a pale aqueous light across a rug set beneath it on the scrubbed floorboards. The rug glowed like a jewel with shades of amber and cream and gold on a red background, the heavy window curtains picking up the same warm colour, as did the embroidery on the seats of the upright chairs. Apart from a round table, a shabby wing chair and a smaller chair set before the fire, the rest of the furniture – three more chairs, a large cabinet with drawers underneath and a glass cupboard above, and a sofa – was placed around plastered walls that looked newly lime-washed. Even the air in here was different, tangy with beeswax and lavender and the spicy aroma of the apple-wood burning in the grate.

So much my senses took in before I hastened to follow Cass to the table and carefully set down the platter of cold meats on the white cloth which was already arrayed with silver cutlery and blue and white china of a fineness I had never seen before. Cass put the covered pot of porridge to keep hot by the fire where a burnished copper kettle already simmered on the hob and a blue and white teapot stood warming on a brass trivet.

Mrs Yelland, with no more than a swift glance in our direction, turned back to the yellow flowers she was settling into a jug on the window ledge.

With her back to us, she said, 'You may tell Mrs Hill, Cass, that I will return Emily to her shortly.'

'Yes, ma'am. Thank 'ee, ma'am.'

Cass bobbed a curtsey at Mrs Yelland's unresponsive back, gave me with an encouraging wink and departed. It was very silent when she had gone – nothing but a faint scratching noise as Mrs Yelland rearranged the flowers to her satisfaction, and the crackle of the fire. I fell to wondering if I should be able to find my way back to the kitchen without going astray. Then, though I had received only kindness so far from Mrs Yelland, the silence as it lengthened became unnerving, reminding me inevitably of Miss Edgar's cat-and-mouse methods. She had taken the utmost pleasure in drawing out an interview with anyone guilty of transgressing her petty rules. Her victim would be subjected to long, tormenting pauses, during which Miss Edgar would smile her false smile as she contemplated some new form of humbling punishment.

But when Mrs Yelland turned slowly to face me, she was not smiling. Indeed, there was a look on her face that made me think my presence was an interruption to whatever sad thoughts had taken hold of her. It seemed something of an effort for her to focus on me and to say softly, 'I have always thought this jasmine such a brave flower, to blossom as it does in the dead of winter.'

'Yes, ma'am,' I said, having little idea of what she meant, flowers having no place at Lady Eleanor's.

Her sigh was no more than a faint breath. 'I suppose its very tenacity is a lesson to us that even in this cruellest of seasons we must have hope.'

'Yes, ma'am.'

'So be it. The flower is a sign of better things to come. As are you, Emily Wroe.'

'Me, ma'am?'

'Indeed, yes. Skinny little rabbit that you are, you represent change and a new order. You have taken no harm from your tumble?'

'No, ma'am.'

'Excellent.' Her movements were brisk now, as she crossed the room to seat herself in the smaller of the chairs by the fire. She settled the fine brown wool of her skirt in orderly folds. 'That you prove hardy is fortunate. There is much to be done here and I have a mind to improvements. But nothing will be achieved without hard work and I have need of willing servants round me. You are the first of a new breed, and come highly recommended for your diligence in performing the duties about the kitchen and scullery that will be required of you.'

And what pleasure Miss Edgar must have had in condemning me to drudgery of the lowest sort.

Mrs Yelland smiled. 'So I have decided you will be my good omen, Emily. My good luck charm.'

'Yes, ma'am?' I said cautiously.

She laughed. The laugh transformed her. In repose the gravity of her expression gave her a matronly look. When she smiled or laughed the matronly image was quite banished. All the energy of a lively intelligence seemed to flash in her green eyes. Even the contours of her face seemed changed, from mere ordinariness to something close to beauty. I noticed then the creamy smoothness of her complexion, the perfection of her small, even teeth, the seductive curve of her lips. Mrs Hill had said Master Harry had been enchanted by his new wife. In that moment it was easy to see that it was nothing to do with spells, but that bewitchment of a very different sort was entirely possible.

'Poor child. You look bewildered. And no wonder. But do not fret at the responsibility. All you need do is work hard and be obedient to my orders, as I understand you have been taught to do —' She broke off to cry lightly, 'Ah, Mr Yelland. Good morning to you. Such a slugabed you are! Why, I have been up and about these three hours.'

I turned to view the man who was my master. My nervous curtsey went unheeded as he yawned and stretched and answered amiably, 'That's as maybe, my love, but you were asleep long before I closed the door on the last customer.'

He shambled towards us, a big bear of a man, slippered feet slapping loudly on the boards, nightcap askew on a round, cropped head and the skirts of a shrunken dressing robe that might once, in its heyday, have been brightly striped in red and yellow, gaping over a round belly to reveal the nightshirt underneath.

I felt embarrassed at the nearness of this large male creature in a state of undress. My upbringing in a world of females had not prepared me for such an intimate encounter. Yet neither Mr nor Mrs Yelland seemed to think the presence of a maid in the least untoward. I noted that carefully. I had much to learn in this outside world. I guessed this would be the first of many such lessons.

Mrs Yelland smiled again, that same dazzling, transforming smile. No, not quite the same. It seemed, as she looked at this man who was her new husband, that there was a fixity to it that had not been there before. As though there was purpose behind it. As though she knew perfectly well how she looked and what effect it had.

'Oh dear, I should not tease you,' she said. 'It is my own fault that I am a lark rather than an owl. I find it quite impossible to break myself of the habit of rising early, as I always had to do at Starlings. I hope you will forgive me for it.'

'Forgive?' He blinked at her, the expression on his broad, jowly face one of honest and simple adoration. 'Why, there is nothing to forgive.' He guffawed, and brushed his bunched knuckles against her shoulder. 'Save that I woke to find only chilly sheets where I expected warm, willing flesh, which was a disappointment – and I thought to 'tice you back, my love, should you feel the need of more comfort than this fire can give.'

He bent to aim a kiss on her mouth, but she turned her head crying quickly, 'Really, Mr Yelland, did you not notice we had company?' so that the kiss slid clumsily to her cheek and he was forced to stand upright again, looking somewhat bewildered.

'Company or no, a man might greet his wife . . .' he began. Then, peering at me as though properly seeing me for the first time: 'And who might this young person be?'

'This is our new scullery maid, Emily,' said Mrs Yelland. 'You remember how that goodwife we met on the coach from Exeter told me of the excellent maid she had obtained from a foundling home in Bristol? I lost no time in writing to the Board of Trustees on the very day I saw off that thieving slut I caught picking the pocket of a drunk.'

'But I always found Poll a good-natured soul. Do you not fancy you were a mite hasty there, my love? After all, one little slip—'

'It was not the first time,' Mrs Yelland said firmly. 'I spied her more than once lurking about the taproom door when she should have been about her work. That was why I made it my business to watch her and so discovered that she was regularly fleecing those whose wits were rendered insensible by drink. What else could I do but put her off?' Again the bewitching smile. 'I was deeply grieved to think that she sought to reward her kind master with such wicked behaviour . . . But you may rest assured, my dear, that you will never be troubled by dishonest and treacherous servants again. It is my duty – and indeed my pleasure – as a wife to take up the domestic burdens of this household which you have carried alone for so long. My only wish is to make your life easier . . . Though I see from your face that something troubles you. Do you find my intentions unpleasing?'

'Of course not, my love,' he said hastily. 'It was just that . . . well, I daresay I'm become set in my ways, being so close to forty before finding the happiness in marriage that has eluded me for so long . . . but I have a responsibility towards those who've served me well over the years and who have no place to call home other than the Thorn Tree. Mrs Hill, for one . . .'

Mrs Yelland affected hurt surprise. 'Mrs Hill? Why, I have nothing but admiration for her cooking. Have I not told you so several times? She is a pearl among cooks. I cannot think why you should believe me capable of such high-handed behaviour.'

Mr Yelland looked abashed. 'I'm sorry, my love. I would not have mentioned it, but—'

'But that yours is a generous and unselfish nature which would more easily put up with discomfort rather than cause offence, even to a servant. I find that wholly admirable. Yet I also know from experience that the best of servants may sometimes fall into lax ways and have need of guidance and encouragement from time to time.' She laid her hand gently upon his sleeve. 'I wish only to make you happier than you have ever been, Harry. Why else should I have striven to turn this parlour into a pretty and easeful chamber where we might be cosy together? Surely you could not prefer it as it was, so bedevilled with the clutter of years that you could hardly stir an inch without barking your elbows or stirring dust enough to make you choke?'

'My dear, I could not have believed that my parlour could look so well. Even King George himself could wish for no better . . . Though it's true that I miss my grandfather's settle and the big table.'

'They are not lost!' she said, teasing again. 'They are merely stored in the barn until I – we – may arrange another room where they will be better displayed. And there are plenty of unused chambers to choose from, are there not? I shall set about spring-cleaning a suitable one as soon as I have completed one or two other necessary tasks.' She frowned, then said, as though the idea had just come to her mind, 'Such a sad waste to have so many empty chambers. Even in this quiet season there always seems to be someone going by, for the parish keeps the road in good repair. Certainly better than many country roads I have had the misfortune to be abroad on in winter. Surely in summer there must be plenty of travellers passing this way to reach the toll road to Bath and Bristol.'

'But we have plenty who stop and take refreshment,' Mr Yelland said, with some surprise. 'You saw for yourself how we were run off our feet last evening. And every bed was bespoken.'

'But only two bedchambers in use,' she protested. 'And those abominably crowded.'

He laughed. '''Tis my experience that there are plenty who would sooner share a bed with three others, or take shelter in the stable loft, and have money left to spend on a good breakfast, rather than sleep in solitary splendour and suffer an empty belly for lack of funds.'

Mrs Yelland sighed. 'So it seems. But then the persons who patronise the Thorn Tree are scarcely the sort to appreciate anything better. Yet here we are sitting in a room you say is fit to accommodate a king.' Her voice was thoughtful. 'How sad that we should not set our sights higher than rustics and labouring men, not to mention those others who are so cunning and disreputable in appearance and manners that I shudder to think by what means they make their money.'

'So long as his coin is good, I take no mind to how a man may look or how he earns his bread,' Mr Yelland said comfortably. 'Ours is a reliable trade and always has been. Besides, my old dad always drummed into me that good food and ale served at honest prices were more important than folderols and fripperies. And I take no argument with that, for the Yellands have always made a regular living at the Thorn Tree.'

'Quite so,' said Mrs Yelland somewhat acidly, and looking as though she had a great deal more to say on the matter. But she did not pursue it. Deftly, she turned the conversation again to the subject of servants and to the unfortunate state of the kitchen and scullery, saying lightly, '. . . though this neglect is something you must not chastise yourself for, Harry, for a woman's eye is keener in these matters. And I shall of course consult with Mrs Hill to discover how best to make improvements, so your fears that I shall distress her are quite without foundation.

As to the other servants, if they are honest, willing and obedient then we shall get along in the utmost harmony, as I was explaining to Emily here a few minutes since, was I not, child?'

'Yes, ma'am.'

Mrs Yelland inclined her head in my direction, her clear gaze momentarily laced with feelings that were not evident in her gracious manner or the tone of her voice. Then she took up the kettle, poured boiling water into the teapot and said, 'You may return to the kitchen now. And pray tell Mrs Hill that I shall be down directly after breakfast to speak with her.'

'Yes, ma'am,' I said, and made my escape, leaving Mr Yelland settling to his breakfast, innocently unaware of the determined and calculating glint in his wife's eyes.

For all Mrs Yelland's talk of consulting with Mrs Hill, it was more a case of Mrs Yelland proposing what should be done and Mrs Hill reluctantly agreeing after the mistress had roundly dismissed any opposing arguments. And no sooner was her intention pronounced than Mrs Yelland descended on the kitchen, sleeves rolled to the elbow, straight-backed figure encased in a sacking apron, to labour as hard and long as any of us. I admired her for that, at least, though she gave no quarter to anyone else either and I fell to my bed each night in a smothering cloud of weariness. Had the other two not been equally exhausted, I daresay I should not have been allowed to sleep so peacefully, for Mrs Yelland did me no favours by constantly pointing me out as an example.

'Put more elbow grease into the scrubbing,' she would cry to Amy. 'Watch how Emily goes about it.' Or, 'Emily will show you the way to get the table properly scoured and white, Cass.' Or the big stewing pot, or the fire irons, or anything else whose neglected condition we were ordered to bring to perfection under the mistress's critical gaze. I earned many a glower from them both in consequence and Amy took to sly and sometimes painful methods of hindering me. Muddy fingermarks would appear on a surface I had just polished; my cleaning rags would go astray; I would return from some outdoor errand to find my bucket had mysteriously upset its grimy contents over the newly scrubbed flagstones ... And once, more seriously, she managed to jog my elbow as I poured fresh water from the kettle into the bucket, causing me to splash scalding water onto my wrist. Her effusive apologies did little to mask the sneering pleasure in her face. But I was well schooled in hiding my feelings. I would not give her the satisfaction of letting her see how much it hurt. Instead I made the excuse of fetching more water so that I could allow my tears of agony to escape in private, and numbed the worst of the pain by holding my hand under the gush of icy water before I returned indoors.

But despite Amy's tricks and the undercurrent of grumbling from Cass and Mrs Hill, the work progressed in what spare time we had from the urgent business of keeping the inn's customers fed and watered. Then, one afternoon, Mrs Yelland climbed down from the chair she had been standing on to give the last energetic polish to the high window and stared up at the scrap of blue sky now clearly visible through the glass.

'You will save on candles from now on, if nothing else, Mrs Hill,' she said. 'You might as well have had blinds up there for all the light that could penetrate ... Now, I do believe we're finished. It all looks very well, does it not?'

But Mrs Hill remained determined not to be reconciled to this pristine version of her old dirty kitchen.

'Handsome, ma'am,' she said in a voice of doom. She shook her head so that her jowls wobbled. 'You've gone to a deal of trouble and I 'preciates it. But what with smoke from the fire and steam from the cooking and fat spitting everywhere when there's meat to be roasted, I fear everything will be as 'twas soon enough and these poor maids will have worked their fingers to the bone for naught.'

Cass nodded sagely. Amy sighed. Both quickly arranged their faces into mournful lines, shoulders sagging as if borne down by the unbearable weight of unnatural cleanliness.

'If I might speak plain, ma'am,' Mrs Hill went on.

'By all means,' said Mrs Yelland in an encouraging tone.

'You being . . . well, p'raps not properly used to the trade of catering for hungry men who'll stand no delay, I tell 'ee straight, there's no point in niceness. They wants their victuals quick and hot and plenty of it. And that's what I aims to provide.'

'You do, Mrs Hill,' agreed Mrs Yelland. 'None better. I have heard it said that wagoners and packmen go out of their way in order to sup here because of your excellent cooking.'

A glint of satisfaction sparked in Mrs Hill's eye.

'I'll be bound not one of 'em cares two hoots whether there's cobwebs in the corners or a bit of fat splashed about, so long as his supper's good and tasty.'

'I agree with you entirely. I'm sure they do not.'

This satisfying response emboldened Mrs Hill to add, 'Master Harry's never had nothing but praise for what I does. Nor his pa before that. Both was glad and willin' to let me take care of everything my own way in my own time. Just as a cook should let be. I been here eight-and-thirty years, ma'am, so I should know what I'm about.'

'You should indeed.'

Mrs Hill, growing more confident by the minute, said, 'I was littler than Emily here when I was took on as scullion. Old Mrs Yelland had passed on by the time I was raised to be cook. Her was a sorry invalid a-many years, and with Master Harry being young then and sent off to school, old Master Yelland said he couldn't never have managed as well as he did without Nellie Hill at his right hand.' She finished on a note of triumph. 'And Master Harry hisself told me the same thing not a week afore he went south to wed 'ee, ma'am. Why, it might have been his own dear pa speaking.'

Mrs Yelland did not answer straight off, seemingly digesting Mrs Hill's arguments, and Mrs Hill allowed herself a small satisfied nod at Amy and Cass. Then by way of emphasising her authority in the kitchen and my place as the unwanted newcomer brought in by this interfering mistress, she said loudly to me, 'What you staring at, girl? Get on with gutting and skinning them rabbits. How many more times must I be on at 'ee, lazy little varmint? Would that I'd not lost poor Polly. Not a patch on her, you're not. Why, her'd have been done with those rabbits long since – and had 'em chopped ready for the pot the way I taught her, not to mention the onions and turnips, which you en't set a finger on yet.'

'Are you then in need of eyeglasses, Mrs Hill?' Mrs Yelland asked in a worried manner.

'Eyeglasses, ma'am?' Mrs Hill blinked in surprise. 'Naught wrong with my eyes.'

'Really? Then perhaps it is your imagination that is at fault.'

''Magination?'

'Well, there is clearly a great gap between what actually happens and what you perceive to be happening, and I find myself considerably worried on your behalf because of it.'

Mrs Hill was quite lost. She stood there, large and solid, arms aggressively akimbo, jaw squared, but suddenly looking overblown as though one more sharp thrust by the mistress would deflate her to a blubbery puddle on the freshly sanded flags.

'In short, you seem not to have noticed that Emily

works twice as hard and in a far more thorough manner than Polly ever did.' Her voice was suddenly cutting. 'I find it very strange that you remain ignorant of Emily's energy and application to her duties much as you did Polly's slipshod ways and thieving.'

'As I say, ma'am,' Mrs Hill blustered, 'this 'un puts on a show when I'm looking—'

'And clearly when you are not. Otherwise the scullery would be in the same disgusting state as it had evidently been for a long time under Polly's slovenly care. So, take note of this, Mrs Hill. The kitchen is now brought to a standard which I insist be maintained. Granted, this is a busy and productive place, but that is no excuse for the neglect of decent housewifely considerations. I have observed for myself that there are certain hours in the day when your duties are less than pressing. I shall expect you at such times to oversee the maids in restoring order and cleanliness.' She fixed the cook with a steely eye. 'A hungry wagoner might not care one jot for a cobweb dangling into his dinner, but I most certainly do, Mrs Hill. As to spilled fat or anything else that makes its home where it should not be, you will see that it is removed and the kitchen left spotless before you retire to bed at night. Every night. Do you understand me?'

Mrs Hill gulped, setting her chins a-quiver. She looked so startled and helpless under Mrs Yelland's unwinking gaze that I felt a twinge of discomfort on her behalf. In the battle of wills there was little doubt who would be the victor.

'Well, Mrs Hill? Is that clear to you?'

Cook could do no more than mutter her agreement. Mrs Yelland, her voice once more light and encouraging, said, 'And speaking of beds, the maids' present sleeping arrangements are most unsatisfactory. Young girls are prone to mischief when they are left unsupervised, witness Polly's unfortunate example. As soon as can be arranged they will remove to the attic alongside your room, Mrs Hill, where you may be on hand to ensure that they remain where they should be during the hours of darkness.' Then with a hard look at Amy, 'And I caution you all: my bedchamber is on the floor below the attics and I sleep exceedingly light. I shall most certainly hear if there is anyone creeping about overhead who should be fast in bed.'

Amy insolently flounced her head as though she did not care, but her lips tightened in anger, prompting me to remember those mornings when Cass and I had woken to find her bed empty.

'Her's out at the privy, I daresay,' Cass would explain a touch too hastily.

But the giggling, whispered conversations with Cass when she eventually sneaked in had given me cause to wonder if there was some other explanation. Now I knew that I was right.

But any pleasure I might have felt in Mrs Yelland curtailing Amy's sleazy activities or the prospect of a new bedchamber was quickly dispelled, for the minute Mrs Yelland left the kitchen Amy pounced on me and twisted her fingers in my hair, yanking on it so hard that my eyes watered.

'You bin sneaking tales to missus, eh?'

'No! I've said nothing!'

'Liar!'

''Tweren't likely Emily said aught,' Cass said quickly, wincing in sympathy as Amy wrenched again at my hair. 'Missus has got eyes in her backside. 'Ee knows that, Amy.'

'A-prowling and a-poking of her nose into what don't concern her,' Mrs Hill said, recovering her belligerence now Mrs Yelland was safely out of earshot. 'The day that woman's shadder fell over Master Harry I swear it brung down a curse on him and on all who dwells under this roof.' She lowered her bulk into the rocking chair and gave a vicious poke to the logs in the grate, saying to Amy sourly, 'Oh, leave off tormenting the girl, else they rabbits won't be ready this side of Easter Day. Make yourself useful by pouring me a mug of ale. I'm that shook up, I shall have to rest for five minutes afore I starts on the baking.'

Amy gave me a final shove that set me staggering, though her expression told me that this was a business far from finished. As I tucked my hair back under my cap and plunged my hands back among the carcasses, it seemed at that the smell of her animosity hung in the air with as strong a whiff as the blood-and-guts odour of the poor dead rabbits.

'Lovely old girl, isn't she?' said Luke Gilpin tenderly, leaning over the pigsty wall to scratch behind the ears of the fat pink and black sow rootling in the straw. 'As pretty as a picture. What do you say, young Emily?'

I shrugged.

I was terrified of the great snuffling creature. She was the biggest of the three pigs and seemingly the most threatening. Each day when I brought out the swill buckets I eyed the gate to her sty with alarm. It looked very ramshackle and she always seemed to be pressing her fat sides against it, regarding me with malevolence.

'You don't need to stand back there,' Luke said, grinning. 'She won't leap the wall.'

I shrugged again. Wishing I could think of something clever or comical to say. But the words would not come. For, in truth, finding myself unexpectedly alone with Luke Gilpin, I was overcome with awkwardness. I did not know how to talk to him. It was something beyond my experience. Although I had envied his cheerfulness and the bold, cheeky way he stood up to Enoch and

Albert, it was one thing to be a mute observer of these things while I cleared the men's plates at mealtimes, it was quite another to have his attention fully on me as he propped himself against the pigsty wall, the pale sunlight making a showy nimbus of his red hair where it fringed his battered green felt hat.

Nervousness made me truculent. Why did he have to intrude on these quiet moments that were so precious to me? Though I was wary of the pig, I always looked forward to bringing out the kitchen scraps. I would make two or three journeys, slipping unremarked round men and horses in the busy yard, cutting down the muddy passage between the stables and the brewhouse and crossing a strip of rough grass to the barn and the pigsties. When I had done tipping the buckets into the wooden barrel, I would steal a few moments to look about and relish the peace and silence.

Today, this time alone seemed especially welcome. I had tossed down the empty buckets and looked with pleasure at the now familiar view. The orchard and the small field beyond it where Master Harry's sturdy grey horse grazed belonged to the inn. Beyond again, a patchwork of fields and hedges melting to the distant blue of hills. The snow and ice had disappeared a few days since and today a soft wind blew from the west, wafting away the smell of the swill barrel and the pigs, replacing it with the fresh tang of green things and growth, though there was not yet a bud on the thick thorny hedge that bounded the orchard and the trees were still bare of leaf.

But soon, I thought. Soon.

The sky was patched with the same blue and white as Mrs Yelland's teacups. It was as I looked up at the drift of the clouds, breathing in the sweet moist air and wishing I could transport some of this tranquillity indoors to dispel the rancorous atmosphere in the kitchen, that I heard the squelch of heavy boots.

I had jolted round, fearing it was Enoch or Albert, who would lose no time in telling Cook that I had been caught idling. But it was Luke, who said, laughing, 'What's this? The scullery maid dawdling when she should be up to her elbows in greasy water?' Then, after his burst of admiration for the pigs and drawing my reluctant attention to the dubious charms of his favourite, he said more gently, as he watched me hurriedly taking up the buckets, 'You don't need to run off. I'll not be telling anyone you've taken a moment's rest. In truth, I'm glad to have the occasion to have a quiet word. I know what being new in a strange place feels like.' His blue eyes were kind. 'I've been on my own since my ma died four summers past, when I was but eleven years old. It's a hard path when nobody cares to give you a kind word or a bit of encouragement.'

I was taken aback at the genuine sympathy in his voice, made awkward by it.

'I'm sorry... about your ma,' I managed stiffly.

'Smallpox,' he said. 'I took it mildly, but I wished at the time I'd been taken, too. Still, I wasn't and I had to make the best of it though they were lean years that followed, having not a relative to care and needing to scratch a living as best I could. So you see I do understand how 'tis to be alone in the world... and I just wanted to say that I'll look out for you should you have the need of it. Leastways, I suppose you've no kith and kin or you wouldn't have come from that foundling place.'

I shook my head, feeling as I did so the rasp of the thin cord against the skin of my neck, the rough scratch of the canvas pouch, which Martha Monday had made for me, against my chest.

'*Mark my words, you got family someplace.*' Martha Monday's voice whispered in my mind. '*The lady that visited knowed about 'em. Her writ it on this paper, I'll be bound, but this scrap was all I could fetch out of the fire. This and the key. You hide it well from prying eyes, my duck. P'raps it'll bring you luck, mayhap even lead you to where you come from as a baby and you'll find what 'tis the key's for.'*

But that was my secret. It was not for Luke Gilpin to know of. Nor anyone else.

'I reckon the missus means well by us,' he went on earnestly. 'It's just that the others are so old and crabby they don't want to see things change. Mrs Yelland's been real good to me and I've no reason to suppose it'll be different for you. Why, but for her I'd still be skulking about inns in hope of carrying a lady's bags, or looking to mind a horse while a gentleman dined. And thinking myself lucky if I found a cart to sleep under by night.'

'Then how did you come here?' I broke off, feeling myself redden at the stab of curiosity that brought the brusque words to my tongue. But he was not offended. On the contrary he seemed eager to explain.

'Mrs Yelland's sharp. Not much escapes her. Why, there must have been a dozen other urchins outside Bristol market, all desperate to carry her basket for a ha'penny. But she picked me out because ... well, I spoke a bit different, I suppose. Acted polite.' He pushed back his shapeless hat and scratched absently at his fiery hair as though lost in wonder at the way fate had worked for him. 'I'd never let myself forget the things Ma taught me, see. Out of respect for her memory I'd promised myself never to sink entirely to the ways of the streets, though I soon learned to curse and use my fists as well as the next. Had to in order to survive.' His voice grew thoughtful. 'Yet in the end it was acting on what Ma told me of good manners and how to speak civil to the gentry that was the saving of me. Missus spied I was a bit different. By the time her basket was full she'd learned all there was to know of my history. Not that it was in any wise an unusual tale ... just that Ma had been abigail to a grand lady at

Clifton before she married my pa, who was a jobbing carpenter, though I remember little of him for he died when I was small. All Ma had learned at Clifton she carried with her all her life.' He smiled wryly. 'Not that it put her in a good case with our neighbours for they thought her proud for someone scraping a living as a seamstress and keeping her son by her well beyond the age when he should have been put out to work... So there you have it, young Emily. 'Twixt one day and the next my fortunes changed. Missus told me Master was thinking of taking on a boy to help about the yard and the taproom and if I should turn up at the Thorn Tree she'd plead my case with him. That was the week before Yuletide.' He chuckled. 'And never a better Christmas did I have in all my life. As much as I could eat, a good bed, a new pair of boots and Matty here, and her sisters, to look after.' He gave the sow an affectionate slap on the rump. 'What more could anyone wish for?'

I resisted the urge to cry out my own dislike of the menial work I had been put to. He would suppose me proud and difficult, as Miss Edgar had always professed me to be. I did not want that. He was trying to be kind and I had not the heart to sour his enthusiasm for his own improved situation by bellyaching about my own. It was not his fault Miss Edgar's spite had landed me here.

'I'm ... I'm glad things turned out well for you,' I said.

'And they will for you, young Emily,' he said cheerfully. 'You'll see.'

'I've dawdled long enough,' I said, turning away so he should not see how his optimism jarred. The dark thread of cynicism and resentment ran too deep in my mind, was too ingrained, to be dispelled by a few easy words.

But I had scarcely taken two strides before his hand came down on my shoulder, twisting me back to face him.

'Emily, I mean it. Don't think yourself alone.' His voice

was urgent and his expression had sobered. 'Fact is, you and me – we're incomers, which is cause enough for the others to be against us. But because Mrs Yelland is the one who got us places here and she's misliked, that gives them an extra grievance against us.'

His eyes suddenly seemed a darker, more intense blue. I sensed, with a jolt of surprise, the silent message in their depths – fought, at first, against the truth of it. Surely it could not be the same for him as for me. He was all of fifteen years and growing rapidly to manhood and little though I knew of boys and men, I understood them to be rational, logical creatures. Girls and women on the other hand were ruled by wayward emotion, which together with their physical weakness and inherent lack of intellect made them man's inferior. Which was God's intention when he created Adam and Eve; the one born to be strong and dominant, the other to serve and obey. Or so the vicar of St Peter's, where Lady Eleanor's girls were marched of a Sunday, had told us. It was a favourite theme of his. He had preached sermons about it on more than one occasion with a stern eye on his faded wife and five fidgeting daughters sitting in the front pew.

So, as I stood there, I tried to tell myself that I could not see loneliness in Luke Gilpin's eyes. Surely that was one of the unruly feminine emotions that the vicar had spoken of so disparagingly. Yet honesty forbade me to deny it. It *was* there, clear as glass. And, once I allowed myself to believe what I saw, I sensed that it was a loneliness no less deep and painful than mine, for all that Luke was so nearly a man.

When I did not immediately answer, Luke dropped his hand from my shoulder. A flush of scarlet bloomed in the spaces between the freckles on his face. So men, apparently, could feel embarrassment, too.

'I've overstepped myself,' he said gruffly. 'I'm sorry. I

should have known you'll not be wanting any truck with a yard boy.'

'What makes you think so?' I said in a level voice.

'You're not like the others.'

'Because I'm a charity girl?'

'I thought that's what it was. At first,' he said slowly. 'After all, you've been raised a deal different, and whatever Cook says out of spite for the mistress, anyone with half an eye can see you've been taught properly how to go about things. But there's something else. It's hard to explain. It's not rightly about the way you look – though how you always manage to be such a neat and tidy little thing when Cass and Amy always appear as though they've just been dragged through a hedge, I don't know. But it's more than that...' He faltered, the colour coming up again in his cheeks, then went on resolutely, 'There's an air about you that sets you apart from the rest. And I don't know how to explain it.'

'Let me help you.' A sigh escaped me. 'Stubbornness? Pride? Contrariness? Dumb arrogance? If that's what you see, I've heard it all before and I don't want to hear any more.'

'Well, perhaps I do see a bit of one or t'other.' Despite his discomfiture, the ghost of his usual grin flickered out. Then he was solemn again, frowning as he groped for words. 'But that's not what I mean. Leastways, I suppose that's part of it... But not everything. You put me in mind of a street player who pretends to be a fine lady or an old crone or a damsel in distress, though you know she's really someone different.'

'I'm no actor in a sideshow,' I said. 'I've never even seen such.'

'I know. Oh, hang it!' He broke off, exasperated. 'I'm not making any sense. I might as well save my breath.' With a violent movement he tore off his battered hat and threw it to the grass, then, meaning perhaps merely to vent his frustration, kicked it into the air. He put out a hand to catch it on its descent, but he had reckoned without the breeze, which whisked it away and over the gate of the sty. The hat landed on a surprised Mattie and dangled from her snout for a few seconds before she wrestled it to the mud and proceeded to gnaw reflectively on this unusual snack.

Any remaining solemnity was gone in a trice.

With a whoop of anguish, Luke leaped to the gate and tugged his hat from Mattie's fangs, but not before a strip of green felt disappeared into her chops.

'Been with me a long time, that hat,' he groaned, tenderly pressing together the ragged edges of the tear. 'Washed up on the tide by Bristol docks, it was, and years of wear left in it.'

It was a long while since I had felt the urge to laugh, but the look of comical dismay on his face, and thought of the pig enjoying her unexpected titbit, brought a great bubble of it into my throat. Before I could string together any words of consolation I was overcome.

Luke jammed the hat back on his head and scowled.

The brim now drooped in two separate pieces either side of his head. To look at him was more than I could bear.

'Your fault entirely, Emily Wroe,' he yelled. 'You're a maddening wench. Driving honest folk to desperate acts. And what are you laughing at?'

But the kind of laughter that comes up from your boots and takes your breath and denies any attempts at subduing it is as catching as measles. Luke could not defend himself against the infection.

'I don't see,' he sputtered, trying in vain to cling to offended dignity, 'anything funny... in a man... having his hat gnawed... by a... a... pig...' His words dissolved to a great guffaw.

So there, by the pigsty, we held our ribs and choked,

gasping out the words 'pig' and 'hat', only to set ourselves off again into another paroxysm.

And in that shared and helpless laughter – laughter that brought more ease to the heart and spirit than any amount of words ever could – the first bonds of friendship were forged.

Chapter Two

Though I did not realise it at the time, my perception of the inn and my place in it began to alter once I found a friend in Luke Gilpin. It was so subtle a change at first as to be hardly noticeable, yet looking back I can see that with the knowledge that I had an ally – even one with as little importance as myself – a small seed of confidence was sown. And that fragile seed was helped to root and flourish by two events that occurred shortly afterwards.

The first was when Mrs Yelland, true to her word, supervised the removal of Cass, Amy and me to a new bedchamber up in the airy attic next to Mrs Hill's room.

Too airy for Amy. Indeed, judging by her scowl there was nothing to please her about the odd-shaped room with its ceiling sloping at unexpected angles and the two small latticed windows propped open to the blowy morning.

'The miserable old bitch,' she hissed, when Mrs Yelland had departed with a caution to take no more time than necessary to dispose our few possessions as we wished. 'Sticking us up here in this freezing hole when we was nice and snug where we was.'

''Tis a bit draughty,' Cass agreed, but she seemed bemused as she surveyed the three narrow beds, each with a new mattress that I had helped Mrs Yelland to make from sturdy ticking and fresh chaff mixed with dried sweet-smelling herbs that she said would help keep the fleas at bay. Clean sheets and a good patchwork quilt were folded tidily on each feather pillow. 'Don't look so bad though, do it?' She stared around, her voice awed. 'A proper tallboy with a drawer each and a looking-glass on top. Never had such before. And we got a chamber-pot apiece 'stead of one to share. Oh, and don't that hooked rug look pretty, all yeller and green?'

'The devil take her and her airy-fairy ideas,' Amy snarled, glaring at the earthenware basin and the jug filled with fresh water standing on a table to one side. ''Specting us to have time for her fancy notions.' She put on an affected voice, mimicking Mrs Yelland. ' "Wash your hands and face mornin' and night and be sure to comb the straggles out of your hair afore 'ee starts work" – as though Mrs Hill or anyone else gives a horse fart how we looks.'

'But missus does, that's for sure.' Cass put down her bundle by the nearest bed and tested the thickness of the quilt with a respectful hand. 'P'raps we'd be best to go along with what her says. After all, her's promised us new dresses for summer. I'd not like her to change her mind, which she might do iffen we don't humour her.' She gave a wistful sigh. 'Save for when we buys new ribbons or kerchiefs or a scrap of trimming off the pedlar when he calls, I've never had naught that wasn't passed on from other folk.'

'You got no brains, Cass,' Amy said scornfully. She stalked across the boards, giving me a jab in the ribs with her sharp elbow when I did not move quickly enough out of her way. She reached up to bang shut first one window then the other, to emphasise her defiance, for Mrs Yelland had said to leave the casement open by day in order to keep the air in the attic sweet. 'I'm not catching no ague out of a gale blowing through. And I got the measure of her, even if you're too daft to see it. You mark my words, we'll be made to pay for what her pretends to be so generous about. Her's just buttering us up so's to make us slave the harder. Her's full of nasty tricks. Did it a-purpose to spite me particler, fastening us up at the top of the house, thinking to deny us what bits of pleasure an' profit might be found here and there.'

Cass giggled. 'P'raps it's as well, Amy Wright. You might have found yourself sickenin' for more than an ague if you'd gone on the way you was doing.'

'I knows how to take care of myself,' Amy said. She had strange-coloured eyes, of a shade somewhere between green and yellow. Perhaps it was the sudden beam of sunlight angling through the window that made the unpleasant yellow in them seem more apparent. 'If things ever do go badly for me, I'll know who to blame.' Her voice was a sibilant, penetrating whisper, the warning hiss of a snake. 'But for her getting her claws into Master Harry, things would have gone very different for me. You knows that as well as I do, Cass. Last summer I had prospecks. Real prospecks. And if *you* care to forget the way things was then, *I* never shall. Never.'

Cass threw me a sideways glance, then frowned warningly at Amy. 'Enough of that,' she said. 'No sense in speakin' out of turn. 'Twas no more than a bit of summer madness. Best to put it out of your mind. Best for everyone and no harm done.'

But Amy gave her no heed. 'There'll come a time when I can pay her back,' she said softly. 'And when it does, make no mistake, I'll not miss my chance to right the wrong done me.'

The cold threat in her voice seemed to intensify the chill in the attic air. I shivered, thoughtlessly rubbing at my suddenly goose-fleshed arms. That small sound was my undoing.

Amy swivelled round, her broad nostrils twitching as though scenting prey. Looking for something or someone to vent her temper on. Finding me.

'And what are you a-staring at, eh? Standing there like butter wouldn't melt in your mouth. Thinks you're too fine for the likes of us, don't 'ee? Never a word to say for yourself, but all the time starin' down your nose as though we was a bit o' dog shit you trod in.' She stalked across the room and grabbed the neck of my dress so tightly that I was half strangled as I was jerked towards her. 'A gutter-born bastard. That's all you are. The leavings of some poxed slut who got you by a scabby beggar on a midden. I can just see the pair of 'em. Her a withered bag o'bones and him riddled with sores and ugly as sin.'

'No! That's lies!' I choked, clawing at her hands, the monstrous picture raised by her words sliding like slime into my mind. 'Get off me!'

'Why should I? Time someone learned 'ee how to behave.' With her free hand she pulled back the side lappet of my cap and took my earlobe between her thumb and first finger. She dug in her nails, twisting and pulling so hard that I could not help but squirm. 'That hurts, do it?' she said with satisfaction. 'Good. Because that's nothing to what 'ee'll be catching off me, if you don't do as I bid from now on.' Her face was thrust close up to mine, her lips drawn back over small, grey teeth in an animal snarl. 'Do you hear? When I calls, you run. And for a start 'ee can make up my bed proper nice. Which is that one there, for I don't want 'ee alongside Cass or me. You can take the one under that low bit of ceiling. If there's heads to be broken, I'd sooner it was yours.'

In spite of my distress, I felt a stab of glee. Because of the odd shape of the attic, three beds could not lie side by side so one was placed at right angles, tucked into a little alcove made by the outer wall and a thin partition that ran halfway across the attic space before stopping abruptly for no apparent reason, though Mrs Yelland had speculated that it was probably left over from an earlier time when there must have been several smaller rooms occupying this space. From the first, I had coveted that near-private alcove where I might almost imagine myself alone. And now it was to be mine – by way of punishment, Amy thought. Little she knew!

'Oh, leave off tormenting the girl and come and look at this,' Cass said. She was investigating the tallboy and had found the lavender bags Mrs Yelland had put in the drawers. She pressed one to her nose and inhaled deeply. 'My, but we'll smell like gentry iffen we keeps our clothes in here . . . and 'tis a real nice-looking glass.' She primped at her reflection. 'I never knowed afore that these blue ribbons 'zackly matched my eyes.'

The painful pressure on my ear eased. The stranglehold on my collar was loosed. I thought for a blessed instant that Cass had managed to distract my tormentor, but Amy had only released me in order to seize something she had spied around my neck.

'What's this you bin hiding?'

She dragged at the cord, tugging out the little canvas bag from its hiding place under my bodice.

'Nothing! Nothing to do with you!' I yelled, clawing frantically at her hand. 'Give it back!'

'Must be something worth having,' she said, smiling nastily, 'or you wouldn't have it kept so secret. Money, is it? A gold piece?'

'No! All I got in the world is three pennies. They're in my bundle.'

'That so? Well, 'tis nice to know. But first, I needs a look in here.' She wrenched at the cord but it was too sturdy to break. Then she tried to wrest it over my head but I clung to her hands.

'You shan't have it! It's mine.'

'That's what 'ee thinks. I believes different.'

Under my scrabbling fingers her hands were slabs of unyielding bone and muscle. I knew, despairingly, that the odds were stacked against me beating her off. She topped me by a good head and was broad and strong in proportion. But I had to try. I drew back my foot and kicked hard. The toe of my shoe cracked smartly against her ankle bone. The yelp she gave was very satisfying, though I had little time to savour it for she immediately retaliated by holding me off with one hand while she punched me hard in the stomach with her clenched fist.

I doubled over, fighting for breath, a black, spinning sickness blanking my sight.

Her taunting voice came at me from a distance.

'That'll learn 'ee to be obstropolous.' A hand jerking my chin up, the cord catching painfully on my burning earlobe. 'Now let me have that bag.'

Her soiled blue skirts swam into focus. Then the tight-laced bodice with the flesh bulging from the top . . . the grey ribbons of dirt on her neck . . . her sharp-featured face with the full lips parted in a triumphant sneer.

'No!' My voice was a husky gasp. I groped wildly for the bag, caught at it with frantic fingers, folded it into the palm of my hand where it fitted, warm and familiar as so often it had when I slept at night, in the hope that I might dream of the woman who had left it for me . . .

I do not know where the thought came from, leave alone the words, but they were there, springing into my head, spilling out in a voice that strengthened with each syllable.

'If you take this from me you'll be cursed, Amy Wright! Your tongue will rot off and your hair will fall out and you'll be full of scabs and boils before you die in horrible agony.'

'Hah! Thinks to save yourself wi' spinning a fancy yarn, eh?'

'It's the truth. What's in there was given me by a witch.'

She laughed loudly. Perhaps a touch too loudly. Hope stirred in my breast.

'You 'ear that, Cass?' she scoffed. 'Proper little liar, en't she?'

'Go on then,' I said softly, staring her in the eye. 'I dare you. Take it and see what happens. But when trouble comes, remember I gave you good warning.'

I heard Cass draw in a quick, scared breath. 'Don't, Amy! Perhaps it's the truth she speaks. Best be on the safe side.'

'It's all a pretence . . .'

'So what's stopping you taking it, then?' I said, loosing my hold on the bag so that it swung free. Amy made to clutch at it, but as her fingers touched the canvas, she jerked them back. She glared down at me.

'Where did 'ee meet this witch?' she demanded.

'I didn't know she was a witch until I did her a favour,' I said. 'How should I? I just helped a poor old lady who'd fallen in the street . . . carried her bundle, stopped a rough lad from throwing stones at her . . . When I got her home she insisted on giving me a charm against evil . . .'

In any other situation I would have found Amy's expression laughable. How could she possibly believe such a rigmarole? But she clearly did and my relief was beyond laughter. As uncertainty and fear began to take the edge off her aggressiveness, my confidence grew and I silently blessed the tales of fairy enchantments, heroic adventures and mystic quests that I had learned at Lady Eleanor's.

Miss Edgar, whose idea of recreation was for one of us to read approved passages aloud from the big Bible as we laboured heavy-eyed over our sewing before bed, would have been appalled had she known that despite her attempts to stifle any independent thought in the cause of raising us girls to be obedient, humble, hard-working – and therefore eminently employable – an imaginative life flourished within the collective bosom of her charges. Indeed, it was possible that because of the narrowness of our existence in that cold, frowning place we seized more avidly on any scraps that might brighten our inner lives. Martha Monday had a deal to do with it. She was a fount of superstition and gossip. We kept abreast of the more notorious doings of the town – from public hangings to scandals among the gentry – through Martha's whispering in someone's ear as they went about the scrubbing or the laundry and doubtless the tales grew with the telling and retelling. But she really came into her own when we were grudgingly allowed by Miss Edgar to be ill enough to remain bedfast for a few days.

Miss Edgar had a fear of contagion. Holding a handkerchief soaked in rosewater to her nose, she would make no more than a brief, daily inspection to ensure the invalid was not malingering before briskly retreating. It was left to Martha to dose us with black draught and report any worsening condition that might indicate the need to call in the doctor.

So, wafting a shovel of burning camphor or lavender over the bed to clear a stuffy head, or bathing us with vinegar water to bring down a fever, she would tell us stories. Magical stories heard, she said, when she was a child herself at Lady Eleanor's before Miss Edgar's time when a kindlier overseer had ruled for some years before the undue frivolity in her nature and laxity in the matter of accounting for extravagance in the kitchen had incurred the displeasure of the trustees.

Out of those stories had come the concoction I wove to fend off Amy Wright. And she believed me! It seemed, indeed, a miracle born of the touch of the little canvas bag and its charmed contents. But even as Amy took a step backwards, shrugging, assuming a bored expression as though tiring of her bullying game, I knew it was less to do with miracles than using my wits to advantage in a moment of desperation.

Superstition. That was the key. On my very first day here I had observed how quickly those in the kitchen had become uneasy when Mrs Hill suggested that the mistress had used unnatural means to secure herself a husband. How useful that knowledge had proved. And how timely that my mind should pounce on it in my defence, when I was clearly disadvantaged by Amy's size and strength.

I was not so powerless as I thought. I saw that with sudden clarity. For neither Amy nor Cass was possessed of any great intelligence. It was not boastful to admit myself superior in the sharpness of my wits, but a plain, honest fact. And, by God, why should I not admit it and use it to my advantage?

I tucked the canvas bag carefully into my bodice.

'You did a wise thing, Amy,' I said. 'For all that you've been so unkind to me since I came here, I'd not have wished you to suffer.' I shook my head. 'Mind, you'd better watch yourself in the next day or two.'

'How d'you mean?'

'You handled the charm very roughly. There may yet be some evil befall you on account of that.'

Her reaction was all that I could have wished. She looked so alarmed that I almost relented and withdrew the threat. But prudence held me. In the interests of a more comfortable future relationship, best to let her sweat over it for a few days. With all the spills and knocks that happened as we went about our work, she'd doubtless find something to blame on the curse. If not, I should find some convincing reason to explain why she had been spared.

Well satisfied, I was now prepared to be conciliatory. 'I'll get on with making up the beds now,' I said brightly. 'And to be sure, Amy, I'm willing to help you all I can with any little errand or task. Just so long as you don't raise your fist to me again. Or keep on harassing me as you have been doing.' I let my hand rise with slow significance to lie on my bodice where the canvas bag was hidden. 'Otherwise, I'll not answer for what mishap the talisman will lay on you – or anyone else who means me harm.'

I stared at her long and hard. She was the first to drop her eyes and turn away.

* * *

The room that had been our old bedchamber, being on the cool north wall and convenient to the kitchen, was to serve in future, Mrs Yelland informed us, as a pantry instead of the cramped cubbyhole presently in use.

'I do believe it was originally intended for some such purpose,' she speculated, rolling up her sleeves and looking round the now empty room before we began on the scrubbing. 'There is a good flagged floor – and see those marks on this right-hand wall, Emily? Rows of shelves must have hung here once. And those rusty old hooks in the ceiling might well have been used to hang game or flitches of bacon . . .'

I was growing to appreciate being selected by the mistress to work alongside her. She was eagle-eyed to find the smallest fault, but at least when she spotted some oversight, I knew it was because of a genuine mistake on my part and not some trumpery excuse she had invented in order that she might take enjoyment from her victim's fear of unpleasant punishment. That had been Miss Edgar's way. It was not Mrs Yelland's.

But I was so bedevilled by the anxiety and apprehension instilled into me by Miss Edgar's methods that I stayed very wary of Barbara Yelland in those early weeks, though it became increasingly difficult to deny that she drove me no harder than she drove herself and seemed genuinely appreciative of my efforts. The fact that she sometimes broke into song as we worked, or fell to chatting of this and that, made the drudgery seem less arduous. Yet still I took care to do no more than murmur, 'Yes, ma'am,' or 'No, ma'am,' as the occasion required. I had had my ears boxed too often in the past for asking questions, or otherwise speaking out of turn, to believe it would be any different here.

But I was wrong about that. That particular March morning, I was scraping the ingrained dirt from the flags behind the door when she called to me to see what she had found.

'This book, Emily. Do you know anything of how it came here?' she said, blowing at the cobwebs that clung to it. Then, answering her own question, 'No, of course you do not. It has evidently lain under this rubbish in the corner for years.' She opened it eagerly, and held it at arm's length. 'I do not have my eyeglasses, and the writing is very small and cramped. Perhaps it is a diary – very old from the look of it. Oh dear, what a pity you are not able to read, Emily, for I shall have to contain my curiosity and not allow myself to be distracted until we have finished our work.'

She seemed so very disappointed. And she need not be. Surely, for once, I might speak out . . . Oh, and the joy of being able to handle a book, to see the pattern of words unfolding on a page . . . I swallowed, burst out more loudly than I intended, 'If you please, ma'am, I . . . I can read.'

'But I understood—' she stopped, stared at me hard, said, 'Yes, well, I find it likely, despite all that was said.' She thrust the book at me. 'What do you make of it, then?'

I wiped my hands on my sacking apron as I stood up. The worn leather felt warm under my fingers. I wanted to smooth it, prolong the business of opening it, savour the anticipation of whatever delights might be found within.

'There's a name here, ma'am, on this first page,' I began nervously. '*Mary Yelland, her boke*. And there is a date: 1697.'

'Would that be my husband's grandmother, d'you suppose? Read on, child. Let us hear what secrets this Yelland goodwife has to reveal.'

I carefully turned the stiff pages. 'It seems to be a book of receipts.' I peered at the cramped writing, picking out the words slowly. 'It says how to make a squab pie . . . and here, to make a pudding of beastings . . . Oh, and this is to cure an ill humour . . . *Take elderberrie wine, one quart, and heat with nutmeg and cinnamon . . .*'

'Do you think, then, I am in need of such?' She sounded amused.

'Oh no, ma'am,' I said, my face hot with confusion, for I had been carried away with the thought of administering such a convenient draught to Mrs Hill.

'I should not tease. Thank you, Emily, for enlightening me about the book's contents.' She took the book off me and put it into her apron pocket. 'I find myself disappointed that I shall not be privy to Mary Yelland's thoughts on being mistress here. It would have been amusing to compare her situation with mine. Still, the finding of it has brought one interesting fact to life. That I harbour a scholar among my servants.'

'Hardly, ma'am,' I murmured, made increasingly anxious by the frowning way she regarded me. 'I'd best get on.'

'Not for a moment,' she said sharply. 'Do you write and number also?'

'Yes, ma'am.'

'You had proper schooling, then?'

'When I was little, ma'am. A lady came by the day to teach us. But she was put off by the time I was nine. Her wages cost too much, it was said. And now the big girls are set to teach the smaller ones.'

'But you— did you not find learning difficult?'

'Oh no, ma'am. The reading and writing came easy to me. And if I was let, though it wasn't often, I loved to help the little girls.'

'Is that so? Well, well.'

The dryness of her tone caused my stomach to lurch with apprehension. She did not approve.

'You were recommended to me as being exceptionally thorough and hard-working in the menial tasks that would be required of you,' she said slowly, 'though unfortunately you were felt to be lacking in intellect. Indeed, it was implied that any tasks other than scrubbing and cleaning were quite beyond your capabilities. "Well suited for duties that make no demand on her intelligence", was, I believe, the phrase employed in the letter which I received from the Trustees. Yet you are clearly not twopence short of a shilling, as I was led to expect. How has this unfortunate situation come about, do you suppose, Emily?'

Even though I had always known of Miss Edgar's distaste for me, I was appalled to realise that she intended her spiteful influence to pursue me into the wider world. To have represented me to the trustees as a near imbecile! And how could those grand gentlemen – whom we so rarely saw in person and who seemed to take more interest in accounting and bookkeeping than in the very foundlings they were meant to supervise – take her word so blindly?

'The overseer – Miss Edgar,' I blurted out, discretion cast to the winds by the injustice of that hateful woman's parting blow. 'It was her doing! She especially misliked me – and quite a few others. But I never thought she would sink so low as to . . . as to lie like that. Though we never pleased her . . . and not one of those that she misliked – and most were good, gentle girls doing their best – was ever sent to be apprenticed to a decent trade or given a place at a grand house when their time came. The best places were for her favourites. The rest might go hang! And those she hated most she intended for the roughest, dirtiest, vilest situations when their time came, as happened to me.' I faltered, stopped, the realisation of what I had implied cooling my rush of anger as though a bucket of icy water had been thrown over it.

'And you were dispatched to a run-down tavern, where you might moulder among the slops and vermin,' she finished. 'I see.'

Now I had done it! I should have held my tongue. God knows, I had had enough practice.

'I . . . I didn't intend—' I whispered.

'Oh, but you did, Emily Wroe. And while you are speaking so frankly, perhaps you would also be so good as to explain the reasons why the overseer took against you. There can be no smoke without a fire. You must have displeased her mightily in some fashion.'

Her sharp green eyes were fixed on me with unflinching directness.

I hesitated, but I had nothing to lose now. She might as well know the truth about me as not. 'She said I was rebellious and stubborn, ma'am. And ungrateful. And high-nosed to the point of insolence.'

'Pride! Stubbornness! Ingratitude! Such sins in a foundling. No wonder the good woman despaired of you.'

'Yes, ma'am.'

'I expect you were well beaten for it.'

'Often, ma'am.'

'And clearly to little effect. Or mayhap the punishment served merely to make you more defiant. Hah! Your manner and your words may appear humble enough, but there is a spark in your eyes that speaks otherwise. Not to mention a certain haughty stiffness of the backbone.'

'Ma'am, I'm sorry, I don't mean to—'

'And unaware of it. Worse and worse. And are you determined to cling to this misguided belief that you, along with others, have been wronged by the estimable Miss Edgar?'

'Not misguided, ma'am,' I protested. 'And she wasn't estimable. She made us suffer for a grudge she held against... against...'

'Against whom?'

'I have been told,' I said miserably, 'leastways, Martha Monday, who's been maid there for years and knows everything there is to know, said she'd always had a down on those orphans who she thought might... might be by-blows of the gentry.'

'And were you then one such natural child?'

'We . . . we were never told directly, ma'am. But there was gossip. I always knew I wasn't one of the ones left in rags on the doorstep or in the church porch. Martha said I was fetched in by a grim-faced woman who said no more than she'd had a long journey and was glad to be rid of the responsibility. She'd thrust me into Martha's arms and hurried off. There was a purse of money, and a paper on which was written my name and the date I was born attached to the warm shawl I was wrapped in. I was finely dressed, she said, in embroidered linen and lace.'

Someone had cared. For a little while. For the time she was allowed. Someone had stitched love into those tiny, perfect clothes. Had she wept over them, too? Wept over the loss to come?

'So your overseer presumed a genteel background and had a predisposition to make you suffer for it. Did your garrulous informant know the reason?'

'Her family had come down in the world,' I said, 'and having no fortune and being ill-favoured, no man ever spoke for the miserable old— for her. Then she was made jealous by her pretty cousin marrying the young man she herself wanted – he was a minor sprig of the nobility – and she was left to earn her living as a governess before she took up the post at Lady Eleanor's. All of which turned her sour.'

Even as I spoke I tensed, ready to receive the buffet about the ears that would surely now be my lot for speaking out of turn about my elders and betters. But it did not come.

Instead, Mrs Yelland said in the same ironic tone she had used all along, 'How very galling for the poor woman to be faced daily by the fruits of lust when she herself was never likely to raise such an emotion in any man's breast. Dear me, the trustees did very well to engage such a suitable person to supervise the welfare of foundlings.' She shook her head. 'You do understand, do you not,

Emily, that it was very thoughtless of you to exist at all. As I see it, the poor soul must have been tormented by the way you survived and flourished, despite every discouragement. And to show sparks of spirit and cleverness, to boot! No wonder she sought to punish you.'

I stared at her, not knowing how to answer. I had expected blows, but she seemed to be inviting me to share in something in which she found wry amusement.

She shook her head. 'So, what's to be done with you, Emily Wroe? If beatings have not reformed you, then it seems I must put up with having a rebel and a scholar in the scullery.' She smiled then, that transforming smile. It seemed to lighten the cold dim room, as though a shaft of sunlight had suddenly penetrated the small cobwebbed window. 'Doubtless I shall think of some method of punishment suitable to such a square peg. I believe I might begin by ordering you to continue you with your scholarly studies.'

I gaped at her, wondering if I had heard aright. Her smile broadened, enfolding me in its warmth, dazzling me with its devastating charm.

'I have a mind to lend you some volumes from my own small library. But let me warn you, miss, I shall quiz you most severely on the contents once you have read them. My books are very precious to me, so if time reveals that your apparent enthusiasm is but a devious way of gaining my sympathy, or if you mishandle them, you will not get another chance.'

I stammered out my thanks, but she was picking up her broom and once again chivvying the detritus that littered the flags into a neat heap, saying in her usual brisk manner, 'Come, we are wasting valuable time. Interested as I am to learn more about your life before you came here, Emily, you may just as well talk as you work.'

So, hesitantly at first, I began to speak. Mrs Yelland listened and questioned and listened again, deeply attentive, and this was such a novel experience for me that I responded like a flower that throws open its petals at the first touch of the sun.

Serendipity. A word I had not heard then but I have thought of its aptness many times since. The making of happy discoveries by chance. Like the finding of that book of receipts lying hidden under the dust of years which was to forge a bond between maid and mistress that has held to this day. If it had remained lost, who knows? I do not care to think of it, though Barbara Yelland has told me often enough since that she would have picked me out for advancement sooner or later.

But had it been later I would have mouldered for a long time in that horrible scullery – years, perhaps. Instead of which, by the time summer was over my circumstances were improved beyond anything I could have dreamed of.

I gradually adjusted to the noise and confusion that had seemed so overwhelming to me when I first arrived at the inn and I was grateful for the measure of order Mrs Yelland had imposed on the rough-and-ready routine of the kitchen. Even Mrs Hill admitted that the new pantry was an improvement when the weather turned hot in May.

'The milk'd have turned by now in the old 'un,' she admitted grudgingly. 'Mind, it was closer for me to get at. And I don't hold with all this whitewashing. Never did like the smell of it. Sets my nose all of a drip.'

I suspected that Master Harry might well have been secretly in agreement. He was not a clever or ambitious man, but his easy-going nature made him popular with the customers. He was proud of the excellent ale he brewed and never happier than when dispensing it – and enjoying it – in the taproom. He seemed bewildered by his wife's insistence on overhauling her new home.

'There's no need to wear yourself out, like this, my love,' I heard him say once, blinking at her bemusedly.

'We shan't use half these rooms even if we get more trade. You might just as well leave them closed up as they've been for as long as I remember.'

'I do not like to think of all the insects and dirt lying undisturbed,' she answered briskly. 'Besides, some of the furniture is good and solid and deserves better than to be hidden by rubbish that needs turning out and burning . . . And speaking of turning out, I had thought you had discarded those old leather breeches and that disgraceful coat. Do you intend to greet your customers looking worse than a wagoner who's been on the road for a week?'

'I've work to do in the brewhouse. No sense in ruining good clothes in there.'

'Then be sure to change before we take our dinner. What is the use of having a press full of good clothes if they never see the light of day?' She spoke teasingly to take the sting from her words. 'Do you not care that I like to see you looking well, husband?'

He looked mournful. 'I mislike playing the dandy, my love.'

'There is nothing dandified in wearing good, well-tailored cloth. And there is nothing fanciful about the shirts I have made you, either. The ruffle on the front is far smaller than those I sewed on the shirts of my late husband.'

'Ah, but he was a prosperous man and mixed in fine company.'

'He thought of himself first and foremost as a farmer, even though he was well set up, and he dressed no more than very plain. But always neat and tidy. The trouble is that you have been too long left to your own devices and have fallen into slipshod ways. But it is not too late. Thank heaven you now have a wife who will keep you up to the mark. Now run along, do, and allow me to get on. And do not let me set eyes on you again until you have made yourself properly presentable.'

'He'd sooner be hobnobbing with his cronies than sitting with her upstairs in that parlour her's got up so fancy,' Amy said sourly. 'Stands to reason. What red-blooded man wants to be a-sat for hours sippin' tea out of chiney cups, all dressed up like a pedlar's monkey as her'd like him to be?'

Mrs Yelland might have chivvied her husband into visiting his tailor, true, but I was less sure that she regretted being deprived of her husband's company. Indeed, she seemed perfectly content to spend her spare hours alone in the room she had made so elegant and comfortable. She took great pleasure from her books and never returned from her visits to Bristol without something new to show me. She also spent many evenings that summer surrounded by ledgers and bills of account.

'I cannot make head nor tail of half of this muddle,' she declared one day when I had been summoned to read aloud a poem about daffodils which I had been memorising from the works of Robert Herrick. She threw down a yellowed scrap of paper and slammed the ledger shut. 'Nothing tallies. Nothing balances. There are no entries at all for the last six months and I have no way of knowing whether half these bills have been paid or are still outstanding. Harry might well tell me that there is no spare money for the further improvements I have in mind, but how can he possibly tell from these accounts? He was willing enough for me to cast my eye over them, knowing that I had helped my late husband with his accounts when he became too ill to manage them alone, but I declare these are in such a mess it will take me the rest of the year to put all to rights!'

It did not take her that long. By July the worst of the hard physical labour of cleaning and clearing the rooms so long neglected was done so she attacked this fresh challenge with her usual energy. Within a short time all debtors and creditors had been visited or requested to attend the inn with a view to setting matters straight. A new ledger was opened and kept meticulously. Inventories were taken. Every item on every bill – be it for the kitchen or the stable – was in future to be checked by her before any account was settled. Old Enoch and Mrs Hill were both interviewed privately on their method of ordering and economy.

'The bossy besom would have me account for every blade o' straw and handful of bran,' Enoch wailed afterwards. ''Tis fearful that a man o' my years and experience do have to knuckle down to a bit of a wench when I never 'ad no complaints from Master Harry in all the time I been trusted to 'tend to things. An' he just laughed when I spoke to him of it. Said he'd no head for figures and missus liked everything orderly and once all was straight we might go on as we've allus done. He's well and truly under 'er thumb, I can tell 'ee.'

'What 'er wants is to be breeding,' Mrs Hill said, breathless with outrage. 'Her needs a babe a year to give her something else to think about 'stead of accusing poor folks as does their best of things they've no knowledge of. No knowledge at all.'

But for all their protests, they were both close-lipped about what had actually been said to them at their interviews and a certain air of caution seemed to hang about them for some time afterwards. It was Luke who enlightened me.

'Enoch and Farmer Ashdown's eldest lad had a nice little arrangement.' He grinned. 'I've seen them whispering together. And coins being passed. I'd wager a gold piece to a farthing that they've been fiddling on what comes from the farm for the kitchen or the stables. Might be other sources, too. Easy pickings with Master Harry being so easy-going and leaving so much to Enoch. Enoch's checks everything that's delivered and often as not Master Harry gives him cash to pay off young Ashdown.'

'But wouldn't Farmer Ashdown find out? Or was he in on it too?'

'I'd fancy not. He might be good with cows and corn, but he's a simple soul and doesn't have any head for book learning. Leaves the accounting to his eldest lad – who's of a different nature entirely. Out for a bit of quiet profit for himself, I'd say, without having to share it with his brood of brothers and sisters. So he adds an extra shilling here and there to the bills. Or maybe slips something onto the account that hasn't actually been delivered. It couldn't work without Enoch and Mrs Hill, so they gets their cut to keep them sweet. Probably gone on for years.'

'But that's thieving,' I protested.

He shrugged. 'Perhaps they don't see it like that. My ma once said some such practice went on in the big house where she worked, with tradesmen rewarding the cook and butler for their patronage. Ah, but why worry about it, Princess? That's Mrs Yelland's business, not ours – and she'll be watchful against such cheating in future. Come on, I'll show you Mattie's litter. All as bonny as maybe and even the runt likely to thrive enough to make a good side of bacon.'

I was willing to be sidetracked. 'I don't know how you can be so callous,' I said, leaning over the pigsty wall to admire the squealing heap of piglets. 'Claiming to love pigs and yet licking your chops over the prospect of bacon.'

'Got to be practical,' he said, grinning. 'Us farmers have to be. Can't afford to be sentimental over beasts meant for the pot.'

'You're no farmer, Luke Gilpin. Only a yard boy.'

'But I will be. One day.' His blue eyes glinted under the thatch of red hair. 'I've made my mind to it. Can't think of anything I'd like better than a nice little house and what shall it be? Forty acres? Sixty? A hundred? Aye, that sounds well. Will you come and visit me, Princess, when I'm set up on my own plot of land with cows and pigs and hens and horses? And men to say "Yes, sir. No, sir," as they scuttle about to do my bidding?'

'To be sure. I'll bring my mother, the Queen, and my father, the King, along too. After all, they'll be wanting to meet the lad who was nice to me for the years when I was lost after being stolen by gypsies . . .' I broke off from the pretence we sometimes indulged in. The news I had could not be held back a minute longer. 'Oh, Luke, I'm to become kitchen maid, with an extra penny a week. Mrs Yelland's taking Cass to be upstairs maid and fetching in a girl from the village to be scullion, instead of me!'

'But that's grand!' he cried. Then he pulled a comical face and said in a wailing voice, 'But say that you'll still speak to me, Emily, when you're become so rich and elevated.'

'Be serious, Luke! That isn't all. Listen what else I've learned . . .'

'I would have preferred you as my personal maid, Emily,' Mrs Yelland had said in her straightforward way, 'but it would have caused bad feeling to advance you too quickly when the others have been here longer. And I do believe Cass will make a good fist of her new duties. She is much improved in her attitude of late and begins to take pride in her appearance. As for you, child, you may be crestfallen that I have chosen Cass over you, but remember this. It is to your advantage that you become thoroughly acquainted with every aspect of kitchen work before you have further advancement.'

'Thank you, ma'am. I'll do my best,' I said, trying not to feel envious of Cass who would be free of Mrs Hill's grumbling and Amy's spiteful antics. I had grown to like Cass. I could not but wish her well. 'But, ma'am,' I said, suddenly struck by a more worrying possibility, 'will this mean . . . that is, shall I be able to keep on with the reading?'

'Of course. I do not intend to give with one hand and take away with the other. In fact I am of a mind to extend your schooling to include simple household accounting.' She rose from her chair and paced to the window, then back, as though full of uncontainable energy and impatience. 'You see, Emily, when the time comes, as I hope – no, as I *insist* it will – I shall have need of people about me who are competent in every aspect of the running of an inn. Not dullards and country clods such as have reigned here too long, but persons with quick wits and ambitions to better themselves. For I have every intention of making the Thorn Tree more than it is at present. Much more.'

'In what way, ma'am?' I ventured, easy enough with her now to know that my question would not offend her.

Yet I feared that I had, for she did not answer directly, but paced again to the window and, with her back to me, said in a low voice, 'I will not be thwarted. I must succeed.' Then, in so faint a whisper it was little more than a breath, 'The waters of despair are so very deep that I shall be entirely drowned if I do not have something purposeful to cling to.' She fell silent, seeming lost in contemplation of something beyond the thick, greenish panes of glass. Then, as if suddenly recollecting my presence and my question, said in her usual brisk tone, 'It might be considered a disadvantage that we are not directly on the turnpike to Bath, but there is a deal to be said for a modest location and the parish does its work well in maintaining the road to a reasonable standard, despite the traffic of heavy wagons and farm carts. There must be many travellers – particularly women journeying alone – who would welcome quiet, clean, inexpensive lodgings not too far out of Bristol. And, yes, I know the yard and the taproom and the rooms on that side are oftimes busy and noisy, but the *respectable* traveller might be housed in this half of the house where it is quiet, and need never set eyes on the rougher element. Let me show you.'

She whisked back to the table and beckoned me to look at a piece of paper spread there.

'Can you make sense of it? I have drawn a rough plan of the inn. There is the main door into the taproom... Here is the kitchen and the rooms that provide the present lodging. But can you see how neatly the building might be divided? All the rooms on this side of the house could have a more discreet access, other than through the taproom, if a new entrance were made here, on the west wall.' Her finger jabbed down onto the paper. 'There is nothing but rough ground outside, which could be cleared and paved – perhaps even made into a little garden. Ladies would appreciate, I'm sure, such a welcoming aspect. The new door would open into this room, which could then be divided into a small hallway and a parlour with the adjoining room as dining chamber. This already gives onto the passage leading from the kitchen to the main stairs. So convenient, you see, for food to be brought up without becoming chilled and for guests to reach the bedchambers on this floor where I would propose to lodge them. And of course there would always be special attention to the requirements of ladies travelling solitary, so as to ensure privacy and peace of mind.'

I followed her blunt, pink fingernail as it pointed, her vision unwinding itself in my head. I saw how easily it might be done. She rapped the paper impatiently with her knuckles.

'Once the alterations were in place and new customers encouraged, who knows where it might lead? I have tried to impress on Mr Yelland that change is everywhere and if we do not adapt to it, we shall be left behind. There are more people travelling every year now the Turnpike Trusts have improved so many of the roads – with new Trusts being set up by the month. It takes no more than forty hours to reach London from Exeter by stagecoach these days. And there is talk of even greater speeds and new coaches that will be able to carry people outside as well as in. Yet I can remember when it took a relative of my late husband's a full week to travel to us from Oxford.' She shook her head at the memory. 'He was fatigued beyond endurance when he arrived at Starlings and continued to be considerably troubled by itching from the livestock he had accumulated while sleeping in unsavoury beds. It took him the best part of his stay with us to rid himself of the great quantity of fleas that had taken up residence in his clothing. His experience has been much in my mind since I came here. Indeed, I have heard similar stories since of hostelries that seem to exist purely to fleece the unwary traveller and send him away ill fed and unrefreshed. And it could all be so different! It *will* be different here at the Thorn Tree.' Her eyes glinted with an almost feverish light. 'I cannot understand anyone not seeing the advantage of it.'

By anyone I supposed she meant Master Harry, but it was to me she cried, 'Do you think I am right, Emily? Come. Speak up. Sometimes I feel that I am the only one standing out against a tide of inertia and sloth! Yet there is something in your bright face that tells me I am not alone in wishing for better things. So do I press ahead and tell – no, *encourage* – Mr Yelland to look beyond his casks of ale? Or do I content myself with letting things moulder on as they have always done?'

Luke whistled softly, his eyes wide. 'So what did you say, Em?'

'Just that I'd no objection to bettering myself and she laughed and pinched my cheek and sent me off.'

'And d'you think it'll come about? What she plans?'

I looked down at Mattie sprawled on the straw with the guzzling piglets a pink, wobbling fringe along her belly.

'I reckon so,' I said slowly. 'She'll not rest content otherwise.'

Luke gave a whoop of excitement.

'Then that's the best news I've heard since she brought me here.'

I let him rattle on about how it was fate we'd both come to the Thorn Tree at the right time when it was ready to go up in the world – and Luke Gilpin and Emily Wroe along with it.

But I looked down at the pigs, not seeing them or hearing Luke, but wondering what sadness lay in Barbara Yelland's past that seemed to drive her as though there were a demon at her heels.

If Luke and I had believed that Mrs Yelland's plans would hasten to fruition we were to be disappointed. Though Master Harry had been happy to allow his wife her head over domestic matters, when it came to any radical change at the Thorn Tree he showed that he had a mulish side to his amiable nature. However much she persuaded and argued, he stayed stubbornly cautious.

'My love, think of the extra work and worry! The superior classes are bound to be more particular and demanding than the working man.'

'Are we then condemned never to raise our standards above the level of carters and packmen?'

'We have always made a comfortable living at the Thorn Tree. My father and—'

'Your grandfather. Yes, yes. You have told me of them often. But if they were alive today do you suppose they would not be alert to the changes in the world and wish to profit from them?'

'But in our little backwater—'

'You are content to moulder and let other people reap the rewards of enterprise.'

'You are too harsh, my love.'

'I merely state the obvious. And I do so out of affection and respect for you, Harry. You deserve so much better than to be master of what is little more than a common alehouse. The opportunity for betterment is there, waiting to be boldly grasped! I should be failing in my duty as wife and helpmeet if I did not present the possibilities to you and offer my heartfelt encouragement and support.'

'And I am not ungrateful. Indeed, my love, I never cease to bless the impulse that carried me to Devon to attend the funeral of my dear mother's last remaining cousin. It was fate that sped me there. I shall never forget that moment when I spied you, so lovely, so helpless in your grief. And even though you were surrounded by people and attended so protectively by your stepson and his wife, I was impelled to force my way through the throng to speak to you. To proffer my condolences, to be sure, yet I felt even then that our eyes spoke of things that could not be uttered by our lips.'

'How true. The workings of fate are wondrous indeed. Bowed with grief as I was, there is no denying that the . . . the interest, shall we say, that sparked between us went a considerable way to easing my sense of loss and loneliness . . . Harry! You are crushing my gown! Leave off, do. You will embarrass Cass. Besides, that wig of yours is moulting. Look at these strands that have detached themselves. And such an old-fashioned heavy thing it is. You really must pay a visit to your wigmaker and bespeak a more modern style, or grow your own hair as it is becoming more fashionable to do . . . But where were we? Oh, yes. You have not properly explained why you have set yourself so against me.'

'Against you? I am the luckiest man in all Somerset to have taken Barbara Bowyer for my wife, as I tell you ten times a day! I would never wish to upset you, my love, especially as you take my wellbeing so tenderly to your heart, but in this you must allow a more prudent counsel to prevail. The alterations you propose will not come cheap and are not to be undertaken lightly. I will think about it, I promise, and in the meantime, dearest, I have no objections if you choose to amuse yourself by making a little garden – as you suggested – in that corner by the west wall. You had a pretty garden at Starlings, did you not? Young Luke may be spared to help you with the heavy work whenever you wish. I recollect my mother grew flowers when I was a child. That was before she became too frail and breathless to tend her gillyflowers and pansies and such.'

He was hopeful, perhaps, that with the passage of time she would abandon her unsettling ideas. But if there were intervals when her purpose seemed to lie dormant, it took little to revive it. Whenever business slackened, whenever some argument in the taproom led to drunken fisticuffs in the stableyard, or when she saw some elegant private equipage passing by – with neither the coachman nor the passengers within giving more than a dismissive glance at the unprepossessing aspect that the inn presented to the road – then she would press her arguments with renewed vigour.

'A lick of paint would make the place welcoming to travellers. The sign alone is so faded that the device can hardly be seen, and it is dangerous to a degree. Have you not noticed it hangs merely by a thread of rust? There'll be a broken head to deal with one of these days... And, really, Harry, it is intolerable that a cartload of steaming farmyard muck stood in the forecourt for a good half-hour this, the hottest day of the year. It is bad enough that we must put up with all manner of disreputable wagons and carthorses standing outside at busy times, but the sight and stench of that was not to be borne... No, I do not care that it was Farmer Ashdown come to quench his thirst on his way to his five-acre field. Surely space could be made so that the more noisome and dirty vehicles might be driven out of sight.'

Like a constant drip of water that slowly wears away stone, so, as season followed season, her exhortations began to have some small effect. The old sign was taken down and repainted and rehung on a new pole made by the village smith. A lick of paint was given here and there to peeling windowframes. After much deliberation and doleful shaking of the head against the excessive expenditure, a small field alongside the stableyard was rented from Farmer Ashdown, to become a new wagon yard so that the forecourt might not become so congested.

To Master Harry's surprise this proved popular among his customers. There had been a spate of thieving in Bristol from wagons left unattended overnight. True, that was in the city where all manner of riffraff abounded and professional gangs followed their light-fingered trade in the congested alleys that fringed the docks, but there were plenty of persons travelling country roads and not all of them respectable. Tales of footpads, highwaymen and their ilk – often gaining highly coloured and gory detail as they were told and retold – abounded in the taproom. The more nervous among the carters – particularly those who preferred to sleep with their loads – were soon loud in praise of the new wagon yard, with its thick blackthorn hedges and a gate that could be closed and padlocked at night. Pretty soon they could all see the advantage of it.

'So you see, I do talk sense, Harry,' said Mrs Yelland.

'Indeed you do, my love,' he agreed.

But he still remained obdurately set against converting the west wing.

If he was wishful that his wife's abundant energy might be diverted by maternity he was, like Mrs Hill, to be disappointed. This second marriage seemed destined to remain childless, as had been the case, we eventually learned, with the first.

Cass revelled in relaying the gossip she gleaned while she was about her work, enthusiastic to show off her improved status. Everyone soon knew that Mrs Yelland's late husband, Mr Paul Bowyer, had been a widower of fifty when she wed him, with a married son little younger than she was herself. For most of the seven years they had together her husband had ailed with a weak chest.

'Likely he never 'ad the energy to tup her proper,' Mrs Hill sneered.

'Or mayhap, 'is pillicock refused to turn playful,' Enoch said with a leer. 'One of 'er frowning looks'd be enough to cause any man's willingness to shrink to naught.'

Coarse speculation provided a deal of amusement round the kitchen table.

There was much I could have added to Cass's gossip, but I had no intention of fuelling their prurient interest. When I came back from my lessons, or from doing some household work alongside the mistress, Mrs Hill would always try to ferret out what had been said, searching for some snippet that would add to her store of grievances. But I never spoke of anything beyond the verses or the passages we had read and discussed, or the mathematical problem Mrs Yelland had set for me. Cook's glowers told me that this was not at all what she wished to hear. Sometimes I would add innocently, 'Do you know the poetry of William Shakespeare, Mrs Hill?' Or it might be John Milton or Andrew Marvell. 'It's very fine and Mrs Yelland reads aloud so beautifully...'

'When have I ever 'ad time for poetry?' she would roar, rising to the bait and shaking her meaty fist under my nose. 'Her's filling your 'ead with rubbish! One o' these days it'll turn your brain to mush! You gets those taters peeled afore I really gets angry and knocks the livin' daylights out of 'ee.'

She was easily diverted.

I gradually fleshed out the bare bones of Mrs Yelland's past for myself, watchful for some clue to the dark misery I glimpsed from time to time. There had certainly been times of unhappiness in her young life, yet it still seemed to me that these were unconnected to whatever still troubled her. Nor did I believe it was anything to do with her first husband. She never spoke other than in affectionate terms of him. He had been helpful to her at the time of her father's death. Her father had been an Exeter corn merchant and from the age of fifteen she had been his housekeeper and companion. 'My father was possessed of a great melancholia after my mother died. He took little interest in the business after she had gone, and after his death I discovered that we had teetered on the verge of ruin for years. The prospect of being cast out penniless into the street was very real and very frightening. It was Paul Bowyer, one of Papa's suppliers, whom I had met from time to time, who proved a true Samaritan. He helped me sort out the muddle so that I could sell the business and pay off the rest of the creditors. For himself,' she added with a fond smile, 'as we had come to be companionable during these trying weeks, he proposed to write off the debt my father owed him if I would consent to be his wife. He thought we should manage very well together. And so we did! He was the kindest, most considerate of gentlemen.'

By now, conversation was easy between us as we sat over our books, though it was mostly about the work in hand or day-to-day affairs. But I loved it when she was in a mood to reminisce. It seemed almost as though her tales helped fill the void in my own past. I hugged the details to myself, so that when I was about the mindless tasks in the kitchen, I could place the imaginary family I had invented – mother, father, sister, brother – into a reality I had no experience of.

'What sort of a house did you come to, ma'am?' I prompted. 'Was it very quiet after living in the town?'

Her green eyes clouded, though her voice was carefully noncommittal as she said, 'The house was – is – charming. It is a farmhouse, of course. The name tells you that: Starlings Barton, a barton being an ancient Devon name for a farmstead. It was built by a Bowyer ancestor – a foreigner, out of France – oh, in the early sixteen hundreds, I believe. The house prospered as the family prospered. It is now a most comfortable residence, set in pretty gardens which I took the greatest pleasure in tending. As to quiet – there was far more lively company visiting there than ever I had experienced in Exeter. Some sad visitors, too, for my husband always offered a helping hand to those of Huguenot stock who had fallen on hard times.'

I frowned at the unfamiliar word. Tasted it on my tongue. 'Huguenot,' I repeated carefully. 'What is that, ma'am?'

'A name given to French Protestants who have been much persecuted in the past by the Catholic majority. And still are, though one hopes a wiser and more tolerant course will eventually prevail. The first Bowyer – he was a Bouvier then – fled to England for sanctuary after a dreadful and bloody time that has become known as the Massacre of St Bartholomew. My husband told me that streets in towns and cities across France ran red with blood for a whole week as innocent people were dragged from their houses by enraged mobs and put to the sword.' She shook her head. 'It seems to me that man has ever been quick to justify his pleasure in bloodshed and torture and warfare, or his greed for power and riches, by claiming his sordid actions give satisfaction to the Almighty. Think of the Crusades! Think of the Spanish Inquisition! Think, indeed, of King Henry plundering monasteries or Oliver Cromwell imposing his stern, cold Puritan creed so harshly that people went about in fear of being punished for taking pleasure in innocent merrymaking or traditional revels.'

She paused and I put in hastily before she could be further sidetracked into reading me a lecture on Royalists and Roundheads or asking me to recite the names of King

Hal's six wives, 'Did you say the name was changed? Why was that?'

'The French Bouvier was difficult for local people to pronounce. It quickly became Bowyer and it was thought practical that it should remain so. Their descendants have so intermarried with Devonshire families that it is almost forgot in the district that they once came to these shores as foreigners. Among themselves they take care to hand on all they remember of their ancestors so that the French inheritance shall be kept fresh in the memory.'

'It must be very sad for them to remember such evil times.'

She laughed. 'Oh, not all the tales are solemn ones. My husband was particularly fond of recounting the story of one Bowyer who had a great scheme of planting mulberry trees so that in time he might breed silkworms. Many of the Huguenots, you see, were skilled in the weaving of silk and Great-great-grandfather Bowyer thought to improve the family fortunes by supplying the raw material to his exiled countrymen. Unfortunately, his plan for breeding silkworms came to naught. Having more enthusiasm than practical knowledge, he planted the wrong kind of tree – the black mulberry, instead of the white. Excellent for fruit, but unsuitable for silkworms!'

'He must have been shamefaced when he found out.'

'Not a bit of it! He took it in good part, put the whole episode down to experience and decided to make use of the field to expand his gardens. He rooted out many of the mulberries, creating grassy rides and shrubberies around those that were left. He set about creating a more formal garden close to the house, but died before it was finished, though subsequent generations have improved and extended it. The lower part of the garden is still known as the Mulberry Field. It is a very tranquil place. I spent many happy hours there myself, when I was not pottering about the flowerbeds. A garden always flourishes well if there is someone who tends it with loving care.' Then, with an impatient edge to her voice which was often there when she spoke of her stepson's wife: 'I fancy Abigail has no enthusiasm for anything that might tax her intellect. She scarcely knows the name of a flower. All she understands of the garden is how to sit in a rose bower looking fetching.' Then she laughed. 'Oh dear, what a sourpuss I sound. Poor Abigail. She cannot help being what she is. But what am I thinking of! Time rushes on and I have not heard the passage that you have memorised.'

I applied myself hastily to John Milton.

> 'Sabrina fair,
> Listen where thou art sitting
> Under the glassie, cool, translucent wave,'

The magic of the words took me over. But at the end of the lesson Mrs Yelland returned to the subject of Huguenots, giving me a further poem of Milton's to study.

'It seems apt that you should read his "On the Late Massacre in Piedmont", which relates to yet another violent episode against the Protestants, this time in the southern Alps. It will have more interest now you understand something of the background.'

I read it by candlelight before I slept. Not perhaps the best time, when the images it raised might have followed me into sleep. But I did not dream of slaughter and gore as I half expected.

But I did dream. And most strangely.

I was in a dark place and cold. Icily cold. There was frozen grass underfoot and above the leafless trees the stars hung in the moonless sky like shards of glittering glass strewn across black velvet.

I was moving among the trees. Mulberries. I had no notion what such a tree looked like, but I knew that I was in the place Mrs Yelland had called the Mulberry Field.

With the certainty that comes with dreaming, I hastened to the biggest tree where I should meet the person who would explain the meaning of the little brass key and the scrap of paper which I held in my hands.

A figure shrouded in a brown cloak stood in the deep shadow, and I knew I was on the verge of a momentous discovery. But the hood of the cloak was flung back and it was Miss Edgar who cried, 'You young fool. Look, you could have read it for yourself, but I'll not let you!' She snatched at the paper and I saw with dismay that it was no longer a charred scrap but a whole sheet of paper.

I clawed at her hands to get it back. But she ripped it to shreds, hissing, 'I sent her packing. You'll never catch her now.'

Then I saw someone running away from me across the frosted grass – a young girl, ghostlike in pale, flowing garments. As she ran she glanced back over her shoulder. She was terrified, desperate. I felt my own response to her pain clutch at my heart. I wanted to run to her, comfort her . . .

But I could not run. My feet were suddenly mired. And the girl was slipping away. Fading like a ghost into the mist that was creeping under the trees, blinding me, choking me.

Then I realised I was back in the coal cellar at Lady Eleanor's and Miss Edgar had thrown away the key and I should never get out and there was no air left . . .

Tugging at the sheet that had tangled itself round my face, I woke to the pitchy blackness of the small hours, awash with relief that I was back in my bed at the Thorn Tree. The nightmare of being shut away and forgotten in the coal cellar was one that I had experienced before and I soon put it out of my mind. It was not that which haunted me as I went about my work later that day. It was the vividness and clarity of the rest of the dream.

I could not help but cling to the idea – foolish as I

knew it to be – that the scene in the Mulberry Field held some deep meaning for me beyond the obvious significance of the scrap of charred paper that had mysteriously become whole. That was clearly due to wishful thinking on my part.

But the mulberry tree? The starlight? The bitter cold?

I had felt that aching cold in my bones. I could have reached up and grasped the lowest branch of the tree, so real it was. The starry skyscape had been so sharp I could have been observing it with my real vision, not the imagination of a dream.

Yet try as I might I could not interpret it. Nor imagine how or why I had dreamed up so lucid a vision out of the fragments Mrs Yelland had told me.

Mrs Yelland's first marriage might have been one of convenience for her, but it had turned out well. As to her second, I could see with my own eyes how Master Harry doted on her, yet there was no more than a teasing fondness on her side and sometimes an impatience with him that she could barely conceal. I wondered why marriage to him had seemed so attractive to her, newly widowed as she was and presumably living in some style and comfort at Starlings.

Something must have occurred to make the prospect of becoming an innkeeper's wife tempting. She was a clever woman. She would not have taken such a step without thought. And she must have understood full well the manner of man she was marrying – amiable, easygoing, but not overly gifted with intelligence or ambition. And even if Master Harry had been rosily over-optimistic about the cosy life she would have at the Thorn Tree, she was clear-sighted enough to have seen through his flannelling and realise that her life here would be no sinecure.

But there were hints to what must have happened. A scornful remark, a curl of the lip whenever she spoke of

Abigail Bowyer. Had this been the source of the friction, a jostling for dominance between two women who both considered themselves mistress of the household? Yet relations seemed to have remained – superficially at any rate – cordial. They still wrote to each other, though it seemed more a duty than a pleasure on Mrs Yelland's side.

I eventually rejected this idea. The more I got to know her, the more I understood that there was a deep and entrenched antagonism between the stepson, Tom, and his father's second wife. No letters ever came from Tom Bowyer. She rarely spoke of him, and then only with a brusque, dismissive note in her voice. Had he always resented the woman who had replaced his mother? Perhaps his resentment had been muted in his father's lifetime, but without his father's restraining hand, and newly master in the house, the difficulties for one so strong-willed as Mrs Yelland could be imagined.

It made sense of why she had seized the chance of an early escape from a difficult situation to a second marriage where there was no one to challenge her authority. At the Thorn Tree there were no resentful offspring nor even the shadow of a former wife to make life difficult, and with Master Harry's parents long gone, no aged relative to interfere neither. She could make a fresh start in a new place and put the past behind her.

But the past cannot always be so easily dismissed. Sometimes the twists and turns of fate bring us full circle and we must again face that very spectre from which we fled in the first place.

It was nearly three years before Master Harry gave way on the matter of the west wing. They might have been frustrating years for Mrs Yelland, but for me and for Luke, who had come to the Thorn Tree with few expectations, they were increasingly good years.

We had to work hard – at busy times to the point of

exhaustion – but there was the reward of good food always on the table, a regular wage, a good bed and, for me, an element of freedom I had never known before.

There were initial fears I had to overcome. Not least having to face the taproom, as it was now one of my duties to help Amy and Luke serve up food to the customers. The night I first arrived it had seemed a terrible place, full of wild, leering faces and ear-splitting noise. But it was not half as bad as I had expected. I realised that my first impression had been coloured by fear of the unknown and the contrast to the habitual, chilling silence at Lady Eleanor's where everybody crept about on slippered feet and scarcely dared speak above a whisper.

Cass had given me sensible advice.

'Iffen they gets too forward – straying hands, pinching and that – and some of them does when they've had a tankard too many – it don't mean nothing. Best take it in good part. They'll have forgot about it by morning when they've sobered up. Decent working men, most of 'em. Got wives and sweethearts waiting at journey's end. Master Harry'll look out for 'ee. He's watchful for trouble for all he looks so soft and easy. Any that gets properly nasty, he's like to cool in the horse trough.' She proudly smoothed down the skirts of her new print dress. 'I has to say I does find my new duties more to my liking than waiting on rough-mannered carters and such. An' I'm glad missus picked blue for me. Mind, that lavender you and Amy have suits you a treat,' she added hastily. 'I've watched how missus does her hair and I'll show you how to curl yours up fashionable like I've done mine.' She frowned. 'Though rags didn't do much for your hair, I has to say. Too straight and heavy by half.' She gave me an assessing look and sighed. 'P'raps tongs'd make sommat of it . . . I daresay I could sneak 'em out from upstairs . . .'

'Oh, you mustn't,' I said in some alarm. My scalp cringed at the thought of Cass wielding hot tongs round my ears. Her heavy-handed ministrations with the curling rags, in which I had been ordered to sleep in the expectation of producing long ringlets by morning, had been uncomfortable to say the least. 'I mean . . . I wouldn't want you to get into trouble on my account.'

'P'raps you're right,' she agreed reluctantly. 'Pity, though. Such a . . . a nice colour, your hair. 'Twould have looked a treat with a bit of curl in it. Made 'ee look real pretty.'

She was just being kind. I could see that from her expression though, being Cass, she had tried to find something consoling to say. I only had to look in the mirror to know that my unfortunate hair was best kept pinned tightly under my cap. When released it hung straight as straw about my face – save that straw has the benefit of a good yellow colour and my poor hair was pale as ash. Amy, of course, missed no opportunity to sneer, calling me 'Milksop' and 'Butterhead' and never failing to remind me how popular she was among the customers whereas I scarcely drew an interested glance, being so skinny and plain and quiet.

It was true. But it was the greatest relief to me that the ribald banter, the playful slaps, and the leering looks scarcely ever came my way. Even as I grew to be a young woman rather than a thin wisp of a child, the men were respectful rather than forward. Which suited me well.

Amy made sure from the first that I was put to waiting on those she personally considered not worth her trouble. Unwittingly, she did me a great favour, for I was comfortable with the quieter, older men who treated me with consideration and kindliness, as, perhaps, they might have treated their own daughters. Amy preferred the lively element – the younger men and the hard-eyed among the older ones.

'They tips the best. 'Ee can have the skinflints and the poor old men, who hasn't a spare farthin' between 'em.'

There was more to it than that, of course. Despite Mrs Yelland's strictures, Amy was not about to give up her other source of income and pleasure so easily. She occasionally managed to sneak out on some excuse or other.

'Had to dash to the privy,' she said one day to Mrs Hill, breathless and grinning, having been missing for twenty minutes. 'Gaw, I did have a gripin' in me belly.'

Mrs Hill, scarlet-faced from the fire, aimed a warning blow at her ear.

'Gripin'? What Jed Smith's got hid under his breeches was troubling your innards, more like. I 'eard he was hanging about the stables. But just think on, iffen you gets into trouble, it'll be me her ladyship'll blame for not keepin' a close rein on 'ee.'

'Don't fret,' Amy said, tossing her head. 'I got ways of managing.' Then staring hard at me, she added loudly, 'It was somethin' I ate, I tell 'ee. That's all. Naught to do with Jed Smith. So don't 'ee go tattling any lies upstairs.'

'I'm not interested in what you're about,' I retorted. 'And I don't ever tattle to Mrs Yelland about what goes on down here. If you're caught out it'll be your own fault and nobody else's, so it's no use scowling. And another thing,' I went on coldly as she opened her mouth to bawl at the little scullion who had scuttled into the kitchen with a stack of clean bowls. 'Don't take your bad temper out on Trudie or I'll scratch your eyes out.'

'You and who else?' she sneered. But she left Trudie alone.

I had quickly learned the language that Amy understood. This and her superstitious belief in the 'charm' I wore did much to ease my lot.

Life, though, was not all work. Whenever trade was slack, one or other of us would be given a few hours off. I was always torn between settling to a good long spell with whatever book I was reading or exploring outside. On fine days the outdoors won.

Bit by bit I became familiar with the lie of the land around the inn. It was a novel experience to be entirely alone with no limits on how or where I might walk. A touch intimidating at first. Would I get lost? Were there any wild beasts waiting to leap out from the hedgerows? Badgers? Foxes? At certain seasons, foxes made dreadful screechings in the night that caused the blood to run cold. Badgers were fearsome brutes with terrible fangs that could tear a dog's throat out and slice an unwary man's fingers off. Luke had told me of baitings, dog against badger, he had seen in Bristol. I had shuddered and put my hands over my ears as he explained with some relish the way the animals pulled each other to bits to the cheers and groans of those who had money to lose or win.

'How could you bear to watch?' I said. 'Poor suffering beasts.'

'Animals don't have feelings the same as us,' he said cheerfully.

'Not even your pigs? They squeal enough to make your skin crawl at slaughtering time.'

'It doesn't mean anything,' he scoffed. 'Besides, it's their fate to be turned into pork chops and bacon . . .'

'I know, I know! A would-be farmer can't afford the luxury of being squeamish. You've told me so a hundred times. Well, that's one thing. It's quite another to catch a wild creature and torment it cruelly until it dies. I'll never believe that's a . . . a *civilised* occupation for any man to indulge in.'

He grinned. 'Ah ha! You've been learning more long words from your books, eh? Well, let me tell you, Princess, the nobs enjoy a good baiting as much as any gutter urchin. I've seen 'em.'

'Then shame on them! And on you, Luke Gilpin!'

He laughed. 'My, but you can talk fierce when your dander's up, for all you claim to be soft-hearted. Still, I suppose it's the lot of females to be so contrary. That's why men are put in the world to have the mastery over them and set them straight when they go astray with their daft ideas.'

It was impossible to put him down. I knew I could not make him change his mind. Perhaps it was as well. It was much more comfortable to view the animal world as being bereft of feeling. Privately, I wished I could be more like him and the others around me who seemed equally hardened to the casual cruelties inflicted on brute beasts. The sight of an old, tired horse being beaten to make him move, a birdcatcher with a cage full of frantic linnets flailing against the wires, the newly born offspring of the stable cats tossed carelessly into the water butt – all these were things that caused my spirit to cry a silent protest. Yet cold logic told me that the old horse must work or the poor carter who owned him would lose his living, the birdcatcher had a family who must eat, the stables would be overrun with cats if the numbers were not kept in check.

But on my solitary walks, I could rejoice in my own freedom and that of the birds and animals that I did see: the rabbits scuttering for cover as I approached; larks flinging themselves skywards in a fervour of song; the rustle in the grass that heralded some small creature – a mouse, a vole – about its business. Once I did see a fox. We met almost face to face at the edge of Brimston Wood. For a heart-stopping instant I feared that this fearsome predator might fling itself at me as it would on a hapless chicken or lamb.

We stared at each other across the glade. Its eyes glinted amber-yellow, its coat was glossy, its brush thick and bushy. It had fed well this summer. And even if it was at some farmer's expense, I suddenly did not care.

I lost my fear in that instant. I was too much taken up with imprinting its lithe handsomeness on my memory. Then it turned away into the undergrowth and was gone on thin, delicate paws that scarcely made a sound on the newly fallen leaves.

I felt privileged to have seen the living creature, rather than the limp, blood-matted carcasses that Farmer Ashdown was prone to string up along a particular fence and which I took pains to avoid after the first time I had passed it.

Much of what I gradually learned of country lore came from Cass. I would take her a flower to identify, tell her of a bird or creature I had seen and she would furnish me with the name. She had been born in the nearby impoverished hamlet of Brimyard where the grandmother who had raised her still eked out a living labouring for Farmer Ashdown.

'Ma died when I was born and Pa went off to find his fortune and never come back,' she told me cheerfully. 'Sad, en't it? Would have liked a pa, but then, what 'ee never has 'ee never misses and I've done well for meself, getting took on 'ere. I can give Gran sixpence and more every time I visits now on top of all sorts o' bits and pieces Mrs Yelland passes on. I'm hopeful I'll be able to look after her proper one day. Her's an old lady now, well past fifty, and full of rheumatics. 'Ten't right her should be picking stones and digging taters for evermore. Her's looked after me and I intends to find a chimney corner for her when I've a cot of my own.'

She blushed as she spoke. Looking after her grandmother in a proper fashion had a great deal to do with Ned Arnold, the eldest son of the tollhouse keeper at Brimston Cross. Sometimes our hours off coincided and it was surprising how often the walk she suggested took us as far as the tollhouse. 'I does so love to look at the grand people passing,' she would explain as our circuitous route along the fringes of Brimston Wood to gather bluebells, or up the slopes of nearby Gibbet Hill in search of the fine blackberries she swore grew there, brought us close to the Bath Road. "Twon't but take us a few minutes out of our way,' she would add, suddenly dropping all pretence of interest in bluebells or blackberries as she hastened towards the real object of our outing.

It was an odd, bashful sort of courtship. If the tollgate was busy, she was quite content to stand at a distance and watch Ned and his father taking the money and opening and shutting the gates. Her round blue eyes lingered dreamily on the object of her devotion, though I was mystified by the attraction he held for her. What on earth did she see in him? He was no more than a raw-boned, heavy-featured youth with a gap-toothed grin and very little to say for himself.

'He's right handsome,' Cass would sigh longingly.

I searched diligently for signs of it.

'He's very like his father,' was the best I could manage, hoping that she would be warned by Obadiah Arnold's surly aspect, which did nothing for looks that had matured and set to florid stoutness.

'A fine figure of a man, his pa,' Cass agreed.

I opened my mouth to explain what I meant, then closed it. Cass would hear only what she wanted to hear. Love, apparently, was deaf as well as blind.

Dumb, too. I was torn between amusement and curiosity at what passed for conversation between them. Cass, normally so gossipy, was rendered practically speechless during these encounters and Ned communicated in grunts and guffaws. Yet these halting interludes were interpreted by Cass later as lengthy conversations when many flowery compliments had been exchanged.

'You 'eard what he said when I told him that I was learning a new way of tying ribbons in my hair? Said I'd no need of fancy trappings, I was pretty enough! And didn't he just redden up when I said as how I thought his coat – as used to be his pa's – suited 'ee much better, Ned not having the belly to stretch it out of shape.' She blinked happily and sighed. 'He and his pa between 'em makes a brave sight. You hear such tales of fisticuffs and worse when travellers gets uppity about paying tolls, makes me properly worried sometimes. But I reckons Ned and his pa could see off anyone turning obstropolous, being so big and burly. Why, you could see how respectful even that fine gentleman on the big hoss was. And Ned spoke to 'im so civil and pleasant and give 'im a proper dashin' bow when he took his coin . . .'

A strange commodity, love.

I pondered later on the alchemy that caused the attraction between these two. It was oddly touching, the way they stared at each other, as though their eyes spoke silently of meanings they could not find words for. The lumbering, tongue-tied youth and the ordinary young woman caught up in a private enchantment, inexplicable to the onlooker – unaware for a few precious moments of the glowering parent muttering of neglected duties, the swarm of small brothers and sisters giggling at them from the safety of the tollhouse door, and me, impatiently nudging at Cass to remind her that time was running on and we'd best make haste.

One damp January day, newly returned from one such walk and tidying ourselves up in our attic room before we went to our work, Cass said, kindly, 'Don't 'ee fret, Em, in a year or two you'll have as good a lad as Ned come a-courting. Course, with all that book-learning you got, and if ever missus gets her way over a better sort o' lodger, you might land yourself a gentleman 'stead of a carter's lad or such.' She cocked her head on one side and eyed me up and down. 'Now you've growed a bit and filled out . . .' She stopped, as though she'd not really looked at me properly for a long time and now could see something that puzzled her. 'I reckon you really has growed up, Em. You'll be what now? Fifteen?'

'Just.'

She frowned. 'You allus was a bit different to Amy and me. Can't put my finger on it proper – I suppose it was being in that foundling place for so long. And with the book-learning . . .'

I laughed. 'What? Have I gone boss-eyed because of reading and writing? Or has it caused my ears to grow like a donkey's or my face to turn green?'

'See, that's part of it,' she said earnestly. 'Oh, not them silly things, but being sharp with answers. Knowing stuff as don't matter to any but scholars. And you got a way with you. But like the missus. Sort of . . . quick and . . . and mannerly.' Then she grinned. 'My, but Luke Gilpin'll have to watch hisself. Some fine bucko'll be snatching you off from under his nose, iffen he's not careful.'

'*Luke?*' I groaned. 'Oh my Lord, spare me from Luke. He's keener on pigs than females.' Then, because Luke had always been kind to me and it was grudging of me to put him down I said earnestly, 'For all his teasing, he's been a good friend, especially in the beginning when I was so new and fearful. He cheered me those first awful weeks, helped me to see the good side of being here. That's typical of Luke, isn't it? Always full of fun and rudery, but soft-hearted underneath. Look how he helps young Trudie. He treats me no different from her or anyone else.'

'I'll grant you that. He'd make a cat laugh, poking fun at things as he does. And I seen how he puts hisself out to give Trudie a hand with the heavy buckets, her being no bigger than two penn'orth of copper.'

'There you are then.'

'But he en't got eyes for her like he has for you. I knows that for certain.'

'Give over, Cass,' I said, suddenly irritated by the smug way she was smiling. 'Being sweet on Ned Arnold's addled your brain. You're seeing things that aren't there.'

'Oh, you're young yet,' Cass said loftily. 'You'll

understand when you gets on a year or two, like me. That'll be the right time for 'ee to be settling your fancy on some steady lad.'

'Well, it won't be Luke Gilpin, I can tell you that!'

She went off, still smirking in that thoroughly maddening manner. I fumed for a while, then found myself wondering why I found the thought of Luke being my secret admirer so alarming. I liked Luke, didn't I? Of course I did. But not in that way.

The thought of Luke and me gazing at each other in the same doltish way as Ned and Cass quite broke my ill humour in a burst of giggles. As if we could or would!

No, no. The whole idea was silly beyond words.

All the same, Cass's remarks set me thinking. Not about any prospective lovers, but about what lay ahead. And what my future would really hold.

I stared slowly round the attic room and at the little alcove with the narrow bed that was my own private space. It had a curtain now that I could draw across for extra privacy and a shelf to hold my treasures: a few books, a bundle of goose quills and a knife well honed for sharpening them; a bottle of ink, a few precious sheets of paper; a tin candleholder and a couple of spare candles.

Was this as much as I could expect in life? Oh, perhaps, an improvement in my situation here would mean a few more trinkets on that shelf, a few more pennies to hoard or spend before I married – if I should be fortunate to get an offer from some farm labourer or stable lad . . .

Was that it?

To Cass such a prospect seemed exciting and fulfilling. But now I saw that she was right to say I was different. Even as my head told me that this was as much as I could expect, and I should be grateful for what I had, a great, mutinous surge of denial surged through me.

No! It was not enough. I wanted – needed – more. There was a deep hunger in me that could not be assuaged by accepting my lot, improved as it was.

Instinctively my hand rose to touch the place between my breasts where the little calico bag hung. I felt through the cotton of my bodice the shape of the key.

Someday I should find whatever it was that the veiled lady had meant me to discover. And I knew that whatever light that discovery threw on my past was something essential to the very core of my being. I should never feel complete until I knew the secret of the key and had some inkling of what the letter had intended to convey to me.

Could I ever find out? Would it be a fruitless quest? Was this sense that I must not settle for the ordinary, but press for something better, yet another treacherous expression of the unfortunate traits of pride and rebelliousness Miss Edgar had done her best to beat out of me? She had reminded me often that my high-nosed ways and dumb insolence would bring me to grief.

Outside the little square of window a brief glimmer of blue appeared between the massed grey clouds. My fingers traced the familiar line of the key.

Cass's way was not mine. I felt that in my bones, in my blood, in my heart.

That frail glint of blue somehow heartened me, strengthened my purpose. As though it was some kind of omen of better things to come. What those things would be and how or when I should achieve them I could not say.

All I knew, as I stood there, was that I was ready to take my chance whenever it came.

Chapter Three

Afterwards I was to remember that moment. How I had been touching the key in that instant of hoping, longing for I scarcely knew what . . .

Although I had spun a tale to Amy about my so-called charm, it was just that. A fairy tale. So what happened the next day was sheer chance. Of course it was. I had to believe that or I would sink to the superstition of kitchen gossip. After all, there had been grumbles about the state of the road for some weeks. A bad downpour in November had swirled away gravel and created deep potholes. Ever since, a succession of carts had become mired or suffered broken axles at a particularly bad place just beyond the bend before Brimyard. It was just another accident. Of course it was.

Early that afternoon Mrs Yelland called me outside to help stake a rowan sapling that had blown over in the recent gales. Although I was usually willing to be outdoors, a biting north wind had set in and I was more than a little reluctant to face it.

The heavy old kitchen shawl I had thrown over my head and shoulders might have been gossamer for all the protection it gave me as I held the stake upright so that Mrs Yelland could secure the little tree. I hoped she would not keep me long. The garden she had created at Master Harry's suggestion was a colourful, scented corner in summer, but a dank, cheerless place on this sullen winter's day.

She had created the garden partly out of frustration that her plans for the house had been thwarted, and grumbled accordingly that it was a waste of her time if no one but herself was to enjoy it. But I knew that it was a labour of love for her. Even the rooting out of thistles and brambles and couch grass had given her satisfaction and she had spent hours walking about the patch and planning where everything should go. Luke had hauled buckets of stable muck to hearten the soil. Paths had been marked out and laid with gravel, herb beds and flowery corners created. A carter coming up from Devonshire delivered wicker hampers lined with moss in which seedlings and thorny twigs with roots bound up in muslin had made the journey from Starlings Barton.

'At least the silly creature has followed my instructions and sent what I asked for,' Mrs Yelland had remarked with the usual scornful tones she always employed when speaking of her stepson's wife. 'I had quite expected she would instruct the gardener to make up a bundle of weeds. She would have been quite capable of it. Such a dunderhead! She seems to have learned nothing since I left. Every letter she writes seems to be a cry for help and advice about some household disaster or other.'

But she soon forgot her scorn of Abigail Bowyer in the gentle rhythm of planting and hoeing. Under Mrs Yelland's loving fingers everything flourished and bloomed. Thyme and rosemary, purple-flowered sage and the vigorous lemon balm, dill and fennel, caraway and marjoram. The thorny twigs grew to bushes which shook out swags of bloom to scent the air in June.

Mrs Yelland had a history for each bush. The rich red Apothecary's Rose was the one claimed for the House of Lancaster while the white was the emblem of York. It seemed incongruous, she said, that such beauty should have symbolised the bitter struggle between power-hungry claimants to the throne that had gone on through the reigns of seven English kings. My own favourite was the pink-striped Rosa Mundi, meaning rose of the world, named for the mistress of the second King Henry who had kept her hidden in a maze. I thought this a most romantic tale.

But there was no aspect of the garden that was romantic this particular afternoon. By the time the tree was staked to the mistress's satisfaction my fingers were numb. I tucked them under my armpits, edging towards the angle of the wall out of the wind and praying she would not find another task to delay me.

But gardening was ended for the day, though hardly in the way we expected. For Luke burst upon us at that very moment, crying, 'Come quick, missus! There's a coach overturned down by the bend and folks is hurt.'

We ran.

We heard the screaming of a horse before we reached the scene. The sound seared every nerve in my body. I had hardly time to slow my steps for fear of seeing what had happened to it before there was a loud bang. Then, mercifully, silence. We rounded the bend in time to see a tall man in a blue coat standing over the still twitching horse he had dispatched. A wisp of smoke rose from the pistol in his hand. The other horse was on its feet and, wild-eyed and shivering, was being extricated from the broken shafts and harness by Master Harry and a man in a torn and filthy coachman's coat.

The man with the pistol looked up grim-faced, ashy pale. He had lost his hat, and his dark brown hair had come loose and hung about his bloodstained collar. A trickle of blood ran down his cheek and dripped off his chin.

'See to my aunt, would you?' he said. Despite his appearance his deep voice was calm and authoritative. 'There are no bones broken, I think, but she needs warmth and shelter while I sort out this sorry business.'

'Of course,' said Mrs Yelland. 'But you are injured . . .'

'It is nothing,' he said curtly. 'Is there somewhere nearby where my aunt might rest and recover?'

'Just beyond the bend. An inn. We shall take care of her. Come, Emily.'

We hurried to where the elderly woman sat on the grassy verge by the overturned coach, a heavy, antiquated sort of vehicle, over which several men who had run from the fields were now clambering to remove baggage and stack it by the roadside. Mrs Yelland and I gently helped the dazed lady to her feet and supported her back to the Thorn Tree. She limped badly, but seemed more concerned for the horses than herself.

'I have only twisted my knee . . . but poor Neptune . . . I could scarce bear to hear his pain.' Her voice quavered. 'Thank God Felix was with me and armed against rogues. What should I have done else to put poor Neptune out of his misery? And what of Hero, my other horse? He was on his feet, but was there any injury?'

'He is being looked after. He is in good hands,' Mrs Yelland soothed. 'You must think of yourself for the moment. Now, can you manage the stairs? I have a most comfortable room where you may rest as long as you wish . . . Ah, there you are, Cass. Run ahead and put a light to the fire in the corner bedchamber. Then bring hot bricks and the warming pan, and warn Mrs Hill that we shall need a strengthening posset.'

The poor lady, a Miss Cavendish, was considerably shaken and distressed, though there seemed no serious injury.

'I have my nephew to thank for breaking my fall,' she said, as we settled her before the fire. 'I tumbled on top of him or I should have been very much the worse. The poor boy hit his head with a terrible crack. Oh dear, I wish you would send for him to come indoors . . . But he would take no notice! Stubborn as a mule, like his poor late papa, God rest him, and to what good? Nothing but ruin . . .'

She maundered on as Mrs Yelland tucked a quilt round her and I took off her shoes, which were soaked from the muddy puddle she had stepped in. Her stockings were very much holed around the toes, I noted, which seemed less to do with the accident and more to do with a previous carelessness over the matter of darning. Indeed, her whole appearance must have been somewhat faded and tattered, even before she had been tumbled about.

The hat I had removed from her tangled mass of grey hair was of fine straw but the blue ribbons were grubby and frayed. Her heavy black cloak was patched. The yellow velvet gown underneath, though perhaps once stylish, was practically threadbare, the lace trimmings hanging off the bodice in untidy loops.

'Thank heaven that Felix insisted Matilda should not make the journey! My maid,' she explained, 'ancient as Methuselah and knotted with the rheumatics, but such a faithful heart. Oh, I shall miss her, I shall indeed.'

I reflected that Miss Cavendish's wardrobe seemed to have been missing Matilda's attention for some time already.

'She was sadly put out when Felix insisted that she rest at her sister's house rather than make the journey to Bath,' Miss Cavendish rushed on, as if anxious to unburden herself. 'Oh, and I do become so very distressed at harsh words and unpleasant atmospheres and she was . . . well, she made it clear she blamed *me* . . . And Felix had to speak very strongly to her. *Very* strongly. It was a most upsetting interview. Yet see how fortunate it has turned out for her! When she learns of what befell us – well, I hope she will feel everything is for the best. Do you suppose she will?' Her faded blue eyes looked hopefully at Mrs Yelland.

'Your maid must surely appreciate such a fortunate

escape,' she murmured diplomatically. 'Now, let me tuck this quilt round your shoulders. Then I think a comfrey poultice will render your knee more comfortable.'

'You are most kind.' But she still worried at the topic of her maid like a dog with a favourite bone. 'Felix, you see, wishes her to stay permanently with her sister. Men can be so overbearing, can they not? He means well, of course, and I do love him dearly, he being the only kin left to me, but I fear he has been impulsive. He intends a more comfortable life for me in Bath now that he has the means – and I do agree that the house is far too large now for one person, and so very cold and draughty with the cost of coals quite prohibitive – but Matilda has been with me since I was small and we are used to each other.' Her voice trembled on the edge of tears. 'I know she has become crabby, but at my age it will be hard to accustom myself to this new person he has engaged in Bath, however well recommended she comes. Felix has assured Matilda that he will provide a comfortable pension, but she was inconsolable. Inconsolable!'

'Times of change can be very difficult,' Mrs Yelland said, gently patting her hand. 'Especially as we get older. I daresay in a little while she will come to appreciate an easier life.'

'Do you think so? It would be such a relief if I could be convinced of it. But there again, suppose that this unfortunate accident has been visited upon us as a sign that we should turn back?'

Mrs Yelland smiled. 'More a sign that the parish is neglected its duties in the matter of repairing the road. It is become almost a daily occurrence for carts to come to grief on that corner. Your accident was no exception, I assure you. Now here is your posset. Try to drink it while it is still hot.'

Her matter-of-fact tone seemed to give Miss Cavendish a modicum of reassurance. Looking fractionally less harassed, she took the posset from Cass and peered at it suspiciously.

'I shall not manage more than the smallest sip. At my age one does not have the appetite one enjoyed in one's youth.'

The evidence of a poor appetite was very clear. Though she gave an impression of bulk as well as height, she was in reality thin as a twig under her layers of garments, as though it was a long time since she had eaten well. She took a wary sip of Mrs Hill's heady concoction. Then, reflectively, another. Two lively spots of colour bloomed on her sunken cheeks as, slowly, the rest of the brew was downed.

She tipped back the last drops, then gazed in surprise into the empty tankard.

'My, 'tis an age since I drank a posset as good as this. It quite takes me back to childhood. My mama had the knack, d'you see. Most reviving to the sickly or the injured. As I remember, it is a matter of the right amount of brandy – never wine or ale – and a nicety with the spices.' She sniffed at the milky dregs. 'Cinnamon there, I'll be bound, and nutmeg. Or is that a hint of cloves?'

'Perhaps you might manage a drop more,' Mrs Yelland encouraged gently. 'And you should try to eat. It will help strengthen you after the shock you have had. A slice of cold mutton or beef? Or a sliver of rabbit pie?'

'Oh, the merest mouthful of beef, if you insist,' Miss Cavendish said, sighing as though she found the pressure put upon her to eat quite intolerable. Then, adding vaguely, 'And you might mention to your cook that a drop more brandy would perfect the brew...'

The heat of the fire, the effects of the double posset and the several slices of beef she had somehow managed to eat set her head nodding. Soon she was snoring steadily, her troubles temporarily forgotten.

'You had best stay with her, Emily,' Mrs Yelland

whispered. 'I will find you some sewing to occupy you while you sit. I must discover what is happening downstairs and whether the gentleman intends to proceed to Bath today.' She shook her head. 'The poor lady looks considerably neglected. Living in genteel poverty in some ancient pile, by the sound of it. No wonder the nephew has taken her welfare in hand.'

At the door she paused, turning to look around the room with satisfaction. Firelight glinted on the polished fire irons, on the freshly laundered blue curtains looped back from the large bed, on the gleaming mahogany of the press.

'I think the young man will approve of the accommodation we are able to offer his aunt. There is plenty of room for her boxes. Mayhap I shall persuade him to allow her to sleep here tonight at least.'

He needed no persuasion.

I had darned two pairs of Mrs Yelland's stockings and decided to light the candles before turning an old sheet sides to middle when there was a tap on the door and he came soft-footed into the room.

He looked a great deal worse than his aunt did. He had cleaned the blood from his face and tied back his hair, but now the angry graze on his temple was exposed and the swelling around his half-shut eye was turning purple. Even the golden flare of candle and firelight could not disguise the pallor that lay over the rest of his face. The skin over his beaky nose and bony cheeks was drawn tight, as though from the effort of keeping pain and shock under control.

He saw my look as, candlestick in hand, I made my bob.

'My battered appearance alarms you?'

'Not at all, sir,' I said, replacing the candlestick on the high mantel. 'But you do look as though you need some doctoring. Mrs Yelland – the mistress – might be able to recommend some potion to ease you. She's skilled in such things.'

'She has already informed me that the best remedy for a black eye is to lay a beefsteak upon it, but I could not settle until I had seen for myself if my Aunt Cavendish was comfortable.' He examined her sleeping face before he sent a quick assessing glance round the room. Then he bent his scrutinising gaze on me.

'You are Emily?'

'Yes, sir.'

'Your mistress speaks highly of your honesty and common sense. I would wish you to attend my aunt while we remain here. I have arranged that you be excused other duties.'

'Really, sir?' I said, delighted to learn that I was to escape the kitchen for a short while. 'You . . . you intend to sleep here overnight, then, sir?'

'Certainly tonight. If the weather closes in – and there is already a little sleet in the wind – I daresay the business I have in Bath might wait a day or two. We shall see what the morrow brings. As I am assured that the cook here is accomplished, I suppose we shall do tolerably well here for a couple of days.'

'Everything will be done to make you comfortable, sir,' I said, knowing Mrs Yelland would be anxious to put on as good a show as possible. 'And the food *is* very good,' I felt obliged to add, prickled by the somewhat cynical tone of his voice. 'Your aunt said the beef she had for supper was the tenderest she'd eaten in an age.'

'But Miss Cavendish has been . . . shall we say, a little *removed* from the finer aspects of good living for some considerable time. Her expectations are not high. Had I but known the truth of it—' He broke off, his expression dark. 'Well, no matter. It is the present that is important.' He looked me up and down. 'Having no other course open to me, I must needs rely on you to see that she is attended efficiently. And with . . . consideration,' he added, his voice suddenly losing its biting edge.

'Of course,' I said. 'I'll do my best on both counts . . . Oh, sir, do you feel faint?' I stepped towards him, putting out a steadying hand.

He swayed, blinked, then with an effort took command of himself again.

'Thank you, Emily,' he said, striving for dignity but suddenly looking considerably more vulnerable – and younger – than the impression he had given earlier. His air of authority had led me to believe he was something close to Mrs Yelland's age, but now I realised he was nearer to twenty than thirty. 'I think I must return to my bedchamber where the beefsteak awaits. Perhaps . . . perhaps you would walk with me.' He spoke stiffly, as though it was an effort to admit to weakness. 'If I put my hand on your shoulder . . . so. I am steady now.'

Though he was trying to make light of it, I realised he must be feeling very dizzy. His hand gripped my shoulder hard and though it was no more than a few steps along the passage to the next room he leaned so heavily on me that I wondered if we should both soon be stretching our lengths on the polished boards.

But somehow I managed to support him into his bedchamber and rather than lead him to the chair that stood before the fire, I steered him to the bed. Once I let him go he collapsed backward and lay there, eyes closed, long legs dangling awkwardly over the side.

'Shall I fetch, someone, sir? Mrs Yelland or Master Harry?'

'No, no. A few moments' rest, that is all I need.'

A sheen of sweat had erupted to gloss his pallor.

'You'd be more comfortable lying down properly straight on the bed,' I persisted out of anxiety for him. 'Shall I help you with your boots, sir?'

He opened his eyes. Or rather one eye, the other being

a mere bloodshot slit. 'I cannot abide being fussed and fretted over,' he said, probably meaning to sound commanding but the thready weakness of his voice serving only to raise my fears for his condition. 'Return to my aunt, girl . . . Leave me to my beefsteak.'

'I don't think it's right you should be left alone,' I said stubbornly. 'You're sicker than you realise, sir.'

'Dammit, girl. Do as I say . . .' His voice faltered, fell away.

'Look, if I get my arm under your shoulders and you hitch yourself round a bit . . . There. That's better.' It was no time for niceties. Ignoring the mud caked on his boots, I heaved up his legs onto the counterpane. 'I'm going for help, sir. You're in no fit state to see to yourself, whatever you say.'

He was swimming in and out of consciousness. He blinked at me in a vague way.

'Damned bossy woman,' he whispered. 'Never could . . . stand 'em.' Then his head fell back on the pillows and he looked so like a dead man that I picked up my skirts and flew for Mrs Yelland.

Sleet turned to snow in the night.

Leaden dawn revealed dense curtains of whirling white flakes riding the back of a northerly gale. The wind clawed and howled round the house all day. Icy draughts found their way through the smallest aperture and set candle flames twisting and streaming. Those who could hugged the fire between chores, thanking heaven that larders were satisfyingly stocked, as always in winter, against the prospect of isolation. The men ventured outside to dig paths across the yard, but as fast as a space was cleared and salted, snow claimed it back. Eventually they admitted defeat and, after fetching fresh water and restocking log piles, they retreated to the horse-odorous snugness of their quarters above the stables, emerging only to grope across to the kitchen for meals.

The storm blew itself out the second night. By the following morning, the landscape beyond the inn was an alien wilderness, with every landmark shrouded in a thick coverlet of white. But the sky had cleared and the sun was out.

'Good news of Mr Winterborne,' I said cheerfully to Miss Cavendish as I plumped up her pillows and set the breakfast tray across her knees. 'Master Harry says he's sleeping soundly after a good night's rest. Mrs Yelland is inclined to think that his injury is less serious than she first supposed. She greatly feared the blow might lead to a dangerous inflammation of the brain, but now she thinks he's over the worst.'

'Thank God for that,' said Miss Cavendish, fervently. 'The poor boy. I have felt so guilty, for it was all on my account that this misfortune overtook us.' But her attention was already diverted. With a greedy glint in her eye she was reaching for the spoon to dip into the bowl of porridge well doused with honey. 'Such a generous helping,' she protested, 'but one cannot bear waste. As for coddled eggs, my appetite will be considerably overburdened.'

Overburdened or not, she finished everything. It had been the same at each meal so far. I had come to the conclusion that it was not so much lack of appetite that had caused her to become so thin and undernourished, but lack of opportunity to eat. Whatever little income she had seemed to have been spent on maintaining the horses for which she had a great tenderness, the coachman to look after them and her ancient maid. An adequate diet for herself had been an unaffordable luxury.

She did not tell me this so bluntly but being with her from morning to night, and she seeming to enjoy the novelty of a fresh audience, she let slip a great deal more than perhaps she realised.

I was certainly an attentive listener, not only to please her and to ensure that the trust Mr Winterborne had put in me was justified in every particular, but out of interest and curiosity to learn what I could about these unexpected and unusual visitors.

Mostly Miss Cavendish leapt from anecdote to anecdote in a most confusing manner, rambling on at length about people she had known in childhood. But she also spoke a great deal and in the fondest terms about her one young sister to whom, because of a great disparity in age, she was more mother than older sibling. This sister had made an impulsive marriage, a love match, she said, to an unfortunate man who was in dispute with a cousin over the ownership of a small estate that had belonged to his grandfather.

'It dragged on for years and the cousin won in the end,' Miss Cavendish reflected sadly. 'The lawyers benefited, needless to say, and the cousin was made even wealthier by the outcome. But Charles was bankrupted. I helped them all I could, for my dear sister's sake, but I did not have the means other than to house them and continue to pay my nephew's school fees, for he was a clever boy. Then the tragedy! And the disgrace for my sister, Sybil, and young Felix, who was only sixteen, which is a most sensitive age . . .'

A doomed love match? Tragedy? Disgrace? I was even more intrigued. The elements of an epic poem or a romantic saga were all here. But, maddeningly, Miss Cavendish had diverted into a tale of an embarrassment she had suffered when she herself was sixteen and I heard no more until just as I was helping her into bed that night, when she said, suddenly, 'I hope God will forgive me for an inability to kneel at present. My prayers will be no less heartfelt for saying them as I lie here.'

The candle flickered and, in the play of light and shadow across the beaky nose and strong jaw, I caught momentarily the resemblance to the man lying in the adjoining room.

'I shall pray,' she whispered, 'for dear Felix to make a swift recovery. And, as I do each night, for Charles and Sybil that they be reunited in heaven, as they were forbidden to be on earth.' Her voice was sad and far away. Her eyes stared unfocused into the shadows inhabiting the corner of the room. 'That was the final straw for her, you see. She did not last a six-month after he was refused burial in consecrated ground. A broken heart, that's what killed her. A broken heart. And he was not a bad man. Stubborn, impassioned and misguided, yes, but not wicked. All the same, it could not have happened worse. She was condemned to be separated for ever from him by the churchyard wall. She in the Cavendish vault within, he without. Sometimes I feel that their souls can never be at rest.'

She fell silent, closing her eyes and clasping her hands together. Her lips moved soundlessly and I withdrew with the candle to the little truckle bed where Mrs Yelland had thought best that I should sleep so as to be on hand should Miss Cavendish need anything in the night.

I knew the implication well enough. Suicides could not be buried in consecrated ground. Felix Winterborne's father had killed himself.

I felt a coldness at my back as I hastily undressed. I was quick to snuggle down under the sheets and when I snuffed the candle the embers glowing red in the hearth seemed to have no power to dispel the weight of darkness flooding the rest of the bedchamber – a sad and heavy darkness, with the moaning of the wind in the chimney filled with voices crying to be let in out of the snow.

When daylight came it was possible to laugh at such imaginings, but I found that the distressing tale still had the power to move me. A tragedy indeed, though I was now more inclined to feel sympathy for the people left to face the griefs of this world, rather than those – lost souls or not – who had moved onto the next.

At least Mr Winterborne seemed to have risen above the tragedy. He had lost his parents and, from all accounts, been rendered penniless. But fortune seemed to have dealt him a kindlier hand since he had left the place of his father's disgrace, swearing he would not return to Somerset until he had the means to live like a gentleman. 'And now that he has,' Miss Cavendish had said mournfully yesterday, 'I think it might have been better had he stayed in London rather than be in this plight.'

But today, with better news of Mr Winterborne and her knee less painful, she was in a much more cheerful frame of mind and less inclined to stay passively before the fire. She insisted on making a brief visit to her nephew and beamed to find him propped up in bed, spooning up a milky liquid from a bowl and grumbling between each mouthful.

'Every drop now, sir,' said Mrs Yelland in that firm voice I knew so well.

He grimaced over his spoon.

'Damned slops,' he growled.

Miss Cavendish's smile wavered. 'Really, Felix, you should not be so bearish,' she admonished gently, with an anxious look at the other woman. 'Mrs Yelland and her husband have watched over you day and night while you have been ill. You should be grateful for their care and not offend them by speaking out of turn.'

'Well, I am recovered now. And bread-and-milk being decidedly *not* to my taste when I am in good health, I cannot see why I must suffer it on my sickbed.'

'Because it is wholesome, sir,' said Mrs Yelland calmly, 'and easily digested. It is as well to stay on a low diet until you are on your feet again.' She smiled reassuringly at Miss Cavendish. 'I believe that irritability in a convalescent is an encouraging sign. It proves that the healing properties of the constitution begin to establish themselves over the invading humours.'

'Oh, do you think so?'

'Most certainly. I have observed it often.'

Mr Winterborne thumped the spoon into his bowl and the bowl onto the table beside the bed.

'I do not care to be spoken of as though I were not in the room,' he said in a tone of ice. 'I pray you, ladies, if you must speak of me in that patronising way, do it elsewhere.'

I daresay his scowl and the frown that drove down his brows might have been deeply threatening at any other time, but his half-closed eye and the black swelling round it gave him such an odd, lopsided appearance that I was forced to look down at my shoes and concentrate very hard on tracing the cracks in the leather in order not to disgrace myself by laughing out loud.

'Thank you for your care of my nephew,' Miss Cavendish said nervously to Mrs Yelland. 'He will understand how much he is in your debt when he is properly in charge of himself again.'

'It is no trouble, ma'am. Especially at this time, quiet as we are and likely to be so for a day or two with the roads blocked. My husband will be up to shave Mr Winterborne shortly and perhaps later he may feel strong enough to sit out of bed for ten minutes.'

'Ten minutes, be damned! I shall be up and dressed as soon as I can rid myself of fussing females. And you,' glowering at me, 'need not stand there smirking. I have a long memory for disobedience. I have not forgot that you took it upon yourself to ignore my orders.'

'And very properly, too,' Mrs Yelland said crisply. 'Had she not summoned help you would have lain unattended in a dead faint, sir, for some considerable time. And even when you did come round your wits were rambling. You were in no position to help yourself at all.'

'Pray, dear, do not set yourself back by insisting on getting up too soon,' Miss Cavendish urged. 'You may undo all the good care that has been taken of you.'

He looked from one to the other of us. Then, with the evident intention of proving that he was perfectly capable of getting out of bed, he heaved himself upright and made as if to throw back the covers. In mid-action, he stopped. He drew in an audible breath, putting his hand to his head and closing his eyes as though sharp pain or dizziness had struck him. He eased himself gingerly back to the pillows. Fortunately, the muttered imprecations that escaped his gritted teeth were too low to be properly heard.

He opened his eyes, said sourly, 'I fear inaction does not suit me, Aunt, used as I am to rude good health. I am rendered foul-tempered in consequence. Take no heed of it.'

If that was meant as an apology I thought it a pretty grudging one.

'Oh, I do understand, my dear,' Miss Cavendish said. 'I think it best to leave you to sleep in peace. Just remember it is better to rest and recover steadily rather than rush things and set yourself back.'

She looked troubled as we made our halting progress to the adjoining room.

'I still wonder if I am doing the right thing in taking up residence with him in Bath,' she murmured. 'He means well, I know, but he has been on his own for so long with no one to please but himself that he may begin to feel grievously encumbered when I am permanently resident under his roof, dependent on his charity and goodwill. You see how he galls at restriction. He was always possessed of a somewhat impatient temperament. I saw it over the business with Matilda. I should so much hate it if he came to resent my presence in his house and regard me as a nuisance, a . . . a millstone round his neck.'

'I think he has a great fondness for you, ma'am,' I said stoutly, feeling aggrieved with the wretched man for having upset his aunt just as her spirits were beginning to recover. I repeated the tale of how, on the night of the accident, he would not retire to his own bed until he had seen for himself that she was comfortable. 'Of course he won't think of you as a nuisance,' I scolded, as I settled her back in her chair. 'That's properly the wrong way of thinking, to my mind. Even if you are to sleep under his roof, ma'am, you won't be under his feet all the time, will you? At least, not if what I've heard about Bath is true. Everyone I've spoken to who's been there says what a fine and lively town it is with so many sights to see. You'll be able to walk out with your maid to take the waters and look in the fine shops like the rest of the fashionable folk and there'll be the circulating library to visit – just think of all those wonderful books you'll be able to read – and there'll be plays to see and I daresay there'll be lots of ladies like yourself to make friends with.'

She did not answer, merely stared into the fire, looking forlorn. I brought the footstool and lifted her feet onto it, then hovered, uncertain what to do or say. Perhaps I had offended her with my outburst. She knew I had been taken out of the kitchens to wait on her. What lady of quality would not be put out by having a mere kitchen maid air her unwanted opinions? Until now, I had been so careful to be quiet and respectful, conscious of the responsibility laid upon me by Mrs Yelland and Mr Winterborne.

'Forgive me, ma'am,' I stammered. 'I didn't mean to be so... so forward.'

She sighed. 'I am not offended. Touched, rather, that you should take my concerns to heart.' She smiled wistfully. 'I wish I could believe that life were so straightforward, that all distress could be restored by imbibing a glass of water or opening a book.' She reached out and laid her hand on mine. 'You have a good heart, child, and you speak good sense. I *should* be thinking of the advantages of living comfortably with my nephew in Bath rather than looking for problems before they arise. Now, reach me the topmost of my boxes, if you would. I have an idea of how I may be useful to my nephew – at least while we are fastened here. With the weight of snow in the lanes, I cannot see that we shall be able to leave for a day or two yet. I shall set myself to entertain him!'

Greatly relieved, I fetched her the box. She opened it and drew out several items, setting them on the table at her side. She regarded them with satisfaction.

'Cribbage board, backgammon set, cards. Ah, dear Felix has spent many a happy hour with me over these games. In fact, I introduced him to cards and dice, my sister not having the same interest and her husband frowning on such frivolous pursuits. My nephew has found these accomplishments very much to his advantage during his latter years in London when he was mixing with the *ton*. I have no doubt he was able to make a good showing in whatever company he played. Do you play at all, child? No? Dear me, am I doomed to play patience or solitaire until Felix is able to partner me?' She looked at me consideringly. 'Of course, should you be prepared to leave off your mending I might be willing to initiate you into the mysteries of backgammon or bezique or cribbage.'

'I'd like that, ma'am,' I said with truth, having no great love of darning and patching sheets.

'Then what shall it be?'

'Cribbage, perhaps? Only I can't play for pennies, ma'am, for I've none to spare.'

'Dear me, no,' she said, smiling. 'Nor I, child. I shall merely keep a tally of who wins and loses. You've seen the game played, then?'

'It's popular in the taproom.'

And in the stables. I had once asked Luke if he'd teach me, but he'd said it wasn't a game for females. 'Stay with your books, Princess,' he'd said, grinning. 'That's a nice ladylike occupation. Crib can be a rough game, best left to menfolk who won't get the vapours over a bit of cussing and shouting.'

Evidently genteel ladies *did* play, though the sedate game that occupied us was a world away from the noisy bouts that went on in the taproom. But then, many a man's wages hung on the outcome, with side-bets spurring the onlookers to curses and cheers.

I had thought these men, who could ill afford it, very foolish to gamble, though once I got the hang of the game I began to understand the seductive element that might tempt them to it. I was drawn into the cut and thrust of competition, eager to pit my wits against the run of the cards. And even though nothing hung on the outcome beyond the tally Miss Cavendish kept, I knew that in the next game or the one after, the marks against my name would grow and I would beat her in the end.

But I mostly lost. I was disappointed how badly I fared.

'Luck, of course, plays a large part in the game,' Miss Cavendish said, attempting to look modest but failing to suppress the gleeful glint in her eyes as she stacked away the cards late that night. 'Nevertheless, there is an element of skill that comes with practice and I am pleased that I still have the knack. Now, to bed. We shall continue our little tourney in the morning.'

The morning brought a change in the weather. Rain lashed at the windows and brought avalanches of snow crashing from the roofs. The morning also brought a visit from Mr Winterborne. I met him in the passage as I was fetching Miss Cavendish's breakfast tray. A very much recovered Mr Winterborne.

The woollen cloth of his dark blue coat and breeches had been brushed and cleaned by Master Harry and was now immaculate. The ruffle of his shirt and neatly tied stock gleamed crisp and white above the long russet-coloured waistcoat. His buckled shoes bore a high gloss. His dark brown hair, freshly washed and glinting with chestnut lights, was tied back with a plain black bow. There was nothing at all dandified about his attire, yet there was a subtle elegance in the cut of his clothes that spoke of excellent tailoring and quality materials. And, too, an assurance about the way he wore them that spoke of someone who took pride in looking well and having the height and figure to show such excellent tailoring to advantage.

I made my bob awkwardly under the weight of the tray. He nodded and lifted the cover on the dish of eggs and kidneys.

'My aunt is eating well?'
'Indeed, sir. She enjoys everything I put before her.'
'And her injury?'
'Much improved. And she'll be pleased to see you looking so much better yourself, sir.'

The discoloured skin around his eye was much less swollen and the rest of his face, though pale, was of a more natural sallowness than the ashy pallor it had been. However, the expression in his eyes gave me no confidence that his temper was much improved by being up and dressed. Their greeny-grey depths seemed as uncompromising as the draught that scurried round my ankles.

'Is she still abed?'
'No, she was up and dressed early this morning. She was thinking to visit you later on.'
'Then I shall save her the trouble.'

Was there any need to frown like that as he said it? Could he not at least try, for the old lady's sake, to look pleasant? And suppose he was as grouchy to her as he had been yesterday? The poor lady would be greatly cast down . . .

He moved towards the door and without thinking I stepped to block his way.

'Sir, Miss Cavendish is set on . . . on pleasing you,' I said, groping for the right words to impress him without giving offence. 'If you could see your way to showing her that you appreciate her company, it would mean such a lot to her.'

He raised one eyebrow, the cold stare intensifying.

'It wouldn't take much, sir . . . just for you to sit awhile and talk . . . and maybe have a hand of cards with her.' I began to flounder. 'It's just . . . just that she worries that you think her a nuisance – which I'm sure you don't – and she needs to feel you're taking her in because you're fond of her, and not grudgingly, out of charity.' I stopped, realising what I had implied, rushed on headlong, instantly making it worse. 'She's such a nice old lady and I don't like to think of anyone hurting her feelings.'

'Meaning that I am likely to?'

'Yes . . . no . . . I mean not *intentionally*.'

He took a step closer so that I was near as trapped against the door.

'Is that so?' His voice was silky soft. 'Tell me, do the wilds of Somersetshire breed a specially troublesome brand of kitchen brat? Who are you to be so free with your insults?'

My fingers gripped the tray so hard that the crockery rattled. It was a great effort not to flinch. But if I had stung him, he had stung me, and my blood stirred to defiance.

'And who are you, sir, to call *me* a brat?' I said, as softly and deliberately as he, though I was glad he could not see how my legs shook. 'Is it a case of the kettle calling the pot? You may dress like a gentleman and call yourself a gentleman, but you will not be a gentleman in the eyes of anyone else if you continue to behave as . . . as *boorishly* to your aunt as you did yesterday.'

'Boorish? You talk too high for your station.'

'I speak the truth! It's not my fault if the truth is

unpalatable. You ordered me to be considerate to your aunt, which I have been, and she is much restored in spirits because I have looked after her just as you wished me to. Now you look to ruin all that!'

'And you look to ruin her breakfast,' he said. 'Give me that tray before your unjustified indignation causes you to shake the eggs to an omelette.'

'Unjustified! When I saw with my two eyes the effect you had on her when you were so evil-tempered yesterday?'

Silence. Then I saw the beginnings of a smile soften the corners of his mouth. A reluctant sort of effort but a smile, none the less.

The fire went out of me as quickly as it had flared up.

'Oh, sir,' I began. Then stopped. What was there to be said? I could not beg his forgiveness for speaking out. I meant every word. 'I don't know about omelette, but those eggs will be cold as charity if we stand here much longer.' I paused and then added flatly, 'Charity can, indeed, wear a cold face, sir. Take the word of one who has experienced at first-hand how something born of the kindliest intentions might turn heartless and grudging.'

'Oh? Pray tell me of it.'

'I was raised in a foundling house in Bristol.' I suppressed a shudder that the thought of Miss Edgar still brought to me. 'It was not a happy nor a comfortable place, sir. And there was no one to speak out for us against the injustice and harsh treatment the overseer took pleasure in.'

'Which is why you take it on yourself to speak up for an old lady you consider equally helpless?'

'It's not at all the same sort of case, sir, but I find that I mislike injustice whatever shape it takes.'

'Meaning my recent display of *boorishness*?' Though his voice was grave, his smile was mocking. I was not sure if the mockery was intended for me or himself. 'Will it put your mind at ease to know that I do not intend to put any difficulties in the way of my aunt having a contented and comfortable old age? My anger had nothing to do with her, beyond the fact that I was exceedingly put out by the deception she had practised on me these last years.'

'Deception, sir?' I said, taken aback.

'Deliberately hiding from me that she was desperately reduced in circumstances due to unwise investment of her money by a rascally lawyer. Not to mention the way she was abysmally ill-served by her crone of a maidservant. It did nothing for my temper, I can tell you, when I saw that her horses were better fed and cared for than she was. And out of sentiment she would not sell them, for fear they might be hard-used!' The self-mockery was clearly evident now as he went on, 'There is nothing like a bad conscience to stir up righteous wrath. I had failed to visit her, you see, in the seven years I had been away, being concerned entirely with my own affairs. I had relied on a correspondence that was invariably cheerful and optimistic on her part. Yet, had I but known it, she could scarcely afford even to pay for the receipt of my letters!'

'So . . . so you were angry with yourself, not her.'

'That is a part of it. There were other matters, but they do not concern you. However, if you will open the door and precede me into the bedchamber before I get a cramp in my arms from the weight of this tray, you may hear for yourself how I intend to make amends.'

He made a very good fist of it. It was not a side of Mr Winterborne that had been evident before, but he now displayed a most charming and attentive manner to his aunt. I wondered, somewhat cynically, how much was genuine and how much play-acting for my benefit. He certainly glanced over to me from time to time, with that same mocking smile narrowing his eyes, as though to say, 'See how I keep my word.'

But his aunt was clearly delighted and that was all that mattered.

When I removed the tray of empty dishes, with orders from Mr Winterborne to take myself off for an hour and then fetch hot chocolate, I closed the door to the satisfying sound of laughter. When I returned I was alarmed to hear raised voices within. But it was only a playful difference. As I entered the room, Mr Winterborne was flinging down his hand of cards onto the table. Miss Cavendish, eyes gleaming, was scooping up a small heap of silver.

'Damme, Aunt Cavendish,' Mr Winterborne said. 'I could have sworn I had the better of you.'

'Ah, luck was on my side.'

'And cunning. You always were too quick for me.' He leaned across the small table and plucked at the bedraggled velvet of her sleeve. I blinked to see that he withdrew a card from it.

'Always as well to have one in reserve,' she cried, unabashed.

'*Another*, do you not mean?'

'I daresay,' she answered airily. 'Still, it is best that I won, is it not? All that you would have gained from me by winning was that old snuff box with the broken hinge.' The tarnished silver box, along with the coins, disappeared into the pocket tied to her dress. She reached greedily for the almond biscuits. 'I declare the excitement of the game has given me quite an appetite.'

'And has lost me all my small change,' said Mr Winterborne. 'Still, I shall have it back off you before long.'

Miss Cavendish gave a mischievous chuckle. 'I shall enjoy watching you try, dear boy. Though I do not guarantee any success.'

Mr Winterborne leaned back in his chair and stretched out his long legs comfortably towards the fire.

'So, Emily,' he drawled, 'I hear you have been inveigled into playing cribbage with a card sharp of the first order. I forbear to ask if my aunt allowed you to win. Losing was never her style.'

I was uncertain how to answer this startling piece of information.

Miss Cavendish saved me. 'Now, now, Felix dear, do not tease the child. With Emily I played perfectly fairly. I would never stoop so low as to . . . well, to play tricks on an innocent. I save my guile for those I consider experienced and deserving of it.'

'Then it is a pity you did not ask Lawyer Merryweather to a game,' Mr Winterborne said drily. 'You might have recouped all the rogue lost for you.'

A shadow crossed Miss Cavendish's face. 'Dear boy, he was not the man for cards.'

'Nor for gambling his own money, I hear, when he might use that of elderly ladies who relied on him to safeguard their interests.'

Miss Cavendish sighed. 'My mama always said that a bad deed never went unremarked in heaven. He will come to justice in the next world.'

'And in the meantime he continues to prosper mightily in this one.'

'He netted himself a bride of considerable fortune, true,' Miss Cavendish nodded gravely. Then she smiled, confiding with some satisfaction, 'I hear his new wife has a mighty shrewish nature. She nags him most severely and there is talk of terrible fallings-out. They cannot agree in any particular about the mansion they are a-building near Wells and she loses no occasion to belittle his taste and countermand his orders. So sad, is it not?' she added happily. 'To gain two thousand a year on marriage and then to discover that your bride is sour and demanding. Oh, I do hope, most sincerely, that the new Mrs Merryweather continues in the same mode.'

Felix Winterborne laughed. 'Aunt, you have a wicked streak in your character. Poor Emily must be deeply shocked to know she has been nurturing a veritable viper in her bosom.'

'But it is entirely your fault, Felix!' Miss Cavendish said with mock severity. 'You bring out the worst in me. It was always the case. I remember how even as a boy you would egg me on to show you the tricks I had learned myself as a girl.'

'And perfected with much practice,' he said. 'Who was it who taught you? The coachman?'

'A footman my father kept. A very pretty young man.' She gave an almost girlish giggle. 'Alas, his angelic face concealed a devil's heart. He eloped with my governess and a considerable quantity of Papa's silver. But before that, seeking any excuse to while away time with his lover, he would spend his spare moments in the schoolroom teaching me the sleight of hand by which he had earned his bread through much of his misspent life. Which reminds me, dear, did I ever tell you of the time your grandfather spied the rogue at Exeter races and gave chase but lost him in the crowd?'

She fell into contented reminiscence. Felix Winterborne, eyes half closed as he stared into the fire, did no more than nod or murmur a comment from time to time. I think he scarcely heard a word his aunt was saying. He seemed to have fallen deep into thoughts of his own, only to rouse from his brooding as a particularly violent gust of wind threw rain against the windows.

'Such weather,' Miss Cavendish murmured anxiously. 'Dear me, there will be flooding, no doubt of it, with this rain after such a depth of snow. The roads will be like rivers.'

'Which tends me to the opinion that we should delay travelling onto Bath for the present,' Mr Winterborne said. 'You are comfortable here, Aunt, are you not?'

'Very much so,' she agreed. 'Indeed, Mrs Yelland and Emily between them quite spoil me. I shall not mind in the least prolonging my stay.'

'So it would not distress you unduly if I left you here

for, say, two days, possibly three, while I attend to some business that I might usefully pursue while I am in the district?'

'But the rain . . . will this business not wait?'

'I shall only have to travel so far as Axbridge to visit a gentleman of my acquaintance. I should think it no more than ten miles from here.' He leaned forward confidentially. 'If I am to take a share in his proposed copper mine, then I would wish to investigate his plans more closely to see if the prospects are as rosy as he made out when I met him in London.'

'Of course, but—'

'I am no Merryweather, Aunt, to be taken in by ephemeral schemes. It is prudence and a clear head for business that has brought me thus far. I have no intention of disposing of my funds other than in sensible investments. I think an unexpected call on this gentleman and a little investigation in the district would be to my advantage.'

'It is just the thought of you being abroad in such conditions.'

'It may have stopped raining by tomorrow and I shall take care to avoid low-lying places.' He smiled at her warmly. 'I could wish I had my own mare with me, but as she has gone lame I had to leave her eating her head off in Bath and must make do with a hired nag.' Then, as though to distract her from fretting over his proposed journey he said, 'I fear news of Grandfather's old chariot is not good. It is a wonder it got us this far from Glastonbury.'

'Whittle did warn us that there was a touch of woodworm.'

'A touch!' He laughed. 'A veritable army of maggots has been at work. Not to mention various degrees of rot. It is not worth spending money on, I am afraid. The kindliest action would be to donate what remains of it as firewood for the poor.'

'Ah, it was a proud sight when I was a girl,' Miss Cavendish said with a sigh. 'So highly polished you could see your face in it and as fine a pair of bays as you could wish to rattle it along at a great speed. Still, you must do as you think best, dear boy.'

'Before I leave for Axbridge tomorrow I will give Whittle orders to ride Hero to my house in Bath on Monday, which is the day I hope will be the latest day I shall return here. Whittle may then bespeak us a chaise to fetch us to Bath on Wednesday next, if that is agreeable.'

She sighed again, but it held more of relief than sadness.

'It is the greatest comfort that I have a man about me now to make these decisions, Felix. I thank you for your trouble. And for taking a tiresome old lady into your care.'

He leaned forward and laid his hand gently on hers. 'Whatever I do is but a poor repayment for your generosity to me and my family in the past.' If there had been any play-acting earlier there was none now. There was genuine emotion in his voice and I thought with sympathy of the tragedy that had clouded his boyhood. Then he smiled, lightening the atmosphere that had suddenly become filled with shadows. 'As to tiresome, Aunt Cavendish, that depends how much money you propose to relieve me of before we sleep tonight. Now, what say you to a further hand of piquet?'

He picked up the cards and tossed them from hand to hand. The cards seemed almost to dance between his fingers. Unerringly he caught them, shuffled them, set them down square and neat on the table.

'Your cut, ma'am,' he said.

They nodded at each other, both straight-faced now and I caught again that family likeness: the beaky down-curved nose, the strong jaw. Unfortunate, perhaps, for the young woman Miss Cavendish had been. Not for him though. In a man's face those particular features arranged themselves far more . . . well, suitably, was all I could think of.

There was something else that linked them. Something that I wondered afterwards had been merely the effect of the sudden flare of flame from the hearth.

For in both pairs of eyes, faded blue and deep grey-green, glittered a positively wicked and mischievous light.

The weather did improve over the following days.

Mr Winterborne left for Axbridge on Master Harry's horse, the inn slowly came back to its usual bustle as the roads cleared and the last grey remnants of snow puddled and drained into ditches and streams. The sun shone from a sky miraculously cleared of all cloud and Mrs Yelland invited Miss Cavendish, now she was able to get about more easily, to dine each day in her own parlour. She fretted that the old lady and her nephew did not have the convenience of a private parlour downstairs.

'But at least,' she said, with satisfaction, 'Mr Yelland begins to come round to my way of thinking over the matter of improvements. Before our unfortunate travellers arrived here, he had no notion of how profitably we might be served by catering to the quality.' The crisp ribbons on her cap danced in time with her pleased nodding. 'But now he has witnessed for himself how well appreciated our hospitality is he is less inclined to brush aside my ideas. And I do believe the generous sum offered by Mr Winterborne for the hire of his horse quite tipped the balance in my favour.'

If she was happy, Mrs Hill most certainly was not. Whenever I showed my face she showered abuse on me for leaving her short-handed.

'It is scarcely my fault,' I said, finally moved to exasperation.

'Don't give me none of your lip!' she bellowed. 'I've Amy and Cass a-sneezing and a-blowing and scarce fit to lift a dish and Trudie worse than useless while 'ee has to be prancin' about 'tending to the gentry. And here's me, scarcely knowing which way to turn!'

Cass was put out with me, too. Mrs Yelland had excused her temporarily from most of her upstairs duties so that she might help Mrs Hill.

''Ten't right and proper, putting 'ee over me,' she said, scuffing her wrist against her dripping red nose. 'I should've been put to looking after the old dame, 'stead of which I'm back here, skivvying. An' me not well. Not well at all.'

'I'm sorry, Cass . . .'

'You en't,' she declared. 'You're only too glad it's me not you that's not been brung back downstairs.'

'I couldn't leave the old lady. Mrs Yelland wouldn't let me. Not with Mr Winterborne's trusting me to look after her while he's been away.'

'I could've done it just as well as you!'

'She's got used to me,' I protested. 'Besides, Mr Winterborne should be back today and they'll be gone altogether by the end of the week. Then everything will be as it was.'

'The sooner it comes the better,' Cass snapped, unwilling to be soothed.

Amy, whey-faced, seemed too fatigued for once to indulge in cat-calling. She skulked by the fire and contented herself with glowers in my direction.

I knew I should be feeling guilty, but I was not. I hated the thought of going back to the kitchen. Sometimes I indulged in daydreams of Mr Winterborne, realising that I had become indispensable, whisking me off to Bath to become a lady's maid and companion to his aunt. But of course, I was not indispensable nor experienced except in kitchen work, and there was a respectable widow, a woman of long experience and exemplary character, already engaged.

In truth when Mr Winterborne returned that afternoon he scarcely noticed me at all, beyond the briefest of acknowledgements as he entered Miss Cavendish's room. He was still wearing the mud-spattered, caped greatcoat and boots that he had travelled in and a waft of horse and of chill outdoor air breezed in with him to compete with the warm, still odours of the bedchamber. His forceful masculine presence seemed suddenly to invigorate the atmosphere as he strode briskly to his aunt to offer her a polite bow and kiss her cheek. He was clearly restored to full health. The bruising around his eye had almost gone and he was bristling with energy.

'I hear Whittle got away early,' he said with satisfaction. 'That means he will be comfortably at my house by early afternoon at the latest, even at Hero's pace. Good. I would not have him travelling in the dark. I would not wish to distress you unduly, Aunt, but there is talk of highwaymen in the district.'

'Oh, my dear, how dreadful.' Miss Cavendish's hand flew to her breast. 'Thank God you are back safe. I should have been so worried had I known of it.'

'I had an untroubled journey,' he assured her. For some reason he seemed more amused than upset at the news. 'And I never go abroad without my pistols.'

'Even so, such villains might shoot first!'

He gestured her protests aside. 'I would not have mentioned it, save that I heard something that pleased me mightily while I was in Axbridge. And I think you yourself will not be grievously upset to hear it. It concerns your former lawyer.'

'Mr Merryweather?'

'The same. He and his bride are reported to have been held up on the road near his half-built new house outside Wells and relieved of their jewels and money.'

'No! Were they hurt?'

'Only in their pride and their pockets.'

'Then I am thankful for that,' Miss Cavendish said, clearly shocked. 'For all that he cheated me, I should hate to think of him involved in bloodshed.'

'Merryweather, apparently, was carrying a considerable sum of money to hand to the architect whom he was to meet on the site. One hundred guineas, I understand. I am reliably informed that his wife lost a silver necklace, a quantity of silver in brooches and a pair of valuable diamond and ruby earbobs set in gold.' He paced across the hearth, swung back to face Miss Cavendish and said with relish, 'Now is that not justice, Aunt, after the way he cheated you and others equally trusting and helpless?'

She thought for a moment. 'Yes, there is a certain irony in such rough justice being meted out to him.'

'Do not sound so doubtful!'

'You are sure there was no injury?'

'Certain.'

'Then I suppose I might allow myself to feel a little satisfaction.'

'Indeed you might.'

'But it would not do to gloat,' she scolded. 'And I wish you would not be so . . . so exceedingly pleased about it. We have yet to travel to Bath, remember. Suppose we ourselves are attacked? What price justice then?'

'Oh, we should be safe enough in daylight,' he said easily. 'And the rogue at Wells appeared to be a more gentlemanly example of the breed.'

'Gentlemanly! What is gentlemanly about robbing defenceless travellers?'

He laughed. 'I have met one myself whom I could class as such.'

'You met a highwayman?' Miss Cavendish said, astonished.

'It happened when I first left Somerset to seek my fortune in London. On the way there I chanced to find employment as a clerk in a candle factory at a place a few miles from London city. I lodged near Hounslow Heath, which was notorious for footpads and other thieves. I fell foul of a mounted highwayman when I was returning from work late one May evening. Fortunately he was not intent on slitting my throat.'

'How can you smile about it, Felix?' his aunt gasped, paling.

'Because I came to no harm and lost only sixpence – and to James MacLean himself, which I suppose is fame of a sort.' He shrugged, dark brows lifting, as though in wonder at the memory. 'It was extraordinary. One minute I was staring into the barrel of the pistol, handing over my purse and believing my last moment had come. The next, the pistol was put away and I was asked, perfectly civilly, a few pertinent questions about my age and status. Then this would-be robber laughed and tossed the purse back to me, saying that he had mistaken me for someone else and was not in the business to make profit from a poor and very young clerk. He told me his name and said that he had extracted one coin, so that I could boast of my meeting with him. It would earn me, he said, many a free glass of ale in any tavern I cared to patronise. And by God he proved right!'

Miss Cavendish stared at him blankly. 'MacLean? Is he well known then?'

'Was, Aunt,' Mr Winterborne said drily. 'Scarcely a month after my encounter with him he and his partner William Plunkett held up the Earl of Eglington and afterwards the sale of a blunderbuss he had stolen was traced back to him. He was hanged, alas, that October, after a year or two of living richly off travellers journeying in and out of London. Plunkett, though, escaped and has never been seen since. Doubtless he is enjoying his ill-gotten gains in quiet retirement somewhere.'

'How can you lament the loss of such a person?' Miss Cavendish said, tut-tutting.

'Because he could have struck me down – killed me perhaps – taken everything I had. Yet he did not. He was courteous – perfectly charming, in fact. I quite see why he was known as the Gentleman Highwayman. As to his other title, the Ladies' Hero, hearsay has it that women, rich and poor, swooned over him. There were certainly plenty of them, I'm told, weeping and wailing outside Newgate Gaol when they took him out to be hanged.'

'I still say that however politely it is executed, a crime is still a crime,' said Miss Cavendish stoutly.

'You are right, of course,' he said, though amusement still quirked the corners of his mouth. 'And I stand corrected and chastened, Aunt, for speaking otherwise.'

'With all this talk of robbers you have not told me how you went on in Axbridge.'

'Oh, it went well enough,' he said, vaguely, as though his enthusiasm had been used up recounting the story of Lawyer Merryweather. 'I think I might risk a small investment . . . But now I must return to my room and rinse off the grime of my journey before we dine.'

He strode off, only seeming to notice me at the last minute where I stood by the bed repacking one of Miss Cavendish's travelling boxes. He favoured me with an impersonal nod to my hasty curtsey. I had been so carried away by this talk of highwaymen that I had nearly forgotten my manners. And as I folded and tidied ancient velvets and threadbare silks into some semblance of order I realised, with a sigh, that life was going to be very dull indeed when Mr Winterborne and Miss Cavendish were gone away.

But I was wrong.

Mr Winterborne had been very generous with his praise of the inn and Mrs Yelland's plans for it, promising that he would spread the word of the Thorn Tree's convenience and excellent food among his acquaintances in Bath. He himself, he said, would be seeking lodgings here again when he was travelling south, as he would need to do from time to time.

He was also exceedingly generous with his tips. I stared open-mouthed at the two golden guineas he pressed into my palm. I had never owned such riches in my life.

'A small token,' he said, waving away my stumbling thanks. 'You have pleased my aunt and cared for her very well. And,' he added in a tone laced with irony, 'defended her bravely against brutes made ill-tempered by blows to the head.'

I felt colour come into my face and wondered why I had ever thought his eyes cold. They seemed now to hold nothing but good humour. But then, why should he not be in high fettle? He was on his way home, he was restored to health, and perhaps some good had come out of his delay here with a successful piece of business executed in Axbridge. I just prayed for the sake of his aunt's peace of mind that this pleasant mood would last.

'I wish you and Miss Cavendish a safe and speedy journey, sir,' I said, adding impulsively, 'I hope when you come again, I'll hear that Miss Cavendish has settled happily in Bath.'

He laughed. 'You still do not trust me.'

'I do, sir,' I said, hoping that my trust was not misplaced. He had been nothing but polite and courteous since his recovery, but I had no idea what it would take to bring out that scowling, impatient side of his character. Had that display of temperament been an unusual and temporary effect, or was it likely to show itself whenever he was crossed or frustrated? 'Your aunt is a kind and God-fearing lady,' I went on as firmly as I dared, 'and she thinks a great deal of you, sir. 'Twould be a pity if her fondness for you was to . . . turn out a disappointment to her . . . Which I'm sure you'll not allow,' I finished in a rush.

'A pity indeed.'

Then, disconcertingly, and with a certain louche slowness, he looked me up and down, examining every inch of me from my shoes to the top of my cap. I had the feeling that he marked each crumple in my apron, the smears of dust on the hem of my dress, every lock of hair that was escaping, as it inevitably did, from the confines of my cap, and found my whole person considerably odd and gauche.

'So what do you propose to do if I decide to treat my aunt badly?' he said, his eyes at last meeting mine. 'Shall you rush to Bath and rescue her? Will you take horse and gallop pell-mell to lay siege to my house? Good God, I must take care to bolt my doors at night and order the constable to keep watch if that is the case. The very thought of a virago of such a great size and brute strength preparing to call me out creates the most desperate fear and confusion in my heart.'

He clutched dramatically at his chest as he spoke and the picture raised in my imagination by his words let me down. I scarcely came up to his shoulder, for heaven's sake, and there was a boldness about him that would have made a hefty man think twice about tackling him, leave alone a skinny little kitchen maid. I did not want to laugh, but I couldn't help it.

'That's better,' he said with satisfaction. 'I was wondering when you would condescend to look at me without either condemnation or fierceness sparking out of those watchful brown eyes of yours.' Then he reached out and closed my fingers over the coins he had given me and said gravely and, I hoped, sincerely, 'I promise I shall take good care of my aunt, never fear. But thank you for championing her so bravely.'

There was lavish praise for Mr Felix Winterborne all round the Thorn Tree after he had gone. And why not? He had been uncommonly generous. Even little Trudie, the scullion, had received sixpence from him when he visited the kitchen to pay his compliments to Mrs Hill in person. Mrs Hill pocketed her sovereign with glee, dropped to a knee-cracking curtsey and declared that it had been no trouble, no trouble at all to prepare food for such gentry. Which quite contradicted the crescendo of grumbles that had actually accompanied each tray of dainties.

Cass, her cold improved, half-a-crown better off and restored to more favourable duties above stairs, condescended to forgive me.

'Well, I'm not one for begrudging good fortune to others,' she said grumpily when she knew of the guineas I had been given. 'Though I thinks those as was put out most should've been favoured above those who gained easy pickings. Still, you're to help me turn out the bedchambers that have been used and I'll make sure you pulls your weight.'

I nodded meekly, suppressing the urge to remind her that we never worked together but that she dawdled and made excuses to remove herself so that I did the bulk of whatever cleaning we were about.

She brightened. 'Any road, Mr Winterborne says he'll be coming back and when he do, in a proper way and not half dead from banging his head, and without the old dame, there'll be no call for 'ee to be running out from the kitchen to 'tend him. No, 'twill be bound to be me as is called upon an' I shall be the richer for it. Ah, such a fine and generous young gentleman, en't he, Em?'

I do not think she noticed the little hesitation before I agreed. To have done other than conform to the generally held glowing opinion of Mr Winterborne would have made me sound sour and ungrateful, which I did not wish to be. I *was* grateful for his generosity. Very much so.

But I could not help but remember that other side to him – the impatience, the scowling bad temper. But was it altogether that? Such things could be excused given the situation in which he had found himself. No, it was the coldness I had seen in his eyes – only the once, to be sure, but I had sensed that the coldness ran deep and strong. I could not entirely dismiss the thought that it was still there despite the altered, benevolent impression he was now careful to maintain. Generous he might be, but he was no angel in my opinion. And that very generosity, that largesse handed out without exception somehow nagged at me. I felt there was something about it – about him – that was, perhaps, not quite . . .

Well, in truth, I was not sure *what* it was about him that made me wary. And what did it matter, anyway? He was gone now and my two guineas were locked away safely in Mrs Yelland's iron chest. She encouraged all the younger employees in the habit of thrift, promising to add an interest each Michaelmas day of a ha'penny for each pound we saved, though only Luke and I paid any real attention. But today she was urging me take something from my little hoard to spend when the pedlar came.

'There is only the paper and ink I ordered on his last visit to settle for,' I said, then added a little wistfully, 'But he did have a bale of pretty cream muslin, sprigged with blue . . . but it would be extravagant . . .'

'Ah, but it is pleasant to be extravagant for once. You deserve a new dress, for walking out in in the summer. I will help you to cut and fit it. And how if I give you what trimmings you need by way of a small thank you for your valiant work this week? Now, make the calculation as to how many breadths you would need, then put the addition and subtraction in the ledger as I showed you and tell me the total.'

I wrote down the sums and made the reckoning. 'I shall still own three pounds, seven shillings and fourpence farthing after the cost of the material,' I said proudly.

'Excellent.' She gave me a warm smile, then sighed. 'I wish you would encourage Cass to be as provident. She no sooner gives me a shilling to save than she has it back to spend on some frippery or other. I cannot seem to make her understand that it will give her a good start to married life if she has a little put by. As for Amy, I have given up any hope of improvement there. At least I have Cass able to write her name, even though she balks at learning to read.' Her lips tightened to a hard line. 'Sometimes I regret that I did not overrule Mr Yelland from the first and send Amy packing. She is sly and underhand, and workshy into the bargain. And I reckon she is still up to her old tricks with the men, clever though she is at covering her tracks. Well, I shall only need to catch her at it once and, by heavens, she'll be off the premises before she has time to draw breath.'

But Mrs Yelland had no need to catch her. Amy was already tangled in a snare of her own making.

Though Cass was soon over her cold, Amy's ague had not cleared. It settled on her stomach and no amount of peppermint tea or sitting by the kitchen fire hugging a blanket-wrapped hot brick seemed to ease her discomfort.

The morning after our visitors had left she vomited noisily into the chamberpot before dragging herself miserably after Cass and me down to the kitchen.

Mrs Hill up until now had been sympathetic, coaxing her to eat and allowing her to sit about even more than she usually did. This morning, though, she waddled in looking thunderous.

'I heard 'ee earlier, heaving your heart up,' she bellowed. 'And that do bring to my mind not so much eating a bad piece o'pork, which you been swearing was the cause, but more a piece of pork of a very different kind put in a very different place.' She clenched her fist and held it under Amy's nose. 'So, madam, what 'ee got to say for yourself? And I want the truth, mind. No tall tales, for if you lies to me and time proves 'ee wrong, I swear I'll knock the living daylights out of 'ee!'

Amy's face crumpled and she let out a great howl. 'I dunno how it happened,' she wailed. 'Never got caught before.'

Cass gripped my arm. 'Her's breeding!' she whispered, aghast.

I did not normally have much pity to spare for someone who was so often prepared to bully others, but she looked so pathetic, cowering on the stool before the fire, that I could not help a pang of sympathy. And something else: some unnamed emotion that stirred and shivered deep in my heart.

'I warned 'ee it'd come to this,' Mrs Hill shouted, 'but 'ee took no heed! All this talk of bits o' sponge and vinegar keeping trouble at bay. More fool 'ee for believing nature wouldn't find a way to get round such hobstacles.'

'Jed brung me herbs to get rid of it – but all they did was gripe me guts.'

'Jed Smith? He's to blame?'

Amy broke into a loud sobbing. 'I en't seen sight nor sound of him since he knowed the brew didn't work. His master says he's changed with another lad and goes down to Bridgewater, 'stead of coming this way to Bristol.'

'That's just the manner o' no-good villain he is,' Mrs Hill said ferociously. Then, in a somewhat softer tone, 'So what you plannin' on doing now, maid? Once you're showin' proper, missus'll have 'ee out . . .'

'Before that, I assure you, Mrs Hill,' said Mrs Yelland in an icy voice.

We all jumped.

She walked to where we stood in a little stricken tableau, her footsteps ringing briskly in the stunned silence.

'So, I am proved right,' she said. She looked down at Amy with hard eyes. 'Once a trollop, always a trollop. The only surprise to me is that you have gone so long without falling into trouble.'

'Takes two,' said Amy, with a spark of her old sullenness. 'He never let me alone. But now he's gone off—' Her face began to crumple again. 'An' I've no one as'll take me in, let alone a baby. There's only Pa and I en't seen 'ee in years since he moved to Taunton wi' his doxy – an' 'er's as hard as nails—'

'So you have no home to go to, no money and the young man you *claim* to be the father of your child has turned his back on you. A sorry state of affairs, is it not?'

'It's his! Jed Smith's! There's been no one else! Honest!'

'I'm afraid I do not rate your honesty very highly,' Mrs Yelland said, but her tone had softened a little as though, like me, she could not help feeling compassion for someone who looked so tear-stained and defeated. She sighed. 'I have every right, you know, to turn you out this minute. You have been deceitful in the pursuit of your lusts. Yet there will be a child, poor innocent thing, and I would not have it punished because of your scandalous behaviour.'

'Can . . . can I stay, then?' Amy said hopefully.

'For the present. Until arrangements have been made.'

'A-arrangements?'

'I shall see if we cannot call this . . . this paramour of yours to account.'

'He'll deny it,' Amy wailed. 'An' he don't have no money. He promised me the draught'd work an' I wish it had, for I don't want no pukin' bastard to look after.'

'Never let me hear you say that again.' Mrs Yelland's voice whipped like a lash into the silence. 'The child has not asked to be born. *You* have created it and it will look to you in its helplessness for the care only a mother can give. The least you can do is prepare to . . . to accept the responsibility and love it in return. Do you understand? Do you?'

It seemed as if Amy might argue, but she thought better of it and mumbled unconvincingly, 'I reckon so.'

Mrs Yelland turned away as though she could not bear to look at Amy any longer.

'I shall see what can be done,' she said coldly.

But as she swept past us, I saw that her expression almost mirrored Amy's in its distress. And that there was the glint of tears in her eyes.

'You're quiet, Princess,' Luke said later. We were leaning companionably on the gate to the orchard. I had slipped out in the slack moments after dinner was cleared away, when Mrs Hill was taking a nap before the kitchen fire and Amy too bound up in her own woes to make some nasty comment. This was the time I usually took my lessons, but Mrs Yelland had pleaded a headache and I, for once, was relieved to have an interlude when I could review my own disturbed feelings.

'I was thinking of the mistress,' I said, which was part of the truth. 'This business with Amy. I think it's upset her.'

'Never,' Luke scoffed. 'She's been looking for a chance to see Amy off ever since she first come.'

'It's not Amy herself. It's the baby.'

He looked at me blankly. 'How so?'

'Well, Amy getting caught and hating the idea, but Mrs Yelland . . . when I saw how she was today I realised it's a great grief to her that she's childless. Yet she never showed it before and I never saw it.'

'What's the odds to that?' Luke said.

'Hard to explain. It makes me feel, after all she's done for me, that I should have understood.'

'You're being too soft. Any road, it's naught to do with you.' He dug me in the ribs with his elbow and grinned, the fringes of his hair as fiery as the sunset behind the leafless trees. 'That's Master Harry's business. Though perhaps you could remind him to go about it a bit more often.'

'Don't, Luke!' I edged away from him. 'I don't want to listen. There's enough of crude jesting about her in the kitchen.'

'It's only a bit of fun,' he said. 'It can't hurt her. Not words. As for t'other one, I'd like a penny for every time Amy's been made mock of about the stables for her carryings-on.' He guffawed. 'Mind, she'll not be as free with her favours now.'

I shuddered, hating to think of Amy's name being in any way bracketed with Mrs Yelland's in ribald speculation. As to that other spectre that haunted me...

I turned away from Luke, pulling the old kitchen shawl tightly about my shoulders. 'It's too cold to be standing here,' I said abruptly. 'I'm going in.'

'No, don't!' His hand shot out and caught my arm, pulling me round to face him. 'Don't rush off. Not seen much of you lately,' he said, with an awkward shrug. 'What with you being busy with the old dame an' all.'

'I'm poor company,' I said irritably, shaking off his hand. 'Best leave me be before I start snapping your head off.'

'What's got into you, Princess?' His good-natured face wore a puzzled expression. 'You've got to be glad Amy's going.'

'Course I am, but—'

'But what?'

'Nothing that need concern you, Luke Gilpin.'

'I hate to see you looking miserable. Did the old woman do something to upset you? Or the gentleman?' He clenched his fists and punched an invisible opponent. 'Just tell me,' he grinned, 'and I'll beat him to a pulp when next he comes a-calling.'

'No! It's not that at all. I... I don't want to talk about it.' To my horror a sob caught in my throat. I gulped it back. 'Let me be, Luke,' I quavered. Then words would not come at all as I struggled for composure.

'Oh, Emily, love.' His voice wobbled, as though my distress was catching. His sturdy arm came round my shoulders. 'Don't cry. Whatever it is, you can tell me. If there's anything I can put right for you, I will. I swear it.'

There was something comforting about the weight of his arm, about the large solid shape of him as I leaned my forehead against the rough cloth of his battered old working coat.

'I wish you could,' I said, getting my voice under control. 'But it's just me being silly – about things that I can't help thinking of. I look at Amy and . . .' I broke off. 'Oh, it's too horrible to say aloud, Luke.'

'No it isn't. Not to me,' he said firmly.

'She . . . she was always calling me bastard. Making up dreadful stories about what happened . . . when my mother and father—'

'I can guess, the filthy-mouthed slut! But I've told you, Princess, words can't hurt.'

'They can,' I whispered. 'Oh, they can. And today, I looked at her and thought . . . wondered . . . if she'd spoken the truth. Suppose someone just like her really was my mother. And my father a snaggle-toothed lout like Jed Smith.'

'Not they!'

'But I don't know, do I? It's more like to be the truth than the lord and lady I always pretended. Amy doesn't want her baby. She hates it already. Suppose . . . suppose that's how my mother felt about me. Never loving me, wanting to get shut of me as fast as she could . . . And there's me always believing that she was still somewhere waiting and hoping we'd someday find each other.'

'But you've got your key, remember?'

I'd almost forgotten I had told him of that.

He had come across me one day last summer when the string around my neck had broken and I was retrieving the bag from a clump of grass where it had fallen. I could have spun him the same cock-and-bull tale that I had given to the others, but I didn't. Luke was my friend. And though I had been reluctant to reveal my secret, I owed it to him to be honest. I had shown him what the bag contained. He had frowned at the scrap of paper with the few scrawled letters still visible though they made up not one complete word. He had held the shining key in his dirty palm while I told him all I knew of it. Then he had tucked both carefully back into the bag and, his irrepressible grin crinkling up the massed freckles on his face, had said, 'See, I always said you were different, Princess. You've got royal blood, for certain. And don't look so bothered. Your secret's safe with me.'

I knew that it was. We never even spoke of it when we were alone, as though by some tacit and surprisingly – for Luke – tactful understanding he knew that this link with my past was too precious to be spoken of easily.

His arm tightened now as though to urge his own conviction and optimism upon me.

'Whoever fetched that meant you to know there really *was* someone who cared.'

'I suppose.'

'No suppose about it!' He chuckled. 'There's never a chance that anyone like Amy's your ma. I spied you for a princess straight off, remember?'

I managed a watery smile.

'That's better,' he said.

'Thank you, Luke.'

'What for?'

'Oh, just for being here when I needed you.'

He did not answer straight off. Nor did he move his arm away. When he spoke again his voice held an unusual, intense note.

'I . . . I'm always here for you, Emily. Always will be. I want you to remember that.'

I blinked up at him. He was eighteen now and had

matured physically a great deal in the past year, his body becoming muscular and sturdy. His face had filled out, too – become fleshier under broad cheekbones. But the freckles and the shock of red untidy hair were the same, and his eyes maintained their bright blue cheerfulness.

But not at this moment. And what I saw there made me wriggle uncomfortably in his grasp.

'Don't go,' he said softly. I could feel the pressure of his fingers trembling against my back. Trembling? Luke? 'I've so much wanted . . . that is . . . Oh, hell's teeth—'

He bent his head and in surprise I raised my mouth to let him kiss me. His lips were cool, the skin a little rough, and he was very tender and gentle, which too was surprising. One thing was certain in my mind as we stepped apart a little breathlessly after some minutes: it was not at all an unpleasant experience.

'I shouldn't have—' he began.

'You shouldn't have—' I began at the same time.

Then we both stopped, looked at each other and laughed.

'You're not angry with me?'

I thought about it. 'No.'

'I'm glad of that,' he said, looking relieved. 'I wouldn't want to put myself in the wrong with you. It was just . . . just I gave in to temptation. I've wanted to do that for a long time.'

'Have you?'

'Don't look so shocked! 'Tis a natural thing between a lad and a maid. And with you growing so . . . so pretty and fetching it's been a torment to hang back.'

'Don't think to flatter me into another kiss,' I warned him.

'It's not flattery,' he said earnestly. 'It's the truth.'

'Go on with your nonsense!'

I did not believe him, though a wayward part of me wanted to. And even more errant thoughts crossed my mind as I strolled, considerably heartened, back to the kitchen.

Kisses and hugs had been rare in my experience.

I had a memory of life with the wet nurse I had been put to for the first four years of my life. A poor, honest woman of the district, as all the nurses were, whose paid duty it was to care for us and, if we survived the separation from our birth mother and the ailments that threatened early infancy, to return us to Lady Eleanor's when we were of an age to be trained in usefulness. I remembered rough kindness and kisses amid the boisterousness of her own large brood and the way I had howled when I was forced apart from her. After that, I had quickly learned to expect little in the way of expressions of affection or compassion.

So my experience of kisses and comforting touches was not great. But even in my ignorance – innocence – I had been taken aback by how agreeable I had found it to be kissed and flattered by Luke. An initial awkwardness, because he was so familiar as a friend, had slid away to be replaced by... what? Curiosity? A growing excitement? A sense of taking a step into realms of emotion which had so far been closed to me but which I might now begin to explore? All of these, together with the realisation that my body had responded instinctively and pleasurably to his touch, without any commitment of mind or thought.

Kissing was an agreeable business altogether, I decided.

I wondered when I should have another chance to continue this very different kind of education.

Mrs Yelland wasted no time in sorting out Amy's problems.

She chivvied Master Harry to ride to Midsomer Norton to explain the situation to the carter and present him with a letter in which she had set out how the situation might be resolved. The carter, a God-fearing man, together with

Jed Smith's father, who was enraged that his son might be dismissed from a steady job without a character if he did not do the right thing by the girl he had got with child, acted promptly upon her instructions. Mrs Yelland, who occasionally attended morning service at the little church in Brimyard – dragging a reluctant Master Harry there when he could be persuaded, though his head tended to be sore of a Sunday morning after a roisterous Saturday night in the taproom – made a private visit to the parson.

The result was that a week later Jed Smith and Amy Wright made their vows in the presence of his still-angry father and Mrs Yelland. Thereafter Amy would make her home at the Smiths' cottage at Midsomer Norton.

Amy went hard-faced to her wedding.

She gave up crying once she knew what was to happen, putting on a semblance of gratitude for an old grey gown of the mistress's which Mrs Yelland hastily refashioned for her, and the three guineas Master Harry pressed upon her as a parting gift. Cass and I found some early violets growing under a hedge and with a few sprigs of rosemary and winter jasmine fashioned a posy twined with white ribbons for her to carry. The grey gown was of a decorous shape, the bodice covered with a muslin fichu, a far cry from the usual tight-laced, low-cut bodices she wore to display her full bosom to its best advantage.

With her hair washed and combed and hidden under her cap instead of bouncing down her back in greasy curls, the effect was sober. She stared fixedly at the kitchen floor, her mouth sullen, looking more as if she was about to go to a funeral than a wedding.

'Well, you looks real ladylike,' Mrs Hill managed, then she threw her apron over her face and bellowed into it, waving us away and crying, 'I'll miss 'ee, Amy. Oh, how I hates partings.'

''Tis all her fault – the missus,' Amy muttered viciously.

'Her could have let me stay where I belongs.'

Cass and I followed her to the kitchen door, Cass saying overbrightly, 'Well, you'll get a husband afore me, you lucky thing. I'm proper jealous, for I was thinking Ned would be speaking up and I'd be the first.' She gave a false laugh. 'But 'tis you getting wed all proper and off to be a wife. Jed's ma'll probably be glad to have another woman in the house, her having no daughters.'

'Hush your rattle!' Amy's head shot up. She swung round to glare ferociously at Cass. 'It shouldn't be me that's going. I got more right to be here than her. I'd not be leavin' if *she* hadn't got her claws into you-know-who when her did. You knows that, Cass. I was cheated.'

Cass shook her head and cast a warning glance at little Trudie, all ears at the scullery door. 'Don't talk out of turn,' she hissed. 'There never was a chance for 'ee there. Now get off with you. Missus is waiting.'

Mrs Yelland had appeared at the corner of the yard.

Amy looked at her through narrowed eyes. 'I've a mind not to go. What's there for me with Jed Smith, anyway, save a life of waitin' on his ma and pa and church three times of a Sunday? I'd be best on my own.'

'No you wouldn't,' Cass said, giving her a push over the doorstep. 'Not unless you fancies being fetched up afore the magistrate for having a babe out of wedlock. In my book that's no competition set against starting off respectable.' Her voice softened. 'It'll maybe turn out a deal better than 'ee expects.'

'And if it don't? Will Lady Muck come and rescue me? Not her! I've made my bed and I'm to lie in it. Or so her thinks.' She raised her chin and smiled, as though taken by a comforting and pleasing thought. 'Well, all I can say is that if and when things turn out badly for me, I'll know where to lay the blame. Indeed I shall.'

Her step was almost light as she tripped across the yard to where Mrs Yelland waited. We waved and shouted our good wishes and she waved back, just as though she were the willing bride Mrs Yelland expected her to be.

But Cass and I both fell silent as we closed the kitchen door and went back upstairs to finish off the last of the cleaning in the bedchamber recently occupied by Mr Winterborne. Amy's smile, sly and gloating, seemed to have blighted any attempt at light-hearted chatter. Which was why, as we shook and pummelled the feather mattress, I said without any preamble, 'What is this grudge Amy has against the mistress?'

Cass looked at me warily. 'Oh, some bee in her bonnet from afore you come here.'

'Don't put me off with fibs, Cass. She's hinted at it more than once. For some reason she thinks she had a chance with Master Harry.'

'Sshh. Don't speak so loud.' She leaned towards me across the bed and whispered, 'You must swear it'll go no further if I tells 'ee.'

'Cross my heart and hope to die,' I whispered back.

'Well, 'twas only once or twice when Master Harry, 'e drunk a bit too much ale and the widow woman he used to visit reg'lar in Brimston had gone off to Bridgewater to look after 'er sister.'

'Widow woman?'

She gestured impatiently. 'You can't think 'e lived to be nearly forty without a woman, can 'ee?'

I had given little thought to it. I had vaguely assumed, I suppose, that he had been content in his easy-going way with his bachelor existence until he fell in love with the woman who was to be his wife.

''Twas convenient to both him and the widow woman,' Cass said, spelling it out plainly with a hint of exasperation. 'Her being past child-bearing, see, there was no chance of her being caught like Amy. And her wasn't looking for another husband or she'd lose the money left her by the first. So, like I say, her's gone off and Master

Harry gets a bit merry one evenin' and I suppose with Amy always wheedling round and her bein' convenient, he forgot himself for once and took her to his bed. Or mebbe two or three times, it bein' summer and hot weather when 'tis a natural time for dalliance.'

'He *slept* with her? In . . . in his own bed?'

'A man has his needs,' she said primly. Then giggled. 'That's not to say women don't but they mostly says less about it. And they having to face any *consequences* is likely to be less willing, if you take my meaning. And there again, if 'tis a wedding band you're set on, then 'tis best to play a bit respectable in that department for it don't do to give too much and too easy, lessen the other party gets to thinking weddin' vows en't necessary.'

I presumed it was a policy she was following with Ned Arnold, but I was too overcome with the picture of Master Harry and Amy entwined in the great carved bed to pursue it further.

The beast with two backs. I had heard that ribald description bandied about in the taproom. It always made me think of the quick rough coupling of Luke's precious pigs when Farmer Ashdown's boar visited them. Was that how it had been? Hasty and loveless? Instant lust, instantly gratified? I shuddered away from the thought that it had been anything more; that the master had entertained any tender feelings towards sluttish Amy.

''Twas only a bout of midsummer madness and a tankard too many on master's part,' Cass said firmly. 'He never was one for foulin' his own nest in the way of chasing and harrying maidservants as some masters do. And he was always quick to see off any doxies who came a-flauntin' their wares at the taproom door.'

'But he turned a blind eye to Amy's tricks.'

She shrugged. ''Twas a case of what the eye don't see the heart don't grieve about, I reckon. And you know, for you've seen it yourself, that her has a way of chatting and teasing as pleases some of the customers. And pleased customers buys more ale and is like to come back often. No, he took no mind of her, so long as her kept her *activities* private, like.'

How convenient that must have been in the slipshod days of Master Harry's tolerant rule.

'And after . . . after what they did – what happened then?'

'Oh, master was generous with her. Put her off in a kindly fashion. You know his way. I reckon he was a bit abashed when he was properly sober again. Gave her the means to buy a new gown and a pair of buckles for her shoes. She was pleased enough with that at the time, though her always had hopes as he'd give up on the widow woman. Then her'd be waiting to pick up where they left off.' She giggled. ''Stead of which he goes to a funeral and comes back besotted with a *different* widow.'

We spread a clean sheet over the now plump and smooth mattress and tucked it in neatly.

'You can manage the rest of the bed-making,' Cass said bossily. 'I has things to see to in the best parlour.' She glanced round the room. 'Thank heavens 'tis all done and tidy. To be sure, I can't think that missus'll find anything to carp about.'

She spoke as though her back had been relieved of a great burden now that the two bedchambers were set once more to receive any future guests. I did not remind her that I had done most of the work because she was forever flitting off on some pretext or other. I was happy to let her go. I was always grateful for a few moments of peace and quiet. Particularly now, after such a disquieting revelation.

'Don't 'ee forget, you're to say naught to a soul,' she warned me before she left.

'I suppose by that you mean Mrs Yelland,' I said drily. 'I imagine everyone else knows, or guesses. How could such a thing ever have been kept secret at a place like the Thorn Tree?'

'What's past is past and forgotten by most,' she said. 'Besides, Master Harry's always been well-liked. Nobody'd willingly tattle to fetch harm on him. There's only me knew how Amy's brooded on it. So don't you go sneaking to Mrs Yelland, you hear?'

'I swore, didn't I? I don't go back on my word.'

Reassured she went off, probably to make the most of the mistress's absence to idle away an hour in primping and preening before the mirror, while I slowly and methodically made up the bed, my mind busy wondering if Mrs Yelland had known or guessed at Master Harry's previous entanglements.

And if she had would it have made a difference?

Reluctantly, I supposed not.

This was the real world, not the romantic world of princes and princesses, wicked witches and magic spells, with which the children of Lady Eleanor's had entertained themselves as an antidote to the aridity of their affection-starved lives. Whatever reasons Mrs Yelland had for entering into a marriage with Harry Yelland, it was certainly not undying love. She had not been swept off her feet by a dashing, chivalrous suitor. It was a way of escape from a situation she found untenable at her previous home.

Yet they managed comfortably enough, even if it was a marriage of convenience on her part.

And on his?

For the first months I had been here he had been her adoring shadow, even though her response was at most a kind of affectionate exasperation. But his ardour seemed now to have cooled. Occasionally they went to church together of a Sunday or to Bristol. Mostly, day-to-day routine kept them apart. He always busy in the brewery or stables or taproom where she seldom strayed; she up in the parlour with her books and ledgers whenever she was not bustling about on her domestic duties. And there were no long evenings spent together in the parlour. He stayed in the taproom until the last customer was gone. She retired to bed early and rose early while he snored on until a later hour.

I twitched the last crease out of the counterpane and wandered over the creaking floorboards to the window. I stared down at the little garden the mistress had made.

Was marriage always a matter of compromise, I wondered? One partner – or perhaps both as in the case of Amy and Jed Smith – going out of expediency or necessity to the altar?

And if Master Harry's example was anything to go by, perhaps it was that romantic love had but a brief blossoming before it lost its colour and became as drab and uninteresting as the dead winter foliage I could see below.

I leaned my forehead against the glass. It struck cold against my warm skin.

If love were such a fickle emotion, I thought, as though the chill of the glass had forged a cold path through the muddle of my thoughts, then perhaps it was better not to fall in love in the first place. Which made it reasonable to believe that it was best to marry for well-judged reasons, rather than as a result of some ephemeral passion. Better to go clear-eyed into marriage than be dazzled by starry-eyed illusion.

Something caught my eye on the rug at my feet, glittering briefly as I moved. Then disappeared. I bent down and felt in the fraying edge of the blue and green striped woven wool. Whatever it was glinted again as I hooked it up out of the clinging strands and set it on my palm.

An earring, fashioned in twisted strands of gold and set with a faceted piece of glass the size of a small pea and three deep red stones. I tilted my hand from side to side and rainbows flared within the glass. I caught my breath.

Not glass or paste, surely. This was too beautiful a thing, too delicately fashioned. Costly. Where had it come from? What was it doing caught up in the rug in what had been Mr Winterborne's room?

Clear as if he stood beside me I heard his deep voice, full of relish.

'... *one hundred guineas ... a silver necklace, a quantity of silver in brooches ... a pair of valuable diamond and ruby earbobs set in gold ...*'

My hand shook. The rainbows winked at me with cold brilliance. Surely not! I was mistaken.

Then whose?

Not Mrs Yelland's. I knew all her jewellery: a brooch of carved jet and a gold locket that held tiny likenesses of her mama and papa painted on their betrothal; her wedding band, and another circled with seed pearls. Nothing else.

Miss Cavendish's then? She had been in this bedchamber once or twice. But her jewels had all been sold long ago. She had told me. She had certainly worn none while she was here.

There was no other person at the Thorn Tree who could own to such a fine thing. And the room had been unoccupied until Mr Winterborne came – scrubbed clean, polished, by Mrs Yelland and myself, every hanging laundered by the washerwoman who came in by the week. Weeks ago I had taken the matching pair of rugs outside to beat and sponge them. After rubbing them dry I had beaten them again until all the accumulated grime was removed. I had examined every inch of the rugs that day and there had certainly been nothing lurking in the frayed edge. No, the rug had accumulated its treasure since then and Cass, who had rolled up the rugs this morning in order to sweep beneath them had, in her usual careless way, flung them down again without a second glance.

The earring had been left for me to find. And if I was

right in my suspicions, I wished heartily that I had not.

'*Now is that not justice, Aunt?*'

How pleased he had been. How eager to spill out the glad tidings to his aunt as soon as he had returned from his jaunt. Quick to reassure her that the robber was of a gentlemanly disposition. No wonder . . .

I looked from the window to the rug. And back again.

Had he stood here against the light to inspect his haul? The purse of guineas, the jewels. Turning them over in his hands. Revelling in the revenge he had extracted from the rascally lawyer. What had happened then? Had he been interrupted? A knock at the door to make him hastily conceal his booty? Or was it merely an excess of high spirits after the success of his dangerous escapade which had made him momentarily careless?

I moved to the chair by the cold and empty hearth and sat down to think.

Had I fashioned this dreadful conclusion because my imagination had been provoked by an inner conviction that there was some coldness, some mystery about him that I could not quite fathom?

It was quite possible.

I stared round the room, as though to catch some echo, some trace of the man who had lain hurt and feverish in the bed, had sat in this very chair before the fire, had strode impatiently about this room . . .

Nothing. Just silence, for it was very quiet at this end of the house. No noise filtered through here from the yard or the taproom and the quiet seemed to deny my lurid imaginings.

But my mind would not let go the picture of a young, impoverished clerk being accosted by a highway robber of charm and bravado and graced with most gentlemanly manners. How remarkable the encounter with James MacLean must have seemed to the young Felix Winterborne. Had the effect of it impressed him so decidedly that he had himself turned to the same wicked and dangerous game? He was clever enough to have seen the possibilities. He could have used his gains to raise himself swiftly to a comfortable gentleman's life.

Everything fitted: the convenient journey to Axbridge 'on business', which might or might not be true, but which certainly had taken him quite near to Wells; the pistols he carried – for his defence, he said – but which might well be used for a different purpose. Even the open-handed largesse with which he had earned – bought – the goodwill of every servant could be seen as a means of ensuring himself a warm welcome should he wish to use the Thorn Tree as a bolt hole again. No one would wish to suspect such a respectable, affluent and generous gentleman of being involved in any nefarious activity. Not unless there was some direct evidence.

The earbob had warmed in my palm. The blood-coloured stones felt almost alive against my skin, as though Felix Winterborne's lifeblood beat there. I closed my eyes. If this ornament should prove to belong to Lawyer Merryweather's wife, then he would have a hard case to answer. All I needed to do was to pour out my suspicions to Mrs Yelland who would, in turn, set in motion a chain of events that could take Felix Winterborne to the gallows.

Justice would be swift and merciless. Miss Cavendish would lose her rascally nephew to the hangman's noose.

I sat bolt upright.

Miss Cavendish. So proud of her nephew who had gone to London to seek his fortune. And found it! And had returned triumphantly to rescue her from the impoverished existence into which she had sunk. If I betrayed him to the justice he deserved, I might as well condemn her also.

Poor lady, I had liked her very well and hoped so much that she would be happy and content in Bath. Little chance of that if her nephew choked his life out on the end of a hangman's rope, with all the resultant scandal. And how could she bear to know that he would go to his death as a spectacle to thrill and amuse bloodthirsty crowds, his body perhaps to be hung in chains at some crossroads in order to be a warning to others. Flesh and firm young muscle turning to stinking decay, those greeny-grey eyes pecked out by crows...

I went icy cold, my fingers closing tightly over the earring.

I could not do it.

Even if he were guilty, I could not be responsible for betraying him to such a ghastly end. The knowledge that I had been the deliberate and direct cause of a person's death and the ruination of a kind old lady's life was a burden I was not prepared to carry, for I knew it would haunt me to my own dying day.

Felix Winterborne would come to grief in his own time and his own way. I would not be responsible.

I would dispose of the earring. Throw it away when I was out in Brimston woods, or on the hill. In the meantime it must not be found anywhere in the vicinity of the Thorn Tree.

I had the little bag from round my neck in a trice. I dropped the earbob inside, to a faint metallic chink as it fell against the brass key. I drew the string tightly and only when the bag was safely hidden again under my bodice did I feel as though I might breathe comfortably again.

The day was not done with surprises.

Cass and I had gone into the parlour as usual as the clock in the corner chimed half-past two, the hour at which Mr and Mrs Yelland took their dinner. Cass busied herself laying cutlery on the table before the leaping fire, while I brought in the hot dishes of mutton broth, jugged hare and buttered turnips and set them on the hearth where they would keep warm until they were ready for Cass to serve up.

Mrs Yelland was always prompt to oversee that all was as it should be before Master Harry joined her. Lifting lids to sniff appreciatively at the contents, straightening a knife here, moving the salt cellar to a more convenient place and taking as much care to commend us for faultless service as to scold us if we were clumsy or forgetful.

Today, though, she made no move towards us. She stood, with her back to the room, looking out of the wide window with its small panes of thick greenish glass. She seemed so deep in thought that I hesitated to speak. But speak I must or I should catch it from Cook, who wished to know whether she should later send up what was left of yesterday's apple pie as well as the new-made one of preserved damsons.

I cleared my throat. 'Ma'am, Mrs Hill would like to know . . .' I began.

Mrs Yelland swung round, startled, her hand going to her throat. In the other hand she held a sheet of paper. Her eyes, for an instant, were frighteningly blank, as though she could not remember quite where she was. She stared at me without recognition.

'Ma'am?' I said, taking a worried step closer. 'Are you feeling ill?'

'No . . . no. Thank you . . . Emily.' Her colour came back with a rush. She blinked and the strange look was gone. 'Just . . . well, unexpected news.'

'Bad news, ma'am?'

'Bad news?' she echoed. She laughed. A forced, false sound. 'I could say yes, but that would be impolite. I could say no, but it would not be the truth. You see, my late husband's son and his wife are to honour us with a visit. Is it not . . . gracious of them?'

'More visitors, ma'am?' Cass said, catching this last. 'Then a good thing the bedchambers is all to rights.'

'Which gives me no possible excuse to turn them away,' said Mrs Yelland brightly. 'Well, I cannot blame you for that, Cass, for I insisted on it.'

'Yes, ma'am,' Cass said, looking uncertain.

Mrs Yelland seemed to collect herself with an almost visible effort.

'Take no notice, I am only jesting,' she said in her usual brisk tone. 'I was taken aback somewhat by the unexpected contents of my letter. It has been a trying day, and my thoughts were still on Amy.'

'She took her vows?' Cass asked eagerly.

'She did. And is gone off to Midsomer Norton with her new husband and his father, where I hope she settles to be a good wife, and in time a good mother. But to more urgent matters. Mr and Mrs Bowyer will be here the day after tomorrow. They are travelling to Bath in search of a cure for Mrs Bowyer who, it seems, has been greatly troubled in the years since the birth of her second child, by megrims and palpitations.'

'Is she an invalid lady then?' said Cass. ' 'Twill be a lot extra work.'

Mrs Yelland gave a wry little smile. 'Oh, you need not worry on that score, she will bring her own maid. And she is not in the least an invalid, though I never did meet anyone who paid such exquisite attention to her health. Indeed, I trust her husband does not let loose of her among the genuine invalids who frequent Bath or she will quiz them unmercifully on their symptoms. She likes to ensure that a well-researched ailment is at her disposal when she is in need of one.'

I smothered a chuckle, glad to see that she had recovered her spirits and her dry wit. Cass looked from me to the mistress with a puzzled frown, having failed to catch the irony.

'What will you need me to do, ma'am?' I said hurriedly.

'They will arrive in time for dinner and sleep here for

one night before they go to Bath, so you need do no more than you usually do and help Cass to bring the meals. Besides, with Amy gone you cannot be spared from the kitchen. I will myself ensure that all is comfortable in the red bedchamber and see to any particular requirements.'

Later that evening, she came down to the kitchen to instruct Mrs Hill on the menu she would require for her guests. I met her in the passage as I was hurrying back from the taproom with an empty tray.

'I must turn my attention to employing some new maids,' she said, frowning at my perspiring face. 'Amy might not have pulled her weight, but at least she was an extra pair of hands. I have been negligent. I will engage a woman from the village to help out temporarily. In the longer term, it has been in my mind to pay a visit to the foundling home to engage a pair of new kitchen maids. They will have some training and it pleases me to think I might offer a good home to them . . . and not in the name of charity, but because I have your excellent example before me every day.'

'That's kind of you, ma'am.'

'It is the truth. I should like you to train them up to our ways before I take you out of the kitchen.' She smiled that warm and charming smile. 'Mr Yelland has promised me that the improvements I have wished for will be put in hand this summer. When all is complete I shall set you in charge of attending to the comfort of our superior guests.'

'Oh, ma'am . . .'

'It will be no sinecure,' she cautioned. 'They will expect a great deal more in the way of service and attention than the working men who come here. I intend, once the building work is completed, to put forward advertisements in the Bath papers and perhaps have handbills distributed which will give notice of the Thorn Tree's many advantages. I shall proclaim a high standard and we must live up to it.'

'I'll do everything I can to make it work well,' I said, overwhelmed that I could look forward to escaping the kitchen and Mrs Hill's uncertain temper. 'But one thing, ma'am,' I ventured, 'if Miss Edgar still rules and you go to Lady Eleanor's in person . . . well, you would make a very good impression on her. Too good. If she thought this inn was prospering she would recommend her favourites . . .'

'Ah, and someone more deserving – such as you were yourself – would be overlooked and relegated to an inferior situation.'

'Exactly, ma'am.'

'In that case I shall be more subtle and make my application in writing.' She laughed. 'If Miss Edgar answers, then I shall leave it to her judgement. We shall between us concoct just the sort of letter that will encourage her to send a couple of her least favoured waifs. In that way, I may hope that they will turn out as well as you, Emily.'

Which was a compliment that kept me glowing through all that exhausting evening and beyond.

Mr and Mrs Thomas Bowyer arrived late the following afternoon in a fine carriage drawn by four horses, with a coachman and a boy in blue and white livery up front, and Mrs Bowyer's maid – a young person whose nose was constantly raised in the air as though a nasty smell assailed her – travelling inside alongside her mistress.

I was somewhat taken aback by how grand they actually were.

Though Mrs Yelland had often referred to her previous husband as someone who took a keen interest in the lands he farmed, I now saw that it was laughable to have thought he might have been merely a superior version of Farmer Ashdown.

If Mr Tom Bowyer was anything to go by, his father had certainly been a gentleman.

Mrs Yelland and Master Harry had rushed out to greet them as soon as the carriage drew up outside. I watched, fascinated, from a window in the taproom as a stocky gentleman in a grey coat descended from the carriage, helped down a tall, slender woman, extravagantly costumed in rose pink and turquoise and with quantities of yellow hair tumbling in ringlets from under a wide-brimmed hat, then attended to the formalities of greeting his distant cousin and his former stepmama.

There was a deal of bowing and curtseying and I wondered how Mrs Yelland felt at this moment, greeting the man she misliked and who had been the cause of driving her from her former home, and the feather-headed woman she despised, who now reigned in her stead at Starlings Barton. She would hate to bring them through the taproom, I knew. It was, for once, empty, but its low-beamed, smoky, ale-smelling dimness was not the best introduction to the inn for people so grand. How she must wish the new entrance through the little garden was ready.

I lost sight of them as they moved round the corner and hastily went to the door to be ready to offer them a smile and a curtsey as Mrs Yelland had instructed me to.

They came in two by two. First Master Harry with Mrs Bowyer on his arm and her maid scurrying after her carrying a quantity of small boxes.

I curtseyed but Mrs Bowyer swept past unnoticing. She was very pretty, with delicate features, a simpering smile and a pair of pale blue eyes that darted about in a somewhat vague manner.

A few paces behind, walking more slowly, came Mr Bowyer with Mrs Yelland.

They did not touch. He stood back to let her go in first. I curtseyed again. Neither of them noticed. I stood back and waited for them to pass, ready to spring out and close the door behind them.

They walked into the dimness of the taproom, took

three paces across the floor and, as if by some mutual unspoken consent, they stopped amid the rough benches and tables and turned to face each other. By this time Master Harry and Mrs Bowyer had exited at the far door. I could hear the sound of their voices diminishing as they moved along the passage and up the stairs.

'Barbara,' Mr Bowyer said, into the silence. 'It has been a long time.'

'Yes, Tom,' she said, equally quiet.

'Are you happy?'

'As well as I may be. And you?'

'As well as I may be.'

He looked down at her. She looked up at him, and her smile blazed out, igniting his. After a moment, very gently, he picked up her hand and held it to his lips. Then slowly he released it and I caught the sad, soft breath of her sigh as they turned from each other and, in silence and apart, walked away from me across the taproom.

I closed the door quietly, and stood there with my back to it, reorganising my shocked thoughts.

Great heaven, I had it all wrong. It was not hatred of her stepson that had driven Barbara Yelland away from her former home. It was love.

Chapter Four

In October 1760 old King George died and his grandson succeeded him. I suppose such important events had a great impact on the nation, but the succession of the third Hanoverian George seemed very remote to us at the Thorn Tree. Our own little affairs were far more important. Like the epidemic of scarlet fever which was sweeping through the district that autumn, old Albert being kicked and half-crippled by a fractious horse and the imminence of Cass's baby, which seemed likely to arrive a prompt nine months after her wedding to Ned Arnold. And for me there was the exciting prospect of a visit with Mrs Yelland to Starlings Barton in Devonshire, where we were to stay for a whole week.

I had never been on so long a journey before and I had Abigail Bowyer to thank for it.

She had been enchanted by her first visit to Bath three years before where submersion in the waters had, she swore, so improved her headaches and palpitations that she was quite a new woman. So the pilgrimage had become an annual event. This year the trip had been made at the end of August and the Bowyers were accompanied for the first time by their two children, a boy of eight and a girl of seven, along with their nurse, who stumbled, green and groaning, from the carriage and looked like to fall to her knees in thanks for being released from the torture of the jolting journey.

Which was why she could scarcely be blamed for what

happened next, when the two children erupted excitedly from the coach after their long confinement and the small girl, Odette, darted straight into the path of a wagon that was rumbling out of the stableyard.

How I caught her I still do not know. One moment I was standing with Mrs Yelland waiting to welcome our guests, the next I had hold of the tails of Odette's cloak and was hauling her backwards out of the way of the carthorse's great hoofs.

The child sat down heavily on the cobbles and began to bawl as the wagon wheels went past her with inches to spare, and later I was summoned to Mrs Yelland's parlour to be properly thanked by a grave Tom Bowyer. He presented me with a guinea, which I was reluctant to take.

'But for your quick thinking, Emily, we should not be sitting here so comfortably this evening.' He shuddered. 'It was a most heroic act.'

'Sir, I was the nearest to Odette, that was all.'

He held up his hand. 'I will not hear excuses. I saw what happened. Kindly take this as a small token of our thanks.'

'Indeed yes,' Abigail Bowyer said, in her high-pitched voice that always reminded me of a sparrow's somewhat irritating chirping. 'I cannot bear to think of the consequences had you not acted as you did. That wretched nurse! I shall rid myself of her as soon as we are returned to Starlings.'

'But, ma'am, she was ill,' I said, feeling sorry for the poor girl who had wept bitterly from remorse afterwards.

'Then she had no right to be while in charge of my darlings,' Mrs Bowyer said pettishly. 'If she knew herself to be a bad traveller, she should have spoken up! But no, she chose to hide the fact. And it is not the first time I have caught her out. So she must go.' She heaved a sigh. 'Dear Barbara, you cannot know how fortunate you are to have such good servants about you. Ah, if only I could tempt Emily to Devonshire.'

'Well, Emily, are you likely to be tempted?' Mrs Yelland said easily.

'I'm honoured, Mrs Yelland,' I said, equally at ease, for it was a subject that had been raised before. 'But the Thorn Tree is my home and I enjoy my work here.'

Which was true. Perhaps I was too entrenched. Luke was certainly of that opinion. I wrenched my thoughts away from that particular source of guilty feelings and I smiled at Mrs Bowyer in order to soften my words.

I did not wish to be impolite, but Mrs Bowyer had nothing to offer which I did not have already. Namely, a considerable amount of standing and responsibility. I had two maidservants and a boot boy directly under my authority and all the responsibility for ensuring that the guest wing functioned smoothly, including the making out of bills, the accounting, and the keeping of necessary records. When Mrs Yelland was not at home, I had charge of the inn. I was not likely to exchange my lot for a position at Starlings, where servants tended to come and go with too great a frequency to betoken a contented household.

'It is naughty of you, Abigail, to try to win Emily from me when you know she is my right hand,' Mrs Yelland said lightly.

'Oh, pray do not scold, or I shall be quite put down,' Mrs Bowyer said, pouting prettily. 'It is just that I seem doomed to be surrounded by dolts and country clods who cannot think for themselves nor be trusted to carry out the most menial tasks without supervision. As you know, I do not enjoy the best of health.' She fluttered a graceful hand to her heart, as though to indicate some serious weakness there, though the rosy lustre of her porcelain-smooth complexion and clear eyes seemed to speak of glowing good health. 'Why, on some days recently, I have been so weak and in so much pain from a malady that settled on my lower limbs that I was afeared of some dropsical condition taking hold. It was all I could do to take myself from my bed to the sofa, is that not so, Tom? Yet you will bear witness, my dear, will you not, that, enfeebled though I was, I still had to deal with that wretched nurse who was hysterical over a dead rat being placed in her shoe. She swore it was young Thomas to blame, when the dear child would never do such a thing and it was clearly the work of the kitchen cat. Ah well, she will not be a trouble to me much longer.'

Mrs Yelland nodded in apparent sympathy as Abigail Bowyer rattled on in the same vein for a few moments. Her expression was carefully bland, but I knew the scornful words that she must be withholding.

That silly goose of a woman! She has not the wit to see that her fickle and lazy ways are the root cause of whatever domestic upheavals she suffers. She has no idea of household management. One minute over-indulging the servants, the next berating them unjustly or driving them to rebellion with unreasonable demands. It is the same with the children. If it were not for their father, they would have no steady influence in their lives ...

She scarcely ever mentioned his name, scarcely even spoke to him directly when they were in company, beyond the necessary courtesies. Tom Bowyer behaved in exactly the same manner. Two people well-schooled in hiding their true feelings. Except that someone who had glimpsed their first encounter after a space of years might notice the way his hand might accidentally brush hers, causing a sudden colour to flare in her cheeks, or her glance catching his and holding it for a fraction longer than was necessary.

If it was more than that – if they ever contrived a few moments to be alone – then they were discreet about it. There was certainly no speculation about them in the kitchen where the merest hint of indiscretion would have been seized upon and embellished. All Mrs Hill ever noticed was that the mistress was in an extra-critical mood when they had left.

'I reckon seeing those grand relations of hers allus rubs her the wrong way and throws her into a temper,' she would grumble. 'Then her takes it out on them as is doing their best. 'Ten't right.'

'I'm sure she didn't mean to upset you, Mrs Hill,' I would say cheerfully. 'Especially as she was so pleased with the roast goose you served up for dinner. She asked me to tell you that Mrs Bowyer was particularly complimentary about it. Now, will you let me give you a hand with tidying up that corner before she looks in again. . .?'

'Well, I s'pose 'ee might – but mind that skirt o'yourn against them greasy pots. Don't want her picking no argument on account of 'ee doing young Bella's work, the idle madam.'

Time and familiarity had eased Mrs Hill's antagonism towards me. And I had grown to be used to her grumbling ways. It was much easier to respect her efficiency as a cook now that I was no longer under her feet all day. And with the responsibilities I had towards the guests who sought shelter at the Thorn Tree, it was an asset to have an ally in the kitchen. Many a weary traveller had been soothed out of irascibility by some delicacy dreamed up by Mrs Hill. The mistress had set us high standards: a courteous welcome; good, hearty food; excellent service and the cleanest, most comfortable beds to be had in north Somerset. We all strove to ensure that she – and our guests – were not disappointed. She even had a device carved over the new entrance by the little garden: 'WELCOME ALWAYS SMILES'. Mrs Hill might not be one for smiling, but her talents in the kitchen had gone a long way towards the growing popularity of the Thorn Tree with the carriage trade.

'I have the most splendid idea, Tom!' Mrs Bowyer clapped her hands and twinkled roguishly at her husband.

'Emily deserves a *proper* reward for saving Odette. How can our daughter's life be set against a mere guinea? She shall come with dear Barbara for a visit to Starlings! And I have already quite decided that I shall not take no for an answer. I have asked you and asked you, Barbara, and always you plead that you cannot be spared from the Thorn Tree. But you are looking tired and Cousin Harry said himself you drive yourself too hard and fell prey to fatigue in the summer on account of it. I declare I shall not move from here until you have promised to come to Devonshire and bring Emily. Think of her if you will not think of yourself. She is deserving of a treat, is she not? What do you say, Tom? Will you not add your persuasions to mine?'

The hesitation was barely noticeable, yet into the little silence came a sudden crackling alertness, like the air when there is lightning about. As though all manner of possibilities, of temptations – of longing – sparked and danced the width of the hearth between the straight-backed woman in the plain grey dress and the stocky man in the dark green coat.

I daresay had not Master Harry chosen then to return to the parlour from the taproom to catch the gist of the conversation that moment of weakness would have passed. Mrs Yelland would have set her chin in that determined way she had and refused. Mr Bowyer would have made some show of persuasion while thinking up a way to distract his wife.

But Master Harry, an unlikely angel of destiny with his bear-like figure encased in coat and breeches that were never anything but rumpled and untidy however well-pressed he started the day, stockings writhing like snakes round his plump calves and with his wig, as always, slipping askew, cried cheerfully, 'Why, that is a most splendid idea, Cousin Abigail! Barbara, I will not hear of you turning down such a kind invitation.' His booming laugh reverberated round the room as he eased himself down into the chair next to his wife and produced a handkerchief to mop his sweating face, managing to set his wig even further out of true, and revealing a good inch of grey and bristly scalp at his left temple. 'I accept on your behalf, my love. A nice rest will set you up for the winter – and I'll not hear a word about you being indispensable here. We can bring in a woman or two from the village to help out while you're away and everything will run neat as clockwork as you've set it up to be.'

Even then she might have raised some argument. But he ended his sentence with a rumbling belch. I saw the flare of her nostrils as she turned her head in distaste from the gust of ale fumes.

'Better out than in,' he said complacently. 'So what do you say, Barbara, to a week or two in Devonshire?'

And she, eyes lowered, said quietly, 'It seems that I am to be overruled. Very well. As you are all so insistent, I will take advantage of your kind offer. Thank you, Abigail. I will make the necessary arrangements for Emily and me to travel to Starlings.'

Only then did she look directly at Tom Bowyer. Then, in the blink of an eyelid turn her gaze smoothly – and smiling – to his wife.

Cass sniffed disparagingly when she heard of the trip.

'If I'd been here, 'twould have been my place to go with the missus,' she said, bracing her now-cumbersome bulk on the stool before the kitchen fire. 'But I shouldn't have looked forward to it. Not one bit, for I hear Devonshire's a poor, muddy sort've county. Besides,' she added with the air of superiority she always assumed as a married woman speaking to a mere spinster, 'I daresay my Ned would have said words agin it, 'e not liking me sent so far off. And I shouldn't have wanted him upset.' She pursed her lips. 'What do Luke say about 'ee going? I'd wager he's not so pleased.'

'Why shouldn't he be?' I said, nettled.

'Because he thinks the world of 'ee. 'Tis natural he won't want 'ee gadding off for the Lord knows how long.'

'Great heaven, it's only one week! Mrs Yelland can't be spared for any longer.'

'He's a good lad,' she persisted. 'You won't find steadier. I don't like to think of him made miserable. For sure, *I'd* not go gallivantin' if I was in your place.'

'Well, you're not, Cass,' I said tartly. 'So just leave it be.'

She had no need to try to make me feel guilty. Luke had already done that. When I had run to tell him my news, he had done his best to share my excitement but his expression had soon turned to the glumness that sat ill on his usually cheerful face. I had seen more and more of that particular expression lately – usually after he had been urging me to name the time when I would marry him.

'I've enough saved now to rent a small place and buy a few pigs and chickens and a cow or two,' he'd say. 'If you'll just give me the word, Princess, we can start looking for a decent smallholding.'

'Not yet, Luke. I'm doing well here – we both are – it'd be foolish to throw away what we've both worked so hard to achieve.'

'So when *are* you going to give me word? Michaelmas? Yuletide? Easter Day?'

'I'll think about it.'

'Promise.'

'Luke, I won't be rushed.'

'Rushed? How long've I been asking? A twelvemonth and more. And still you won't be straight with me. You say you care for me, yet you seem to think more of pleasing Mrs Yelland and all those fancy folk you 'tend to than me.'

'Oh, Luke, don't speak like that.' He would look so sad and bewildered at this point that I was always moved to say, gently, 'I just need a little more time to decide. Be patient a little longer...'

We had been having these bickering little conversations since the summer and to be honest I could not fathom why I was so intent on deferring a definite answer. I was never happier than when I was with Luke. I loved him. He was my dearest friend. We shared the same hopes and aspirations for the day when we would not be beholden to anyone but ourselves. We both saved hard towards that day of independence when Luke would take a tenancy on a small farm and we would marry and I would become mistress of my own household.

I found the images raised by the thought of sharing the rest of my life with Luke entirely comfortable and pleasant. He was personable, kind, full of good humour. I enjoyed his kisses. The urgency of his caresses awoke an equal urgency in my own body, though we were both agreed – difficult thought it was at times – never to risk the possibility of a child. My own bitter experience as a foundling was something that cautioned me against bringing any baby into the world lest it was born wanted and secure. When Luke's ardour seemed like to overwhelm him and carry me with it, I was always aware of some detachment, some element in my mind that seemed to be on watch, guarding me against rashness. It would bring me rapidly to my senses with its chill of common sense, causing me to disentangle myself from Luke's embrace, to hastily retie loosed ribbons and pin up my dishevelled hair and to retreat behind smiles and joshing. Sometimes Luke's emotions overrode his caution and he seemed bewildered that I had pushed him off, though he was always abject later.

'Sooner we're wed the better, Princess,' he'd say, grinning. 'Then we shall have no need to be good. Think of it, our own feather bed and the dark of night to make merry in and to breed a tribe of young 'uns.'

There was pleasure in anticipation, true. In Luke's wholesome young body I should find the complete satisfaction that eluded me now. Yet still something prevented me from taking the one step that would turn dream to reality. As though that same inner voice cautioned me to wait. But why? And to wait for what?

'No, 'twouldn't be kind to overset Luke, when he thinks the world of 'ee,' Cass said stubbornly. She scratched absently at one grey-stockinged leg she had exposed to the warmth of the blaze. 'Still, no use harking on it, for I suppose you'll please yourself.'

Cass visited us as often as she could, even though she was now but a month short of her lying-in. Mostly, it seemed, to give herself the chance to crow about her married state, though it was my opinion that the overcrowding at the tollhouse where she now lived with Ned Arnold, his parents and Ned's five siblings, was such that even gregarious Cass liked to find some excuse to escape. Not that she would have admitted it. Nor did she criticise the coarse food that was the regular fare at the Arnolds', nor the hours she and her mother-in-law spent toiling over the washtub and hot iron, for the family purse was tightly stretched and had to be helped by the taking in of washing for their neighbours. All was rosy and perfect to hear her talk. But I saw the pastiness of her complexion that emphasised the tired shadows under her eyes, the raw state of her hands from the hot water and lye, and her swollen ankles and feet from being on her feet all day long, and drew my own conclusions.

'I knows you'd fret to know if the babe'd come early if I didn't visit 'ee,' she said, this being her most recent excuse for making the trudge to the Thorn Tree. I reckoned that the attraction lay more in the chance for her of an hour's peace by a warm hearth, the tasty bowlful of whatever was simmering on the hob, roasting over the embers or baking in the bread oven, and the generous basket of leftovers Mrs Hill always sent her home with. Today, though, even before she began sniffing appreciatively at savoury steam and hinting that she was hungry, she had gossip to impart.

'Do 'ee knows who I seed two days since?' She paused dramatically, round eyes bright, ''Twas Amy! Amy Wright as was and who wears Jed Smith's ring – though I tell 'ee, 'twasn't Jed her was travelling with, but a rough, gypsy-looking man.'

'Amy?' Mrs Hill, feet crossed on the hearth, had been gently rocking herself to a doze as was usual in this slack hour of the afternoon. Now she pulled herself upright, stilled the rocking chair and gaped at Cass. 'So 'twas true what we heard. As her'd run off and left her man and her child.'

'Zackly,' Cass said importantly. 'Told me so herself. Said she couldn't stand living with him – nor his ma and pa. Lasted with 'em no more than it took to wean the babe afore she run away with the tinker I saw her with.'

'Well, I never,' Mrs Hill gasped.

'And what's more,' Cass said, glancing round and, even though the young maids were nowhere to be seen, lowering her voice to a confidential whisper, 'between us three here – for I wouldn't breathe a word 'cept that we all knows her – she's not aiming to stay with the tinker much longer. Says he beats her when he's drunk – and he surely has a rough tongue for he cussed something terrible about payin' his dues at the tollgate. No, her's got an eye on someone younger and handsomer, she says. Fixed up to meet with him secretly once her and the tinker gets to Bristol.'

'The little hussy!' Mrs Hill said, looking pleasurably indignant at such an interesting piece of gossip. 'Well, I has to say it don't come as a surprise. 'Twas always her nature to be fickle.'

'And what of the child?' I said.

''Twas a boy, as you'll remember. Doted on by the grandparents, seemingly. At least that's in her favour for she left him where 'e's better off, 'stead of traipsing him about with her. Though how she could've borne to leave him, I don't know. *I* never could.' She patted the swell of her stomach, and said, in the smug and complacent manner she assumed when the opportunity arose to emphasise her authority in these matters, 'You'll find out one day, Em, what it means to carry a babe for nine months and the sort of feelings you has for it, even before it's born. So I knows all those feelings must be ten times – an 'undred times – more after, when it's out of 'ee and a living and breathing infant. God willing, o'course,' she added hastily, with a placatory glance at the ceiling, as though the Deity hovered there. 'For there's sickness and accidents and hazards a-plenty lying in waiting for the little mite. Fair bothers me, already, the thought of it do.'

'Amy never wanted that baby,' I said shortly. 'In or out of wedlock.'

'Too easy-going by half to want the bother. And too fond of anything in breeches for her own good,' Mrs Hill pronounced. 'I could see the way she was bound and I warned her she'd need to shape up if she was to make anything of herself, but she never took no notice.'

'Her was never properly suited after Mrs Yelland come,' said Cass, unable to prevent a somewhat nostalgic glance round the kitchen with its freshly limewashed walls, sanded flags and scrubbed table, a far cry from the dark and squalid cavern it had once been. Even Mrs Hill had eventually come to realise that her working day was made much easier if everything was clean and in its place and that one hard-working maid was worth two or more lazy Amys. And the Thorn Tree kitchen must look especially comfortable to someone now confined within the cramped conditions at the tollhouse. I wondered if Cass spoke more on her own behalf as she added, 'I reckon Amy didn't know when she was well off.'

'There's more than her found that out when it was too late,' Mrs Hill agreed, small eyes glinting in their layers of flesh as she saw an opportunity to repay Cass for the annoyingly patronising comments she was too free with these days. She folded her meaty arms complacently over her vast bosom and gave a significant jerk of her whiskery chin in the direction of Cass's stomach. 'Thank the Lord, I never was tempted to become one man's unpaid slave,' she said. 'I'd sooner be mistress in my own kitchen with money to spend every quarter, than be a poor man's skivvy with naught to show for it save to be breeding every year.'

'In order to be wed you has to be asked,' said Cass, rising to the bait with a scornful toss of her head. 'Course, there's plenty who never get asked at all.'

'If you means me, my girl, then I'll have you know I had chances a-plenty when I was young, so don't give me none of your lip...'

I left them to their familiar squabbling and went back to the guest wing to check that all was in order before the Taunton coach arrived.

It came in twice a week in the summer months – once a month if the roads were passable in the winter – stopping on its way to Bath and again on its return. It was not one of the fast coach services patronised by the gentry who had the means to pay for speedy transport, but a slow country machine that took an age to jog from small town to small town, delivering and collecting packages and passengers.

The acquisition of this business had been Mrs Yelland's first major triumph. It was followed by others, so that this year there had been four days in the week when we were kept busy with the regular arrival and departure of coaches. Master Harry had been persuaded to take a share in the one that ran between Bristol and Wells. It was proving profitable, even though he was now responsible for providing and keeping the necessary horses, and he was – at Mrs Yelland's prompting – contemplating extending his interest.

Though the passengers were not as free-spending as those of the carriage trade, being for the most part small tradesmen and their wives, minor clerics, perhaps a governess or other upper servant travelling to a new place, they were decent folk who appreciated a good table and the chance of a short rest before they resumed their journey.

Out of habit I glanced through the window as I walked down the passage from the kitchen to check that the front yard was still empty of vehicles and people, but my thoughts were on Amy and how word of her still had the power to grate. I had never set eyes on her since she had left the Thorn Tree and we had had little news of her over the years, yet whenever her name came up, it lodged in my mind like a bramble thorn caught in a stocking which stays invisible among the stitches but reminds you of its presence by a continual scratching.

It was a warm and mellow early October day with the fires laid in the rooms but not yet lit. I commended Joseph, the boot boy, for the tidy state of the hearths and the neat log piles he had made beside them, and spoke warmly to the maids who had covers spread over the parlour table and were busy scraping the old wax from the brass candlesticks and polishing them to a good lustre before the new candles were set in.

Attention to such detail might have seemed pernickity, but I knew that small things contributed to the overall welcoming atmosphere as much as the comfortable chairs with their red linen slip covers that were regularly laundered so as never to look in the least overused, and the cheerful pictures on the walls.

I could not suppress a lift of pride and pleasure

whenever I moved about these rooms. It was not only that I had helped Mrs Yelland in the arranging and setting up of them, but that I felt this to be my own little domain in which I was mistress. Of course I was responsible in turn to Mrs Yelland, but now that a routine was firmly established and I was well experienced in how to handle awkward customers and settle any disputes that arose, I seldom had to call upon her as I had done in the early days. Under her tutelage I had learned to listen carefully to any complaints and to be fair, firm and tactful in the resolving of them. I did my level best to ensure that no traveller ever left the Thorn Tree other than full of praise for its excellent service – even if that traveller was so high-nosed that he – or more generally she – refused to enter the inn at all and demanded that refreshment be brought out to be consumed in the privacy of his or her carriage.

But thoughts of Amy intruded into my pleasure today. So, once I had seen that all was in order, and the two present lodgers – a pair of elderly gentlemen who were making a walking tour of the district – had not yet returned from their day's outing, I retired to the little cubbyhole that had been created between the new entrance hall and the guest parlour where I had a small desk and a shelf for my ledgers. I took one down and opened it, ready to enter the outstanding receipts, but my pen remained undipped in the ink. Instead I absently chewed the end of the quill and gave myself up in some irritation to wondering why I should be so bothered by news of her.

I did not have to look far for an answer. Amy was trouble wherever she went. What distress she must have caused to the Smiths at Midsomer Norton. And now she seemingly planned to cuckold her present lover. Her sly, gloating smile loomed up in my imagination. The thought of what had happened between her and Master Harry still had the power to disturb me – before he had married, true, but the idea of them together at all was highly disquieting.

Determinedly, I dipped my pen and began writing. I would give her no more thought. After all, she had not turned aside to visit us, but had gone on her way to Bristol. With a bit of luck her path would take her far from the Thorn Tree. And keep her permanently at a safe distance

We were to go to the Bowyers for the third week in October. The season had been dry and there was a settled look to the weather as we departed on the slow Taunton machine. It was convenient to leave directly from the Thorn Tree and we were to take it as far as Bridgewater where we would spend the night before bespeaking seats to Exeter on a faster vehicle.

Everyone who could had come out to wave us off.

Luke and I had said our private goodbyes the previous evening, he extra ardent at the thought of my being absent for a whole week and myself endeavouring to match his mood. In truth, though, half my mind was occupied with all the details I must attend to before I left and the other half was filled with excited anticipation of the longest journey I had made in my life.

But Luke did not want to share my excitement.

'I thought we were to take a stroll, and here you are impatient to be off!' he said, grin fading.

'It's near dark, we couldn't have gone far.'

'Never stopped you before. We could take a turn round the orchard.'

'But I have so much to do! You know all the rooms are full. I have only slipped away while our lodgers eat supper, and there are still the bills to be made out.'

'But you're happy enough to leave Margery in charge for the whole of next week. Can't she see to things tonight?'

'But I want everything in order before I go. Oh, Luke,

don't let's fall out. I hate it when you're angry with me.'

In the dusk I saw the stiff set of his shoulders sag as the spurt of temper fell away. He was wearing his good coat and a clean shirt, and his fiery hair was still damp from its dousing under the pump. He had wanted to look his best for me and I was touched and remorseful that I was upsetting him.

'I'm not angry,' he said. He pulled a rueful face as he reached out to take my hands and pull me close. 'Leastways, not with you, Princess. With myself. For taking note of daft feelings I've been having.' He hesitated. 'Dreams.'

'What sort of dreams?' I said in surprise, for he was the most down-to-earth person I knew.

He shrugged and said, somewhat reluctantly, 'You'll laugh if I say.'

'I won't. Promise.'

His grin was never far away. But now it was a half-hearted affair. 'It'll make me sound like Mrs Hill mumbling into her ale about omens and portents . . . But I keep having the same nightmare. I had it last night and it was worse – more real – than it'd been before. I was running with sweat when I woke and shouting.' He stopped short, then burst out, 'It's you I keep seeing, Princess. You're in a river, being carried off into a great boiling flood and I can't do anything to save you. When I try to run, I find I'm fastened in mud up to my knees and I can't shift. And I can hear you laughing.'

'Laughing?' I said carefully.

'Aye, you might well look like that, because it's the daftest part,' he said. 'The more you laugh in my dream, the more I'm bothered. Because you're heedless of the danger.'

'What sort of danger?'

He shook his head. 'If I knew that it might not be so . . . so blasted fearful. But there's something out there – not the water itself – something that's waiting.'

'To gobble me up?' I touched his rough cheek. 'Dream monsters are harmless and well you know it.'

'But it's the *feeling* I get. Of . . . of such fear. And it doesn't go away when I wake up. It's like burrs clinging to me, even now. I can't stop thinking the dream must have meaning. Suppose it's a warning that something terrible will happen if you go away.'

'I should think it's more a caution not to eat too much cheese for supper.'

'There, I knew you'd make mock.'

'Oh, Luke,' I sighed. 'Can you not see how it looks to me? That you've worked yourself up to a grumpy state because I'm going off and you're being left behind. This dream just gives you an excuse.'

'You can't say that. I've never minded when you've gone off before.'

'But I've never slept away, have I? Never been further than Bristol market with Mrs Yelland, and that rarely. It's all right for you, I suppose, those times when you've left for days at a stretch, fetching back horses when they've been hired out—'

'That's different.'

'Because you're a man?'

'Anything could happen on the road. You know it. You've heard tales a-plenty. Accidents, robbers, rogues who don't think twice about wielding knives or pistols. What if the dream means you'll come to harm if you go?'

I broke apart from him. 'And what if it means that you're jealous of my good fortune? If that's so, shame on you, Luke Gilpin.'

And there it was, another tetchy little argument flaring up, and though we kissed and made up before I hurried back indoors, a certain spiky defensiveness lurked below the surface of our farewell. So I was greatly relieved to see that Luke had recovered his usual good humour by morning. Whatever demons had haunted him seemed to have dissolved away in the misty morning light.

'Enjoy yourself, Princess,' he whispered in my ear as he handed me into the coach. 'I didn't mean to cast a cloud.'

'I know. But a week will go in a flash. And I'll have so much to tell you when I come back.'

'I'll not rest easy,' he said, 'but I shouldn't have made such a fuss. I want you to go off happy, not cross with me.'

'Of course I'm not cross,' I said, smiling up at him. 'And I suppose I was a bit strung up too. Put it down to excitement.' I chanced to tease him: 'Just make sure you don't have any silly nightmares, while I'm gone, that's all.'

There was an instant of hesitation. No more than half the time it takes to draw breath. It was a trick of my imagination that caused me to believe the sudden tensing of his shoulders, for he gave a guffaw of laughter and said easily, 'Bread and cheese won't pass my lips, I promise.'

So it was all right. We were friends again. I sat back against the scuffed leather of the hard seat and waved. He made a comic show of an exaggerated bow. Then with a jolt the coach moved forward to the pull of the four horses.

Barbara Yelland was not someone to whom enforced idleness came easily and she was soon fretting at the slow pace of the Bridgewater coach. But whereas every drag up long hills and every stop to change or water the horses and take on or disgorge passengers set her foot tapping impatiently, I was not one whit bored. Every aspect of the journey was interesting to me, from the other travellers on the road to the passing scene. We went through the hilly reaches of the Mendips as we moved south and west, and down to the great flat plain of the Somerset Levels, with its withy-fringed streams and ditches and little villages jostling for a foothold on every rise of ground above what, in times of heavy rain, could quickly turn to a vast shallow sea. While Mrs Yelland made desultory conversation with the other two passengers – a task near impossible on one stretch when we were joined by a harassed young woman with a fractious and continually whining three-year-old, who spent most of the time kicking at me as he squirmed about the seat – I was content to spy what I could through the thick, dusty glass. I more than half-wished I could sit up with the guard and coachman with the breeze in my face and the rich smells of the countryside flowing past instead of the stuffy odours of the carriage.

Only one gentleman, old, withered and deaf, travelled the whole way with us, but a chatty farmer's wife enlivened the final stage of the journey after the flushed and bawling infant was borne off, to the apologies of his mother. 'He's not usually like this,' she said. 'Don't know what's got into him today.'

'Sickening for something I'll be bound,' said the farmer's wife, settling herself down and delving into her basket. 'I've raised twelve and I'd say that his hectic colour's a sign of trouble a-coming, poor little soul. Now I've a few slices of fresh-baked bread and pickle and a roast chicken cut up handy, if any of you ladies is feeling peckish and would like to share it.'

We made an early start from the inn at Bridgewater, Mrs Yelland quietly satisfied that in no fashion did its amenities match those of the Thorn Tree. We had shared the only bed that was available in a small, shabby room that smelled of damp.

'At least there seems to be no livestock,' she said after a careful inspection among the dingy sheets and blankets, 'though judging from the feel of the mattress it may well be that we have an exceedingly bony carthorse as well as its hair to sleep on.'

Which seemed very much the case when we ventured to ease our tired and aching limbs under the bedclothes.

'Really, I do begin to believe we should have taken the flying machine and made the journey in one stretch,' she said, hunching about crossly under the sheets. 'Thank God we have but a few hours in this bed, for I declare I have a complete hoof sticking in my ribs.'

'Only one?' I said, beginning to giggle. 'I'm sure there are at least six under my back.'

'What? A seven-footed horse?' Her voice quavered. 'A singular beast, indeed.'

'More . . . more a *plural*-footed one.'

'Perhaps we should make off with the mattress in the morning,' she said in such a dry voice that I was convulsed again. 'What a fine sideshow it would make. Roll up! Roll up! See the seven-footed horse mattress . . .'

Eventually we stopped the giggling that had overtaken us, mopped our eyes and composed ourselves to what sleep we could catch.

'I cannot remember,' Mrs Yelland said drowsily, 'when I lost myself so wholeheartedly in laughter. Goodness me, how it takes me back to childhood . . . my mama's time. Such a deal of laughter then.' She yawned, fell silent, then murmured, half-muffled by the pillow, 'Well, perhaps it is a good omen. Dear Mama would have thought so . . . As good a tonic as any physician's potion, she would have said . . .'

It might have been that bout of laughter, it might just have been the fond remembrance of her childhood or the knowledge that the worst of our journey was over, but whatever it was, there was a subtle difference in her after that. I knew her better than most and I could see it in her face, in her smile, even by the light of the one spluttering candle the maid left with us when she roused us at four and we made our hasty toilette before descending to the noise and clatter of the yard.

It was as though something inside her that had been long suppressed had been released and the spirit of the young girl she had once been had burst through the carapace of responsibility and duty.

The night spent in that shabby inn seemed to mark a kind of transition from careful wife to carefree young woman. A woman who had deliberately closed her mind to everything she had left behind at the Thorn Tree and now with a light and eager step went towards whatever awaited her in the home of the man she loved.

We emerged from the coach in Exeter into the dusty yellow light of late afternoon and looked about us for Mr Tom Bowyer, who was to meet us.

Even after such a long and arduous journey, Mrs Yelland still managed to look neat and trim, her brown hair coiled smoothly under her straw hat, her green skirts seeming little crushed, her cheeks only warmly pink from the airless confinement of the coach. I, by way of contrast, felt sticky and grubby, and I knew my hat had slipped to an unbecoming angle as I had been endeavouring to anchor my hair which was threatening to escape the pins with which I had secured it. Not that it mattered too much, I thought wryly. Whatever disorderly impression I gave, Mr Bowyer was not likely to notice.

He strode through the press at the door of the inn, his eyes fixed only on Mrs Yelland. His face reflected her warm smile as they greeted each other. She curtseyed, he bowed. They exchanged a few polite words. All perfectly proper. No more and no less than other meetings and partings in the small cobbled square where several coaches and carriages were drawn up to disgorge or claim passengers. Yet I do not think they saw anything of other people in those few moments of meeting and I felt an intruder.

Not that I minded particularly. I stepped a little to one side and took the opportunity to look about me at the old half-timbered buildings, with the upper floors leaning out over the square, and others built of the rich red sandstone that coloured the soil hereabouts, all squashed in or towering up high in a higgledy-piggledy manner. Pigeons wheeled above the chimneypots and dived down to join sparrows pecking at chaff blown among the cobbles. Their little voices were lost in the noise. Wheels and hoofs clattered on cobbles, horses whinnied, urchins raced about begging to carry baggage or to mind a horse. A church bell was tolling nearby. Mrs Yelland had told me that it was a town of many churches, not to mention a great cathedral, which we had glimpsed as we drove in, standing squat and solid above the River Exe which curled like a great silvery snake around the hill on which the town of Exeter stood. This was an ancient place and as the coach had plunged through a deep-arched gateway in the old walls I had felt awed to think that these fortifications had stood solid and protective since the days when the Roman legions had conquered the land.

I do not know quite how I caught the sound through the background clatter, but I did. I stiffened. It came again. A yelp, trailing to an agonised whimpering, the kind of noise that sears the nerve ends. An animal in pain. I looked round. No one else seemed aware of it, or cared if they did.

Another yelp and a burst of screeching laughter. I had it. There, in a narrow alley between two of the top-heavy houses. A pair of ragged youths. One had a string in his hand. He jerked it roughly, so that the cruelly tight noose around the neck of a scrawny mongrel pup bit deeper into the bloodied fur. The other youth held a sharpened stick. I saw him jab it down. Another heart-sickening yelp, the scrabble of claws on stone as the puppy desperately tried to escape its tormentors. And was hauled onto its back this time, paws flailing . . .

I moved. Forgetful of Mrs Yelland and Mr Bowyer, I flew across the cobbles, not stopping to think how I could persuade the youths to give up their horrible game, or to bother that they were both bigger than me. All I knew was that I had to do something.

I understood later that I would not have had the strength or authority to overcome these street-hardened villains. Indeed, I fear I should have put myself in some danger, for they had evil in their eyes and compassion for no one and nothing. But I was not, thank God, the first to reach them.

It seemed that he materialised from nowhere. One moment I was alone at the mouth of the alley, the next he was past me. Two gloved hands reached out and in one smooth movement gripped both youths by the scruffs of their necks. At the same time a booted foot shot forward and kicked the bigger of the two in the seat of his ragged breeches. Then the gentleman pitched both of them forward into the alley where they fell to a sprawling, swearing heap.

The puppy, abruptly released, dragged itself to the wall where it cowered, trembling. The gentleman bent his long length and very gently and carefully took it up.

'Well, hound,' he said drily, 'a fine specimen you are to demand rescue.' Then to me, urgently, as one of the youths sprang to his feet. 'Here. Hold this while I—'

Too late. The youth leapt forward. Something glinted in his raised hand. The gentleman bunched his fist and struck down on the lad's wrist. The knife clattered to the floor, but this was a youth nurtured to street-fighting. He had the knife up again in a flash, struck . . . and was gone, following the other down the alley and away.

'Oh, sir,' I cried, 'you're hurt.' The soft leather of his glove was ripped above the base of his thumb. A red trickle dripped down to the flags of the alley.

'The devil take it, *I've* been bloodied as well as this ugly little hound,' he said. 'Not to mention a new pair of gloves ruined. What is the condition of the brute, ma'am?'

I eased the string from the raw place round its neck. 'It's half starved and filthy, but at least it's alive.' I stroked the soft, flapping ears. The ragged wisp of a tail fluttered. It tore my heart to see the trust, the willingness to please in its eyes as it looked at me. So must it have looked at those . . . those evil devils, and they had rewarded it with cruelty, laughed to watch it suffering. Probably would have continued to torment it until it died. I shuddered.

'Yes, it takes one like that, does it not?' said the gentleman, very quietly. 'It is the helplessness, the trust, that spears the conscience and the heart.'

For the first time I looked up at him. Properly looked. His attention was on the pup as he wrapped a handkerchief round his injured thumb. Blood was already soaking through it as he touched the pup's black nose. A pink tongue lapped at his finger.

'What's to be done with you, eh, hound? Are you able to take charge of him, ma'am?'

I swallowed. My eyes fixed on his face. I found my voice. If it sounded husky and uncertain, it was scarcely to be wondered at after such an unpleasant experience. 'Sir,' I managed, 'my circumstances . . . I don't think it's possible . . .'

'No? Does it mean, then, that I have to put myself forward as guardian?'

He raised his eyes and looked into mine.

It might have been yesterday that I had stared into their greeny-grey depths. Or a million years. Or a mere instant.

The slow thump of my heart marked the seconds as we stared at each other.

It took a few of those heartbeats before full recognition came to him. But into that interval, as his conscious mind struggled to put a name to the face, it seemed that on a different level altogether a kind of awareness sprang across the space between us. As though this meeting was inevitable – irrevocable – and our separate paths had drawn us to this shadowy alley, at this moment, on this day, for a purpose which would define our lives for ever.

And nothing, ever, could be the same again.

Two more thumping beats, setting the blood hot and strong in the pulses at my wrists. I drew in a deep, steadying breath.

'We can't leave him, can we, Mr Winterborne?'

'I remember . . . of course I do. Emily? Can it be Emily?' he said softly. 'Ah yes, I see it. Though I wouldn't— That is, you've changed a great deal. Grown up.'

The conscious me was suddenly aware that my hat had come off and was hanging by its ribbons down my back. My disastrous hair was slipping and sliding round my face, and my hands, being full of scruffy and undeniably odorous puppy-dog – which was doing no good whatsoever for the elegance of my lace mittens – I could do nothing about my untidy appearance.

Oddly enough it did not seem to matter. Not to me. Not to him.

'Well, well,' he said. 'This is a happy chance, indeed. How long has it been? More than two years since I was at the Thorn Tree.'

'You came but the once after that first time. I was back in the kitchen by then.'

'I remember. You were hefting pans as big as yourself about. Still a slip of a thing, I see . . . but no longer a child. Very much not.'

He smiled. I smiled back.

'Your aunt?'

'In wonderful health and spirits. A marriage in the offing, would you believe? A retired admiral whom she allows to beat her at cards from time to time.'

'My good wishes to her.'

'I will be sure to convey your sentiments,' he said gravely.

And all the time our eyes held, spoke differently, of

more important things. I wondered if I had always known that those strong features had melded to a fierce sort of beauty. Known, but not appreciated – until now. The curve of his nose, the long jaw, the smudges of shadow under the high, bony cheeks . . .

'You had best hand the hound to me,' he said.

He took the puppy. A strand of my hair caught against his glove. He regarded it as it lay, silvery pale against the dark leather, before he blew at it gently so that it slid free.

'I am glad to see,' he said, very quietly, 'that you no longer wear the ugliest, most concealing cap in all England.' Then lifting one dark eyebrow as I began to fumble with hat and hairpins, said softly, 'What is that line? "A sweet disorder in the dress Kindles in clothes a wantonness"? Some poem or other . . .'

'Robert Herrick,' I said.

'Ah, yes. And something about ribbands flowing in confusion and tempestuous petticoats.'

'If my petticoats are in a turmoil it is because I have been travelling for two days.'

'And you stay in Exeter?'

'Outside. At a place called Starlings Barton. And you?'

'I have lodgings in the town. Are you travelling alone?'

'With Mrs Yelland. We visit relatives of her previous marriage.'

There was urgency in the questions. In the answers. Out of the corner of my eye I could see Mrs Yelland and Mr Bowyer coming towards us.

'You will want to know how the dog does,' he said quietly. 'I will arrange it.'

That was all.

A flurry of explanations, of introductions, of scoldings on Mrs Yelland's part because I had run off and, when she knew the circumstances, of horror at my recklessness.

'Such a happy surprise that you were here, Mr Winterborne. Goodness me, Emily, what were you thinking of to put yourself at such risk over a stray dog? Have you thanked Mr Winterborne properly for coming to your rescue? What must he think of you, acting so foolishly. I am quite shocked that you forgot yourself in this way, when you are usually so sensible.'

Sensible? I felt as though all sense, all reason had detached itself from me and I had become a different creature, with a churning whirl of emotion and sensation where my mind had previously been.

The two men were exchanging politenesses as Mrs Yelland tugged the strings of my hat straight and brushed ineffectually at the mud, blood and dog hairs that clung to my cloak.

Then it was more curtseying and bowing and a flurry of farewells.

And we parted.

I looked back as we walked to where the Bowyers' carriage waited.

Felix Winterborne stood unmoving. He nodded an acknowledgement. I half raised my hand. Then he turned and disappeared into the dark maw of the alley.

I stood at the open window of the room I had been given and looked across the gardens stretching behind Starlings Barton.

Everything was very still. It was a wide and beautiful panorama, with the distant heights of Dartmoor a purple bruise on the horizon and dusk blooming in soft blue shadows between the bushes in the gardens directly below. Half an acre, perhaps, of formal beds before it became grassland with trees and shrubs spreading away down a gentle slope. I could see the roof and chimneys of another house nestling in the dip before the land curved upwards again and folded itself into fields and rounded hills.

I had washed the dust of the journey away and changed

my dress. The family normally ate, Mrs Bowyer had informed us, at three o'clock, but they had delayed tonight because of our visit. As I was to have the honour, she had added somewhat tartly, of dining *en famille* throughout my stay, as dear Barbara had requested, she hoped I would not cause unnecessary delay by spending too long primping before I came to the dining parlour. Nor offend by rough manners at table, her frown said.

Mrs Yelland had made it plain while the Yellands were still at the Thorn Tree that I was to travel as her companion, not as her maid. 'If it is to be a reward for saving the life of young Odette, then I am sure you would wish to treat Emily as an honoured guest,' she had said lightly. It would have been churlish of Mrs Bowyer to do anything other than agree, though she had clearly since regretted her generous impulse towards me.

'I know her sly ways,' Mrs Yelland had said privately to me. 'For all her generous talk, she probably has you marked as an unpaid housemaid or nursemaid to those unruly children for the duration of your stay. Well, I will not have it. I have claimed you for my companion and that is what you shall be.' She smiled fondly at me. 'In truth, Emily, if I had ever been fortunate enough to have a daughter, I should have wished for a sensible, intelligent girl such as you. But as you are not my daughter, I shall like you very well as a companion for I shall enjoy showing you the delights of Starlings and the countryside around.'

Sensible. That word again.

Sensible, hardworking, reliable – I had always been so proud when Mrs Yelland described me so. For the six – nearly seven – years I had been at the Thorn Tree I had wished for no greater accolade.

Now such attributes seemed cold and remote. Irrelevant.

The Emily who stood at the window, gazing dreamily at the view, seemed to have become detached from the practical Emily who attended to her work with thoroughness and vigour.

This new Emily seemed to be caught up in a turmoil of emotion and sensation, aware as she never had been before of the mingled scents wafting in through the window, the beauty of the dusk-laden garden, the texture of the muslin ruffle on the sleeve of her flower-sprigged dress.

And all because of a chance encounter.

I still was not sure what had happened. No, that was wrong. I knew. My heart, my emotional inner self was fully aware of it, accepted it, even if the rational part of my mind struggled ineffectually to deny it.

Yet could it happen so? That you looked at someone and there was instant and devastating attraction? Something so profound that you felt dazzled, dizzied, *overwhelmed* by the surge of feeling? Was it merely lust?

Perhaps that was part of it – some blind animal instinct that had been roused by his bold and efficient dispatch of the two ragamuffins, by his chivalry and his undoubted handsomeness.

Part of it, but not all.

The rest was . . . was inexplicable. Some deeper affinity that could only be experienced, not explained. And I, bookish and rational creature that I thought myself to be, was bewildered to discover that I had no words to describe it.

A breeze rattled the dry wisteria leaves that twined about the window and puffed at the muslin of the drapes. There was a sharpness in the air, as if the clearness of the sky betokened frost, and I felt the prickling of gooseflesh on my arms as I pulled the casement closed and prepared to face the others.

Starlings Barton was a solid, red-brick house, not by any means overlarge and intimidating but a comfortable family home. It was still possible to see its origins as a substantial farmhouse, though Tom Bowyer's great-grandfather had converted dairies and outhouses to other uses when his assets were such that he could afford to pay other people to tend his beasts and farm his land. It was he who had turned the fields immediately about the house into a pleasure ground where his family might walk and ride without being assailed by the noise and smell of livestock.

'The house, as you may know, was built by the first Bowyer – Bouvier, as the name was then,' Mr Bowyer told me, as we strolled sedately, two by two, around the flagged paths of the formal garden the following morning. 'He had escaped from Paris after the massacre of St Bartholomew.' He shook his head. 'Sad to think that occurred almost two hundred years since and there are still persons today in France who are in danger of execution because of their religious beliefs, though one hopes the mass slaughters of innocent people will never occur again. Jean-Paul Bouvier was the only one of his family to survive at that time and then only because he had mercifully been away from home delivering a commission of jewellery. They were craftsmen – silversmiths – the Bouviers, and comfortably off.'

'It must have been a most dreadful time,' I said. 'To lose everyone and everything so horribly. How did he escape?'

'With the aid of a sympathetic Catholic friend. And Jean-Paul did not escape entirely penniless, thanks to this same friend who smuggled him back to his home by night. Though the house had been ransacked, there was a secret place in the cellar where a box containing the family's gold and jewellery was kept. Miraculously it had escaped the murderers who had taken everything else of value.'

'Oh fie, Tom,' Mrs Bowyer said, turning to pout at him. 'Such a horrid story. Pray speak of something else, for I have heard it a hundred times. And I am quite sure

Barbara must be equally tired of it, for your dear father needed no excuse to pour out all these dreary stories of his ancestors.'

'Oh, I do not mind,' said Mrs Yelland easily. 'And it may be of some interest to Emily. Perhaps you could show her the diary you have of that first Bouvier, Tom. And the translation you have made of it. I had thought I had found something similar when I first went to the Thorn Tree, but I was disappointed to find it was merely a book of receipts.'

'Oh, I am sure *Emily* will enjoy it,' said Mrs Bowyer, in a tone which dismissed me to the lowest rank of the dullest company. 'But we are family and not obliged to be polite.' She linked her hand in Mrs Yelland's arm and cried gaily, 'Come, Barbara, we shall sit over there and I will tell you of the new dressmaker I have found – perfectly up-to-the-minute in fashion . . .'

They moved away to a seat under an arch of roses that had shaken out a final late flush of yellow flowers. I stood awkwardly with Mr Bowyer. I was growing less sure that Mrs Yelland had been wise to insist that I should be treated as her companion. Mrs Bowyer clearly thought I was better suited to waiting on table than sitting at it. Every look had told me so at dinner yesterday and she looked at me often, as though waiting to pounce on any lack of nicety, any gaucheness, on my part.

I had been careful not to offend. From the first weeks at the Thorn Tree I had learned how to conduct myself from the good example set by Mrs Yelland. In recent years I had had the opportunity to witness every manner of addressing oneself to one's food from the uncouth to the genteel and had schooled myself in the correct ways of behaving. But I had not been comfortable under Mrs Bowyer's scrutiny and there were many more meals to come when I should be under her eye. I was beginning to wonder if I would have been better off helping the maids and sleeping with the servants in the attic. At least I would not have laid myself open to being unbearably patronised by Mrs Bowyer.

Yet even if I had, I might not have been any better off for it was evident that all was not well with the servants. Despite the comfort of the house itself, a general air of disorganisation was obvious to the trained eye. Little things: the fire irons in want of polish; fluffs of dust lurking under chairs; a dulling bloom on some of the furniture. Certainly I should have been greatly ashamed had the serving of dinner to guests at the Thorn Tree been so slow as it was here yesterday, with things forgotten and having to be fetched and the footman barely civil in his attitude and exchanging winks and grimaces with the pert maid when he thought himself unobserved.

'Shall we walk a little further, Emily?' Mr Bowyer said, in his courteous way. 'That is, if you would care to hear how Jean-Paul came to settle in Devonshire?'

'Sir, I should,' I said firmly. 'And to see the diary, if you would allow it.'

'I would be most happy to do so,' he said, looking pleased. 'Perhaps we might adjourn to my library later. Mrs Yelland has told me that you are something of a bookworm. I believe she has much enjoyed passing on her knowledge to someone with such a receptive mind as yourself.'

'Without her my education would have been a poor thing,' I said. 'I can never repay her for what she has done for me.'

'I am sure she seeks no reward save to know that her efforts have been so well appreciated,' he said gravely. Then, as though to put me at my ease after his wife's deprecating remarks, 'I have never been of the opinion that the female brain should be discouraged from scholarly pursuits if it is inclined to such. I have always known the satisfaction to be gained from studying for its own sake.

Why should it be different for a woman?'

He glanced sideways as he spoke, an involuntary movement, hastily controlled, towards the bench where the two women sat; his wife in her stylish dress of mustard-coloured brocaded damask with its long bodice laced with green over the stomacher and the expensive gypsy hat set at a fashionable angle over her blonde curls, and Barbara Yelland, no match for such finery in mouse-brown tabby. Yet somehow, in the mellow sunlight of the dying year, the smaller, more sober figure of the older woman seemed to exude a quiet elegance that fitted perfectly into the ambience of a garden that had a sleepy dignity of its own in this late season, whereas Abigail Bowyer struck a garish and artificial note both in her dress and in the harsh persistent chirruping of her voice.

The differences between the two ran far deeper than the superficial ones of dress and deportment, and if the disparity struck clearly upon me, I daresay Mr Bowyer observed it too, and painfully, but nothing of his thoughts showed, save, perhaps, in the overhasty ushering of me onto the end of the formal garden where three shallow stone steps gave onto the grassy area. He continued with the history of his ancestor as we walked.

'Once he arrived in England, being a prudent young man, he travelled the country for some months searching for the place where he could feel most secure and comfortable. He had a mislike of cities after his experience and decided to put his money into land. So he built himself a house exactly in the middle of the acres he had purchased. He had a fancy, you see, to be able to stand at any window and rejoice that everything he could see was his.' He pointed ahead. 'That was where he lived while the new house was built. It is the original property. Perhaps the grass is too dewy for you to walk further where we may have a better view.'

'Not at all,' I said stoutly. I was delighted to be out in

the air and away from Mrs Bowyer's grating chatter. 'I could see the chimneys from my window and wondered what it was.'

'It is the original Starlings Barton, but known as the Old House since the new one was built. It was much decayed when Jean-Paul bought it and even though repairs have been put in hand over the years, only one wing is now usable.'

'But someone lives there,' I said, noting the plume of smoke drifting from the chimney.

'An old lady with her housekeeper,' he said. 'The latest – and one would hope the last – of the many Huguenot refugees who have taken shelter under its roof. I have hopes that the policy in France will soon turn more tolerant towards those whose religion differs from the Catholic majority and the Old House will no longer be needed as a refuge. It has always been the intention of the Bowyer family, you see, to offer help as the need has arisen, to those dispossessed from their homeland.' He looked about him. 'The Bowyers have been very fortunate. Most of what they touched has turned out well. They have acquired much through their own far-sightedness. And through marriages arranged with prosperous families in the district. "Work hard and honestly, turn no deserving man from your door and preserve the land by whatever means you may." That is what Jean-Paul wrote in his diary, which I shall show you, and in the will he left. These precepts have been passed down the generations, father to son.'

'A great responsibility,' I said, feeling that some comment was needed.

'Indeed,' he said in a somewhat sad manner. I wondered if this quiet and scholarly man sometimes found his duty towards Starlings more of a burden than a blessing. But then he smiled and said cheerfully, 'We Bowyers have not always been as clever and prudent as our honourable ancestor would have wished. The matter of these mulberry trees, for example.'

'Oh, yes. The breeding of silkworms was proposed but the wrong kind of mulberry was planted. Mrs Yelland told me of it. But if this is one of the mistakes, it deserves to live for its own sake. It's very handsome.'

We paused to look up at the spreading branches, the almost heart-shaped leaves, turning brown and dry now, and many already fallen.

'To be sure. And we have an excellent harvest of fruit, too,' he said, 'so it is pleasing that so many were saved when the grounds were laid out. But come, if we walk this way you may see the Old House from a most picturesque angle. Are you at all artistic, Emily?'

'I'm afraid not, sir,' I said ruefully.

'A pity. Those of our guests who have sketched this particular view have enthused over the romantical and dramatic effect.'

I could see why.

The land fell away among trees, and the house crouched snugly against the side of the shallow, wooded valley. The building was long and narrow, the far end looking quite ruinous, with tumbled thatch and walls draped with creeper and moss. The nearer end was in good repair, the thatch replaced with stout tiles.

'On her better days, Madame Crespin tends the little garden there. She has it very pretty.'

The small area of flowers and shrubs stood out bravely in the shadow cast by the hill but for all that the scene was so picturesque, I was glad I did not have to live down there. Even on this sunny autumn day the house was cast into deep shade. In winter it would be exceedingly gloomy, with the trees cutting off what light managed to creep above the hill. Just to think of it set a prickle of goose-pimples creeping up my arms.

'The old lady is ill?' I said, for some reason not wanting

to look at the house more than necessary.

'Age and tragedy have caused her to become very frail in mind and body.'

'Has she no family?'

'Dead, now. Or gone abroad.' He sighed. 'I'm afraid she will end her days a stranger in a strange land, with no kin of her own to tend her. One does what one can, but it is little enough set against the losses she has suffered.'

A mood of melancholy seemed to have descended upon us. It was almost as if the shadows that hung over the house had crept out to embrace us with their dank gloom.

I was quite glad when Mr Bowyer suggested that we retrace our steps.

I should have been perfectly happy if I had been left to my own devices at Starlings. The gardens were a delight and Mr Bowyer's library a positive treasure house. And I had, for the first time in my life, the leisure to enjoy everything to the full. But the first two days promised to be the pattern for the rest of the week, with all the daylight hours occupied with walks or drives to visit old acquaintances of Mrs Yelland's, and the evenings set aside for entertaining other guests who had been invited for supper. Which left little time to browse along the library shelves or just sit quietly in the garden and relish the peace and quiet which was such a contrast to the constant noise and bustle of the Thorn Tree.

Perhaps it was as well.

When I did have a few moments to myself from the novel and sometimes daunting experience of playing companion to Mrs Yelland my thoughts had a tendency to drift into ridiculous daydreams which centred on Felix Winterborne. With a consequence that I must spend a considerable time later feeling guilty and ashamed, because I had no right to such thoughts. I was to marry Luke, my dear friend, and I told myself time and again that I had no business to be attracted to anyone else – leave alone someone of whom I knew practically nothing, *and* had once suspected of the most shocking crime.

The recollection of the moment when I had discovered that gold and ruby earbob at the Thorn Tree came back to me with full force. I could see it as clearly as if it lay in my hand now, even though I had rid myself of it in Brimston Wood within days of discovering it. I had dug a hole with a stick among the leaf mould, thrown it in and heaped earth over it before I stamped it down and covered the place with bits of twig.

To my knowledge there had never been any enquiry over it. I had been back in the kitchen working when Felix Winterborne came a second time but Cass would have relayed to all and sundry such an interesting piece of news as a lost earring, however casually he might have mentioned it.

Had I been wrong? Had my imagination been fired too easily? I had felt so certain in my assumption then. But time had blunted that certainty. And now I found myself wanting desperately not to believe it. Surely a man of such sensitivity that he could respond to the distress of a stray puppy would not deliberately involve himself with wreaking terror on his fellow kind. And in any case, how could any of this possibly be relevant to me?

Our paths had crossed briefly. There was no reason to suppose I should see him again. Oh certainly, he had said he would arrange something of the sort, but he had probably spoken without thought. Besides, he could be married with a wife waiting for him at home in Bath, or at his lodgings in Exeter. He might be the thorough scoundrel I supposed him to be, in which case it was entirely for the best that I did not clap eyes on him again.

Oh, but I wanted to! With all my heart and soul I wanted to.

And, knowing that my deepest, most secret self

nurtured the very betrayal of Luke that my mind informed me was both cruel and unworthy was the worst torment of all.

Mrs Yelland blossomed at Starlings Barton. There was no other word for it. I began to see a side to her that I had never expected: that of a sociable and lively woman, with laughter in her green eyes and a spring in her step.

At the Thorn Tree she moved briskly through the day with a composed and watchful air, a woman with her hand firmly on the reins, whose leisure time was spent quietly with her books. Occasionally the vicar or his wife called and took tea with her, usually when some good cause was in need of subscriptions from charitable persons. She was always generous, though she attended church infrequently.

'I would sooner say my prayers in private rather than in the company of gossips and those who pretend piety but are really more interested in what fashions one wears than in the whiteness of one's soul,' she once excused herself tartly.

But perhaps there was another reason, in that she wanted no opportunity to mingle with those who might make demands on her by seeking her friendship.

Though I had never thought much of it before, assuming, I suppose, that her busy life left her with no inclination to be sociable, it came to me now that she had made no effort whatsoever to make friends in the years I had known her. Master Harry might continue to entertain his own friends to supper in the taproom as he had always done, but Mrs Yelland, though always coolly and correctly civil when she met these friends of her husband's, issued no invitations to her parlour. Nor through them, to their wives.

It was as if she had deliberately decided to keep herself as self-contained and solitary as it was possible to be when she was not about the business of playing her public role as innkeeper's wife. And even in the privacy of their bedchamber, I doubted that Harry Yelland had ever witnessed his wife so smiling and light-hearted.

It was not only the presence of Tom Bowyer that caused the alteration in her. Not by any means. It was the house itself.

On the day we arrived she had stepped down from the carriage, then stood quite still on the gravelled drive, her hand flying to her throat as though to hold back a barely containable emotion.

'Is it not the most beautiful house, Emily?' she had breathed, her voice catching. 'I had nearly forgot – no, tried not to remember – how very much I once loved it.'

And still did. It was clear in every warm glance as she entered any room, as though to imprint its likeness on her memory. In the way she ran her fingers, gentle and possessive, across a piece of furniture or touched the drape of a curtain, saying by way of excuse, 'This blue calamanco has worn well. I remember how pleased Paul and I were when we saw it hung.' Or, 'This oak chair belongs to Jean-Paul's time. It was the first piece of furniture he bought in England, along with that carved chest . . .'

I saw, too, how the slackness of the servants and the unruliness of the two children affected her. Every time the children came screeching and sliding down the hall or bounced a ball down the stairs or flung a door wide so that it smashed back against the wall, her nostrils flared and her voice would sharpen as she said, 'Really, Abigail, those children will damage themselves if you allow such hoydenish behaviour.' Though I think she feared more for damage to the plasterwork and the ornaments than for the children.

I could see she itched to take everything in hand. To set the servants in order and give the impudent footman a piece of her mind. To take a stand over the children and their harassed new nurse.

'They are well on the way to being ruined,' she said, sighing. 'Their mother cannot see it, silly woman. Whenever their father attempts to discipline them, they run to her – and what does she do but give them sweetmeats and countermand his orders? It is to be hoped that young Tom is sent off to a good school soon, for the longer he remains under his mother's influence, the more he eggs Odette on to mischief. And he is a good boy at heart. Just woefully managed.'

Privately, though I liked Mr Bowyer, I thought him equally to blame for not asserting himself, though I owned this was difficult when his wife was such a spoiled, headstrong woman. She being the only child of doting parents herself, it was little wonder she had no judgement about her own children.

'Mr and Mrs Bowyer do seem very opposite characters,' I ventured.

'Hah! He never should have married her,' Mrs Yelland said. Then sighed, 'But she is an only child and something of an heiress. My late husband and her father were great friends and arranged the match, seeing it as very advantageous to both sides. She will inherit the whole of her father's estate near Crediton, you see, when he dies. And, of course, she is very pretty... and Tom was always a dutiful son to his father. They were new married when I came here and happy enough at first...' Her voice fell away. She shrugged. 'Well, no matter, even if I had been here and had spoken against the match, my opinions would not have been taken into account.' Then, lightly, 'Lord, how solemn we get. Come, Emily, we must get ready to go out a-visiting.'

So that was how it had been. I could set the rest in place. The stepmother who was but a year or two older than her stepson. Two families living under one roof and the drawing together of two people with similar interests... Whether it had been a long, slow dawning of affection or a sharper, more intense realisation, I did not know. But Barbara Bowyer must have understood how untenable and inherently difficult was her position once she was widowed – dangerous too, in the temptations it offered. So she had taken the most honourable and drastic action that circumstances allowed.

She had encouraged Harry Yelland. Preferring, perhaps, to be independent of any charity that might have been proferred by the Bowyers, even if it meant marrying a man she did not love. Or did not even admire.

She had left the house she loved, the man she loved, taking nothing but the pieces of furniture she had brought to the house from her parents' home.

Now she was returned, with all responsibility temporarily cast aside. Back in the house she adored, close to the man she loved.

Perhaps it was as well that we only stayed a week.

I awoke on the morning of the third day feeling distinctly out of sorts. My throat was sore, my head ached and my normally excellent appetite deserted me completely when I caught the waft of the beefsteak set before Mr Bowyer at breakfast.

Fortunately, my lack of appetite was not noticed. A piece of news had been brought to Mr Bowyer that set everyone exclaiming and tut-tutting indignantly – and that caused me to abandon the one piece of toast that I was trying to force down.

Not half a mile from here, just after midnight on the Exeter road, a most outrageous and bold robbery had been committed by a masked man who had relieved a Mr Timothy Jenkins of several hundred guineas won earlier at cards at a private gambling party in the town. What is more, to avoid any threat of pursuit, the armed villain had forced Mr Jenkins to strip naked and taken away his clothes and his horse, though the beast had been released later. It was the horse returning riderless to its stable in the small hours that set off the alarm. Mr Jenkins had been found by his servants wandering in a daze in a stubble field.

'No doubt drunk as maybe,' Mr Bowyer said drily, 'for he is neither a sober man nor one I should care to invite to my own home for all that he has connections through his mother to the Duke of Devonshire. However, that is not the point. He might be an uncouth braggart, but he is not a hardened criminal. Which the perpetrator of the crime evidently is. And the thought of such a dangerous man on the loose around our peaceful lanes makes my blood run cold.'

'And it happened not half a mile from here!' Mrs Bowyer fluttered. 'Oh, he could be lurking in the gardens at this minute . . .'

'I think that hardly likely,' Mrs Yelland said calmly. 'He has had all the hours of darkness to make his escape. No doubt he is fast asleep in his bandit's lair in the stews of Exeter and well-pleased with his night's work.'

Mr Bowyer nodded agreement. 'I should think it altogether possible that Jenkins was followed from Exeter.'

'The robber probably knew that he carried a considerable sum of money,' said Mrs Yelland.

'Quite. Information of that sort might always be bought from a servant or other such accomplice.'

Mrs Yelland laughed. 'Goodness me, we shall have solved the crime before we have finished breakfast.'

'Pray do not laugh so, Barbara,' Mrs Bowyer cried. 'I do not find it in the least amusing. And I insist, Tom, that you send the menservants to scour the grounds before any of us sets foot outdoors. As to driving to Exeter this morning, as we proposed to do, I fear that we cannot possibly contemplate such a journey now. Why, my nerves would not stand to pass the spot where the crime occurred.'

'As you wish, my dear,' Mr Bowyer said.

'In fact, I think I must lie down,' she said. 'I have gone quite faint from the shock. Tom, Barbara, if you would each give me an arm to the parlour I think I might manage to reach the sofa . . .'

She closed her eyes dramatically, though her colour stayed determinedly rosy. As Mr Bowyer and Mrs Yelland bore her off into the adjoining parlour she kept giving little gasps so as to emphasise the grevious state into which she had been plunged.

But I was not amused, as I would normally have been, by this display of histrionics. My mouth had gone dry and not only from the cold in the head that was brewing. I swallowed the dish of green tea and hastily poured myself another. Then tried to compose myself.

Coincidence, surely. I must not, *must not* jump to conclusions. He was in Exeter, true. So were hundreds – thousands – of other people. Good people, wicked people; plenty of rogues among them. Not him. Not him . . .

'Mrs Yelland will sit with my wife until she feels better,' Mr Bowyer said, returning to tackle the remnants of his cooling beefsteak. 'I do apologise that we shall have to postpone the outing to Exeter. I know you were looking forward to it. Perhaps tomorrow . . .'

'Think no more of it,' I said, with some relief for I did not think that I should have much energy for sightseeing. 'I'll be just as happy to sit and read. With your permission, sir, I'll choose a book from the library.'

'Of course, of course.'

'Then if you will excuse me, sir, I'll go to the library straight away. Then I shall not have the need to interrupt you should you be working there later on.'

I snatched almost the first book I looked at and went back to my room, catching the maid flicking a duster round the furniture in a desultory manner. I sent her off and sat myself in the chair by the window, the book unopened in my lap.

I wished my mind would focus properly, but it seemed woolly and disorientated this morning, with no ability at all to reason and rationalise. However I tried, I could not stop it from throwing up lurid pictures of Felix Winterborne lying in wait as the drunken man on the horse came by. Of the glint of those cool, greeny-grey eyes through the slits in a black mask as he surveyed his naked, shivering victim, snatched away his horse... Wicked eyes. Dangerous eyes. Dangerous to me...

A tap on the door made me start. I had drifted to a half-doze.

'Are you there, Emily?' Mrs Yelland's voice.

'Come in.' I hastily stood up, pinned a bright smile to my face.

'Ah, there you are. I have left Abigail to her maid. I could not stand her hypochondria another moment. Come, get stout shoes and your shawl for there is a breeze this morning. We will take ourselves off for a walk.' She laughed. 'If we meet a highwayman, we shall hope he is chivalrous to ladies, though I think the sight of the gardeners examining every bush will have sent him packing... I think we shall take the longer walk around the boundaries of the property, which is always too far for Abigail's legs. I never knew such a person for having aching legs when faced with the prospect of more than five minutes of walking.'

I thought to say that I was not too enamoured of a long walk myself this morning, but she looked so brimming with vitality that I did not wish to disappoint her. Besides, the fresh air would perhaps blow away this incipient head cold and clear my fuzzy brain.

We stepped out briskly, though I soon found myself unusually breathless and making excuses to pause and admire the view. I had not been as far as the western boundary where the land rose to a small hill, with a seat conveniently placed. I was grateful to be allowed to sit for a moment or two while Mrs Yelland pointed out various landmarks, though the breeze felt quite keen and even when I drew the shawl tightly about my shoulders I could not get properly warm.

'You see, there is Exeter two miles off... and the stretch of road on which the crime of exposing Mr Timothy Jenkins to the elements took place. Goodness me, he sounds such an unpleasant person – Tom says he is boorish and rough-mannered in the extreme – that I think the story of his humiliation will become an amusing talking piece at many a dinner table this winter.'

'The house looks well from this angle,' I put in hastily, to distract my own thoughts from the unpleasant incident as much as hers.

'Indeed it does,' she said. 'And with all the improvements that have been put in hand over the years I am sure old Jean-Paul would be proud to see how his descendants have cared for it.' She shaded her eyes with her hand. 'I do believe we have a visitor. See, there is a man on a horse riding up the drive. I did not think we expected visitors today, though I cannot make out who it is. Probably someone to see Tom.' She turned her head as her eye was caught by a pair of figures plodding slowly up the path from the Old House. 'And there is Madame Crespin taking the air with her housekeeper. Poor old soul. I am surprised she still clings to life. She was already a poor thing when I lived here, though her wits were then not entirely addled. But now, Tom says, she is nothing but skin and bone and has quite lost the ability to speak. Tom does not think her housekeeper is a very kind woman and does her duty grudgingly... Still, it is not our place to interfere. There is a daughter living abroad who pays her keep. Shall we walk that way back and pass the time of day with the poor soul?'

I stood up and followed her down the hill, hardly hearing – or caring – about the old woman.

I knew who the visitor was. It was more a sixth sense than the sharpness of my eyes that recognised the man in the blue coat seated straight and easy on the brown horse, some instinct that set my heart leaping and my blood coursing so fast that I could feel the throb of it even in my fingertips.

How could I have felt cold a moment ago? My skin burned fiery now. He was here, as he had promised. Nothing mattered in the world but that I should see him again. I wanted to go straight away to the house, to be there indoors and waiting when he arrived.

But Mrs Yelland was striding determinedly in the opposite direction, set on intercepting the old French woman.

I followed after her, all the time glancing towards the house and imagining him dismounting, walking to the front door, being admitted . . .

It seemed a very long walk down the hill on legs that grew increasingly heavy and had a curious tendency to wobble. When I did reach level ground it seemed extra soft beneath my shoes, making my tread uncertain. But with an effort I caught up with Mrs Yelland as she reached the old Frenchwoman. She was very bent and crooked of back, with a mass of fuzzy grey hair peeping from under a high-crowned hat. She leaned heavily upon the arm of a somewhat squat woman with a heavy, square-jawed face. They were both dressed entirely in ancient black garments, layer upon layer flapping in the wind – like two black crows with moulting feathers, I thought. Which struck me as wildly funny, so that I had to turn my face aside to smother a laugh.

. . . And saw him coming down the steps from the formal garden with Mr Bowyer.

I blinked. How strange, I seemed to have some

difficulty in seeing them properly. Though the sun still shone and the white clouds scudded briskly across a blue sky there was a strange sort of greyness muting the colours, the outlines of the garden . . .

'Ah, Madame Crespin!' Mrs Yelland cried. 'How good to see you out and about. Do you remember who I am? I was Mrs Bowyer and lived here once.'

I tore my eyes away from Felix, tried to concentrate on what was happening nearer at hand.

The old lady's face was heavily wrinkled, her bluish lips working soundlessly at toothless gums as she stared with rheumy, uncomprehending eyes at Mrs Yelland. Then at me.

'Madame remembers nothing now,' her companion said gruffly.

'Ah, Mrs Kemp, is it not?'

The woman nodded.

'It is very sad that she has become so . . . so distracted,' said Mrs Yelland.

'Better that she lives without her wits than spending the day forever bemoaning her lot,' Mrs Kemp said, with a harsh laugh. 'At least it's a lot more peaceful. For her and for me.'

'Is that so?' Mrs Yelland frowned. 'I am sure, however, you do your best—'

Whatever she was to say next was lost for ever.

With a wild cry, the old woman suddenly leapt at me.

I staggered back as a pair of clawing hands reached for my face.

What was it I had heard? That the old woman never spoke? She was certainly speaking now. Gabbling loudly in a language I did not understand and, strangely, with tears pouring down her face. Sobbing out the words, her fingers reaching, touching my cheek, dry and cool. Little bony bird claws that did not scratch but seemed infinitely tender and gentle as they stroked and petted.

And not frightening. Not frightening at all.

Astonishment had frozen Mrs Kemp and Mrs Yelland where they stood. Now they too leapt forward, took the old woman's arms and dragged her back.

'No!' I cried. 'She means no harm! She didn't hurt me. Please, let her go . . .'

'Great heaven! What has happened?'

Now the men came running over the grass – Mr Bowyer, Felix Winterborne, their figures wavering in the strange aqueous light that had taken over the garden. That was slipping and sliding round me like watery fog.

Stop! Stop! I'm not hurt. She meant no harm. Don't upset her!

The words were there in my head and I thought that I spoke them aloud. But nobody seemed to take any notice and I really didn't care, for I felt so strange and disembodied. And dreadfully sick to my stomach.

The trees, the grass, the sky spun about me, turned black. I had one instant of clarity when I saw Felix's face loom above me.

Then I fell into a dead faint in his arms.

Chapter Five

I was carried inside by Felix Winterborne and laid upon the sofa in the parlour. That much I know because I was later told of it. I swam back to consciousness to the acrid waft of the feathers that had been burned under my nose, though it was still too much of an effort to open my eyes.

A voice. *His* voice. Deep, anxious. 'She is still very white.'

'Such an unfortunate incident!' Mr Bowyer now.

'That madwoman!' Mrs Bowyer. 'I have said before she should not be allowed to wander at liberty!'

'It is so unlike Emily to be overset by such a thing. She is not at all given to vapours.' Mrs Yelland's hand cool against my forehead. I heard the catch of her breath. 'Dear God, she is burning hot. There was I marching her round the grounds and she said not a word about feeling ill! Perhaps she had best be taken up to her bed.'

Then I whirled away again on a tide of confusion with the vaguest impression of being lifted and carried – faces looming and fading. When I came to properly it was to the bliss of cool sheets and a strong smell of lavender.

'Thank heaven,' said Mrs Yelland, tenderly wiping my face with the lavender-water-soaked cloth. 'I was beginning to wonder what next to do to bring you out of your faint. Silly girl! Why did you not tell me that you were in no state to go out walking?'

'It's nothing,' I whispered. 'A sore throat . . . I'm sickening for a cold in the head I think.'

'I hope that is all,' she said, looking worried. 'Well, I shall make up a tisane for you and see if that will reduce the fever.'

'Oh, Mrs Yelland, whatever must Mr Bowyer and Mr Winterborne think of me?' I said, distressed as full memory returned. 'To cause such a to-do. I'm so sorry . . . But perhaps when I've had a rest I'll be able to get up.'

'You will do no such thing,' she said sternly. 'You will stay in bed until the fever has abated.'

Ill as I felt, the wash of disappointment was very keen.

'Did . . . did Mr Winterborne say how the puppy was? The one he rescued?' I managed weakly. 'I do so hope it lived.'

Tell me of the man who had saved him, my heart cried. *Let me at least hear how he is, how he does*.

'Goodness me, bothering your head over a stray dog,' she scolded, then relented and patted my hand. 'It so happens Mr Winterborne made a special journey to tell you that it is recovering from its injuries. Was that not kind of him?'

'Please . . . please thank him for me.'

'Most certainly.'

'And my apologies to . . . to everyone for the upset I've caused.'

She chuckled. 'I fear you have put Abigail's nose severely out of joint. The silly creature quite believes that swooning is her prerogative. Though it is my opinion that in her whole life she has been far too robust ever to have genuinely experienced such a thing.'

I managed a shaky smile.

'And the old lady?'

'Mr Bowyer is exceedingly concerned and embarrassed about what happened,' she said gravely. 'He has given orders to the Kemp woman that Madame Crespin is not in future to be allowed beyond the garden of the Old House.'

'I can't recall it too well,' I said. 'But I don't think she meant to hurt me.' I put my hand to my cheek, frowning. 'She didn't scratch or hit me.'

'She has never shown any inclination to violence previously. Indeed, when I knew her and she still had lucid moments, she was an exceedingly timid woman. I do not have any French, unfortunately, but my husband often tried to engage her in conversation. When she could be persuaded to speak, he said she mostly spoke harmless nonsense.' She shrugged. 'Still, one cannot take risks with someone whose wits are seriously addled. Abigail, of course, would have her put away in some Bedlam—'

'Oh, no!'

'Yes, indeed. Though I think it too a harsh solution myself, I can in this instance understand her fear for the children. However, Tom, being of a kindlier nature and feeling responsible for his tenant, is to write to the daughter and acquaint her with the circumstances. It is likely to be months, though, before any communication will be received from her for her husband is a sugar planter and she lives on some tropic island near the Americas.'

I shivered. The sheets that had felt so pleasantly cool a few minutes since now struck icy against my skin.

'I could wish for some of that tropic sun at this minute,' I said, barely able to keep my teeth from chattering.

Mrs Yelland sprang to her feet.

'I shall order hot bricks to be brought. And see to that tisane.'

'Such a t-trouble for you. I'm so sorry... s-spoiling your holiday.'

'Nonsense! How can you help being indisposed? Now lie back and try to rest. There is nothing like a good sleep for restoring the body to good health. I daresay by tomorrow you will be much recovered.'

I was not. I was, instead, covered from head to toe with a bright red rash. I could hardly swallow for the soreness of my throat, my head throbbed and the fever was worse.

The doctor was sent for, a rotund little man, who set the grey curls of his periwig bouncing as he nodded enthusiastically over my prostrate form.

'As clear a case of the scarlatina simplex or the scarlet fever as I ever did see.'

There was a squeal from the doorway, where Mrs Bowyer hovered holding a pomander to her pretty nose.

'Oh, my poor children,' she shrilled. 'She has brought infection to my house. Whatever shall I do?'

'Nothing, madam,' said the doctor brightly. 'Just wait and see if the children are to take it. They may or they may not. It is all in the ordinance of a higher intelligence than ours. It is my experience that the infection takes three, possibly five days to make its appearance once a person has been subjected to the offending miasmic humours. You will know within the week whether anyone else in the house is to fall victim. In the meantime I would advise the children be kept in isolation, on a low diet, with a minimum of exercise, so that their system does not become at all overstrained and weakened.' He beamed at Mrs Bowyer. 'As few people as possible in and out of the sickroom would also be advisable in order to lessen the risk of the infection spreading.'

With a look of horror, Mrs Bowyer backed through the door and fled.

The doctor turned back to me and patted my hand in a reassuring manner.

'The disease will have to run its course, but we shall soon have you out and about again. I shall make up a cooling draught to bring down the fever and provide an infusion of rose leaves and cayenne vinegar with which you must gargle every four hours. This will be most effective for soothing the hectic state of the mucous membranes.'

He took a few steps away from the bed to where Mrs

Yelland waited anxiously. They spoke together in low voices. His was much subdued and without the hearty tone he had used to me or to Mrs Bowyer. The snatches I heard made little sense to my sluggish brain.

'... scarlatina maligna rather than the simplex ... glands much swollen, the head pains ...'

'... she has no family to summon ...'

'... tomorrow we shall try a blister if she comes through ...'

'*If?* So bad? Great heaven ...'

I was too weary to stay awake any longer.

Sleep. Not the refreshing slumber I was used to. Lurid nightmarish figures loomed and fretted behind my lids whenever I closed them. A highwayman with Mr Bowyer's face galloped on a giant horse that bounded over high, high hedges as though it had winged feet ... Luke called to me across a wide river, boiling with brown flood water, 'Danger! Go back! Danger!' ... A flock of black crows burst through the bulging walls of the room. They dug their claws into my scalp, sunk their sharp beaks into my neck. I tried to scream for Felix who was walking by with Miss Edgar. But she said, 'Take no notice. She is a madwoman and must be sent to the coal cellar.' And Felix turned his back, uncaring that the crows were killing me. 'I cannot arrange anything, after all ...'

Then, mercifully, blackness. A deep, deep void into which I slipped, floating, floating ... at peace ...

'Emily? Emily?' Mrs Yelland's voice was calling from a long way off.

Reluctantly I began to open my eyes.

'Too bright.' My mouth was dry. It felt as though my lips were splitting into cracks as I formed the words. Why could she not put out that dazzling light? 'Too bright ...'

'It is just the candle, my dear.' A gentle hand stroking my hair. 'I will move it away. There. Is that better?'

'Sleep ... must sleep ...'

Another voice. Unfamiliar. Did I remember a doctor being called? Long ago. 'I think we are over the worst. The fever is abating . . .'

The next time I woke the room was no longer the whirling, distorted place of my nightmares. Early morning light. Clear and pale. A pleasant little room, but strange to my eyes because it was not my own bedchamber at the inn. And why was Mrs Yelland sitting dozing in a chair by my bed, fully dressed but with her hair in the long plait as she dressed it at night?

Then I remembered. Of course. I was at Starlings Barton. I must have been quite ill for Mrs Yelland to have sat up with me.

She woke suddenly as I stirred in the bed, blinking the sleep from her eyes. An unguarded moment. A moment when I witnessed how drawn and strained her face had become, all its healthy plumpness seemingly fallen away. There were dark shadows under her eyes and a mesh of crepey wrinkles seemed to have sprung up around the sockets. As though overnight she had aged ten years.

Then her face lit up and the impression – the illusion – was gone. She was herself again, whispering, 'Oh, my dear child, you are back. Thank God.' She took up my hands and held them tightly. 'I thought . . . I thought you were lost to us.'

To my surprise her eyes were bright with tears.

'Was . . . was I so very bad in the night?' My voice was a frail croak.

She gave a shaky laugh. 'Indeed you were. But not just one night, Emily. You have been in a delirium for three days and nights and there were moments when we quite despaired of your life.'

I tried to take in this shocking news.

'Three? Then . . . then the week is gone . . . and we travel home tomorrow –' I broke off, wincing. 'Ouch . . . my neck, when I move . . . so sore.' She released my hands and I touched the tender spot, realising as I did so that there was an unaccustomed nakedness around my neck.

Alarm must have shown on my face, for Mrs Yelland said soothingly, 'The canvas pouch you were wearing is safe here on the bed table. I thought it advisable to remove it as Dr Lodge felt it necessary to apply a blister to draw out the inflammation in your throat. As to going home, my dear, it will be some weeks before you are fit to travel. The good doctor – and I have grown to have great faith in his dedication and good sense – tells me that once the rash has gone the skin will peel away. This takes some time and the condition cannot be hurried. Until you are free of all evidence of the infection you must remain quietly indoors for fear of complications.'

'But they expect us—'

'I have sent word to Mr Yelland. They will have to manage without me for a little while longer, for I could not possibly leave until I am sure you are properly on the road to recovery.' She released my hands and smiled. 'Now, no more questions or you will tire yourself out and undo all Dr Lodge's good work. I shall plump up your pillows and make you comfortable, then I will fetch you a dish of the beef tea that I ordered to be got ready against the time you were awake.'

'You're very kind. I am so sorry that I have caused such upset . . . spoiling everything for you.'

Unexpectedly she bent and kissed my forehead. 'My dear girl,' she said softly, 'you must not blame yourself. If anyone is to blame it is me, for allowing my better judgement to be overruled.'

I struggled to comprehend. 'I . . . I don't understand.'

She stepped back from the bed, smoothed down her dress, said lightly, 'Why, we would not have come here at all had I not decided to . . . to indulge myself. And you might not have picked up the infection, which I do believe – and the doctor agrees – you might have got from that wretched child on the coach. But there it is and regrets get us nowhere. We must look forward, not back, and learn from our mistakes.' Her bright smile did not quite reach her eyes. 'At least my punishment is less harsh than I thought it was to be, for you did not succumb to the fever. If you had been lost . . . well, I should never have forgiven myself. But it seems I have been given a second chance. And I know now, for I have had a great deal of time to think about it during the long night hours, that self-indulgence always bears the possibility of unforeseen consequences. I shall not allow myself to be so foolish again.' She was already turning from me, walking in her brisk way to the door. So I was not quite sure that I heard her say, very softly, 'Though God alone knows the cost,' before the door closed behind her and I sank back to sleep.

The house was very quiet. Mrs Bowyer, I learned, had fled with her children to her parents' house near Crediton.

'To no avail, the silly goose,' said Mrs Yelland, 'for word has just come that Odette has taken the scarlet fever, though mildly, and young Thomas is believed to be sickening. So now she has caused the infection to spread to another household, though her husband warned her there was little point in running away.' She shrugged and said in the old mocking way, 'But she had a fit of the hysterics and in the end he was obliged to let her go.'

'Mr Bowyer is still here, then?'

'He will leave for Crediton this afternoon,' she said. 'Naturally, he is very worried about his children. Had Abigail not been so silly, there would have been no need for him to go rushing off. And the children would have the advantage of being physicked by Dr Lodge and nursed in their own home. But that is not my business. Mine is to see you better and to return as soon as I can to my duties elsewhere.'

Somewhere in the last days the light-hearted, carefree – young – Barbara Yelland had disappeared. Mrs Harry Yelland of the Thorn Tree was firmly in control. Perhaps a little less brisk than usual for she had sat up most of the three nights with me and was in need of sleep, but her straight back, the determined set of her chin, the cool and impersonal manner of speaking, informed me that the carapace of duty and responsibility was firmly back in place.

'And what of Starlings? Have any of the servants become ill?'

'Mercifully, so far, only one of the kitchen maids, though she is not too ill and is taking great pleasure from being confined to her bed and being waited on by the parlour maid, Jane. Jane, apparently, suffered the disease in her childhood and is not like to catch it again. She has been helping out in here as well and proved herself quite useful under proper supervision. Now let me tidy you up. Mr Bowyer wishes to see you before he leaves.'

He came in bearing an extravagant basket of fruit.

'They have just been delivered from Exeter,' he said, 'with Mr Winterborne's compliments. He has sent each day for news of you, being greatly concerned for your recovery, as we all have been.'

'Look at all this, Emily,' Mrs Yelland exclaimed. 'Peaches and apricots and a pineapple, as well as pears and grapes. You are thoroughly spoiled, my dear.'

'It's . . . it's very kind of him,' I said weakly, wondering if the flush of heat I felt in my face was visible through the fading rash.

'It is indeed,' she said warmly.

'He seems a shrewd young man,' said Mr Bowyer, settling himself on the chair beside the bed. 'He tells me he has acquired a piece of land near Southernhay, not far from the cathedral, and is set upon building a terrace of genteel houses there. Apparently he has completed a similar scheme in Bath and it has proved so profitable that he decided to look further afield. He had heard that Exeter was a considerably thriving town due to the manufacturing of serges and the preponderance of wealthy merchants and gentry living here, and came to investigate the possibilities of profit for himself.' He shook his head. 'But I digress, Emily, and I do not wish to tire you with too much talking. I came specifically to tender my apologies for the most unfortunate incident that occurred with Madame Crespin.'

It was not tiring me the least to hear of Felix, but I could not say that. Instead, I murmured, 'Please don't worry about it, sir. She did me no harm.'

'Which was fortunate. However, I assure you I have taken steps to prevent any recurrence. Mrs Kemp has promised to keep her confined to the gardens of the Old House in future. So as long as you remain here, my dear, you will not be troubled by her any further.'

'It seems hard on the poor old soul,' I murmured. 'If I'd not been sickening for the fever . . .'

'We cannot escape the fact that she flew at you in some sort of a tantrum,' he said firmly. 'And she is still my tenant so I must bear the responsibility for her conduct. But I have made it clear in my letter to her daughter that the Old House is no longer a suitable place for her mother to live.'

'But . . . but where would she go if she has no other family?'

He shook his head. 'That is for her daughter to decide. I regret having to make such a decision, but I could not possibly risk any injury to my children.'

'Of course you could not,' Mrs Yelland said sharply. 'And you should not be worrying your head about her, Emily, or you will become feverish again. Now, Tom, say your piece, for I can see that our invalid is becoming tired.'

He looked at her. He did not smile and nor did she.

Their glances met across the width of the bed, lingered, broke away. She turned her head and stared fixedly out of the window. He sighed. His eyes were very sad, as he rose to his feet and said courteously to me, 'I wish you to know, Emily, that you are more than welcome to stay here at Starlings until you are fully recovered. I am anxious about my children, so I must be on my way to Crediton and it is quite likely, in the circumstances, that I shall be away for some time. However, while you convalesce, pray use the library, the parlour or the gardens as you wish.'

'Thank you, sir. I'm very grateful.'

I don't think he heard me. He looked again to Mrs Yelland. She brought her attention back from the window and accompanied him to the door.

'This is goodbye, then, Barbara,' he said softly.

He took her hand and raised it to his lips, as I had seen him do that time at the Thorn Tree.

'Yes, Tom,' she said.

'And you will not change your mind and visit us again?'

'I think not. It is for the best. For all of us.'

For a second her free hand came up as though to touch his cheek. Then she let it drop again. Their eyes met and held. He released her hand, took a pace back, bowed. And was gone, leaving her to close the door softly after him.

I made a steady recovery. Dr Lodge visited me every day for a week before he pronounced that I might get up and sit, well wrapped, in a chair.

'But for no more than an hour today, and it is important you do not sit in a draught. You are fortunate, so far, that no complications have arisen, but you must immediately send to me should you experience pains in your joints or your ears, or a return of the sore throat. Continue to apply the hartshorn and turpentine embrocation to the chest and take the aperient powders every other morning. Good morning, ladies. I shall discontinue my daily visits and will call again in a week's time.'

Though I felt so much better, I found myself weak as a kitten when I took the few steps to the chair that had been set by the fire. But my strength slowly came back and in a few days more I was taking walks about the room and becoming able to concentrate on the book which I had taken so summarily from Mr Bowyer's library, or in a little light sewing to alleviate the boredom of the long days. Though the fine weather had disappeared as dank and dismal November set in, I was longing to feel fresh air on my face. On the morning I was allowed to dress for the first time, Mrs Yelland reminded me, sternly, that though I might now think of going downstairs for a little while, I was forbidden to go outside.

'I know, I know,' I said, sighing at my reflection in the glass. 'In any case, I would probably frighten the birds looking as I do. I hope my skin leaves off this ugly peeling soon, for I look as though I have draped myself in a lace curtain of a very peculiar pattern.'

She smiled. 'Be patient. Nature cannot be rushed. And do not stand there in your petticoats or you will get a chill. Here, let me help you.'

When I was dressed and cocooned in shawls to her satisfaction we made our way slowly downstairs to sit by the good fire that blazed in the parlour hearth. When I had recovered my breath from what seemed a very long walk, I looked about with pleasure at the comfortable parlour. Even this little change of scene made for a diversion after being cooped up in one small room for so long.

She passed me the sewing we had set ourselves to do. In Mrs Bowyer's absence she had made an inspection of the linen cupboard and found much of it in need of attention. 'I do not think Abigail even knows where the linen is kept for I cannot think that she has bothered to look in there or roused the maids to attend to repairs since I left. At least I might make myself useful in darning and patching while I am here. And perhaps you might help, Emily, as and when you feel able to without tiring yourself.'

We sat companionably chatting, thoroughly aware of the cosiness of the parlour each time we glanced at the windows to see fine drizzle blurring the glass and no view at all because of a heavy fog that gave no more than a few yards' visibility. Mrs Yelland was fretting a little at the weather.

'The roads will become quagmires if this rain keeps up. And I know it is not fair on my husband to stay away longer than needs be, though I shall so hate to leave you when you are not yet fit to travel, yet go I must.'

'What harm can I come to now?' I said. 'Master Harry needs you at the Thorn Tree more than I do. I promise to follow Dr Lodge's instructions to the letter. Not that he recommends anything more now than that I have plenty of rest and eat little and often and drink the horrible revitalising physic he left yesterday.'

She smiled. 'True... Well, perhaps I might arrange to catch the flying machine from Exeter to Bristol the day after tomorrow... Oh, and while I think of it, I have a little something for you that I fancied to make from a scrap of velvet I had by me.' She delved into her sewing basket and pressed a small black pouch into my hand, saying carelessly, 'If you think it suitable, pray use it for your mementoes instead of that somewhat battered affair you have hung around your neck.'

'Oh, but it is beautiful!'

I was very touched. Mrs Yelland's skill with the needle was far greater than mine, but she still must have spent many patient hours sewing it so finely. It was lined with silk and lightly padded. On the front she had worked an embroidery of coloured flowers and my entwined initials. It hung on a fine silver chain.

'The chain is an old one that I never use,' she said with a dismissive wave of her hand. 'You may as well have it, rather than let it hide away at the bottom of my jewellery box. Am I forgiven, then, for giving you a fright when you thought you had lost your odd little necklace?'

'Whatever is there to forgive?' I said, overwhelmed by her generosity. 'I was foolish not to have realised you had need to remove it.'

'And was keeping it perfectly safe,' she scolded.

'It's . . . it's very precious to me.'

'When you explained,' she said gently, 'it made me very upset for you. And angry. That dreadful woman at the orphanage! How could she have been so malicious as to destroy something that might have held a clue to your parentage. Such a pity the letter was so badly burned.'

'And it is no more than scraps now,' I said sadly, drawing the old pouch from round my neck and removing the little brass key. I transferred it carefully to the new pouch before I tipped out onto my lap what was left of the letter Martha Monday had given me all those years ago. The charred part had fallen to dust and the brittle remains of the rest had crumbled to fragile flakes. 'I'd not thought to look at it for a long time, so I hadn't realised it had crumbled almost away. I suppose the constant movement, the key pressing against it . . . Well, no matter. I shall save out of sentiment the little that is left.' I sighed. 'I once had hopes that the letter would somehow magically lead me to my mother even though I could never make out one word that made sense. But I think I must make my mind up that I never shall know who she was.'

'Quite so,' Mrs Yelland said in a brisk tone. 'As I have said to you before, it is always best to look forward, not back. After all, if you did ever meet her she might not live up to your expectations.'

'Quite possibly.' I fastened the key and the scraps of paper into the pouch and slipped the chain round my neck, tucking the velvet pouch into my bodice. Then I looked at her directly and said quietly, 'And even if she did, I could never forget how kind and generous you have been to me, Mrs Yelland. I have so much to be thankful for. Most of all that I was sent to the Thorn Tree. It was the best thing that ever happened to me – though I didn't think so at the time.'

'My dear child,' she began, then cleared her throat and it was a few seconds before she continued, somewhat huskily, 'I . . . I think I, too, could express similar sentiments. To watch you grow and blossom – it has given me the greatest satisfaction. For there were times at I was first at the Thorn Tree when . . . well, let us just say that some of my happiest moments were when we were snug with our books in the parlour.'

'Mine, too.'

Though I had expressed what I had said straight from the heart, I was not of a sentimental turn of mind to speak such things easily. Neither was Mrs Yelland and I was glad when she broke the somewhat embarrassed little silence that followed, by laughing and saying, 'We are in danger of becoming a veritable mutual admiration society, are we not, Emily? It is a good thing we do not have other company here to eavesdrop on such a mawkish conversation.'

She picked up the tablecloth she had let fall in her lap and carefully began to set out the patch she had made to cover a threadbare place. Her eyes on her work, her fingers busy with pins she said lightly, 'There is something else I should like to mention before we leave off with compliments. I should like you to know that before you succumbed to illness, I found your conduct as my companion was exceedingly pleasing, both in company and out of it. So I propose that when we return to the inn, you adopt that role permanently.' She looked up at me then, her green eyes regaining some of the sparkle they had lost in recent days. 'What do you say? Should you like to take the step?'

I stared at her. 'I ... I'm ... that is, but what ... what would it mean? How should we go on differently than we already do? And my work ...?'

'It is in the matter of *nuance*,' she said. 'You would have similar responsibilities, but I should like you to feel that you are more *family* rather than a mere servant. Oh, we can work out the details later, but in *principle* would you be agreeable?' A pause; then, almost carelessly: 'After all, you have no mother, I have no daughter nor am likely ever to have that ... that privilege. And though we are not linked by blood, I believe affection and friendship might not be so poor a substitute ...' Her voice trailed away.

My own was handicapped by the lump that had risen into my throat.

'Indeed not,' I managed after swallowing hard. 'I'm honoured. That is, I shall be honoured to ... to accept ...'

I was saved from the embarrassment of being too overcome to find any more words by a tap on the door and Jane's bustling entry into the parlour.

'Ma'am, there's a visitor come,' she said, bobbing a curtsey to Mrs Yelland. 'Mr Winterborne, ma'am, who begs leave to be admitted, for he says to say he'm not afeard of no scarlet fever and do mightily wish to find out how Miss Wroe's mending.'

'Then please ask him to step in,' Mrs Yelland said, her voice somewhat muffled by the handkerchief she had whisked from her sleeve and was pressing to her nose. 'Oh dear, I think the smoke from that fallen log is like to set me sneezing. Pray attend to it, Jane, before you fetch in our visitor.'

And while Jane poked at the innocent ashes and placed fresh logs on the blaze, Mrs Yelland and I composed ourselves, each in our different way, to receive this unexpected visitor.

* * *

'Mrs Yelland. Emily.' He bowed to each of us in turn. 'I hope you will forgive this intrusion, but my mare was in need of exercise and I bethought me to ride this far to enquire about the invalid.'

In the few seconds before I turned my head away because I could hardly bear it that he should see me made so greviously ugly by my flaking, blotchy skin, his image was imprinted with blinding clarity on my mind.

He had disposed of hat and greatcoat, but raindrops clung to the edges of his dark hair, which was drawn back to a neat black tie, and dulled the gloss on his riding boots. Other than that his appearance was immaculate: dove-grey breeches, darker grey coat, with a short claret-coloured waistcoat visible underneath. Starched white stock at his throat, and the crisp ruffles there and at his wrist the only hint of decoration. His cheekbones were flushed from the exercise, his greeny-grey eyes seemingly extra brilliant against the healthy glow of his skin.

It was as though he brought a great draught of energy, of masculine vitality into the parlour, making me cruelly aware of the peeling pallor of my complexion and the invalidish lassitude that was my condition at present.

I had so longed for this moment when we should meet again, but the last thing I wanted was for him to see me as I was now. If only I had a veil, or a fan to hide behind! But I was possessed of neither. All I could do was to turn my head and take a keen interest in the fire and hope that he would not come too close.

But he did.

Out of the corner of my eye I watched him advance.

'I thought, Emily, you would like to see how the pup did.'

He brought his hand from behind his back and dropped something into my lap. And it was no use trying to hide my face any more, for the wriggling, licking bundle of rough fawn- and white-coloured fur would not let me. It scrabbled its paws against my hands, tested needle-sharp teeth on my thumb, then rolled on its back, legs flopping in the air and fell to ecstasy as I scratched its fat pink stomach.

'Oh, but it can't be the same animal!' I cried.

'I assure you it is. And a greedy little hound it has proved to be, as you may guess from the way it has grown. Judging from the size of its paws, I think it is like to match my horse inch for inch by the time its body is grown in proportion.'

I searched among the soft fur. 'The injuries have healed?'

'They were no more than superficial. By the time he was bathed and the blood removed from his fur they were barely visible. Now they are quite lost in a layer of fat.' He bent and poked the pup gently in the ribs. 'What kind of misbegotten beast are you, eh? A blubber hound? A belly-on-legs hound? There is certainly nothing respectable or handsome in your parentage that I can make out.'

The pup grabbed at his finger, feathery tail frantic with delight.

'Don't be so unkind, sir,' I said. 'I find him rather fetching, if somewhat . . . unusual in shape. He has a fine coat, at least, and a pretty streak of white down his nose. Have you given him a name?'

'I thought you might like to have that privilege.'

I looked up at him, forgetting for a moment the unfortunate state of my complexion. He was smiling. And there was such a warmth in his eyes that suddenly it did not matter how I looked, for it was as though such superficialities were unimportant. As if that indefinable, unspoken sensation I had felt so strongly when we met in Exeter had sprung into joyful life again, linking us in some deep and mysterious way that made no sense of pride or embarrassment or formality.

'Then thank you. I shall put my mind to it.'

'Pray do sit down, Mr Winterborne, and take some refreshment with us,' Mrs Yelland said, adding cautiously, 'though we shall quite understand if you should wish to make this a brief call.'

'I am not in any hurry,' he said, promptly settling his long length on the chair Jane had set for him. 'I have always been of the fatalistic opinion that ailments and disease will strike how and when they may and that too nervous an attitude towards them serves only to render life impossibly restricted.'

'Bravo, sir,' Mrs Yelland laughed. 'We are starved of company due to an excess of caution on the part of other acquaintances and shall welcome news of the wider world. Now, will you drink hot chocolate or tea or a glass of wine?'

I envied them their hot chocolate as I sipped the clear broth that I took on Dr Lodge's orders at mid-morning. It was a weak and tasteless brew, that spoke of hasty making, rather than the long simmering of bones and meat and vegetables, the careful flavouring of herbs and spices, that characterised Mrs Hill's excellent soups and broths.

For the first time since I had been ill, I felt a stir of impatience at the dreary blandness of Dr Lodge's invalid diet which Mrs Yelland had been conscientious in administering. He had insisted that undue stimulation of my digestive system was dangerous – indeed stimulation of any sort was to be avoided in my present condition. I had been content – grateful – until this moment, to be cosseted, to let myself drift lazily and passively on this protective tide of kindness and good intentions. But I could not go on for ever in that way, could I? And this . . . this dishwater was not helping to restore my good health and energy. I might just as well have a glass of plain water as this uninspired stuff.

I had worked myself up to feeling quite cross – and

resolving to make my feelings plain to Mrs Yelland – by the time I had swallowed the last insipid dregs. Then I was distracted from these ungracious thoughts by the antics of the puppy-dog.

I had put him down when Jane brought me my broth, whereupon he had lolloped round the room on fat paws to sniff every chair leg and every inch of floorboard and carpet. Now he had returned to the hearth in which stood what I had learned was called a chimney board or companion piece, representing a small boy carrying a lantern. The pup took exception to this realistic, if immobile figure and backed off growling, the hair on his back standing up like bristles on a hairbrush. After a few moments of intense scrutiny of this dangerous object, he put his head down to his paws then sprang forward in an ungainly bounce.

The pandemonium that ensued reduced me to giggles. The chimney board went flying into the fire irons with a terrible clatter and the puppy yelped and scuttled for shelter under my skirts where I could feel him trembling against my ankle. With laughter, my crossness dissolved away. And in any case, I realised, these ill-tempered feelings were just a symptom of the sudden revival of my spirits which needed to find an outlet, and less to do with Mrs Yelland and Dr Lodge than with Felix himself.

I might be physically languid and lacking energy, leave alone ugly from the peeling rash, but since Felix had walked into the room I felt as though the real heart of me – my thoughts, my emotions – had become livelier than they had been for many days. His presence was a tonic far more effective than the evil-tasting physic Dr Lodge had prescribed. And this rejuvenation of my spirits made me, for the first time since the onset of the illness, impatient to be properly well again.

'I think you may have a hard time training that animal, sir,' Mrs Yelland said, frowning. 'I myself think dogs and cats are best kept out of doors, where they may properly do their work of guarding the premises or catching vermin. The parlour is certainly not the best place for this clumsy creature.'

'Blaze,' I said suddenly. 'Do you think that a good name for him? Because of that white streak down his face.'

'I have heard horses called so, but, yes. It suits him. Excellent.' Felix smiled at me, then cast Mrs Yelland a rueful glance. 'I apologise on Blaze's behalf, ma'am. Perhaps it is best if I take my leave and trouble you no more with his unseemly presence.'

'Oh, I think he'll be quiet now,' I said quickly. I felt under my feet and scooped the pup onto my lap again. 'See. He's had such a fright that he's ready to settle down quietly.' Blaze licked my hand. Two golden eyes looked hopefully into mine. I looked equally hopefully at Mrs Yelland. 'If I could have a few more moments with him, I promise I'll keep him good.'

She shook her head and smiled wryly. 'At least the horrid beast's antics have brought a little colour to your cheeks, Emily, which is all to the good. I wish I could take pleasure in such a silly creature, as you clearly do, but, alas, I cannot. I have always been nervous of dogs since I was bitten as a child. However, I do not at all wish to hurry you off, Mr Winterborne, when you have had the courtesy to call on us, so if Blaze – or perhaps Trouble would be a better name – keeps quiet then he may stay.'

I felt a wash of relief that Felix was not to be dispatched. Blaze, seeming to realise that he was in disgrace, quickly curled himself into a ball and fell asleep under the comfort of my hand.

My relief, however, was short-lived for the conversation soon took a turn into matters that I would have preferred not to be reminded of.

'Have you heard if the highway robber who attacked Mr Timothy Jenkins has been caught?' Mrs Yelland enquired casually.

My hand stopped its stroking. I felt the breath catch in my throat. I could not help but look straight at Felix, as I had been trying so hard not to do ever since he had arrived.

Not by a glance or a movement did he betray any sign of anxiety.

'I believe not,' he said smoothly. 'In fact I was speaking on that subject only yesterday to a gentleman who has a brother a magistrate in Heavitree. Current opinion is that the man has fled the district. No one else has been attacked before or since in quite so –' his dark brows lifted – 'original a manner, so it is thought that the robbery was the work of an opportunist rogue passing through the town.'

'I do hope so,' said Mrs Yelland. 'I am to travel back to Somerset, you see, the day after tomorrow. The thought of that exhausting journey to Bristol is bad enough, never mind the prospect of bandits abroad.' Her lips twitched in an effort not to smile as she asked solemnly, 'Have you heard how Mr Jenkins has been since his dreadful ordeal? Mr Bowyer told me you had an acquaintance with him.'

'A very slight one, I assure you,' Felix answered, equally solemn, equally endeavouring to control inner amusement. 'We have been in the same company once or twice and I had the misfortune to be present at the card party that fateful evening.'

'Ah, I heard that there had been an incident of some sort.'

'He caused a most disgraceful scene. I will not sully your ears with the grosser details. Suffice to say that he got obnoxiously drunk and, with his run of luck on the cards causing him to become even more boorish than usual, made disgraceful remarks about several of the gentlemen there. So he was asked to leave. Or rather our host's footmen, with the aid of a burly coachmen and a couple of young grooms, put him outside. Whereupon a cheer went up from the rest of us, though the mood of the evening was quite ruined and the party broke up shortly afterwards.' A grin broke through. 'However, I would hazard the opinion that every gentleman present that evening felt a certain satisfaction in the justice that was served upon Mr Jenkins later.'

'Or could it be that one of those present *ensured* that justice was done?'

The words were out and I could not bring them back. They fell like hailstones into the warm air, wintry and chilling.

My eyes were fixed upon him and his gaze came sharply round to meet mine, an instant of frozen time when a cold glitter lit his eyes. Then it was gone, so that I could scarcely believe it had been there at all.

He turned back to Mrs Yelland, smiling still, thoroughly at ease. Or giving a handsome show of it. 'As to the *wish*, I believe the thoughts of all the company might not bear too close a scrutiny. But the execution of such a daring deed? Well, who am I to say? A black heart may as easily be concealed under the respectable waistcoat of a banker or a merchant or an esquire as under a poor man's tatters.'

'You may tease, Mr Winterborne, but Emily has raised a pertinent point,' Mrs Yelland said. 'Indeed, Mr Bowyer and I speculated at the time that the robber might have had information of Mr Jenkins being flush with money from someone in the house.'

'And you may congratulate yourself on your perspicuity,' Felix said. 'For that is now understood to be the case.'

'Really? How interesting.'

'Though the authorities think it was not a deliberate act of a paid accomplice, but merely a result of the manner of Mr Jenkins' noisy exit. There were plenty of bystanders, you see, who were drawn to the fracas that ensued in the street. And the servants who eventually got him onto his horse and saw him on his way were naturally open with their version of events to those who had enjoyed the free entertainment. It is believed that among the onlookers must have been either the robber himself or someone who passed on the information.' He laughed. 'So there you have it. And as we have gone a long way from your original question, I will tell you that I have heard not a whisper about Mr Jenkins' present state of mind or health, as he has taken himself off to Yorkshire to visit a cousin.'

Mrs Yelland chuckled. 'For which Exeter society is thankful?'

'While extending feelings of commiseration for the cousin,' he said gravely. He frowned, looking now at me. 'So you are leaving on Thursday, Emily? Are you then ready to make such an arduous journey?'

'Most certainly she is not,' Mrs Yelland put in. 'She must wait until Dr Lodge gives the word. It is regrettable that we must travel separately, but I cannot delay my return to Somerset any longer. Dr Lodge tells us that the period of Emily's convalescence must not be curtailed as there is still the chance of complications occurring if she becomes chilled or overtired. As you may see, she is far from herself yet. However, I shall not cease to worry until she is reunited with us at the Thorn Tree. With each week we are closer to winter and that is no time to be on the road, with rain and flood and frost and heaven knows what other hazards to cause delays and mishaps.'

'Quite.' A pause. Then, 'In the absence of Mr Bowyer, ma'am, should you wish me to meet you in Exeter on Thursday I would be happy to see you safe on the Bristol coach.'

'That is most civil of you, sir. But I fear it will be a very early hour and I would not wish to impose—'

'It would be my pleasure. Have you bespoken a seat?'

'I was going to send today.'

'Then allow me to attend to it for you.' He brushed her

thanks aside. 'It is no more than a few moments out of my way.'

'What can I do but accept such a kind offer with good grace?'

'And if it would relieve some of your anxiety, ma'am, I shall be pleased to offer the same courtesy to Emily if Mr Bowyer is still absent when the time comes for her to leave.'

'That would please me very much,' she said warmly. 'Is it not kind of Mr Winterborne, Emily?'

'Very kind,' I said. 'Thank you, sir.'

'It may be even that I might be able to accompany Emily for part or all of the journey,' he said, drumming his fingers lightly on the arm of the chair, as though suddenly struck by the thought. 'I do have the need to return to Bath sometime this month.' He shrugged, shook his head. 'Though the date of my departure will depend on how my business continues in Exeter.'

'If it is at all a possibility...'

'I cannot make any promises. But knowing the situation, I will do my best to arrange my affairs accordingly.'

He looked at me as he spoke.

Wicked eyes. Drawing me into conspiracy. As clear as if he had spoken aloud I knew everything he had said to Mrs Yelland was part of the secret game he and I were engaged in. A game in which charm and gallantry and good humour served to keep the outsider innocent of any deeper purpose. A game in which he was well-practised and I was not. A dangerous game.

He was, I guessed, a card sharp. Possibly a highwayman. I had once seen his eyes very cold, his temper short. He could well be a womaniser, who had left a trail of heartbroken women all the way from here to London...

I was better off with Luke. Safe, kind Luke, who all these years had loved me and whom I loved – of course I did – in return, yet whose features I could not at this moment clearly recall. Only the red of his hair, and a distant feeling of guilt.

Better off with Luke?

Yes! Yes!

I should retreat this minute from Felix, cut him dead. Refuse to take one step along the tempting path on which he stood beckoning me forward. How could I know where it would lead? To a cliff edge, perhaps, over which I should tumble to the jagged rocks of heartbreak? To a deep, impenetrable forest where I would be lost for ever?

But never to know. Always to regret. To live my life in ignorance, in despair, by sending him away.

'I shouldn't wish you to put yourself out on my part, sir,' I said. 'I daresay I'll manage tolerably well even if I must travel alone. But I confess that to make such a long journey solitary – well, I should be glad of your company, Mr Winterborne.'

How very calm my voice was. Yet Blaze stirred and opened his eyes to look at me, as if his senses were alerted by some indefinable tension in my soothing hand.

Felix smiled. There seemed no guile in it, none at all. Or did I merely read into his expression that which I wished most desperately to see?

It was a question to which I did not have any answer.

The house seemed extraordinarily empty without Mrs Yelland.

She left Starlings in the middle of the night – or so it seemed.

She came softly into my room when she was dressed. I started awake as I heard her voice in my ear.

'The curricle has been brought round, Emily. I must go now. I shall write as soon as I am at the Thorn Tree. Do you have the money safe that I gave you to pay for the receipt of letters and your other expenses?'

I struggled out of the clinging strands of sleep to acknowledge that I did.

'Do exactly as Dr Lodge recommends and write as often as you feel able. Go back to sleep now. God bless.'

A light kiss on my forehead and she was gone, a black shadow against the yellow flare of the candle she carried. I heard, far off, a mumble of voices, the slam of a door . . .

It was difficult after that to recapture sleep. The sound of the door closing seemed to echo and re-echo through my dreams, jolting me awake each time I fell to a restless doze. There seemed a deep significance in that sound, as though of something ending . . . something beginning. A sound that unexpectedly frightened me. I wanted to feel joyful and excited about what the future might hold but I could not. Whatever that beginning might signify, I could find little comfort in the welter of my thoughts as I lay restless in the dark hours before light began to filter through the curtains.

Once I was properly awake I tried to throw off the low mood that had seized me. But the sight of my breakfast – dry toast, thin gruel, a glass of buttermilk – did nothing to raise my spirits, and Jane, normally given to chatter, was only half awake and spent the time in helping me to dress mostly in yawning and grumbling that she had had to rise in the middle of the night to get Mrs Yelland on her way and how she'd get through the day without falling asleep she didn't know.

When I eventually left my bedroom, my sense of isolation increased.

I think that I had never felt so alone as I did that dank November day in the shuttered house. I had not realised quite how much Mrs Yelland's brisk presence had kept me cushioned – cocooned – against the fact that most of the house was now shuttered and cold, furniture draped in dustsheets, carpets covered with drugget. With only Jane willing to come near me, and the other servants reduced to glimpses of a skirt or the tails of a coat whisking away from me round a corner, the sense of isolation became more acute as the hours dragged on. I even found that the shutters in the library were closed when I crept there, shivering, to exchange my book. I was near reduced to weak tears because I had to search out a candle and make a light in order to see what I was reaching off the shelves.

It was the lingering effects of the illness, of course, that made even the walk as far as Mr Bowyer's library an ordeal that sapped my energy and made me prone to be weepy and self-pitying. That and the atmosphere of the house that had seemed so cheerful and welcoming when the family was at home, but now was reduced to emptiness and gloomy silence.

So I told myself, and it was true in part. But I also knew that there was a cause that went much deeper. The compound of desire and of guilt, of fear that he might not come to me and fear that he might; of terror that I had wrongly misinterpreted everything he had said to me; of heart-wrenching longing in moments when I was certain I had not...

So my thoughts seesawed about. I could not settle to read. Sewing made my fingers ache. My indifferent appetite failed me completely when faced with my mid-morning broth and I sent it back to the kitchen untouched. The sight of the coddled egg and the cup of barley water which was my luncheon turned my stomach and I could do no more than pick at the slice of boiled cod that appeared for my dinner at three o'clock. It scarcely seemed worth while to leave the comfortable chair by the fire to take the few steps to the small table that had been set for me in the parlour, for the sake of such unappetising fare.

The fish had a stale taste and I could manage no more than a few flakes before I abandoned it in favour of the rice pudding, which bore so little resemblance to the creamy, nutmeg-laced concoction of Mrs Hill's making that it might have been a different species of pudding altogether.

I was trying to force a little of it down when Jane came in.

'Mr Winterborne's here, miss,' she announced. 'I told 'en,' she added helpfully, 'you was dining and p'raps 'twouldn't be convenient, so don't 'ee go putting yourself out none for callers.'

I choked on the glutinous mouthful.

The moment had come. The one I longed for. Dreaded.

Still not too late. I had no need to see him. Jane would turn him away. Tell him that I preferred him not to call again.

I dabbed the napkin to my mouth, then slowly replaced it on the cloth.

'Kindly clear the table, then ask Mr Winterborne to step in.'

I cannot say what I truly expected to happen. In the world of imagination, the moment we were alone, he would have swept me into his arms; or fallen to one knee and sworn eternal love.

There could be nothing so satisfyingly simple in reality.

We greeted each other with formality and, coolly courteous, he seated himself so that the width of the hearth separated us.

'How are you today, Emily?'

'I believe I make some improvement. Will you take some refreshment, sir? A glass of wine, perhaps?'

'Thank you. Will you join me?'

'I'm not allowed. Dr Lodge—'

'Jane tells me that you've scarcely eaten anything today. No wonder you look peakier than you did when I last saw you. Though if your dinner, which I glimpsed in passing, was a sample of the good doctor's diet, then I cannot blame you for spurning it. I told Jane as much.'

'You have no cause to interfere, sir.'

'I promised Mrs Yelland that I would look in each day to see how you progressed. I think she would be most put out if I allowed you to starve yourself to death. Ah, Jane, did you bring what I asked? Good. Now watch what I do.'

There were two glasses on the tray that held a decanter of Mr Bowyer's sherry wine, a small cream jug, a sugar bowl, an egg and a fork. Felix broke the egg into the jug with a little sugar and whisked vigorously with the fork before adding sherry wine to the concoction. He sniffed at it, nodded approvingly, then poured the contents of the jug into a glass.

'Hand this to Miss Wroe, Jane.'

'But Dr Lodge, sir, he'm set against wine or spirits for invalids,' Jane said anxiously.

'Then we shall not tell him,' Felix said, pouring sherry wine into the other glass.

'But, sir, Mrs Yelland said—'

'For God's sake, girl, would you see Miss Wroe fall into a decline for lack of food?'

'No, sir, course not.'

'Then hand her the eggnog,' he said. 'There is nothing finer in my opinion for stirring up a reluctant appetite. And while we're about it, what fruit is in the house?'

'Fruit, sir?'

'Fruit. You know – apples, pears, oranges.'

'With master and missus away, sir, there's little call—' She broke off at his thunderous expression, said hastily, 'There's apples, sir, stored from our own crop.'

'Then fetch me a good, crisp eating apple and a knife.'

She scuttled away and he said to me, frowning still, 'Did Dr Lodge allow you to eat the fruit I sent? No, I can see from your face that he did not.'

'I had one of the peaches and a little of the pineapple,

which I had never tasted before, and it was delicious,' I said. 'But then he—'

'But the old fool found out and disapproved? And Mrs Yelland?'

'She was greatly impressed by his attention to me when I was very ill and it seemed I might die. She took great care to follow his instructions because he said a relapse might be caused by an overexcited digestive system.'

'Overexcited! What would he have your digestive system do, then? Die from boredom? Ah, I have made you smile. That is an improvement. I had thought you had forgotten how. Now drink!'

I sipped cautiously at the frothy liquid. It slid down easily enough.

'I seem to recall, Mr Winterborne, an occasion when I thought you might hurl a dish of bread-and-milk at Mrs Yelland. Don't you fear that I might rebel in a similar manner against your orders?'

He laughed. 'I made an exceedingly boorish invalid, as you so kindly made a point of telling me. You occupy that position far more gracefully. I am sure you would not forget yourself in such an unmannerly fashion.'

'That is your opinion, sir.'

'You think me high-handed because I have challenged Dr Lodge?'

'I didn't say that.'

'But you think it. You are not drinking. Take a sip.'

'I think Mrs Yelland did not intend you to come here and bully me.'

'Stop talking and drink.'

The eggnog was smooth and rich and warming. When Jane rushed back with a rosy apple, Felix carefully cut it into slivers and arranged it neatly on the plate. He gave the plate to Jane to hand to me, then leaned back in the chair, crossed one long leg over the other and took an appreciative sip of the wine. 'If you do not finish that apple, I shall think of something else to torment your stomach with.'

In truth the apple tasted better than anything I had eaten recently. And when I had finished, Felix set Jane running back to the kitchen again.

'I'm an expert with the toasting fork,' he said, crouching over the hearth to dangle a slice of bread at a glowing log. He spread the toast thickly with the butter I had been forbidden, then with honey. He cut it neatly into fingers. 'You have my permission to leave the crusts.'

'So magnanimous,' I murmured.

'Sarcasm, Miss Wroe? A poor return for my efforts to wrench you back from the brink of starvation.'

I managed one finger of toast, then another, while he relished two butter-soaked slices. Jane lit the candles before retreating to the shadows to await further orders. The glow of fire and candlelight spilled round me, round Felix, encompassing us, linking us together, in warmth and light.

He smiled. 'Well done,' he said gently. 'That wasn't so bad, was it?'

I half expected my stomach to have rebelled against this excess of richness, but thankfully it had not. Indeed, it felt more settled than it had all day.

'More agreeable than thin gruel or buttermilk,' I conceded with a grimace at the recollection.

'Then I will make sure that you are not served with such pap again.'

'This is not your house, sir,' I reminded him gently.

'So you are saying Mr Bowyer would approve of me allowing you to fade away, despite the evidence of my eyes that you need nourishment, not punishment?'

'No, but—'

'But nothing.' He paused, then said softly, 'If I appear overbearing, forgive me. I do not like to see you looking as if a draught would blow you over. I want to see you well again.'

'I . . . I appreciate your good intentions.'

'You can send me off with a flea in my ear if you feel that my presence is an embarrassment to you.'

'I think that . . . unnecessary.'

'So you will allow me to call again tomorrow?'

'If you have the inclination. But I wouldn't wish the duty Mrs Yelland placed upon you to lie too heavily upon your conscience.'

A log fell, sending a shower of sparks flying up the chimney, the flare of red-gold emphasising the shadows and planes of his face, glinting on the teasing light in his eyes.

'I assure you it is not my conscience that impels me to visit you,' he said gravely.

I smiled. 'The need to exercise your horse, perhaps?'

'Ah, Miss Wroe, how perceptive you are.'

All awkwardness, all the tension I had felt earlier, seemed to have smoothed away and I felt the mood of melancholy that had harassed me all day lift and fade as if it had never been. Even after Felix had gone, the echo of his presence seemed to banish those bleak thoughts of myself abandoned and isolated in the shuttered house. What did it matter if most of the house was cold and dark? The parlour was comfortable, my own bedchamber was warm and cosy, Jane was doing her best for me. And how could I consider myself alone when there were at least half a dozen other servants left in the house, even if they were sensibly keeping their distance from me?

And Felix would be here again tomorrow.

When Dr Lodge paid his weekly visit he exclaimed his satisfaction at my progress.

'The peeling of the skin is becoming less evident, and you are brighter in spirits, I think. So, a slice or two of well-boiled fowl or mutton might safely be added to your diet, perhaps some buttered turnips and an egg custard... Though take care not to overindulge. If the improvement has been sustained when next I call, I shall permit you to take a little exercise out of doors if the weather is suitable. Then, the possibility of your return to Somerset might be considered.'

Jane burst into giggles when he had gone. 'To think what you've been eating, miss! If he but knew!'

'Well, he doesn't,' I said crossly. 'And I'll thank you, Jane, next time he calls not to stand pulling faces behind his back.' Then I could not help but laugh myself. 'I had the devil's own job to look humble and grateful – which he clearly expected – when he advised I might eat a little chicken.'

'Whatever would he say if he knew 'ee'd been eating victuals near the same as us in the kitchen? Never mind that pineapple as Mr Winterborne fetched 'ee and eggnogs twice a day.'

'Throw an apoplexy, I don't doubt.'

'Well, ten't your fault, miss. That Mr Winterborne'd have to speak up for 'ee,' she said stoutly. 'For he'm to blame.'

'Well, he's not to blame for what I propose to do now,' I said, staring grimly into the looking-glass. 'I can't stand the state of my hair any longer. It's sticky and sweaty and dull as dishwater. Fiddle to catching a chill! I'm going to wash it.'

To Jane's horrified protests I did.

''Tis asking for trouble,' she moaned as she wrapped my clean, wet tresses in a towel and rubbed vigorously. 'Even if 'ee were in good health, which 'ee en't properly yet, 'tis a bad time o' year to be thinking of hair-washing. You'm not to stir one inch from this fire until it's dry, miss! Do 'ee hear?'

I meekly did as I was bid, near roasting myself in the process. And Jane, mollified when I did not appear to have taken instant harm, insisted on brushing out the tangles for me, then produced a handkerchief from the pocket of her apron.

'That high-flown maid of Mrs Bowyer's do swear as a silk handkerchief brings up the shine on hair.'

'Where did you get such a fine thing?' I asked.

She winked. 'Least said, miss. And her's to Crediton with missus so what her don't know can't hurt. I'll put it back straight after I've done with it . . . Pretty hair you got, miss. Pity it don't curl, but the colour's real unusual. Now I'll put it up for 'ee, if 'ee'll pass the pins, miss. I always likes doing up hair. Did my sister's when I was home and the maids here when they lets me. I'm hopeful, see, of being a proper lady's maid one day.'

'And you have the makings of a good one,' I said, staring into the looking-glass in some surprise. She had brought up a gloss on my hair that I had thought impossible after the ravages of my illness, and arranged it in a manner not so different from the way I usually wore it, yet it was looped up in a softer fashion with a ribbon cleverly threaded through the coils. 'As you've put a blue ribbon in my hair, perhaps I should change into the blue sprig gown.'

'It's a bit thin for a cold day, miss,' she cautioned.

'I can wear an extra petticoat and my warmest shawl.' I wrinkled my nose at my reflection. 'Pity about my complexion, though. What isn't peeling is so pallid.'

'Not nearly so bad as it was,' Jane said stoutly. Her hand dived into her pocket again and she produced a small pot. She grinned at me in the mirror. 'Just happened to come across this when I borrowed the handkerchief.' She held it under my nose. 'Smells lovely, miss. Smooth a bit on where it's peeling.'

'Mm, violets . . . but I shouldn't if it's Mrs Bowyer's.'

'Her's more creams and potions than a body can count. Here, let me.' She gently worked a little of the cream over my face and stood back admiringly. 'You can't see those rough patches near half as clear.'

It was true. And the delicate scent of violets seemed to linger, so that after luncheon when Felix arrived, I could still catch the faint aroma when I moved.

The hair-washing, the changing from the plain wool gown to a lighter, fresher one tired me more than I cared to admit to Jane.

But it was worth it – because I saw the way Felix looked at me when Jane showed him in: differently.

No longer seeing me solely as an invalid who needed his care and protection, but as the woman I had been before illness struck me down. As I had been the day when we met in that Exeter alleyway.

And that was when he broke from the courteous formality that had so far kept him carefully distant from me. Instead of taking his usual seat across the hearth, he walked across to where I sat.

'How well you look today, Miss Wroe,' he said softly.

'I believe I am making good progress, Mr Winterborne.'

He reached out and took my hand. It looked very white and thin in his. He held it very gently, his thumb lightly moving over the back of my hand where the blue veins showed.

Then he released it, bowed, returned to his usual seat.

No more than that.

But enough to colour those moments before I drifted to sleep that night with thoughts that sent me smiling into my dreams.

If I look back now on the week that followed, I see myself drifting in a rosy cloud of contentment.

A week in which Mrs Yelland sent me two letters, one of which enclosed a note of three laborious sentences, sadly blotted and misspelled, and ending, 'Your obdt servent, Luke Gilpin.' I could imagine the quill-chewing and frowning this letter had cost him, yet it gave me no more than a momentary pang. I answered in a bright and cheerful vein. And to Mrs Yelland's lively letter, too. The things she spoke of seemed so remote from me. Of course, I was delighted Cass was safely delivered of a daughter, that Mrs Yelland had restored order once more where things had become lax in her absence, that Master Harry had bought two new horses, that everyone sent good wishes and hoped to see me back soon . . . But such things seemed to have lost the importance, the immediacy they had once held.

A week in which I steadily recovered my strength, so much so that one afternoon, in defiance of Dr Lodge, I took a turn with Felix around the rose garden.

It was a delight to be outside. Distances were shrouded with fog and it was very still – a day lacking colour, everything grey and dun, with only the lacing of dewdrops on bare branches and spiders' webs lighting to a brief glittering whenever the weak sun pierced the mist. I inhaled deeply of the moist, cool air. To someone who had been confined indoors for so long, the rich odour of wet earth and sodden foliage, the tang of the gardeners' distant bonfire, combined to a scent more desirable than any a perfumer might perfect.

And my pleasure was compounded by the fact that my gloved hand lay tucked securely into the crook of Felix's arm and that we were truly alone together. We were visible, of course, from the windows of the house or to any of the gardeners who might chance by, but at least there was no Jane hovering and our talk slid so effortlessly from the formal to the informal that I called him by his first name without thinking. Then I blushed and asked his pardon and he laughed and said that he had been about to ask if I would please stop calling him Mr Winterborne, for it made him feel old when he had always called me Emily.

'Because you still think of me as the kitchen maid I once was.'

'A forward hussy, I recollect, even then, when you were no more than fourteen or fifteen. And what are you now, Emily?'

'Nearly nineteen.'

'Does twenty-seven seem a great age to you? For that is what I am.'

'Immensely aged,' I said gravely. 'But you carry it well. You conceal the dodderiness of your step most cleverly and whatever the pomade you use to hide the grey in your hair it gives an exceedingly natural effect.'

'Such compliments!'

'Think nothing of it.'

In light-hearted banter, in shared laughter, we began the discovery of each other. He told me anecdotes about his childhood, making himself out to be a mischievous and rumbustious schoolboy, with no thought beyond scrumping apples or playing tricks on schoolmasters.

'But I know you were something of a scholar and considered clever,' I contradicted him, 'Miss Cavendish told me so.'

'Ah, there is nothing so ruinous to a man's character as an overfond aunt. What other scandalous titbits about me did she sully your ears with?'

I hesitated. 'Not a great deal . . . although . . .'

'Although?'

I was not sure that I should raise such an unhappy subject, yet he was looking at me so warmly, and I only wished to let him know that I understood and could share his pain.

'She . . . she did tell me of . . . sad events,' I said carefully, 'the loss of your father and mother. And I am so very sorry.'

We had come to a halt at the end of the formal garden where the steps gave onto the grassy slopes of the Mulberry Field. He stared straight ahead, very still, before he said in a voice so cold that it instantly dispelled all the light-hearted ease between us, 'So my aunt told you my father did away with himself and my mother died of the disgrace and the grief?'

Oh Lord, I had miscalculated! But the words could not be unspoken. 'She . . . she prayed that they would have found peace,' I said.

'Then I hope to God she is right. I know I never have.' He turned to me and the haggard look in his eyes, the whiteness around his mouth where deep lines seemed to have sprung to prominence, speared me through. 'Do you know how it happened?'

'Of course not! Miss Cavendish wasn't gossiping! She only mentioned it out of the grief she carried for her sister.'

'Well, I have relived it a million times in my head but never spoken of it. Not to a living soul. What makes you, Emily Wroe, think I should wish to speak of it now?'

'Then don't!' I cried. 'I did not intend—'

'You did not intend what? To pry? To hurt? Good Lord! I fight constantly to forget what I saw that day. And you, of all people, at this moment, to remind me!'

I groped for the right words to say. I felt his pain as my own, yet there was a spark in me that refused to fear the harshness of his words, the bitterness and anger in his eyes. That reached out to him from the chill and unhappiness of my own years at the foundling home. Wanting to ease and comfort . . .

'Perhaps it was the wrong time to speak of such . . . such a painful event. But I have known harsh times, too, when I did not have a friend in the world to speak for me, or to offer a kind word, and I . . . I know the comfort I should have had from talking to such a person, of expressing my despair.' I pulled my hand from his arm and drew back from him, but holding myself straight and meeting his eyes without flinching. 'I did *not* speak out of curiosity or anything of that nature, but out of . . .

of affection and gratitude for your kindness to me.'

We stared at each other across a small space that seemed to me to have grown to the depth and width of a great chasm.

Then his glance not wavering from mine, he said in a low, quick voice, as though the words had been dammed back for a long time and now tumbled over themselves to be released, 'I was the one to find him. He had hanged himself from a rope thrown over a beam in the stable. The sight of him, my misguided, gentle, beloved father, turned into that . . . that grotesque, distorted *object* . . . That is the image that ended my boyhood. That I would wish, as a man, to bury in the depths of my mind, and to forget. But it is impossible.'

'Oh, Felix,' I said softly. 'How dreadful.'

'So now you have it, Emily Wroe,' he said, as though I had not spoken. There was anger now in his voice. 'And I cannot think why I have allowed myself to speak to you as I have never spoken to anyone else since that dreadful day.' His eyes raked my face as though he read there something that defied comprehension. 'What are you? Who are you? God help me, I have known many women – more beautiful, more striking, more suitable women than you will ever be. Why should I have found it possible to unburden myself to you? What is this . . . this fascination you hold for me in the shining darkness of your eyes?'

'Please don't be so upset. Would you like to go back inside?'

'For God's sake, Emily, I am not angry with *you* – how could I be? – but with myself, for this . . . this weakness that has allowed me to break my silence. The weakness that has gripped me, ever since I saw you ready to battle over a tormented pup with a pair of youths twice your bulk. Perhaps so far back as when a scrawny little maid spoke out in my aunt's defence.'

I was pulled into his arms so roughly that my hat was

knocked backwards and my chin caught sharply against one of the silver buttons on his coat. Afterwards I found I had a graze to show for it. I felt nothing at all at the time. Nothing, that is, but the surge of joy as his mouth found mine. And the hunger, the wild abandoned hunger that cared not a fig that a servant might glance out of the window and see us. That there were two gardeners walking across the Mulberry Field with scythes across their shoulders who might be nudging each other and grinning.

I was lost. It was an experience beyond anything I had felt with Luke. A melding of all my senses, of physical desire, into one fusion of *rightness*. As though I had waited all my life for this moment and now it was here I did not want it to end.

But, of course, it must.

When he released me he carefully set my hat straight and retied the strings under my chin, saying with a gruffness that belied the gentleness of his touch, 'I must confess to you, Emily, that in my saner moments I have not been pleased to discover myself gripped with a madness I have always been at pains to avoid.'

'If you are mad, then I am stricken with the same malady.'

'I did not ask or wish to be so affected,' he said. He frowned down at the stray lock of my hair he was twisting about his finger.

'Nor did I.'

'I do not wish it now. It is highly inconvenient.' He carefully tucked the strand of hair back into the coils at my neck. 'In fact, there is a young woman, far more suitable in every way, eagerly awaiting my return to Bath.'

'How could I expect otherwise?' I said, unable to keep the tart edge from my voice born of the stab of envy I felt for this unknown young woman – and those others that he had spoken of so lightly. 'You are not a monk.'

He shrugged. 'You yourself cannot be without admirers.'

'There is someone who wishes to marry me,' I said. 'Someone that a gentleman such as yourself would consider eminently *suitable* for someone in my position.'

'And will you marry him?'

'I have led him to suppose so. What of this ... this young woman in Bath?'

'I have led her to suppose that I shall ask her papa's permission.'

'And will you?'

'She is pretty and rich and amiable.' He shook his head in puzzlement. 'And at this moment she seems the least desirable creature in the world.'

'Do you suppose this ... this madness will pass?' I whispered.

'Perhaps it will. Perhaps this time next week or next month we shall come to wonder why we succumbed as we did.'

'And in the meantime?'

'If mischievous fate has contrived to put this spell upon us, then who are we mere mortals to deny a goddess her sport? Shall we go along with her machinations for the present and see what prevails?'

We smiled at each other. He took my hand and replaced it in the crook of his arm. We walked decorously back to the house and I closed my mind to everything but the realisation that even if this desire – this joyous, baffling attraction – that we felt for each other were to prove a fleeting, transient affair, for the present moment it consumed me with delight.

Chapter Six

The hours when we were able to be together seemed to be pitifully few when set against the long, dragging hours when I was alone.

Felix could not come oftener than he did as his affairs in Exeter claimed a deal of his time.

'I wish I had not tied myself up so,' he said, 'but if I do not chivvy the builders, I shall not see the foundations of my houses put in before I leave with you for Bristol. And I am keen to see progress as this is the first time I have ventured into the actual building of houses, rather than improving on property already in existence.' He brought the plans to show me, enthusiastically pointing out the features. 'It is a terrace of six houses, each of three storeys with basement below and an attic floor and with a stretch of garden behind. There is a spring of good water on the site and I have employed an excellent engineer who is supervising the laying of a conduit to each kitchen.'

'The scullery maids will be in your debt,' I said, remembering the days when it had been my duty to fetch water from the yard pump. 'Keeping a house provided with water is a laborious chore.'

He nodded thoughtfully. 'It is my aim to make things convenient for the servants as much as their employers. I have been to too many dinners where the food has been considerably chilled by the time it reaches the table, not due to any negligence on the servants' part but by reason of the distance they must walk between kitchen and dining chamber. This will not happen in my houses.' He jabbed a finger at the plans. 'Here, you will see a shaft rising from the basement kitchen to the dining chamber. It will house a platform on which food may be placed in the kitchen below, which will then be raised by a person standing in the dining chamber directly above. It will operate on a system of ropes and pulleys that will move smoothly and with little effort on the part of even the smallest maid.'

'So the maids will not have to carry heavy platters and tureens up and down the stairs. How excellent.'

'The cupboard housing the apparatus will be disguised in an appropriate manner in the dining chamber, so that its purpose is not evident and it will not intrude into whatever furnishing scheme is put about.'

'And what other labour-saving ideas do you have for the kitchens?'

He looked up from the plans which he had spread on the parlour table. 'I wondered if you might have any suggestions.'

I thought for a moment. 'Well, Mrs Yelland was telling me of a new kind of iron oven with its own grate underneath, which she was wondering about installing at the Thorn Tree.' I laughed. 'She is considering broaching the subject to Mrs Hill, though I don't think it will go down too well in that quarter. Our cook is not one for innovation. From what I hear, though, it might add considerably to the convenience of the kitchen as it stands alongside the fire and uses the same flue and chimney. I think it is known as a perpetual oven.'

'Mm. Thank you, that is useful to know.'

'And if you really do wish to make the life of the servants more comfortable,' I added, 'might I suggest you also give some thought to the attics where they will sleep.'

'In what way?' he said, frowning.

'We're lucky at the Thorn Tree. The walls of the attic are thick and there's a proper ceiling, so we're protected somewhat from the cold or the heat outside, but I think the maids in many places – here, for instance – are not so fortunate. I went last week to visit the scullery maid who took the fever from me. She is back at work today – and glad to be, I should think. The attic where she sleeps has no means of heating and even at this time of the year, before the worst of the frosts set in, the room is very cold, being open to the rafters. In summer, she said, it becomes quite unbearably hot, making it difficult to sleep.'

'Then I shall give consideration to that also.'

Though we spoke on such ordinary things a great deal, and when Jane was there we never strayed from formality, there was always now that different, exciting undercurrent. It threaded everything we did and said – the touch of a hand, the glance of an eye, a smile. We made the most of the snatched minutes when we were alone, though they were surprisingly difficult to find. If we were indoors there was Jane, who faithfully kept to her promise to Mrs Yelland to keep me under her eye. And now that I was pronounced by Dr Lodge free of infection, the other maids were much about, not to mention the footman who resumed his proper duty of announcing Felix's arrival and showing him to the parlour. He had, to me, the sly look of a man given to listening outside closed doors, but at least he had no excuse to follow us outside. I was always glad when the day was suitable to go out of doors.

I grew steadily stronger and our walks increased in length. In my stout shoes and warm-hooded cloak I took no harm, though the still and misty days had given way to showery weather with a penetrating wind out of the north-west. Several times Felix brought Blaze, who was growing fast and who bounced about us on gawky long legs in between dashing off to chase blowing leaves or fetching the sticks we threw for him.

'He's an intelligent hound for all his odd appearance,' Felix said one day, watching the feathery tail disappear into the long grass at the bottom of the Mulberry Field. 'I have taught him already to sit and wait for his dinner until I give the command.'

'But he is not yet too good at coming when you call,' I said, laughing, as Felix whistled and shouted for Blaze to follow us along the path that would take us in a circular route back to the house.

Blaze had other ideas. He went scuttling in the opposite direction, towards the Old House and disappeared down the slope among the trees, with only his excited yelps to tell us that the pursuit of a rabbit was far more interesting that walking meekly with us.

We turned off the path to a spot from which we could see where he had gone.

The Old House was clearly visible now that the trees that surrounded it had lost their leaves. We could see the patch of garden, no longer colourful as it had been a month since, and there was someone out there: Madame Crespin, a bent black-robed figure, moving slowly around the plot and pausing here and there to examine a shrub or pluck a weed, as gardeners will, whatever the season.

I shivered and Felix's arm came round my waist.

'Blaze will find his way back,' he said gently. 'There is no need to stand here to be reminded of how you were attacked.'

'Oh, I'm not frightened,' I hastened to assure him. 'Not of her, poor old soul. It is just that her situation – it's so sad. Her daughter gone and no one to love her, for I think that Kemp woman is not very kind. And to live in that dark house where the sun never gets in winter. And worse – the prospect of being put into a madhouse.'

Even as I spoke Blaze erupted out of the trees and skidded to a halt by the garden gate. The old lady looked up. Blaze, evidently having chased the rabbit to its burrow, was diverted into greeting her, barking and wagging his tail enthusiastically. Slowly, Madame Crespin hobbled towards him and put a tentative hand through the bars of the gate.

It was then that Mrs Kemp appeared at the open door, her very stance betokening belligerence. She was evidently no animal lover. She bent to pick something up and threw it at Blaze. The shower of stones found its target. Blaze yelped and scuttled off, tail between his legs, leaving Mrs Kemp bawling some imprecation after him. Then she took hold of Madame Crespin's arm and dragged her roughly towards the house. She was still shouting, the words indistinguishable from here, as she thrust the old lady inside and shut the door with a bang.

It was all over in a minute. No time to run to Madame Crespin's defence, though I felt myself tense with the need to do so.

Felix's arm tightened round my waist.

'It is not our business,' he said grimly, 'though I see what you mean about the dragon who guards her.'

'I feel we should do something,' I whispered.

'I think our only course is to believe that the old woman, being mad, is not as sensitive to her situation as we would be,' he said, in an attempt to reassure me, which it did not. 'Now come away before you get cold standing here.'

A chastened Blaze at last responded to Felix's whistle and we moved along our chosen path.

'I'm not so sure she does not – nor any mad person – have some comprehension or understanding. How can we know?' I persisted. 'Perhaps she's returned to a kind of childhood. After all, a child may know that it is hurt, or lonely, or unhappy even when it does not have the words to explain. Or if there is no one prepared to listen if it does.'

'As was your case in that foundling home?' He stopped and drew me close into the circle of his arms. 'Poor little Emily. At least I had the advantage of a happy childhood to look back on, even if it all ended tragically.'

'I envy you that,' I said frankly, 'even though I know that I have been incredibly fortunate since. Mrs Yelland says it is best always to look forward, not back. And I know she is right. But I think no amount of counting my blessings and looking to the future will ever quite remove the emptiness I feel because I never knew who my parents were.'

'Have you ever thought of trying to find out?'

'How would I do that?'

'Well, for a start, have you made any proper enquiries at the orphanage?'

'I can't believe they know anything more than Martha Monday told me. She lived all her life there, first as a foundling herself, then a maid. All she ever said was that I wasn't left on the doorstep, as often happened, but taken there by a woman. She said I was dressed in fine baby clothes and wrapped in a beautiful shawl when I arrived so I must have come from a good family.' I shrugged. 'But perhaps she said that to comfort me, I don't know. She had a kind heart and I was glad to accept the story at the time. Miss Edgar always enjoyed telling me that I was the bastard product of peasants. So take your pick. I cannot say that either tale is true.'

He lifted his hand to my neck. I had told him of the key and the half-burned letter. Through the thick cloth of my cloak I felt the gentle pressure on the silver chain hung round my neck. 'But she might know more of the woman who left you the key. Things that she kept back from you.'

I smiled sadly. 'I think not. Martha heard the conversation. There was only talk of the woman making the visit on behalf of her friend, and if there was an address on the letter, it was burned along with most of the rest.'

'You have never approached any of the trustees, to see if there were records kept or if they hold any other correspondence relating to the time you were taken in?'

I looked up at him in surprise. 'Would there be such things?'

'There might well be. Mind, with the delicate nature of such details, the trustees may keep anything of that nature close. Even the overseer might not be privy to it, though she could have given you the impression that she knew.'

'Which means Miss Edgar could have lied,' I said slowly.

'There is only one way to find out,' Felix said. 'And as we are soon to be in Bristol, why do we not take advantage of being there and call at the orphanage?'

'No!' My response was instinctive. I went cold at the thought of that bleak, harsh place. The words tumbled out in a voice that trembled. 'I have never wished to go back there. The last time I heard – two years since when we took on two girls – Miss Edgar was still there and things were no better. She hated me! She would turn me off and I would learn nothing. All it would do would revive horrible, horrible memories that I prefer to forget.'

Felix put his hands to cup my face so that I could not turn my head away. He looked deep into my eyes.

'Emily, she has no power over you now. You are not the helpless child you were, but a grown woman. A beautiful, intelligent woman.'

'All the same, I—'

'I would not wish to compel you to take such a step. But I do believe you should give it some thought. Will you promise that you will?'

I nodded reluctantly, to please him more than anything else and intending to give it no thought at all.

But the seed was planted. And it threw out roots and shoots with alarming speed over the succeeding days. So that by the time Dr Lodge had pronounced that I was fit to travel and could make the necessary arrangements any time I wished, I had come round to thinking that Felix had presented me with an opportunity it would be foolish to miss.

So I left Starlings Barton resolved to return to Lady Eleanor's once we were in Bristol. With Felix at my side, I would face up to Miss Edgar. And I would not go meekly! However the lost, frightened child trembled inside, Miss Emily Wroe would present a very different picture to her tormentor. I would show the old besom what I was made of. And if the chance came I would tell the trustees a few home truths, too!

Our journey was to be a slow one, with no rising in the small hours to catch early coaches or continuing our travel late into the night. I could have kissed Dr Lodge, had he but known it, when he issued his pompous recommendations. Anything that delayed the moment when Felix and I must part – if only temporarily, should our plans go smoothly – was be welcomed.

'It is best that you do not get overtired,' he said sternly. He was somewhat reluctant to leave on this last visit and dawdled a long time before the parlour fire, warming his not inconsiderable backside at the flames. He smacked his lips over the glass of brandy that Jane always fetched for him. 'As fine a drop as ever did touch my lips. Mr Bowyer keeps a good cellar. It is always my pleasure to be called to Starlings Barton where I am favoured with such generous hospitality... Ah, thank you, a drop more would not come amiss. As I was saying, I would recommend that you travel no more than five hours in any day which, at this time of the year, will encompass the daylight hours only. Take care to have at least ten hours' sleep each night, breakfast modestly – I recommend the usual dry toast and a dish of green tea – in case your digestion becomes disturbed by the action of the coach, and be sure to stay out of draughts as much as possible.'

'I will try to do as you suggest,' I said meekly.

'Always remember that you have come this far and done so well by carefully following my instructions. I would not like to hear from Mr Bowyer that you had undone all my good work by choosing to disregard the words of one whose opinion is founded upon many years of experience. And I hope you will make a comfortable and uneventful journey back to Somerset.'

'He'm a right tosspot,' Jane laughed when he had gone. 'Three great glasses of brandy he drunk – and he'd have looked for another save you never offered. He be proper down in the mouth today, for he'm known for a tight pocket and there'll be no more fees to be got out of Mr Bowyer. I daresay he thought to keep 'ee an invalid as long as he could, but 'ee don't look the least poorly now. Proper rosy you been looking these last days.' She winked, said airily, 'Mayhap Mr Winterborne do have something to do with that, eh, sooner than doctor's physick?'

'Jane, hush, someone will hear,' I said, feeling my face hot. 'You . . . you are imagining things.'

'Oh, 'tis clear as daylight to me,' she said, giggling. 'I saw 'ee a-cuddling and a-kissing in the garden, leave alone the way 'ee eyes each other. But don't fret none. I'm no telltale. Good luck to 'ee, I say.' She gave me a nudge with her elbow. 'But don't go getting up to no mischief while 'ee's from under my eye. He'm a fine gentleman, but a rich man may lose his head as soon as a poor 'en, and be wanting more than a maid should give. Iffen you want my opinion, keep him a-dangling until he'm hooked. He'm a good catch, miss. I hears there's a few grand ladies in Exeter been a-sniffin' round his coat-tails.'

'It isn't proper to be talking to me like this, Jane,' I said, making a show of scolding her, though I was riveted to hear more. I knew from experience that there was a network of gossip among servants that often spread wider and more comprehensively than their employers might have guessed.

Jane was unabashed. 'There's naught but good words ever spoke of him,' she said cheerfully. 'He'm a very charitable gentleman, we has proof of that, for Cook's cousin has a sister living in Edmund Street, and her husband's brother do tell as how Mr Winterborne saved a friend of his from the poorhouse not a month since. Found the man work with a wheelmaker and set his family up in fresh lodgings. *And* paid their debts for they was put into the street for owing rent, no matter that his wife had a babe in arms and three infants round her skirts, poor soul.' She gave a knowing nod. ''Twas not the first time Mr Winterborne has reached into his pockets to help a poor unfortunate, and he'm well thought of on account of it. But I'll say this, if he do go a-choosin' 'ee, miss, then he'm a lucky man, too.' Unexpectedly, her eyes filled with tears. 'I never thought it at first, but I've been happier these last weeks than I've ever been in this house.' She lowered her voice to a whisper. 'Missus en't as patient as 'ee. And her don't see what's under her nose, that's for sure, for there's them 'ere as is lazy and won't lift a finger, excepting when missus or master is looking, and gets innocent folk in trouble on account of their own idleness.' She jerked her head in the direction of the footman who was making a show of adjusting the parlour curtains to prevent a stray low sunbeam from striking the carpet. 'Not to mention that he'm one I don't care to meet on my own, for he'm far too free with his hands, if you take my meaning.'

I did indeed. It only confirmed my own impression of the footman. I was touched at Jane's confession and promised, should she ever have need of it, I would provide her with a character. She had proved a good, willing girl which I had not thought her to be at first. All she needed was the right sort of encouragement. From the sound of it, she was unlikely to get it at Starlings.

I was in debt to her, too, and considerably diverted by

what she had told me of Felix. He had not given me the slightest hint of these charitable activities. Nor about any of the ladies who apparently vied for his attention. I instantly took a dislike to all these fashionable society women he knew, seeing them in my mind's eye as copies of Mrs Bowyer: pretty, twittering, mindless creatures to a woman. Then I laughed at myself and the one-sided picture I had painted. How foolish to descend to the pettiness of unfounded jealousy. Such a useless emotion. I should be proud that I was the one he cared for. Proud, too, that he did not boast of his acts of generosity, but performed them quietly when he saw the need.

When I mentioned to him what Jane had said, he brushed it aside, saying that the debt was paltry.

'Not to a poor man without the means to pay it off.'

'But I am not poor, Emily,' he said lightly. 'It was no more than a night's stake on a friendly game of cards.' He smiled. 'As I have confided in you, good luck has played a big part in my rise in the world. Who knows if my luck will always hold? Perhaps the day may come when I am penniless again and need a helping hand. So if I appear generous, there is more than a little in it of a superstitious need to placate the gods of fortune against an uncertain future.'

I did not entirely believe his explanation. His generosity was not the kind to be all show and no heart. But it was true as he told it that his fortune had been founded on luck, even if it had been furthered by shrewd investment. I had been right to suppose the first work he had obtained in London had scarcely been of the variety to cause him a swift rise to success. It had been his skill with the cards that had been the key.

'And, perhaps, the ability to spirit the most useful ones from your sleeve?' I had enquired.

He had laughed uproariously. This particular day being too wet to go outside he had brought with him a backgammon board and we were sitting opposite each other at the parlour table while he showed me how to play. Now he paused before he shook out the dice and said, still laughing, 'Honesty was a commodity in short supply among the company I speak of, so I have no qualms on that count.'

'But how did you get mixed up with such people? I thought you had work as a clerk in a candle factory.'

'So I did. It was actually an older clerk in the counting house who lured me away from the straight and narrow. He took me to a tavern one evening to meet his brother and his friends.' He shook out the dice and moved his counters. 'It was a trick he had played before on others at the candle works who had secretly warned me not to go. But, being curious, I did – and I played the part of a gullible lad up from the country so well that I believe the company was mystified at my run of luck. So much so, that they asked me back the next night. They intended, of course, to wrest back all they had lost and more besides. But instead they lost as much again.'

'It's a wonder they did not turn on you!'

'I did not give them the chance.' His eyes held that mixture of mischief and devilry that I had so often observed. 'As I had earned more than a year's wages in two nights, I thought it politic to leave off clerking straightway, flit from my lodgings and move swiftly to Hampstead. After which I moved on as the need arose to other districts in and around London where my face was not known.'

'Playing the same role?'

'Quite. A green lad from the country with guineas to spend who wanders innocently into a tavern of a certain sort – not in the rookeries where pickpockets and cutthroats abound, nor the ones frequented by respectable men, but the middling sort of place – will always be an attraction to touts greedy for a quick profit. Alas, there were quite a few who learned a sharp lesson on that account.'

'The stage, it seems, has lost a great player in you,' I said drily.

He grinned. 'I tired of the role after a while. And of the constant need to shift about and assume a new name and identity. I had always taken care to save a good proportion of my winnings, so I had steadily built up a substantial nest egg. That was when I reassumed my own name, set up as a gentleman in quiet lodgings near Mayfair and began the business I seemed to have a nose for: that of acquiring land at modest cost and selling it at a profit. And, because I see the question hovering on your lips, I employ only honest tactics and drive as fair a bargain as I am able.' He threw out his hands. 'No hidden cards. No loaded dice.'

'I'm glad to hear it,' I said with mock sternness as I threw two sixes, pounced on an exposed counter of his and removed it.

'Ha! Beginner's luck!' he growled, throwing to retrieve it and turning up only a five which I had protected, so blocking his progress. He waved me on to throw again. 'No... I rely entirely on my own ears and eyes and memory, the trick, if you would call it a trick, being to evaluate where and when may be the fashion for people to live, or what would be an excellent spot for a factory or an extension to a business or a place of entertainment. And to learn who may be short of ready cash and willing to negotiate a quick sale or what neglected corner might usefully be revitalised. But of course I do not sell all that I buy.' His smile had a bitter twist. 'I believe that my experiences as a child – my father wasting all that he had on lawyers' fees in pursuit of his cause against a rich and conniving cousin, my mother forced to live hand-to-mouth and eventually being reduced to dependence on her sister's charity – made me hungry for land and property and the security it brings.'

'That is understandable,' I said gently.

It was his turn to throw again. Instead, he reached across the table and took my hand. His voice was very quiet. 'My dearest Emily,' he said, 'I value your understanding more than you can know. Your understanding . . . and your love.'

I caught my breath. It was the first time the word had been spoken between us. For all the snatched kisses, the laughter, the confidences, there had remained an element of reserve. Both of us had been watchful, I suppose, for some evidence of change in the other that might indicate an ebbing of interest; ready to put up defences against rejection and hurt. For my part, certainly, I had faced the possibility of Felix's attention being fickle. I had looked squarely at the prospect of the attraction that he felt for me proving to be no more than an illusion. Or that my feelings would alter once I was properly well again and the whole episode would turn out to have been nothing but a flirtatious diversion.

It had not happened. Each meeting had seemed to me to be more exciting than the last. Each moment we spent together seemed to strengthen the bond between us. And now he had spoken of love.

He raised my hand, turning it to press a kiss into the palm. Then he held the hand trapped between his own.

'I believe that I am truly in love with you, Emily,' he said softly. 'I had thought myself momentarily bewitched and I would soon break free of the spell. But now I begin to realise the enchantment is of a different order.'

We had set a candle on the table against the gloom of the late November afternoon. A draught set the flame bending and swaying, so that the shadows beyond the charmed circle of light in which we sat were set swooping and dancing about the corners of the room. The candle flame threw the strong jaw, the beaky nose into relief, causing his eyes to seem darker, more grey than green – full of an intensity of feeling that set my blood coursing hot and heavy through my veins.

'I . . . I feel that I am caught under the same spell,' I whispered.

'Poor Thomasina in Bath. I regret I shall not be speaking to her papa.'

'Poor Luke. I shall have to disappoint him also.'

'Which means we are left with each other.'

'So we are.'

He smiled. 'Does the prospect of my continuing to come a-courting find favour, Emily?'

I smiled back. 'I think I may learn to be easy with the idea.'

A thump at the door, the rattle of china and Jane came in with a tray of cups and plates, followed by the footman bearing the kettle and spirit stove.

Felix raised his eyes to heaven, released my hand, said softly, 'We will talk again when we may be more private. There is much to plan.' Then, louder, 'Ah, tea, Miss Wroe. How very pleasant.' And closed one eye in a conspiratorial wink.

That had been the day before Dr Lodge had pronounced that I might return home.

'The good doctor cannot know how obediently I shall obey his instructions,' Felix said with a laugh when I told him. 'I think he would agree it reasonable to allow several days to return to the Thorn Tree, as even by the fast coach the journey to Bristol takes a day and a half and I shall certainly forbid that you travel at that headlong rate. No more than twenty miles a day at maximum! That is the limit I set. Then there is the visit to the foundling home which we must make. Oh indeed, I can quite believe our journey might well run to five days.'

I chuckled. 'You are perfectly wicked.'

'Just think of it, sweetheart! Four long days to be together without Jane hovering within earshot!' He frowned. 'I just wish I did not have to abandon you as soon as we have reached our destination. But I must return to Exeter to set all in order there and to fetch my favourite mare back to Bath for the rest of the winter.'

'And Blaze,' I prompted.

'How could I forget Blaze when he was the means of bringing us together?' he said solemnly. 'Mind you, my landlady in Exeter will probably have thoroughly spoiled and overfed him in my absence as he has her utterly under his ungainly paw, so his allegiance may have been bought with marrowbones and soft cushions. However, if he still deigns to remember me when I return to Exeter, I shall hope to arrange a reunion between you and Blaze at my house in Bath at the end of December. My Aunt Cavendish will, of course, play chaperone as is perfectly proper. I would not have your reputation ruined in the eyes of Bath society.' He grinned. 'After all, my dearest Emily, I want nothing to mar that moment when I walk into an assembly with you on my arm.'

Such plans, such dizzying hopes I could scarcely believe that it was happening to me; that such a world now beckoned. And all because I had fallen in love with – and, amazingly, was loved in return by – a man favoured in every way. A rich and handsome man of property. Not that the material things mattered. I felt in the deepest part of my being that the same spark would have caught and flamed to passionate life whatever his circumstances. Had he been the lowliest, poorest labourer it would have been the same. I had a sense of such completeness when I was with him, that it was almost frightening to contemplate the time when we must be apart.

But part we must for a little while. There were things that had to be done – and not very pleasant things either. I might be gloriously happy, but my commitment to Felix meant that all Luke's long-held expectations of marrying me had to be dashed. I had to face him and tell him. I had contemplated putting some hint in a letter in order to soften the blow, but I realised that would only ease the awkwardness for me, and hurt Luke the more. For him it would only stretch out the time of anxiety and bewilderment. No, I could not play the coward in this. Only by being honest with him and explaining face to face in the kindest and gentlest way I could would I be able to live afterwards with my conscience.

Then there was Mrs Yelland. My interview with her, I felt, would not be easy either. She was my mentor, my friend, and her letters were full of the new schemes for the Thorn Tree in which I would be prominent, when I returned with a new status, as her companion. She had written that she had already moved my belongings down from the attic floor.

> I bethought me of the small chamber which we were using as a store for unwanted furniture left by my husband's family as being possible to bring into use for you. I have had it cleared out, which it much needed as there were many items that had lain there for some years and which might be renovated and brought into use or sold. Once empty, the room proves a decent size, as I remember it when I first put it to use as a store because its nearness to our own parlour did not make it convenient to be let to persons lodging here. I think you will find it very quiet and comfortable as I have set it out, but I should wish you to decide on whether the curtains I have cut down from an old pair of good-quality yellow cotton are to your taste. If not I have another pair, in harrateen, tho' the colour is not so pretty, being a sombre dark brown ... I so much look forward to your approval or otherwise. I have selected one or two pieces of furniture from what we had in store, but there are other pieces you can choose from if they do not suit ...

I should have been so thrilled even a month ago at the prospect of a room all to myself away from the cramped attics, to have this new status. Instead I felt uncomfortable that Mrs Yelland had gone to so much trouble when my own aspirations had so completely altered. I felt a deep affection for her as she did for me. She looked upon me almost as a daughter. She had said so. I had never known my own mother, but the respect and warmth I felt for Barbara Yelland, her kindness and encouragement, had gone a long way towards compensating for that lack.

Yet the feelings I had for Felix were so overwhelming that all else paled into insignificance: my life at the Thorn Tree, Mrs Yelland's affection, Luke's love. I wanted nothing more than to be with Felix, to share his heart and his life. It was sad that others must be hurt or upset in consequence – yet if they had the affection for me which they claimed, they surely would understand and wish me well.

So I comforted myself. And for the present I put aside all thoughts of the uncomfortable interviews to come and prepared to enjoy what time Felix and I had left together.

The journey to Bristol was very different in every practical detail to the one I had taken to Starlings Barton with Mrs Yelland. The damp room Mrs Yelland and I had shared in the slatternly inn at Bridgewater was not to be the pattern of travelling with Felix.

It was quickly apparent that Felix was a seasoned traveller who had the means to demand and get the best. And this was not at the noisy inns where the coaches set us down, but at smaller, quieter establishments which he had patronised previously and where he was welcomed as a familiar and honoured guest.

'Miss Wroe is only recently risen from her sickbed,' he informed our hosts at Wellington and Highbridge where we slept, 'and requires every attention.' So I was ushered to the best bedchamber and fussed over by the maids while Felix made do with a lesser room, even though he himself was looking somewhat less than his best on that first day. He had, he explained when we met in Exeter, stayed up late at the home of his architect where he had been invited to supper while the final amendments to the house plans had been settled. Then on the way home in the moonlight his horse had been startled by a fox bolting out of a hedge.

'I was damn near unseated,' he grumbled. 'Fetched up against a garden wall by the time I had her under control. Wrenched my leg and barked my knuckles against the wall in the process.' Then he grinned and admitted shamefacedly, 'The architect had several bottles of excellent port recently delivered. He insisted we drink a fair sample so I was perhaps not quite as alert as I should have been when Master Reynard startled my horse. And the aching head I have this morning, in consequence, probably serves me right for indulging too freely. Still, the business is settled satisfactorily and I can go away for a few days knowing that all is in order. Even at such a cost to my person.'

At both hostelries we ate in a parlour set aside for our use at breakfast and supper. And, once the maids had cleared the supper dishes and made up the fire each night, we were left to be private.

Perhaps it was as well that Felix insisted that I retire early and, in truth, I found myself aching and weary from the unaccustomed jolting of the coach. I was not yet as strong as I had been before my illness, and Felix, for all his joshing about the doctor's strictures, was concerned to ensure that I did not get overtired. He was very careful of my welfare and courteous in public to a degree that could not be faulted. In private, though, it was difficult to contain the passion that sprang like a fierce blaze between us now that kisses and caresses need no longer be hasty, snatched affairs.

So I cannot say that parting each evening was easy. It was not, neither for him nor for me. And, tired as I was, sleep did not come easily.

As the restlessness of my body and my senses kept sleep at bay, I began clearly to understand how different it had been with Luke, how much less of myself I had been willing to give. I had always known that there had been a part of me that urged caution, but now I saw how indifferent I had actually been to Luke's lovemaking.

But with Felix there was such desire, a hunger that burned to be assuaged, a hunger that encompassed all my senses, that swept me along in its heady, feverish embrace, and laughed at reason and caution and correctness. A hunger that, unsatisfied, was a physical and emotional torment.

Poor Luke. Had he felt like this whenever I pushed him away? Cheated, hungry for something I could not, would not give him? Because he truly loved me and wanted me, and I could not love him in the same way, but only offer him a pale shadow of what I felt now for Felix.

Luke would have been content with that, thinking that my reserve marked me as a good, respectable girl saving herself very properly for her wedding night. But the truth was very different. I was not a good, respectable girl at all. Where Felix was concerned I had no shame. My feelings towards him were shockingly and profoundly unseemly.

One thing I grew to be sure of. If Felix had opened the door to my bedchamber as I lay tossing and turning in my lonely bed, I knew my heart would not have cried 'caution' and turned him away.

We arrived in Bristol in style, Felix having decided that he had had enough of public coaches and ordered up a post chaise for the last part of our journey. I knew we were to stay at an inn at Clifton Hotwells, and I expected to drive out there first, but Felix had other ideas. When we approached the town he called to the postboys – a title which made me smile as both were gnarled men of middle years – to enquire the way to Lady Eleanor's.

'Best to give you no time to brood,' he said, holding tightly to my hand as the chaise negotiated the narrow thoroughfares and the press of traffic. 'The sooner you beard the lioness in her den, the better for your state of mind.'

I did my best to appear calm and collected, but my stomach lurched when I recognised the church to which we children had been marched, two-by-two, each Sunday, And this was the road we had walked past the houses with their trim gardens, where people lived who might smile and nod at the pretty, orderly sight we made as we passed, but had no notion of the reality of our day-to-day existence. Follow the bend to the right. And there, across the narrow cobbled street, the solid walls of Lady Eleanor's, with its high, arched windows and formidable oak door, black with age. The door that had closed me in and shut out the world for all the years of my childhood.

The sudden silence as the horses were pulled to a halt and the wheels ceased their rumbling over the cobbles froze me to my seat. I did not want to move. I wanted Felix to order the chaise on. I did not want to go into that horrible place and be reminded of how it had been.

But Felix was already getting to his feet, still holding fast to my hand so that I had no option other than to go with him. Then we were facing the door, and he was hammering on the brass knocker in the shape of a lady's hand, shaped, they said, to Lady Eleanor's own. The hand that offered a charitable welcome to those who had nothing. Cold, cold charity, under Miss Edgar's bony, grasping fingers.

The door creaked open. An unfamiliar face. A bright-eyed young girl who bobbed respectfully, and smiled, glanced past us to the bright yellow livery of the waiting chaise and asked us to kindly step inside.

The flagged hallway, the austere walls, the chill of old stone. That smell . . . the odour of repression and fear.

'Will you wait in here, please, and I'll find Mrs Aldridge?' Another bob and the maid pattered off.

This room. Miss Edgar's room, where I had stood so many times awaiting judgement. For an instant I saw it exactly as it had been. The one narrow window piercing the bare walls, the few smoky coals in the grate. I saw myself standing before the table placed exactly in the centre of the floor, with Miss Edgar sitting behind it, her eyes glittering with pleasure as she contemplated what my punishment should be.

I blinked. The table was gone. The whole room was different.

There were green curtains at the window, a row of framed samplers hung along one wall; against another was set a wooden chest with a large urn upon it in which were set dried flowers and grasses. A half-circle of chairs stood companionably around the fire. And such a fire as I had never seen in that grate; a robust bank of glowing coals whose warmth I could feel from where we stood.

'Miss Wroe? Mr Winterborne? I am Mrs Maria Aldridge, the overseer of this establishment. Will you please take a seat by the fire? Such a cold day, but pleasant in the sun. Now, what may I do for you?'

'Miss Wroe has come on a quest,' Felix said, then, gently to me, 'Should you like to explain, Emily?'

I looked into the pleasant face with its welcoming smile, the kind blue eyes and found my voice. It sounded faint and whispery. 'I was expecting to find . . . that is, I thought Miss Edgar would be here.'

'I'm afraid I must disappoint you. She left here in

September, when I was appointed in her place by the trustees.'

'Disappoint me?' I swallowed back an impulse to near-hysterical laughter and burst out, 'I'm not disappointed. Rather, I'm grateful that I do not have to speak to the old witch!' Then, realising I had overstepped the bounds of politeness, I pulled myself together, said quietly, 'Forgive me. I . . . I did not find her to be a sympathetic woman when I was a foundling here.'

'Ah, yes.' Mrs Aldridge did not seem put out by my outburst, rather she was regarding me with sympathy. 'I can imagine how it was. Such tales that I have heard . . . But we will talk of that later. Now if you would like to explain to me what this quest is about, I will do my best to help.'

Of all the things I might have expected to find here, it was certainly not kindness and understanding, which Mrs Aldridge had in abundance. Hesitantly at first, then more confidently, I told her.

She shook her head when I had finished. 'I doubt if I can tell you much more than you already know. I shall look out the books, of course, and see what is entered. As to the trustees, the minutes of their meetings are held in my strong box, but they deal mostly with the accounting and the other administration. However, let me show you.'

She removed the urn of flowers and opened the chest with a key from the bunch she kept at her waist. She brought the ledgers she removed to where we sat.

'This is the year when you arrived.' She turned pages, ran her finger down columns. 'Here it is. *Emily Wroe, born 10th January 1742. Parents Unknown*. Then there is a list of clothing, shawl, dress, petticoats, bonnet, et cetera said to be of fine quality, and a sum of money entered. Twenty guineas.'

'So much!' I said.

Mrs Aldridge nodded. 'A generous donation. Would

that we always received such bounty with our little ones, but then most of the poor women who must part with their infants have not a farthing to call their own.'

'So Miss Edgar did lie to me,' I said grimly. 'It was Martha who told me the truth – Martha Monday,' I explained. 'Is she still here?'

'Indeed she is,' said Mrs Aldridge. 'Should you like to reacquaint yourself with her? She has easier work now, helping to look after the littlest ones when they are brought back from their wet nurses. Perhaps you would care to accompany me to the nursery when we are done here.' She folded one ledger, picked up another. 'This is the minute book. Let me find the date – yes, your name is properly entered amongst the other business of the day. But that is all. The money will be listed in this third book, yes, here. But nothing else, I'm afraid.' She smiled sympathetically. 'Just the bare details, as I expected.'

I had thought that I had not built up any hope. But now, as disappointment gripped me, I realised that I had truly wished for some extraordinary detail to be uncovered.

Mrs Aldridge put her books to one side, leaned over and took my hand.

'I can see you are disappointed, my dear. But, alas, that is the way of these unhappy situations and perhaps it is for the best. After all, even if you had found a clue to your parentage in these books, I think you might have found yourself in an even worse dilemma.'

'In what way?'

'Why, your mother's situation might be exceedingly delicate. She is perhaps married with other children. The circumstances of your being brought here make it more than likely that you were born out of wedlock. If that were the case, and your birth had been kept secret, she would scarcely want you to reveal yourself openly.'

'No, but if I just knew who she was . . .'

'If you knew, the temptation to seek her out might be too great. No, my dear, I think it would be wiser to accept that you will never know. Look to the future, not the past.'

An echo of Mrs Yelland's words. And, sadly, she was right. There was no other course. I must accept what could not be altered.

'It seems so,' I said, with a sigh. 'And I must be grateful that you were here, Mrs Aldridge, in place of Miss Edgar, and such information that you have you were willing to share. I think she would not have been so forthcoming.'

Mrs Aldridge shook her head. 'I think my predecessor was . . . well, shall we say unfortunate in her dealings. Indeed, I think if you will be discreet about what I am about to say, you deserve to know that she left in some disgrace, the trustees having found her out in the matter of her accounting.'

'That doesn't surprise me,' I said grimly. 'Martha said I was once left money by a visitor who called and Miss Edgar took it for herself.'

'It is my opinion that there might have been many similar instances. But nothing of course could be proved. What did come to light, through one of the tradesmen becoming disgruntled with his treatment at her hands, was that not all the money with which she was entrusted found its way to the proper place. That is, for the benefit of the orphan girls.'

I looked at her appalled, remembering the meagre food, the darning and patching of clothes until they were threadbare, the lack of any comfort or pleasure.

I felt a surge of anger, too, as I remembered the brief visits of the trustees, who had seen only what they wanted to see, who had praised Miss Edgar for her economy and good management.

'How could she?' I whispered. 'And how could they – the trustees – have been so blind? Could they not see what manner of woman she was?'

'We have a different system in place now,' Mrs Aldridge said firmly. 'There is no possibility of any dishonest practice occurring again. The previous lax system, you see, was easy to manipulate for someone whose moral judgement was, shall we say, weak in the face of temptation.'

'And what has happened to her?' I asked, hoping to hear that she was languishing in some prison cell as black and unsavoury as the coal cellar.

'She was removed quietly. She was requested to leave the district without delay and is retired to Keynsham on the Bath Road, I believe. The trustees felt it best not to take the matter further in view of her advanced age and in the interests of Lady Eleanor's girls. It was feared that some benefactors might withdraw their charity if the matter became common knowledge.'

'And, naturally, any advertisement of the trustees' incompetence in their guardianship of the orphans would seriously damage their reputation.'

She raised her eyebrows, said diplomatically, 'I would not wish to comment on that, save to advise that several of the trustees resigned immediately and a new board is now formed. And whatever mistakes occurred in the past, it will be different in the future, I assure you. I have always been of the opinion that a child does better when its natural intelligence and spirit is encouraged rather than suppressed. I raised my own three daughters to adulthood on those principles, during which time, being widowed young, I made my living by opening my house as a small school for young ladies. So I do have the practical experience to support my theory. Perhaps you would like to come with me to see the changes I have put about here in order to further my principles.'

Afterwards, I was to remember the sound of young voices. That, above everything else, marked for me the difference, the astounding improvement that had taken place in the few months since Mrs Aldridge had become overseer.

The atmosphere of fear and repression had entirely gone. No one tiptoed about the passages scared that an unwary footfall might arouse wrath. No one shrank back at the overseer's approach. Yet there was respect enough. As we came upon them girls stopped their work to make their bobs, but there were smiles where there had once been scared looks, and easy chatter where terrified silence had prevailed.

'Oh, 'tis unbelievable, the difference,' Martha said, when the greetings and hugs were over. She looked round at the nursery where the little ones were playing at tea parties. 'The bigger ones has proper lessons now of a morning, as it used to be afore Miss Edgar stopped 'em and though they still must help about the house, 'tis done in a different spirit altogether. *And* they gets some time to do as they please. As for these little 'uns, Miss Edgar would have had 'em whipped for not sitting still and practising their stitches. But Mrs Aldridge says there's no need for such yet. Plenty of time, her says, for them to be set to learning.'

No need yet.

Mrs Aldridge was giving her charges time to be children, not dumb, uncomprehending slaves to a relentless system, I thought with pleasure, as the chaise rattled towards Clifton Hotwells. Felix was crestfallen, though, his mind running more on the lack of success in tracing my family than on the positive improvements at Lady Eleanor's.

'Perhaps I should not have encouraged you to think that we should learn more of your mother. I hate for you to be so disappointed.'

My hand was warm in his. I smiled at him. 'But I'm glad that we went, truly. To see the changes, to see the girls happy and know that Miss Edgar has been banished

– that comforts me more than I can say.'

Which was true, though I thought it best to say nothing of the anguish and revulsion that had gripped me when we had walked along the passage onto which the cellar door opened. There was no need to speak of it. It would have troubled him the more and I did not want that. But in those few moments I had been a child again, feeling all the dread and horror of that black place, so that my legs had trembled and my heart set up such a breathless pounding that I thought it would fly out of my chest. Somehow I had managed to keep moving, turning my head from the others as though to examine a picture on the wall, so that my expression would not give me away. By the time we reached the end of the passage the feeling had subsided. It had been nothing, I told myself. Best not spoken of. Best forgotten.

Yet the incident returned to haunt me that night, and though the consequences of that seemed both right and desirable at the time, I can look back now and see how foolish I was to imagine that happiness was something that, once achieved, never diminished but flowed on like a deep, ever-welling spring.

I know now that happiness is a rare and precious emotion, and we are lucky if we are able to drink one heady draught from its bubbling waters before it soaks back into the earth and is lost.

The inn, set among the elegant terraces and fine houses of Clifton, was quiet, the fashionable season for taking the waters being over, though a few stalwart – or desperate – people still remained. People who were not interested in balls or card parties, but genuinely in need of a cure. Among them was an acquaintance of Felix's from Exeter, a Mr Bryce, a manufacturer of serges, who had brought his ailing wife to drink the waters.

They had arrived earlier on the same day, having taken

the flying machine to Bristol. We came upon them as we went into the inn and they were walking out on their way to visit the fountain before the daylight properly faded. Poor Mrs Bryce leaned heavily on her husband's arm, her thinness, the flush of her cheeks and the cough she did her best to suppress betokening a consumption that had a strong hold on her.

'We sleep the night here before travelling to Bath,' Mr Bryce said, after exclamations of surprise at the chance meeting, and introductions had been performed. He was a thin, sallow, sad-looking man of middle years, with an air of worry about him as heavy as his full-bottomed wig. 'It is a bad time of year for my wife to be travelling, but she was done so much good by the Hotwells water I purchased in the summer that I felt we must break our journey here to order a further supply from a genuine source. The last I bought, d'you see, did no good at all. On the contrary it upset her stomach greatly. I fear I had been gulled into buying some made-up article instead of the real thing.' He shook his head sadly. 'I had not realised that people would sink so low as to bottle up ordinary water and pass it off as from a medicinal spa. And I was charged near seven shillings the dozen bottles instead of the six shillings which is the proper price.' He sighed, then said earnestly, 'As you are only just recovered from the fever, Miss Wroe, I would urge you to take a case or two of the genuine article home with you. It is a most effective restorative.'

'Thank you, I will most certainly consider it.'

'And you will drink the waters at Bath also, ma'am?' Felix said gently to Mrs Bryce. 'I have heard good reports of it.'

'I shall, sir,' she said, in a husky whisper.

'And on to Cheltenham, if she finds no improvement in Bath,' Mr Bryce said.

Mrs Bryce smiled tremulously at her husband. 'But I

am sure that will not be necessary, my love. I shall be quite restored after a whole month of idling. Come the spring I shall be quite my old self again.'

'Poor woman. I fear that she may not live to see the spring,' Felix said grimly when they had gone. 'I only met her the once before and I am shocked to see the difference in her in such a short time. It will hit Bryce hard when she goes. He is devoted to her. He was always at the gentlemen's card parties when I was first in Exeter – though never the life and soul of them, I confess, for he is a man who always looks on the black side, even at the best of times – but I can see clearly now why he has set everything aside in order to care for her.'

I did not expect to see the Bryces again that evening, but when I was washed and changed and had joined Felix in the small room where we would take supper he told me he had met them on their return from the spa.

'They will have supper in their chamber,' he told me. Then, looking a little crestfallen, he said, 'But the man looked so deuced careworn that I felt compelled to ask if he would like to take a glass of brandy with us before he retired. I thought it might take his mind for a short while off his troubles, though I half expected him to turn the invitation down. Unfortunately, he seized upon it. I am sorry, sweetheart, but I seem to have got us company for the evening. He will join us when his wife is settled for the night.'

I could not be cross with him, though my heart sank that we would not be alone for this, our last evening. But I told myself not to be selfish. In a few weeks Felix and I would be together again. We were young and had our lives before us. The Bryces were not so blessed. Far from it.

So I managed a smile and said, 'It was a most understandable and sympathetic impulse, Felix. And to be truthful, I think I shall be glad to retire early myself after such an eventful day. Should you mind if I excused myself once Mr Bryce joins us?'

'I suppose I must not,' he said gloomily. He took my hand and slowly kissed the palm, in the way that he had that set all my senses shivering. His eyes were dark and intent in the flare of the candlelight. 'Perhaps it is as well that we are not alone tonight. The thought of not seeing you after tomorrow – well, let us say that the prospect tends me towards a regrettably lustful frame of mind.' Another kiss, his mouth moving from my palm to where the pulse beat at my wrist, the heat of his breath against my skin.

'Oh God, Felix, stop,' I whispered, half laughing. 'The supper will be here in a minute.'

'When will we marry?' he said lazily. 'I have the taste of your skin on my tongue. It makes me hungry for more.'

'We . . . we have not spoken of marriage.'

'Did you suppose I had dishonourable intentions?'

'I was content to drift. To hope. After all, we have known each other for so short a time.'

'Should we then waste months and years being cautious? Or should we cast caution to the winds and take our chance at the game of love?'

'Ah, there speaks a man with gambling in his blood.'

His hand slid up my bare arm, smoothed the fall of lace at my elbow, drifted to the neck of my dress. His mouth followed the same seductive route.

'So? Your answer, madam?' he said, breathing soft against the curve of my breast.

I closed my eyes, allowed myself a moment to drown in pure, sensuous pleasure, said, on a sigh, 'I am ignorant of the ways of the gaming table. But I do know that I love you, Felix—'

A rattle of footsteps, voices, the latch on the door lifting. Felix released me. We smiled at each other as we straightened ourselves, prepared to present an illusion of propriety to the landlord's wife, who bustled in bearing a laden tray, with a maid behind her fetching a scuttle of coals.

'We will set the day when we meet tomorrow,' he said softly. 'Will that suit you, Miss Wroe?'

'Perfectly, Mr Winterborne.'

But, as it turned out, we did not wait that long.

I was thankful not to have to linger with Felix and Mr Bryce. I knew it was unkind to think in such a way, but I wanted nothing to cast a damper on my happiness, as Mr Bryce's doleful manner seemed like to do.

So, as I had told Felix I would, I bade the gentlemen good night and retired to my bedchamber.

It was a plain room, very clean, and I was glad to feel the softness of a feather mattress cradling me as I snuffed the candle and settled to sleep.

Sleep was a long time coming.

Physically tired as I was, my mind was annoyingly alert. One minute it was repeating, step by step, my visit to the foundling home. The next it was rushing ahead, imagining where and when I should be married and where we should live and what Miss Cavendish would say — and Mrs Yelland. Then, somehow, Miss Edgar's face slid into my drifting thoughts . . .

The nightmare, when it came, was as bad as it ever had been when I was a child. I was in a coach going to my wedding and I knew we were on the wrong road, going to the foundling home, because Luke kept his pigs there, which had to be fed, and he was driving . . . Then I was inside Lady Eleanor's with Miss Edgar dragging me along the corridor. 'You come from the gutter and I shan't stand by and let you get above yourself.'

I was shouting for Felix, but my voice was a croak. The cellar door was open. The steps pitched steeply down into the blackness. And I was falling, falling. The door slammed. And the monster in the dark came moaning and crying at my heels as I scrabbled back up the stairs which swayed and melted and tipped me backwards into the slavering jaws... 'Emily,' it growled. 'Emily, I have you now...'

Then it was Felix's voice. 'Emily! For Christ's sake, Emily!'

I came up out of the pit of terror, the sheets tangled round my legs, the flicker of a candle, Felix's hands on my shoulders shaking me...

I was shuddering against his shoulder. His hands smoothed my hair.

'Hush, hush, sweetheart. You will wake the house. I could hear you shouting as I went past the door on my way to bed. I thought some villain had crept in and was attacking you!'

My trembling eased. A bad dream – that was all. But as Felix moved to release me, I clung to him, not wanting to let him go. The ghostly creature of the nightmare still cast its evil shadow into my mind. Miss Edgar's eyes glittered maliciously on the edge of my vision.

I did not want to be left alone to slip back into that pitch-black place where monsters lurked.

I took a breath, knowing what I was asking. Knowing what I wanted.

'Stay with me, Felix,' I whispered.

'But I—'

I reached up and put my hand over his mouth. 'Stay with me.'

Then I turned my head, blew out the candle and drew him down beside me.

Some of the night we must have slept, tumbled together, naked limbs entwined, sated with lovemaking. Then one of us would stir, the other would drift drowsily awake and move a hand to seek the eager flesh of the other, and sleep was no longer possible...

There had been pain at first. But he was very gentle, very skilled, taking his time, allowing me to pause and wonder and appreciate the sensations his lovemaking aroused. And presently the pain was nothing against the greater pleasure.

He kissed me and left me before anyone was astir, carefully pulling the covers up to my nose, which I was very glad of when I woke fully, for the maid had come in to put a cup of hot chocolate on the bed table and draw back the curtains.

'A bright frosty morning, miss,' she announced cheerfully. 'I'll stir up the fire, then fetch your hot water.'

When I had washed I stood naked before the small looking-glass on the mantelpiece, looking at my body this way and that and surprised that I looked no different. Oh, there were traces of pink marks here and there where kisses had grown demanding, perhaps a certain, knowledgeable glow in the smile I exchanged with my reflection. I had scrubbed anxiously at the smudges of blood – the other stains – on the sheets, with a cloth soaked in cold water. They had paled almost to insignificance. Apart from these small signs, there were no outward traces that I was no longer the virginal creature who had walked into the inn yesterday.

But I knew. Felix knew. And I hugged my arms around myself in delight as I realised that the intimacies that we had shared somewhat prematurely would soon be ours within the bounds of marriage.

Easter, we had decided in the small hours, when the spring came. I would carry a posy of spring flowers, I thought dreamily as I dressed, primroses and sweet-scented violets, and wear a gown of the same soft primrose colour...

We sat primly before the maid at breakfast, talking only

of what we would do before we should set off for the Thorn Tree.

'I shall speak to the caretaker and see if we might be shown round the Old Room, where the most fashionable assemblies are held. Such a pity you cannot see it in its glory, but we shall come back in the proper season. There are other excellent buildings, too. The ladies' tearoom, for example. It is so commodious that balls are held there twice a week.'

But the little secret smiles we shared spoke of different things.

Mr Bryce looked in as we were finishing breakfast to say goodbye before he left for Bath.

'My wife had a tolerable night,' he said to our queries. 'If we have no delays she will stand up well to the journey, I believe, being well rested. I hope you, too, will travel comfortably.' He seemed a touch less doleful this morning, as though heartened by the bright crispness of the day. 'It is not raining, it is not snowing, and we set off in the hope that we shall arrive on time at our destination.' His pale smile faded. 'There is always the risk of robbers on the way, of course.'

'I doubt it,' Felix said heartily. 'Not in broad daylight.'

Mr Bryce shook his head, agitating his heavy wig into anxious motion. 'One never can tell with such rogues. I tell you, Mr Winterborne, I would not have believed the audacity of that . . . that villain I told you of last evening, who set upon poor Mr Powys only four nights since.'

'That was Exeter, Mr Bryce,' Felix said, 'not Bristol.'

'But Bristol is a veritable rats' nest of riffraff!' Mr Bryce exclaimed. 'The docks in particular abound with low creatures from the ships that tie up there. If Mr Powys can be attacked within yards of his own house in a decent, quiet place like Exeter, then there must be an even greater chance in a big city for villains to grow fat by highway robbery – and worse.'

Four nights since.

'I think you are unduly pessimistic, sir,' Felix said, his voice holding a firm, reassuring note, but his glance when it caught mine was somewhat wryly amused because Mr Bryce was not to be shaken from his belief that the whole world, in every particular, was against him.

I tried, with all my will I tried to respond, to signal that I shared his wry understanding of Mr Bryce's character. But I could not. I could only fix my gaze again on the scabbed knuckles of Felix's right hand, where it rested on the white cloth.

Four nights since.

'What exactly was it that happened to Mr Powys in Exeter?' I said quietly.

Mr Bryce was eager to advise me. 'It was quite scandalous, Miss Wroe. He had been to call upon his brother who lives in North Street and taking a short cut through an alleyway near St Bartholomew's burying ground on his way home, he was near ridden down by a masked man on a horse.' Mr Bryce's wig performed distressed pirouettes. 'The villain had a pistol and demanded Mr Powys's valuables which Mr Powys made a show of giving him, but being a quick-thinking gentleman, and averse to the loss of his property, when the robber leaned from his horse to take the watch and purse, Mr Powys snatched the pistol away. Whereupon the villain leapt from his horse and a most ferocious tussle ensued for the possession of the pistol. And it being after midnight and not a soul about, Mr Powys quite thought himself about to be killed, for the villain was a giant of a man and immensely brutal and strong, who cursed and swore most horribly. Eventually the villain wrenched the pistol back, leaped on his horse and galloped away into the night, unfortunately taking Mr Powys's purse with him, which he had managed to repossess.'

'Such a loss!' Felix exclaimed. 'Still, it was lucky that a

villain of such a deep dye did not decide to fire his pistol and make an end of Mr Powys.'

'Indeed, indeed.' Mr Bryce shuddered. 'He should have let his valuables go without protest. What is money when set against the prospect of losing one's life?' The clock on the mantel chiming the quarter-hour set him on another fretting track. 'Dear me, I told the landlord to have the post chaise at the door by nine and I see no sign of it. I trust he has not overlooked my orders. I had better see him to find out what the delay is, else the daylight will be gone before we are in Bath.'

He departed in a flurry of bows, fervently expressing the hope for our safe return home and somehow managing to make the possibility sound unlikely.

Felix laughed. 'It cannot be more than fourteen miles to Bath from here. It will be a slow equipage that takes the whole day about it. What a worrypot the man is. He sees phantoms where none exist.'

The clock ticked on the mantel. Outside the window there was the rattle of wheels and hoofs – Mr Bryce's chaise, no doubt. We were alone for the moment. I wished we were not, that the maid would come in and that we did not eat privately, but in some public room where I would not be able to say what must be said.

I braced myself to speak, very quiet and composed. 'That was evidently no phantom that attacked Mr Powys.'

'Powys?' Felix looked at me sharply. 'Surely you have not been alarmed by Mr Bryce's maunderings?'

I stared at him unsmiling. 'Felix, what I have to say . . . it is difficult, because I may be wrong. I hope I am. If I am wrong you will have every reason to be angry with me for even thinking such a thing. But it is something that has worried at me for years and I must now speak and take a chance against your anger.'

'For heaven's sake, sweetheart, why the gloomy looks?' He raised his dark eyebrows in comic dismay. 'You surely have not caught the infection from Mr Bryce!'

'I want you to cast your mind back, Felix, to that first time you were at the Thorn Tree with Miss Cavendish.'

'What is this about, Emily?'

'Did you lose anything while you were there? Were you disappointed when you delved into your pocket and discovered that one half of a valuable pair of earrings was missing? A pretty thing made of gold and set with rubies and diamonds?'

As I spoke I saw the change in his expression – the cold wariness that came into his eyes, the tightening of the corners of his mouth.

'I have no recollection.'

'No? You described such earbobs to your aunt when you returned from your jaunt to Axbridge. They had belonged to Lawyer Merryweather's wife, you said. Stolen from her by a highwayman.' I paused. Said into the silence that hung chill and fraught between us, 'Were you that man, Felix?'

'Me? What is this rigmarole, Emily?'

He laughed. But it was a harsh sound and did nothing to lighten the coldness in his eyes.

'I found the earbob in your room after you had left, caught up in the rug.'

'So what did you do with this . . . this trinket you suspect me of stealing?'

'I took it out into the woods and buried it. Do you know why I did that? Because I could not speak to anyone about it. I was fearful that you would be called to account and the hangman would get you. I did not want that on my conscience. Nor could I bear the thought of Miss Cavendish's distress. My feelings on that are no different now.'

'If it is Lawyer Merryweather's misfortune that bothers you still, I assure you he is not a man to waste sympathy on.'

I reached out and ran my finger lightly across his grazed knuckles. 'Nor Mr Powys? Nor Mr Timothy Jenkins?'

'Oh, come, Emily!'

'I have most desperately tried not to believe any of it.' I did not take my eyes from his. 'Tell me I'm wrong. I hope that I am.'

He did not move. I think in that moment his mind sought a way to continue the deception, to formulate some lie to put me off, then realising that would not do, tried a different tack. He thought to coax me to make a joke of it, like a schoolboy caught in mischief.

'Emily, sweetheart, I see I am undone! You prove yourself too clever for me. But it was not so clever to get rid of a valuable trinket. At the very least it might have provided you with a reward, even if it had proved my downfall. You would have been made famous – a heroine for poets to write splendid odes about – for unmasking a highwayman.'

I snatched my hand away as he sought to grasp it. 'Felix, how could you?' I cried passionately. 'It is not a joking matter. How long has this . . . this game being going on? No! Not a game – a cruel, violent, deadly business!'

He shrugged. 'If you wish to give it a name, call it common justice.'

'Justice! Oh yes, I see. Your aunt was wronged by Lawyer Merryweather so you set yourself up as some kind of . . . of knight errant.'

'If you like.'

'I don't like! And what of the others? How many others?'

'Oh, from time to time, if I see a man who will never be taken to task by the law, but who is a villain in all but name, then I may decide to teach him a lesson.'

'So this is how you made your money in the first place, not at the gaming table but at highway robbery!'

'No!' His eyes narrowed. 'No. I did not lie to you about

that. Whatever I take I find a way to give to those who have been wronged. Only once did I ever keep the proceeds of a robbery and it was a mere handful of guineas which I removed from the breeches of my father's rich cousin, whose pride and avarice caused my father's downfall.' A faint cold smile touched his mouth. 'I allowed him to remove his breeches first. And his shirt, and his hat. In fact all his garments. And made him dance, all dangling, shivering flesh in the moonlight, in front of his stiff-necked, swooning wife and her mother and the coachman. It was the sweetest moment of my young life.'

I shivered. 'Oh God, Felix, I can understand, after all you had suffered. But I could never condone—'

'No? Well, if it offends you, I am sorry. You wanted the truth and you have the truth. But now you have prised out my guilty secret what's to be done about it, eh? About us?'

He eased himself back in his chair. The width of the table was between us. It was a gulf a thousand miles wide.

'You . . . you will keep on?'

He was not laughing now. His eyes were narrow and steely, his jaw set.

'Shall I tell you something, Emily? The reason I kept myself free from women's apron strings all these years is precisely because one day I might sit opposite someone like you having this exact conversation.'

'But you were ready for offer for this Thomasina. You said so.'

'I dallied with the idea because she is amiable and pretty and rich. And malleable to a degree. She would have been easy to deceive. However, I met you and that was the end of Thomasina.' His voice softened. 'I want you, Emily. I never lied to you on that. But I will not be turned into what I cannot be because you see things differently.'

'And have a conscience?'

'My conscience impels me in a different direction.'

'But it isn't right for you to set yourself up as judge and jury and executioner!' I cried. 'And there is such danger in it for you! Look what happened with Mr Powys. If he had been armed, you might not have got away as you did. If you will not think of yourself or your victims, have you no concern for your aunt who loves you? And you say you love me, but how can I trust what you say when you spin me tales about your horse being frightened by a fox? You lied to me, Felix! And so easily. What else do you lie to me about?'

'I did not lie,' he said calmly. 'My horse *was* startled by a fox when I was returning from the architect's house.' He held up his damaged knuckles. 'I caught my hand on a wall. You made the imaginative leap, linking my bruised fist to the imagined fight with Powys.'

'Imagined?'

'It is my recollection that the moment I came on the man he practically threw his money at me. If it is his fancy to make himself out a hero, so be it, but I tell you, for most of our interview he was on his knees begging me not to kill him. Not that I would have done, but he was not to know that. I just needed to give him a taste of the fear and humiliation he puts others to. You see, the man's an importer of fine wines, but he has a secondary business as a usurer and employs brutes to collect his interest. He has no compassion for the poor people who, once in his grip, have little prospect of escape. Why should I feel shame because I cause him a few moments' distress?'

'Because it's wrong,' I said stubbornly. 'And theft is theft, however you dress it up to sound worthy. Oh, it sounds clever and plausible, but how do you know that you do not make matters worse for those you wish to help? You took money from Mr Powys, yes? So, if he's the kind of man you say he is, he'll want to make up for that loss. What happens to the poor people in debt to him then? Will he squeeze them even harder?'

'All I know is that what I took from him means one family, possibly two, will escape his nasty little trade. That is enough for me.' He leaned across the table, said urgently, 'Emily, sweetheart, it need make no difference to our plans. I want you with me always. I love you. But I have to be what I am, without pretence. And you must accept that.'

The clock ticked on, marking everything that united and divided us. Even then, for all my protests, I might, just might, have weakened. There was something dashing and romantical about his trade. About him. If I could only overcome my fears for him. And I loved him so . . .

'Felix, I don't know.'

'Sweetheart, we will go for our walk as we planned.' He stood up, holding his hand out to me. 'You will get used to the idea.' He laughed, at ease again, my warm, kind, caring lover, all that cold, dangerous side to him hidden away. Then he said, lightly, teasing, 'If you find it difficult to understand what I do and why I do it, think of that woman from the foundling home who was so callous with you. Would you not have liked to wreak vengeance on her for what she did to those in her care? Good God, had she not been a woman I might have dreamed up some scheme to discommode her myself!'

The clock chimed the half-hour.

Miss Edgar. I thought about her. She had been cruel, yes – I did not like her and shuddered at the memory of her – but what was done was done. Best put down to experience and forgotten. How much more pleasurable to do well in spite of what had happened, to make a good fist of the future and not waste time looking back bitterly at an irretrievable past or on plotting revenge.

In an instant of icy clarity, I saw how my life with Felix would be. Not romantical at all – far from it. I remembered the times when I had seen that wicked, teasing glitter in his eye; how buoyed up and full of inner excitement he had been that time he had returned with the news of Lawyer Merryweather's downfall. However much he might try to justify himself, I could guess that it was the element of danger and challenge that appealed to him as much as this crusade for what he called justice.

I could never share any of that.

I would be the one waiting at home, worrying, watching, dreading to hear that he had been taken, or injured. And I could not play Thomasina's role. I was not malleable. I would not meekly turn a blind eye and pretend to be easy about his activities. And how long would it be before the underlying tension pulled our love to pieces?

I drew my hand back the instant before it slipped into his.

'I think I will not need to go walking,' I said steadily. 'I know my mind, Felix, just as you know yours.'

His eyes searched my face. All the memory of the night we had shared was in that look and every fibre of my being craved his touch. I wanted him so much. Wanted him to take me in his arms, kiss me, tell me it was all a mistake and he would change because he could not let me go...

But he did not move. And I did not either. He stood there, unyielding, his greeny-grey eyes like chips of ice. I stood there frozen by sorrow for everything I had lost.

Then he bowed, formally. I curtseyed. And it was over.

I left the inn at noon, alone, in the chaise that Felix had ordered. I would not let him come with me as we had planned, nor would I allow him to pay for the journey.

'I have enough by me that Mrs Yelland left,' I said. 'And there is no need to see me off. I am quite capable of giving the postboy instructions and it is best that we do not prolong our parting.'

But he was there, waiting, when I was ready. He handed

me inside, where I busied myself settling my skirts neatly as the horses pulled away.

I did not intend to look at him again. But I did. He stood there watching us go and I found myself pressing my face to the glass of the window to catch the very last glimpse of him as the chaise turned the corner.

Then I leaned back and gave myself up to the tears that I could hold back no longer.

Chapter Seven

'Here, you hold Ellen a minute,' said Cass, thrusting the baby at me and retying her bodice. 'Hold her up over your shoulder and pat her back. That's it.'

The baby's silky-soft head nuzzled at my shoulder. She gave a milky burp.

'You got the knack already,' Cass said, grinning. Then she frowned. 'What's this I hear about 'ee and Luke, eh? I met him as I come in the yard and he could scarce give me the time of day he was that miserable. And no wonder. Oh, you can't mean it, Em! You can't not marry the lad. He's been sweet on 'ee all these years. And he's been that worrit about 'ee and so looking forward to 'ee coming home.'

'I'm sorry,' I said. 'I had a lot of time to think about it while I was ill. It's for the best.'

'Not the best for him, that's for sure.' She pursed her lips reprovingly. 'Or is it 'ee's got too grand now for him, what with being missus' *companion* an' all?'

I had been back at the inn for over two weeks. Sometimes I could almost imagine I had never been away. Like now, sitting by the kitchen fire with Cass, as we had done so often before, Mrs Hill dozing in her rocking chair, a cauldron of good thick pottage bubbling lazily over the glowing embers and scenting the air with savoury vapours.

But it was not the same, though I might pretend that it was for a few minutes in the day.

'No it isn't,' I said sharply. 'That's nothing to do with

it. It's just . . . just being away from him, I realised I don't love him enough. I like him – of course I do – as a dear, dear friend, but it's not like you and Ned are, and it wouldn't be right to marry him, Cass. So there's an end to it and I'd be obliged if you wouldn't keep on about it.'

She sniffed. 'I'll speak my mind, if I think 'tis right to do so. And I still thinks 'ee's a daft moppet. I know you got a room to yourself now and a lot of fancy furniture, but that don't compare to settin' up with a decent lad in a place of your own. Well, come New Year he'll be gone and I hopes you'll not regret it. Just think, he'll be rattling around by himself in a house as needs a proper family to fill its rooms. And twenty acres to farm, he says.'

'It's his choice, Cass. I'm not forcing him to take on the tenancy. And I'm not going to say another word about Luke, so leave it be.'

I could hardly bear to remember the interview with Luke: the ashy whiteness of his face under the freckles, his desperate pleading, and finally, his complete dejection when he had seen that I was adamant. It had been so cruel and I had nearly been in tears at the end of it. But I knew it had to be done. I could not go on pretending. And it would have been even crueller to allow him to cling to hope.

I carefully drew Ellen down to the crook of my arm. She was a good baby. She was instantly, deeply asleep after her feed, her lashes minute gold fans on her cheeks, the tiny perfect fingers of her left hand gripping my finger. She made little contented snuffling sounds.

I had not wanted to hold her today, though I had been eager enough before. It seemed too ominous, an omen. Ellen's baby fingers gripped and held tenaciously. Yesterday there had been no sign of my courses, always so regular. Nor today. Did that signify that a tiny and similarly tenacious little creature now inhabited my own body? Or was it just the result of the fever that had caused my system to delay its natural rhythm? I told myself it was the latter. Of course it was. It had, after all, been only one night. One night with Felix which was all I should ever know...

I wrenched my thoughts away.

'Have you heard any more about the Turnpike Trust taking over our road?' I said. I reckoned there was not much she could tell me that I did not already know as it was a topic on everyone's lips at the moment, but it was a sure way of diverting Cass, who had a very personal interest in the scheme.

'Oh, 'tis all set up,' she said eagerly, which Mrs Yelland had already told me, there being considerable implications for the Thorn Tree. 'My Ned heard it from the vicar when he went to plead his case to be favoured as gatekeeper at one of the new tollhouses.' She grinned. 'From what the vicar said, 'tis certain sure we stand a good chance of it, he and his pa always being straight with the accounting and that, not like some who's too fond of slipping pennies into their own pocket.'

'But that's splendid news,' I said, genuinely pleased for Cass.

'There's to be a gate t'other side of Brimyard where we'd dearly love to be. So we must hope that's the one we'll get, for we could take my gran in with us, dear old soul, and we'll be nice and close to everyone we knows. Course, it won't all be done in a minute, but p'raps by next year me and Ned might be eating Christmas dinner by our very own hearth.'

'Then I hope you are,' I said.

'I daresay missus is happy about it, an' all,' she said, nodding knowingly.

The road was to be much improved and some of the steeper sections rerouted to easier gradients. For anyone travelling to and from Bristol it would provide a safe and convenient link to the road that led to Wells. Even if they should then have to pay for the privilege, there was undoubtedly the prospect of a considerable increase in traffic.

'Very happy,' I said. 'She's already planning how we can take advantage.'

'That's 'er all over,' Cass chuckled. 'I'd wager Master Harry's not so bothered. He was always one for a quiet life. Which 'e never has got much of since he wed the missus.'

'More fool him for marrying her then.' The voice cut like a knife into the cosiness of our conversation.

Cass and I both near jumped out of our skins.

She was standing not a yard from us. For a moment I did not recognise her. Then, as Cass burst out her name, I saw that it really was Amy. She had opened the kitchen door without a sound and advanced across the flags without us hearing, because, I saw, her feet were bare, though so grimed with dirt that she might have been wearing boots. She was hung about with a ragged red dress, her shoulders covered by a filthy shawl. She carried a bundle in one hand, a piece of grey cloth, the corners pulled together and knotted. An acrid, animal odour wafted from her, overlaying the good smell of the pottage.

'What a cosy little picture,' she said grinning, looking from one to the other of us. She had always had a certain blowsy attraction with her black curls and full bosom. That was gone now. She was thin to the point of scragginess, there was a fading bruise on one cheek and her grin revealed that she had lost half her front teeth. 'Like as if nothing's changed since the old bitch pushed me out, save that 'ee's whelped, Cass. What, only one ugly brat? I'd a thought 'ee'd have had a litter the size you was when last I seed 'ee.'

Cass bristled. 'You watch what you says, Amy Wright!' she cried, her jaw jutting belligerently. 'I'll not stand to be insulted by the likes of you.' She took Ellen from me and snuggled her protectively to her bosom. 'What're you doing here, any road?'

Amy made a mocking curtsey. 'Come a-callin', haven't I? Couldn't pass the door and ignore old friends, could I?'

I stood up and faced her, saying sternly, 'Well, now you've said your piece, I'll thank you to go.'

'And who are you to set yourself up in Mrs Hill's kitchen?'

Mrs Hill, hearing her name, harumphed and woke from her doze. She blinked at Amy, her jaw dropping.

'Well, I never,' she gasped. 'It can't be Amy! My heavens, maid, what a sight 'ee looks. Whatever happened to 'ee?'

For an instant, Amy's hard expression wavered, then she tossed her head and said, 'Oh, been travellin' here and there. On the road with friends.'

'And got a wallopin' off someone by the looks of things. Some man got a bit rough wi' 'ee, did he? What did 'ee do to deserve that?'

Amy put her hand to her cheek. 'Got betwixt two of 'em when they was fighting, that's all.' She ran a careful tongue over the gaps where her teeth had been. 'Pity me smile's ruined. Still, it's not every girl as has two men out of their heads over her, is it? Mind, I wasn't much for either of 'em. I'm fickle, me. Love 'em and leave 'em, I say. So I'm off on my own again. Footloose and fancy free.'

'And half starved from the look of 'ee,' Mrs Hill muttered, heaving her bulk out of the chair. 'Give me that bowl, Em, then go cut a wedge off the loaf and fetch a spoon.' She ladled out the hot soup and thrust the bowl at Amy. 'That's for old times' sake, but don't look to me for a soft touch. I don't hold wi' what you done, leaving your husband and child, I tell 'ee straight. So drink your soup and be off afore missus catches sight of 'ee. Her'll not have 'ee hanging about stinking like a polecat as 'ee does.'

Amy did not wait for the spoon. She dropped her bundle, grabbed the bowl and put it to her mouth, slurping the pottage down, then taking the bread from me and mopping up what was left at the bottom.

Shaking her head, Mrs Hill refilled the bowl. Amy ate more slowly now, savouring the taste, smacking her lips when the last drop and crumb were gone.

'You was always the best cook in Somerset,' she said.

'I knows that, so no need to think 'ee'll flatter me into letting 'ee stay.'

'Did I ask to stay? No! Wouldn't thank 'ee for it.' She looked round the warm cave that was the kitchen. Her expression was scornful, but something feral and calculating glinted yellow in her eyes. She reminded me of the half-wild cats that lurked about the stables; always alert for opportunities to steal a scrap of food or fight for possession of a rat or a sparrow. 'I'd nearly forgot how cosy 'twas here. You're all snug as bugs in a blanket. Not a care in the world. And things like to get better, I hears, with the new turnpike. Why, in a year or two Master Harry'll have coffers a-bursting with guineas and 'er he took to wife, the bitch, will have a different silk dress to wear every day of the month.'

'We'll have none of that talk, else 'ee'll feel the weight of my fist as well as what 'ee already knows of,' Mrs Hill growled. 'Em, cut a slab of cheese and give 'er to take with the rest of that loaf. Now be off with 'ee.'

Amy took up her bundle, unwrapping it to put the lump of cheese and bread inside, then tying it up again around her few possessions. She slung it over her shoulder.

'So nice an' welcoming,' she said with a sly grin. 'I'll have to make sure I call again when I'm passing.'

'Don't 'ee put yourself out none over that,' Mrs Hill said sourly.

'Oh, it's no trouble. I knows 'ee always liked my company.' She padded to the kitchen door, pulled it open. 'I'll be back, never fret. Old friends is best, I say. Can't neglect old friends, can I? 'Twouldn't be proper.'

The cackle of her laughter was flung back at us in the draught sweeping in at the open door. The door banged. And all that was left of her was a fading, rank taint in the air.

Mrs Yelland was not best pleased to hear of Amy's visit. As well as visiting the kitchen, Amy had hung around the stables for some considerable time and had even tried to cajole Enoch into letting her sleep the night in the hayloft.

'Thank heaven he packed her off,' she said. 'But I have told Enoch – and I tell you now, Emily – if she comes again I must be called immediately. I shall let her know in no uncertain terms that she is not welcome here. She is no more than a common whore. I will not have such a person befouling the good name of our inn which we have worked so hard to attain. Now come, my dear, I would appreciate your opinion on how we may partition the north bedchamber. It will make two, possibly three smaller rooms, which would be a great advantage, but I do not want to make them too cramped. We must consider quality as well as quantity. When the new turnpike comes we may well have need to cater for more of the gentry – even the nobility – as well as the middling sort of folk we accommodate now.'

When the turnpike comes . . .

It became a sort of litany, firing Mrs Yelland to new heights of ambition, stirring even Master Harry to wonder if he should think of extending the stables.

'Why, that is a most splendid idea,' Mrs Yelland said with her brilliant smile when he tentatively suggested it. 'I had been thinking something along those lines myself, though of course, I should not have dreamed of setting myself to interfere with matters in which you have so much experience.'

I had noticed since my return a certain softening in her attitude towards her husband. She seemed less inclined to the ironic mocking of him, more ready to encourage his opinion warmly than override it with her own ideas. It was as if the time with the Bowyers had wrought a subtle change in her, perhaps the realisation that whatever her feelings for Tom Bowyer, she must put all thoughts of him behind her and make the best of what she had. Perhaps the mere fact that the Thorn Tree's fortunes were set to improve dramatically made her more amenable.

Whatever it was, Master Harry looked the more lively for her encouragement. Always amiable, he seemed even more cheerful than usual, and I caught him looking at his wife with the worshipping air he had displayed when they were first married.

The winter months were always the slackest of the year, though with the weather holding dry there was more traffic than usual, and I was glad of it. I wanted to keep busy, though no amount of activity served to remove the constant ache in my heart, or allowed me more than a few moments' respite from grief. It had to be faced: Felix had not loved me enough to give up the dangerous trade he was in. And I had thrown away my chance of happiness because I loved him too well to have borne the uncertainty and dread which would have been a constant nightmare to live with.

I was forced to encompass Luke's grief as well. I had done him a dreadful injury and guilt was a close companion through the days leading to Christmas. As I took my meals now with Mrs Yelland and Master Harry, I no longer had to face him across the kitchen table, and I took care to avoid the places where he would be working. But it was inevitable that we would meet sometimes and the accusation in his blue eyes, the dejection that wrapped him like a dark shroud, was a most bitter image to carry with me.

I should have to face him at Christmas, though.

The tradition was that everyone at the Thorn Tree ate dinner together in the kitchen on Christmas Day. As those who usually patronised the inn made an effort to be at their own homes that day, it was rare that anyone but the people who lived and worked here sat at the two big tables put together, with Master Harry presiding at one end, and Mrs Yelland at the other.

Last year Luke had sat beside me and held my hand under the cloth and whirled me off in a jig afterwards when the tables were pushed back and Enoch was persuaded to fetch out his fiddle and scrape a few tunes. And there was a kissing bunch hung from the ceiling and games and sweetmeats and wine and ale and cider flowing. And a deal of laughter and talk and good fellowship.

Last year and all the previous years had been keenly anticipated occasions. This year it loomed ahead of me like a threat. I had done my best to keep the depth of my unhappiness hidden and if I appeared to others somewhat quiet, well, I had been ill, hadn't I? And Luke being popular, there were others beside Cass who looked at me accusingly for causing him distress and thought it no wonder that I kept myself to myself more than usual.

But I could not drag either excuse out much longer. Indeed, Mrs Yelland had begun to look at me with a worried air and once she had said, gently, 'Emily, dear, this business between you and Luke, I think you should not blame yourself too much. If you wish for my opinion, I think you are being very sensible not to tie yourself down too young.'

I had made some embarrassed comment – embarrassed because I could not confess the whole truth of the matter – and she had said briskly, 'You are fretting without a good cause. You did quite the right thing, my dear, if you were uncertain about settling down. Luke is a most pleasant and hard-working young man and I am sad that we are to lose him. However, I must say this – and I hope you will not be offended – but I have always felt that you did not quite suit. I could never picture you stuck away on some lonely little farm with only sheep and pigs and cows to talk to. Ah, I have made you smile, so perhaps I am not so far off the mark. But even such a fate as that would be very desirable if you were to share it with someone who meant the world to you. But I do not think Luke is that man. Not for you, Emily. Tell yourself that even if he goes around very hangdog at present, he will get over the disappointment and make an excellent husband to some decent country girl, who understands all about barley and beef.'

I tried to do as she said. I told myself that Luke would get over my infidelity. I silently repeated that I would, in time, stop loving Felix.

There was only one problem that I could see. I could not bring myself to believe any of it possible.

On Christmas Eve a great ash log was brought in and put on the kitchen fire and we all drank a glass of hot punch to welcome Christmas. On Christmas morning Mrs Yelland bore Master Harry off to church with those maids who could be spared, while I stayed to help Mrs Hill with the preparations and to supervise the setting up of the festive board.

I was glad that I did not have to go out. I had woken that morning feeling queasy and out of sorts. The thought of all the food I should have to face sent me scuttling for the chamberpot, though I was not sick and by the time I was washed and dressed the feeling of nausea had eased.

When I had woken feeling so uncomfortable I had held the faint hope that it might be that my body had at last resumed its normal working. But it had not.

I stood by the window for a moment before I went downstairs, bleakly realising that what I had suspected was now more than likely confirmed. I was carrying Felix Winterborne's child.

Outside the window the tree branches bent to the force of the strong wind. Heavy clouds gusted from the northeast and there were only a few scraps of blue sky showing. It was noticeably colder this morning. Perhaps we should have snow.

I thought of Amy out on the road, fending for herself in the harsh winter weather. Amy, forced into a marriage that went against her feckless nature because she had found herself in the same situation that I was in now. How she would jeer at my predicament if she knew. I could almost hear her taunts.

I leaned my forehead against the cold glass, thinking of Amy, my mother . . . all the women down the years who had submitted joyfully to the demands of their own bodies and been forced to pay a bitter price. Amy had walked away without regret from husband and child and the bonds of marriage. My mother? Well, I should never know the reasons why she had given up her daughter. Or whether she was happy or not about it.

I clasped my hands over my stomach. Flat and hard now, it would soon begin to swell and there would be no hiding my condition.

But I knew one thing, whatever happened, however I was persuaded or vilified, I would keep this child. I would love it and protect it and never, never put it into the hands of strangers. It would not be easy. A woman alone with a bastard child. No, not that! A love child. A child born out of a night of happiness. Felix's child.

I turned slowly from the window. A child to love and be loved.

Such a thought!

A tiny thread of light seemed to lighten the gloom that

had weighted my heart close these last weeks. I would hold to it. It would give me purpose to get through the difficult days and months that lay ahead.

The Christmas feast was easier to cope with than I had imagined. I put on a determinedly cheerful face, joining in the toasts, the ribbing, the giggling, the snatching of kisses under the mistletoe. It was made easier for me because Luke, too, had regained much of his spirit. I daresay he, like me, was putting on a good face. I certainly did not want to cast a gloom over other people's well-earned festivities and I could not think that he did either.

We carefully avoided each other. No snatched kisses for us. No dancing to the raucous scratching of Enoch's fiddle. I left that to the younger maids, who were only too eager to take a turn with the one presentable – and available – man present. I made myself busy taking as much as I could of the burden of preparation from Mrs Hill and helping Mrs Yelland with the clearing up afterwards so that the hardworking little scullery maid could take her ease for this one day of the year.

The feeling of nausea had passed and I was thankfully able to try all the dishes from roast goose to plum pudding. Several glasses of crisp golden wine that Master Harry had been saving especially for this day also had a welcome blunting effect on thoughts that were too sharp. I did not care if the effects were only temporary, it was nice to view the proceedings through a mellow haze. Even the mountains of dirty dishes Mrs Yelland and I had to tackle while the others clapped or danced to Enoch's music-making seemed less formidable under its heady influence.

Even on such a holiday the animals must be seen to and Enoch eventually put down his fiddle – to allow our ears to recover, Mrs Yelland whispered, raising her eyes thankfully to heaven – and the men went off to tend their charges while the women regrouped around the hearth. The great ash log had shrunk around its glowing edges but it would clearly see the day out and probably tomorrow as well. We were poking chestnuts into the hot ashes that surrounded it when Luke came running back inside, his face near as red as his hair with panic.

'It's Amy Wright,' he cried. 'Come quick, missus. She's drunk – got herself up into the hayloft with a lighted candle. She's threatening to set the place on fire!'

The wind that met us in the yard was like an icy hand that snatched away all the cosy expectations of the day, the grey dusk made weightier by the sullen weight of louring cloud. We plunged into the dark of the stables where the men stood grouped about Master Harry, watched by the horses who put inquisitive noses over their stalls, ears pricked, the homely smell of them mingling with the sweet scent of hay piled up in the loft above.

Master Yelland was at the foot of the ladder, looking up, saying, 'Now come down, girl. No one's going to harm you. I'll come up a step or two and you can pass me the candle, then I'll help you down . . . and you're welcome to eat with us.'

'Oh, aye? What then, Harry? What then?' Amy gave a giggle that ended in a hiccup. 'S'pose I'd be put off again, eh? No feather bed for me. Not your bed, Harry . . . not no more. Not while the bitch still shares it.'

She sat cross-legged at the edge of the square-cut hole that gave access to the loft. In one hand she held a lit candle. In the other she had a dusty bottle by the neck. She tipped it up and took a swig, the candle in her other hand sending a wild flickering light round her as she moved.

'Ah, thass better,' she said, smacking her lips. 'Brandy. 'Tis warming.' She swayed backwards and forwards, grinning her broken-tooth smile. 'Stole it from 'ee, Harry. Taproom. Easy. While 'ee all was stuffin' in the kitchen.

An' the can— candle.' She belched. 'Thought me to hang on here. Better'n a hedge on a cold day. Have a little chat with 'ee, Harry.'

'And I'd be happier to talk inside the house, where it's nice and warm,' he said encouragingly.

'Soon get warmer 'ere, if you likes.' She giggled and thrust the candle perilously close to the hay. Then she pulled her hand back and leaned so far forward that it seemed she might tumble. But she did not. She blinked down at the faces looking up to her. 'Oh, the bitch is here. Welcome, Bar— Barbara. Nice of 'ee to call, bitch. I'd offer 'ee a splash o' brandy but wouldn't give 'ee the dirt under . . . under my fingernails.'

One of the men moved – Enoch – whispering in Master Harry's ear, 'Best shift the horses just in case.'

'What you whisperin'?' The grin was gone. She scowled as Enoch began to sidle away. 'Come back 'ere, you, or else . . .' The candle flame dipped close to the hay again, swayed back when Enoch stopped moving. 'Thass better. Do as Amy says . . . no harm'll come.' She thrust her face forward. ''S Barbara I'll speak to. Stand away, Harry. Her an' me – us'll talk real nice. Proper ladies we be . . .'

Mrs Yelland moved to the foot of the ladder. Her voice came very cool, very steady, 'Amy, there's food and drink a-plenty inside. You're welcome to join us and to stay as long as you like.'

She giggled. 'Thass kindly . . . Harry's bed, you offering? Warm 'im up, I can. Better'n you . . . Thass what I wants. New gown . . . every day . . . proper lady, thass me.' Another swig from the bottle, a choking cough. Then her voice lowering, hissing, 'Come up 'ere, Lady Barbara. We'll talk private. Then we'll see.'

'Don't!' Master Harry, caught his wife's arm. 'Don't. She's mad – dangerous.'

'Leave 'er be, Harry . . . Up 'ere I says.'

A moment's hesitation, then Mrs Yelland said, 'I'll have

to go. She's too drunk to know what danger she's putting herself in, never mind the horses.' She smiled at him, her face a pale oval in the gloom. 'If I can manage to put the candle out you can come up after me and we'll try and persuade her down.'

'Oh, my dear.' He bent and kissed her cheek. Then, anxiety written all over his heavy face, he took his place again at the foot of the ladder as she began to climb.

Amy shuffled back as Mrs Yelland's head came level with the loft entrance. Then, as Mrs Yelland continued to move up the ladder, her body blocked our view of Amy. So what happened next could only be guessed at. Whether she kicked out at Mrs Yelland with that black, calloused foot, or whether she struck her with the bottle I could not say.

Mrs Yelland came tumbling backwards.

The image was engraved so clearly on my mind that afterwards, whenever I thought of it, I saw her falling with infinite slowness. The arch of her back as she tipped into space, the crack of her head against the rough planks of the loft entrance, the swish of her skirts flying up as she plummeted down onto Master Harry. And Amy's eldritch shriek of laughter following after her . . .

It could not have happened like that, I know. The tumble took seconds rather than minutes. But that is how I remember it. That, and how we all stood rigid, aghast, before someone broke the terrified stillness, stepping forward to the two crumpled forms that lay silent on the cobbled floor. Was it me? I cannot recall, but I know that it was the signal for a chaos of noise and movement.

That laughter – harsh, wild. Then not laughter, but howls of pain and terror as above us with a great crackling rush of light, the sweet dry hay caught, and the horses began to panic, screaming and pounding their hoofs against the wooden panels that held them prisoner.

We got them out – Mrs Yelland, Master Harry and the

horses – a mad, urgent, race against the fire that gobbled up the hayloft and the rafters, then danced outside to greet the wind that roared it a greater power.

We could not save the stables. We could not save Amy. There was hope for the brewhouse and the barn, which lay in the path of the wind, if every bucket and pitcher was grabbed and a human chain formed from the pump. Then, like an answered prayer, the touch of damp in the wind. Not snow, but rain. A drizzle at first and then a sleety, steady downpour.

I was indoors by then, with Mrs Hill. The men had fetched Mrs Yelland and Master Harry into the kitchen and gone back to the fire. Master Harry had been placed on the flags at the back of the kitchen. Mrs Hill, weeping silently, had straightened his limbs and his clothes and his wig and put pennies on his closed eyes. I thought, with a lump in my throat, that Mrs Yelland would have been pleased to see him so tidy for once, however unnatural it was. For it was not really Master Harry lying there, but a grey, waxen shell. Mrs Yelland's fall had sent him staggering back against the stable wall, breaking his neck. Killing him instantly.

Mrs Yelland was laid on the hearthrug. We had gently wrapped her in quilts and burned feathers under her nose, but she remained unconscious. We could not properly say what her injuries were beyond those we could see. There was a cut on the back of her head and her left arm above the wrist was bent at an unnatural angle with the bone glinting through the broken skin.

We did what we could for her, until her eyelids fluttered and a little colour came back to her cheeks. Eventually Luke and Enoch, their best clothes grimy and soaked, carried her upstairs to her bed. I worried that there was no doctor within miles that I knew of, certainly none at Brimyard. We mended and nursed each other with homemade simples when the necessity arose. But there was a bonesetter, a good one I had heard, who worked as a charcoal burner. We should have to send for him in the morning and hope that there were no worse injuries.

I sat the night beside her bed, as she had so recently sat by mine through the fever. Daylight came, wet and grey and cold. The stables still smouldered, the dank stench of sodden ash filling the yard, but the fire had not spread. The men, whose quarters were at the other end of the hayloft from where the hay was kept, had lost all their belongings. So I took it upon myself to open the chest where Mrs Yelland kept the money and gave them each enough to furnish themselves with spare clothes and boots and other necessaries. Then I got the maids to find pallets and blankets so that the men could make themselves comfortable in the barn where the horses had now been put into makeshift stalls.

The bonesetter came. Mrs Yelland had roused now and we persuaded her to take some of the draught of poppy juice and camomile that he had brought which he said would numb the pain. He was very practised and surefingered, but it was an unpleasant business and I was glad when it was over and the arm splinted and bound and Mrs Yelland fallen to an exhausted sleep.

The work of the inn went on. I thanked God for the efficient routines Mrs Yelland had set in place, everybody knowing what they should do and how they should do it, though it was felt that, as a mark of respect to Master Harry, the taproom should remain closed for the present.

There was a great deal that fell to me. That first day, Mrs Yelland could scarcely take in that her husband was dead, leave alone make arrangements for his interment in the family plot at Brimyard church. So I took it upon myself to write to Mr Bowyer, the only blood relative of Master Harry's that I knew of, to inform him of the sad accident. I sent for the vicar to discuss the funeral, and the village carpenter who would make the coffin, and set the maids to making the black hat and arm bands that would be presented to the mourners.

I helped Mrs Hill lay out Master Harry's body properly in one of the downstairs rooms. We put a black cloth on a table where the coffin would rest and placed a sprig of rosemary between his icy fingers, and draped the window and the empty grate with black crepe.

I think nearly all the people in Brimyard came to pay their last respects. He had been born here, he was part of the little community and was greatly liked. Mrs Yelland herself felt able to make the journey downstairs on the following day and she asked to be left alone with her husband for a while.

'I owe him my life,' she said afterwards, very quiet. 'He shall have the finest funeral that can be afforded. I can give him that at least, though he deserved better than to die so untimely. He was a kind man.'

'Yes, he was,' I said softly. 'And he loved you very much.'

'I believe that was the case,' she said with a shivering sigh. 'And I had grown . . . fond of him. I regret it could be no more than that. But I hope he looks down at me from heaven and understands.'

Mr Bowyer, to my relief, arrived on the morning of the funeral. I had done everything that I could for Master Harry and Mrs Yelland, but there was one gruesome matter that I greatly preferred someone else to deal with.

The day before, work had begun on the clearing of the ruined stables and the remains of Amy had been found. I think we all had hoped that there would be no traces left, that the fierceness of the fire had done its work thoroughly. But Enoch, whey-faced, had come to tell me that our hopes were dashed. The remains of what had been Amy Wright now lay where they had fallen among the ashes, hastily covered with sacking and boards.

Mr Bowyer, thankfully, saw to all the practical details,

notified the authorities that had to be notified, arranged for her burial. The work of clearing the stables recommenced.

But that was all later, after Master Harry's funeral, and it was the evening of that day, when everyone had left, that Mrs Yelland sprung a surprise on Mr Bowyer and me.

She sat by the parlour fire in her funereal black, a colour which did not suit her. Against it her skin had a yellow, exhausted tint. She looked old and tired sitting there with her arm bound in a sling across her breast. Yet her voice held some of its usual briskness as she called to Mr Bowyer and me to come and sit down as she had something to tell us.

We had been moving furniture and setting the room back to its usual order and I had thought to retire early to my bedchamber as soon as it was polite to do so, for I had suddenly felt exhausted after all the strain of the last few days. However, I made an effort to stifle my yawns and sat beside her, with Mr Bowyer on the other side of the hearth.

'I have come to a decision,' she said, 'and as it closely concerns you, Emily, I wish you to know of it first. I have been made an offer for the Thorn Tree and I have decided to sell.'

I was thunderstruck. It was totally unexpected.

Mr Bowyer was taken aback, too.

'Now, Barbara,' he cautioned, 'you should not do anything in a hurry. You are still in an emotional state and in a week or two you may regret you have been so hasty.'

She shook her head. 'It is not so hasty. A few weeks back, when we knew of the turnpike coming, Harry was made the same offer – by Mr Charles, who runs the coaches that come here and who uses our horses. I knew Harry would never sell, but the idea was not so unpleasing to me even then. Now, with Harry gone, there is no reason to force myself to continue here.'

'Force yourself?' I said. 'I thought . . . I thought you were ambitious to see the Thorn Tree prosper.'

'Of course I was. When there was no alternative.'

'And what alternative do you have in mind, Barbara?' Tom Bowyer asked quietly.

She paused, looking into the fire, then said slowly, 'I have been, Tom, a daughter in my father's house, and twice a wife to husbands already set in their ways, to which I have adapted as best I could. Now I wish to be . . . to be myself. I am forty years old and I have a notion to please myself for once. To choose a place to live that is agreeable and convenient for me and where I might do exactly as I wish.' She turned her head to look at him. 'Is that so difficult to understand?'

His gaze was sad and gentle.

'There will always be a place for you at Starlings Barton, you know.'

'You are very kind,' she said, 'but much as I love it, I cannot now look upon it as my home as it once was when I was married to your father. Perhaps I may take advantage of your hospitality while I look for a place of my own, for I have a fancy to return to Exeter, where I was born. But no more than that.' She turned to me and smiled. 'You have been a tower of strength this week, Emily, as you always are. And though I will not try to persuade you, because it would not be fair, if you would like to continue as my companion and make your home with me in Exeter, then I should like that very well.'

'But . . . but the Thorn Tree . . . what will happen to everyone here?' I said, bewildered.

'Mr Charles wishes everything to proceed exactly as it does now. He is a careful man, and a kind one, I think. He has watched how we have improved and prospered over the years and hopes to continue as we have done. He will keep all the servants who are willing to stay and help him.

He particularly asked me to tell you that he would like you to stay as housekeeper, with all the responsibility that entails. So you see, I am being very fair to him and to you in showing you that you do have an alternative to accompanying me.' She patted my knee. 'Poor Emily, there have been too many upsets this week. I do not want your answer straight off. There is no rush after all. You must think very deeply about it. The lawyers tell me that my husband's will is straightforward. I am the sole beneficiary. But these things take time. I cannot envisage that I shall move before the spring. Now to bed with you. We will talk more fully in the morning.'

Mrs Yelland was wrong in believing that I had two choices. There was a third.

On the first day of the new year, Luke Gilpin left to be tenant of his own farm. Though we had been careful to avoid each other since my return, today he came to the little cubbyhole in the guest wing where I was making up my accounts.

He stood at the door and I put down my pen and rose slowly to my feet.

'I came to say goodbye, Emily,' he said quietly. 'I couldn't leave without settling this ill-feeling between us. I . . . I wanted to say that I've behaved like a daft lad, not a grown man.' He twisted his hat between his fingers. 'I was hurt, I confess it. I thought it was the end of the world, but the world does go on. You can't make folks love you that aren't able. I think at the back of my mind I'd always known that I was more . . . more set on you than you was on me.'

'I'm sorry, Luke,' I whispered. 'I didn't want to hurt you. You have been my dearest, dearest friend. And I do love you.'

'But not enough. And not in the same way. I know.' He sighed. 'Well, I can't say this is how I planned moving to my own place, but there it is. It's done. It's what I want and I intend to make a good farmer. Still, Princess, if you think to change your mind . . .?'

The question hung in the air. So tempting, so very, very tempting. I could go with Luke. No need to delay our marriage. He would take me without question. I could pretend the child was his, born early, a perfect solution to an age-old dilemma.

But how could I live with myself if I did?

I put my hands on his shoulders and kissed his cheek. He turned his head so that his lips lightly brushed mine.

I stood away from him. 'I wish you all the luck and success in the world, Luke.'

'And you, Princess.'

He bowed, the red of his hair a bright, untidy beacon. Then he was gone.

On the day before Mrs Yelland and I left the Thorn Tree to embark on a different life, I went to pay my last respects to Master Harry.

I walked down to Brimyard churchyard on a March morning of sudden showers and dazzling sunshine that sparked rainbows against the purple rain clouds. I carried two bunches of primroses. I laid the first among the daffodils Mrs Yelland had already placed on Master Harry's grave and stood there a moment recalling his good nature and amiability.

He was buried with his parents. His ancestors were all around, some of the headstones so blurred with age that the names could hardly be deciphered. He had been a gregarious man and it was a happy thought that even in death he had the company of his own family, leave alone the many other people, familiar to him, who lay at rest in the graveyard.

Amy's grave was harder to reach. It was in a patch of rough grass hard by the churchyard wall and already the weeds had begun to repossess the rough soil thrown over her coffin. Amy had not gone to a pauper's grave. Mrs Yelland had insisted on paying for a decent burial though there were those who glowered and said that she should have been thrown in a limepit where common murderers ended.

'I never liked her,' she said. 'Few did, save the men who took their pleasure of her. But if things had been different – had she been raised properly, learned gentler ways, who knows? No, I will not take revenge on her in death. And she has no one else who cares a fig about her passing.'

Mrs Yelland never admitted that she knew what had happened, long ago, between her husband and Amy. And I could not ask. But perhaps this final gesture was an acknowledgement that Master Harry had always tolerated Amy in his amiable way.

I bent and pulled up a leggy bindweed shoot that was already sprouting up through the soil. Then I laid the primroses against the small rough cross which gave her name and the date she died.

I smiled. Amy would have been slyly pleased, I thought, to know that the place of her death had already gathered a reputation. The scullery maid swore she had seen a ghostly figure carrying a candle drifting through the half-built new stables. There was talk of cold draughts and strange knockings, and none of the maids would go near that end of the yard after dark.

So Amy had got what she wanted after all. Her name would be for ever linked with Master Harry's when the infamous tale was recounted down the years.

Long after Mrs Yelland and I were gone and forgotten, the story of Amy Wright would be remembered, a story that would be passed on and grow in the telling until it was a full-blown legend.

I did not begrudge her any of it. I was so much luckier than she had ever been. I would start a comfortable new life in a new place and I would keep my baby.

I had had to tell Mrs Yelland why I could not go with her, nor accept Mr Charles's invitation to stay on at the inn as housekeeper.

When she had recovered a little from the shock, I said quietly, 'I have some money saved, as you know, and I will move away to a good-sized town where I'm not known. I shall make myself out to be a widow and take up respectable lodgings. In my condition it's unlikely I shall find any sort of live-in post, so I could advertise myself as giving lessons to young children, or take in sewing.'

'Oh, my dear Emily!' Mrs Yelland had looked at me tearfully, then she had put her arms around me. 'It would be unbearably hard without friends and with hardly any money. I cannot let you do it. Now come and sit down. We must talk.'

'There's no other way. And I have decided.'

'No other way? Do you suppose I give a fig what people say?' She frowned, thinking for a moment. 'Oh, we might cook up some tale of you being a widow when we move to Exeter. But not on account of my reputation, but to save your feelings, if that is easier for you and will benefit the child.'

'But if we are to stay with the Bowyers . . . Mrs Bowyer in particular would think it scandalous.'

'Then we will not stay there! After all, nothing is settled. And, to be honest, I think I would sooner take lodgings in Exeter while I search for a house.' Her face fell. 'But perhaps, Emily, the associations . . . Mr Winterborne. Great God, I had no idea he was a man of that nature. To take advantage of a young girl left in his charge!'

I shook my head. 'It was nothing like that. I think . . . I think that you could almost say I took advantage of him, the way it happened. I loved him so much. I still do.'

She fell silent. Then she shook her head and said softly, 'I cannot reproach you. I have known true love . . . but circumstances were against me. Had they not been – well, who knows what might have happened?' Then she went on more crisply, 'So if it is not to be Exeter, where shall it be?'

'That is where you want to settle,' I said firmly. 'So I will happily settle there, too. As to Felix, well, Mr Bowyer says in his letters that he has hardly been in Exeter this year save on the briefest of visits. And there is speculation that once his houses are finished he will move on elsewhere.'

My voice was quite steady as I spoke. I was becoming familiar with the idea that Felix's declarations of love had been no more than a passing fancy. All his fine words about loving me and wanting me had been so much chaff in the wind. I had not stood a chance against the tug of that other more sinister passion that ruled his life. I should always hold the grief of it somewhere in my heart, buried deep. But the grief of loss would ease with time, as all grief did.

So it was all arranged. Mrs Yelland and I would take up our new lives in Exeter. She had already spoken to Mr Bowyer about allowing Jane to come and be maid to us and he had agreed. Mrs Yelland was full of eager plans.

'I do not intend to live a social life, that has never appealed to me – so much time spent in idle gossip and frivolous occupations. No, no, I have always wished to learn the classical languages, so I shall engage a tutor to teach me Latin and Greek. And if I am in need of company I shall seek out other ladies of a similar mind. Perhaps form a reading group, so that we may discuss suitable literary works . . . or invite scholarly persons to speak to us. Or, who knows, I might write a scholarly work myself! And when your child is born, Emily, whether it be a son or a daughter, it will have the advantage of being raised in a most cultured atmosphere.'

It sounded very fine and I said how pleased I was, and

how grateful. But there was still a great sadness in me that my child would never know a father's love and care.

I left the churchyard and walked back slowly to the inn, swathed in my all-embracing cloak. A little heavy for the day, but it was best to be discreet. I still did not show too much and I had so far managed to hide my thickening waist by letting out my skirts and making up a light shawl to wear about the house. But I should not like to mar our departure tomorrow by inviting gossip.

I looked about me at the familiar road, the green-springing hedges, the grass beneath them starred with the flowers of spring; up the rise and round the bend which had been the scene of the disaster that had brought Felix into my life, and where a gang of labourers was working. I edged round the ruts into which the men were tipping broken stone and acknowledged the greetings of those who were creating new and deeper ditches either side so that rainwater could drain away. There were gangs like this busy all along this road, and the foundations of the tollhouse where Ned and Cass would be gatekeepers were already in place.

Change was already advancing rapidly towards Mr Charles's new possession.

I quickened my steps as the familiar buildings of the Thorn Tree came into view. The Bristol coach would be in by now. I might as well offer my services to the new housekeeper, for my boxes were packed and there was nothing else I had to do.

The dog came at me like a great shaggy fawn and white hearthrug on legs, leaping up at me as though to greet an old friend. It lashed its wet tongue against my face, feathery tail wagging so hard it looked likely to separate from its body with excitement.

I looked dazedly at the familiar white flash on its nose.

'Blaze?' I said.

Then, in disbelief, looked slowly past the dog to the

elegant dark brown mare and the man sitting on its back. A straight-backed figure in a blue coat, the bright March sun casting a deep shadow from his tricorn hat across the sharp planes of his face.

I stopped dead in my tracks, the dog bounding and snuffling round me.

As I stood there, transfixed – with hope, with a kind of desperate fear – Felix dismounted, throwing the reins to the yard boy who had come running out. The horse was led away, hoofs clopping over the cobbles. Felix walked slowly across the space that divided us.

'Blaze has not forgotten you, I see.'

His eyes were more green than grey in this light. They looked into mine with unwavering concentration.

'He . . . he's grown.'

'Overgrown, I might say.'

His voice, so deep and warm. Why had he come here? I felt a spurt of anger. How could he turn up like this? Just when I was getting used to being without him. He was cruel! Unthinking!

'Emily.' He cleared his throat. 'I . . . I had to come.'

'Why?' I demanded.

He took in a sighing breath. 'I have done my damnedest to forget you, but I cannot. My life is nothing if you will not share it with me.'

He looked tired, I thought. There were bluish shadows under his eyes and a stubble of dark beard along his jaw as though he had been journeying for many hours.

'But . . . that other business. You know what I feel about it.'

Even as I said it the reckless thought came to me that even knowing what I knew of him I still wanted him. I wanted to put my arms round him, comfort him. What did it matter who he was or what dangers he attracted? He was Felix. For good or bad, I needed him, as he needed me.

He did not answer directly. 'I am going away. I thought to ask if you would come with me.'

'Away? Where to?'

'I need challenge, Emily. I cannot endure to be always proper and respectable. If I stay in England . . . well, no matter. Perhaps I was wrong to ask. You have a secure life here, among friends.' His voice was flat, expressionless. 'I can only offer you uncertainty at best. Possibly even danger, for God knows what hazards there will be and it is probably best that I face them alone.'

'You're going abroad?'

'My aunt is married. I have no other responsibility. I have bought a piece of virgin land in the part of America known as New England.' He smiled wryly. 'It is a gamble. It is supposed to be good, fertile land, on the edge of a growing town, but whether I have been gulled or not remains to be seen.'

'You were always one to take a chance,' I said softly.

'Indeed.'

'And among the list of hazards you forgot to mention love.' I held out my hands towards him. 'Perhaps there is more of the gambler in me than I was aware of. Shall I take a chance on love, Felix? The greatest gamble of all?'

Felix hesitated only a moment, then he stepped forward and took my hands, while the dog bounded round us in an ecstasy of delight.

Epilogue

Tom Bowyer stood at the window of his bedchamber and gazed across the formal garden to the Mulberry Field.

He could see the thin plume of smoke rising from one of the chimneys of the Old House and, closer to hand, the small, black-clad figure standing under one of the mulberry trees. She had been there for some time and he wondered what it was that kept Madame Forestier so rapt and intent.

He had not spoken to her yet. He had learned from the footman that she had arrived this morning while he was out with his land steward. Not only her, but a brood of children, all presumably now down at the Old House with their poor grandmama. No husband had come with her, though. He must have stayed behind. In fact, there had been no word from her all this time and it was quite possible that his message had not reached her but that she had been on the high seas by the time his letter had crossed the ocean.

Well, when he had washed his hands and changed his breeches, which he had got muddy walking over a ploughed field, he would go down and welcome her back to Devonshire.

Under the mulberry tree, Renée Forestier, who had been Renée Crespin, breathed deeply of the cool sweet air and smiled. The air of freedom! She could not get enough of it. Claude, her husband, had died six months since, yet it had never been quite believable that she was free of him when she was still in his house, on his estates, with his servants and slaves. And all through the perilous voyage home she had been pursued by thoughts of his petty cruelties, his unyielding nature, half expecting that she would find it all a dream and that he had pretended to be dead from blackwater fever as a means of some extra malicious torment. Only when she had walked down the gangplank in Bristol and set foot on English soil had she begun to believe that she truly was a free woman.

Not entirely free, of course. She had her two stepchildren, her own three and their inheritance to guard. And poor Maman. She must bear responsibility for all of them, though that was a burden she was joyful to shoulder now that she was her own woman.

She would get rid of that terrible Kemp woman for a start. She had taken account of the situation there in an instant, no matter how Mrs Kemp fawned and smiled and made excuses. Maman had been grievously neglected, that was clear. And bullied. Well, she knew all about bullies. And that one would be sent off by nightfall. Tomorrow there would be lodgings to look for while she thought about the next stage of her plans for her growing household. There was no one to stop her now. No one to arrange for Maman to stay fastened up in that grim old house for years and years, as Claude had decided once Aunt Jeanne and Uncle Pierre had died, though she had begged him to allow Maman to come out to them or for herself to be allowed to return to ensure Maman was in good hands.

No one, indeed, to stop her going straight to that bleak orphanage place the day she arrived in Bristol. Not secretly and veiled, as she had done before she left for Barbados with Claude. But openly, to demand, from the old hag who had been so vile to her, the whereabouts of her first daughter.

But the old hag had gone and the helpful woman in

charge had told her how Angelique herself had been making enquiries about her origins. How miraculous that had seemed! She had followed the trail to the inn where her daughter had worked. And that trail had led straight to Exeter, where she was destined anyway. Tomorrow she would go to the address they had given her, where Angelique was living with her employer. They had only left a week ago, though there was some talk of a marriage and Angelique going abroad. And there was a connection through this Mrs Yelland to Starlings Barton, which was a strange twist of fate indeed.

Mon Dieu, she hoped she was not too late to see her little Angelique again. She would always be Angelique in her mother's heart. Angelique Le Rou. That was how she had sent her baby out into the world. Angelique her chosen name, Le Rou Maman's maiden name, so as not to bring disgrace on the name of Crespin. But Uncle Pierre had changed that – called her by an ugly English name, Emily Wroe, so she had no clue at all that she was not English but Huguenot French. And what had happened to the letter and the money and the key she had sneaked to the child?

That was a mystery still to be solved. But it would be interesting to see if the little jewel box she had buried all those years ago was still intact.

This was the tree, she was certain. She saw the house from here at a particular angle and the window where she had been incarcerated by Uncle Pierre that terrible winter and where Angelique had been born. When the iron frost had eased she had come out here and dug a hole and buried a little treasure for her daughter, not knowing how and why she would ever get word to her about it. She had written about Louis and herself. She had told how she was to be married off to a widower with children. She told Angelique how she had loved her and wanted to keep her, but it had been impossible. Then she had put her few bits of jewellery in the box – a child's silver and opal ring, a gold brooch her father had bought her for her twelfth birthday, a locket with a miniature of Maman. Lying to Aunt Jeanne later that she had mislaid her jewel box and could not find it.

Well, if it was here she would give it Angelique tomorrow.

She took from her pocket the little trowel she had found among the jumble of garden implements rusting in the garden.

Then she crouched down and began to dig away the turf between the spreading roots of the mulberry tree.

At The Toss of a Sixpence

Lynda Page

At eleven years of age, Albertina Listerman loses her parents in a terrible accident. Approaching her twenty-first birthday, she experiences further tragedy: her half-brother commits suicide, having squandered the family fortune, and Ally is no longer acceptable in the elegant Victorian society of her childhood.

Robbed of her very last penny, Ally is thrust into a world of hardship for which she is ill-prepared. Her only salvation comes from meeting Jack Fossett during one of the worst rainstorms in Leicestershire's history. Jack is a kind, caring young lad who takes pity on the beautiful, bedraggled girl, and he and his younger brother and sister welcome Ally into their hearts.

But Jack's mother, Flo, is deeply resentful of all gentlefolk. And time must pass and secrets must be revealed before Ally and Flo can see eye to eye – particularly when they discover that Ally is in fact not as destitute as she thought...

0 7472 5504 0

HEADLINE

Where the Mersey Flows

Lyn Andrews

Leah Cavendish and Nora O'Brien seem to have little in common – except their friendship. Nora is a domestic and Leah the daughter of a wealthy haulage magnate but both are isolated beneath the roof of the opulent Cavendish household.

When Nora is flung out on the streets by Leah's grasping brother-in-law, the outraged Leah follows her, dramatically declaring her intention to move to Liverpool's docklands, alongside Nora and her impoverished family. But nothing can prepare Leah for the squalor that greets her in Oil Street. Nor for Sean Maguire, Nora's defiant Irish neighbour...

'A compelling read' *Woman's Realm*

'Enormously popular' *Liverpool Echo*

'Spellbinding... the Catherine Cookson of Liverpool' *Northern Echo*

0 7472 5176 2

HEADLINE

If you enjoyed this book here is a selection of other bestselling titles from Headline

WHEN TOMORROW DAWNS	Lyn Andrews	£5.99 ☐
MERSEY MAIDS	Anne Baker	£5.99 ☐
THE PRECIOUS GIFT	Tessa Barclay	£5.99 ☐
THE CHINESE LANTERN	Harry Bowling	£5.99 ☐
RICHES OF THE HEART	June Tate	£5.99 ☐
LOVE ME OR LEAVE ME	Josephine Cox	£5.99 ☐
YESTERDAY'S FRIENDS	Pamela Evans	£5.99 ☐
FAIRFIELD ROSE	Sue Dyson	£5.99 ☐
SWEET ROSIE O'GRADY	Joan Jonker	£5.99 ☐
NELLIE'S WAR	Victor Pemberton	£5.99 ☐
CHILDREN OF THE STORM	Wendy Robertson	£5.99 ☐
MAGGIE'S MARKET	Dee Williams	£5.99 ☐

Headline books are available at your local bookshop or newsagent. Alternatively, books can be ordered direct from the publisher. Just tick the titles you want and fill in the form below. Prices and availability subject to change without notice.

Buy four books from the selection above and get free postage and packaging and delivery within 48 hours. Just send a cheque or postal order made payable to Bookpoint Ltd to the value of the total cover price of the four books. Alternatively, if you wish to buy fewer than four books the following postage and packaging applies:

UK and BFPO £4.30 for one book; £6.30 for two books; £8.30 for three books.

Overseas and Eire: £4.80 for one book; £7.10 for 2 or 3 books (surface mail).

Please enclose a cheque or postal order made payable to *Bookpoint Limited*, and send to: Headline Publishing Ltd, 39 Milton Park, Abingdon, OXON OX14 4TD, UK.
Email Address: orders@bookpoint.co.uk

If you would prefer to pay by credit card, our call team would be delighted to take your order by telephone. Our direct line is 01235 400 414 (lines open 9.00 am–6.00 pm Monday to Saturday 24 hour message answering service). Alternatively you can send a fax on 01235 400 454.

Name ....

Address ....

....

....

If you would prefer to pay by credit card, please complete:
Please debit my Visa/Access/Diner's Card/American Express (delete as applicable) card number:

Signature .... Expiry Date ....